Praise for "Stay With

"*This is a warning: the book you hold in your hand is compelling and well-written and you may find it, as I did, impossible to put down. It's a romance that's not trashy in any way, one that illustrates what a novel of this sort should inspire in its reader. You'll also be sharing this book with every woman you know!*"
Sarah Reinhard, author and blogger at SnoringScholar.com

"*A romance of rare quality. It takes you to the heart of passion, through various trials of a real life relationship, and into the power of sincere love. And it's hilariously funny!*"
A.K. Frailey, author, *The Deliverance Trilogy*

"*... a beautiful Christian love story that will put a song in your heart. It will make you hungry for Rebecca's bakery but also hungry for true love that can best be understood in light of John Paul II's Theology of the Body.*"
Theresa Linden, author *The Liberty Trilogy*

"*... a poignant and believable love story about two young adults from very different backgrounds. The characters are richly depicted and memorable, including the secondary characters. The story is sprinkled with humor and contains the perfect balance of reality and sweetness and her writing entertains while radiating substance and depth. Stay With Me is a journey of discovery, forgiveness, and redemption—a beautiful journey of two hearts that long to beat as one.*"
Therese Heckenkamp, award-winning author, *Frozen Footprints*

"*A tale packed with desire and determination, pain and longing, healing and hope, not to mention peopled with flesh-and-blood characters who sweep the reader away into a world we all know with struggles so much like our own, Stay With Me delivers the very best of the inspirational romance genre. Highly recommended!*"
Erin McCole Cupp, author, *Don't You Forget About Me*

Stay With Me

A Novel

by
Carolyn Astfalk

FQ Publishing

Pakenham Ontario

Stay With Me

copyright 2015 Carolyn Astfalk

Published by Full Quiver Publishing

PO Box 244

Pakenham, Ontario K0A 2X0

www.fullquiverpublishing.com

ISBN Number: 978-0-9879153-9-9

Printed and bound in the USA

Cover design: James Hrkach, Carolyn Astfalk

Image courtesy Shenandoah National Park/Neal Lewis

Couple on motorcycle: Rossella Apostoli (123rf.com)

NATIONAL LIBRARY OF CANADA

CATALOGUING IN PUBLICATION

Copyright 2015 by Carolyn Astfalk

Published by FQ Publishing

A Division of Innate Productions

To my husband,
Michael

"Therefore a man leaves his father and his mother and clings to his wife, and they become one flesh."

Genesis 2:24

"Do not think that I have come to bring peace to the earth. I have not come to bring peace, but a sword. For I have come to set a man against his father, and a daughter against her mother, and a daughter-in-law against her mother-in-law; and one's foes will be members of one's own household."

Matthew 10:34-36

1

Where Are You Going?

The directional sign suspended from the ceiling read Aisle 13, but Rebecca couldn't have been more lost if it were written in ancient Greek. She may as well have worn a sandwich board proclaiming her unfit to care for small children. Her leaden feet rooted themselves to the floor, and she shrunk in shame as her niece's frilly green skirt upended, showing the world her soggy, store-brand diaper. Emma's back shimmied on the tile, probably giving it the best polish it had ever had, and her orange Dora the Explorer Crocs thudded against the floor one after the other as she let out an ear-piercing screech punctuated by sobbing gasps.

Abby would know what to do.

She silently pleaded for help from her five-year-old nephew, Ricky. He shrugged his shoulders and meandered over to the yogurt multipacks.

Her chest tightened. Had she discovered yet another area where she didn't measure up? If she couldn't handle two children on her own for a day or two, what kind of mother would she make? The knot in her chest loosened, leaving in its place a familiar, sad ache. She had a better shot at becoming the next *American Idol* than at marriage and motherhood. She'd be lucky if she snagged the interest of any decent guy, let alone one that passed muster with her domineering dad.

At least she'd done something right. Putting forty miles — the distance from Gettysburg to Harrisburg — between her and her dad was proving to be the best decision she'd ever made.

Momentarily paralyzed by the stares of the other shoppers, Rebecca took a deep breath and scooped Emma up off the floor, cradling her against her chest. To her amazement, Emma calmed. She continued to sob and hiccup as Rebecca stroked her silky, golden hair, but the thrashing and screeching subsided, ending as suddenly as it started. Who knew the little girl would get so upset about being denied the Mickey Mouse DVD on the end of the aisle?

She placed Emma on her feet, held her hand, and headed toward the dairy case where she spotted Ricky. The boy's thin frame looked even lankier as he stood on tiptoe to scan the selections.

"Emma, honey, it looks like there's only one Chocolate Underground left." The moment the words left her mouth she wanted to take them back. What was she thinking? She was all but begging the child to have another tantrum.

Emma's face fell. You'd think her favorite Disney princess had died. Rebecca braced for a second outburst.

"Chocolate Underground?" said a masculine voice to her right.

She turned to see a young store clerk.

"I'll see if I've got some more here," he said, squatting to peruse the boxes on his dolly.

Did he get some kind of dairy commission? Never had she come across someone so helpful in the supermarket.

After a few moments he added, "It's not looking good."

He shifted boxes of yogurt cups from a cart filled with a variety of cartons, apparently having overheard Emma's favorite flavor. Had he witnessed the tantrum at the other end of the aisle? Probably. When he stood and gave her a look of bittersweet disappointment, heat rose in her cheeks.

He was young. And good looking. Very good looking. Short dark, almost black hair, blue eyes, and a beautiful, dimpled smile that radiated joy.

"Thanks for checking. It's a major staple of her diet." She turned to Emma, whose little hands clutched the last of her beloved chocolaty yogurts.

"You could try the pudding." He pointed to the tapioca cartons on the top shelf.

"Thanks, but I like to hold onto the illusion that because it's yogurt, I'm buying her health food. You know, all that good bacteria and stuff. And it's organic."

He gave her a bright smile that lit his whole face. How long could she draw out a conversation about yogurt?

A gangly teenager emerged from the swinging double doors at the end of the aisle carrying a carton of what looked to be cream cheese. "Hey, Chris."

Rebecca's ears perked at the use of his name — Chris. As in Christian or Christopher? She smiled at Chris one last time. "We'll get out of your way now." She grabbed a box of organic yogurt tubes with one hand and held onto Emma with the other.

"No problem."

She didn't know what she expected him to say then. Something along the lines of, "In that case, I'd like to take you away from here and spend the rest of my life meeting your milk-related needs." Instead, he went back to work.

She gathered the kids and headed down the aisle.

Two near-tantrums and two frozen food aisles later, Rebecca struggled to find the shortest line at the check-out. While the kids twirled around alongside the cart, Rebecca couldn't help overhearing the fracas in the next lane.

A cranky toddler whined and pulled at the drawstrings of a thirty-something guy's hoodie from where she sat in the shopping cart. The man grumbled and cursed. A slew of children's cough and cold medicines lined the belt of the self-checkout. The young man working the registers approached and asked him if there was a problem.

"My credit card hasn't been activated, and I forgot my cell phone. Watch my little girl here for a minute—I have cash in the car." He extricated the child's hands from his hoodie, kissed her forehead, and jogged through the sliding doors. Faced with a fussy baby, who had now dropped her pacifier beneath the cart and broken out into a howl, the cashier looked like a deer caught in the headlights.

Rebecca longed to help, but she couldn't leave Emma and Ricky unattended.

Chris approached the self-checkouts and handed a yogurt multipack to the flustered cashier, who said something to him before gesturing toward the little girl in the shopping cart. Chris nudged the cashier aside. "I got this."

Smiling at the little girl, he said, "Hey sweetie, where are your toes?" At first she offered only a scowl, but then as Chris gave the underside of her knees a little tickle, she giggled. "Where is your nose?" This time she placed a finger near her nose. After cycling through the main body parts twice, he started a game of peek-a-boo. That's when she pushed him away and let out a wail.

Rebecca couldn't suppress a smile.

Chris must have felt her staring at him because he stepped back from the cart and looked at her with a smile and a shrug that made her cheeks heat.

She glanced away, but when she turned back a couple of seconds later, Chris's gaze and his smile remained fixed on her until the little girl's daddy jogged back, money clip in hand, and broke the spell.

Rebecca's attention turned back to her own lane as she finally moved forward. She checked to make sure Ricky and Emma were still in tow and discovered Ricky examining the cover of *Cosmopolitan. Great. Bounteous cleavage at his eye level.* She thanked God he couldn't read yet and lifted the magazine up and turned it around in its rack. "Help me with the groceries, Ricky," she said as she placed her items on the belt.

A candy and magazine rack obstructed her view. *Where had Chris gone?*

***

Chris watched the pretty brunette stop in front of the sliding glass doors. She zipped the little girl's jacket and pulled up the boy's hood.

Trey, the cashier with no kid skills, stood watching with him. "Cute."

Chris's gaze didn't stray from her as she pushed the cart through the exit. She couldn't be more than five foot four, and her wavy brown hair hung well past her shoulders over a short fleece jacket. She wore a long loose skirt that flowed to her ankles, revealing flat white sneakers. "Very cute. Nice, too."

He stood rooted to the floor for a few seconds and then realized Trey might have been referring to the children as cute, not Rebecca. He turned and noticed Trey's gaze fixed on her behind. Nope, not referring to the children. "I think I'm supposed to go after her."

"You're supposed to? Why? Did she lift something?" Not only was he bad with kids, Trey was not the sharpest cheddar in the dairy case. "Hey, where are you going?"

"I have to ask her for a date." Chris jogged through the exit and rushed through the doors. It took a couple of seconds for him to spot her. Halfway up the second row of cars, the little boy dragged a couple of bags and tried to hoist them into the trunk of a silver minivan.

He started toward the van, realizing too late that it had rained, and he sloshed through a giant puddle. Cold rainwater splashed his shin, making his pants adhere to his leg.

She emerged from the side of the van where she must have been buckling the little girl. She relieved the boy of his burden, placed it in the trunk, and shooed him into his side of the van. By the time she secured his belt, Chris reached her.

"Can I help you with the rest of these?"

Her eyes widened, but her lips turned up in a trace of a smile. Good, maybe she liked him. He certainly hoped so, considering what he was about to ask.

"Thanks. I don't know how my sister does it."

Her sister? So, the kids *weren't* hers.

"I guess it takes practice." He reached into her cart, pulled out a fistful of bags, and laid them in the trunk. Bottles and cans clattered together noisily, so he checked to make sure nothing broke. *Smooth move, idiot.*

"Then there's hope for me yet," she said and placed a gallon of milk in the trunk. She slammed it shut and moved to take hold of the cart.

"I'll take care of that for you."

She thanked him, and an awkward silence followed.

"My name's Chris." He held out his right hand for her to shake. "Chris Reynolds."

"Oh, nice to meet you, Chris. I'm Rebecca Rhodes." She grasped his outstretched hand.

Her hand was warm compared to his cold fingertips. Stupid refrigerated section.

"You're babysitting?"

"Yes. My sister is in labor. My niece and nephew are with me until their baby brother or sister is born."

"Well, maybe I'll see you here again. Do you live nearby?"

"Not anymore."

"If you're in the area again, could I meet you for coffee, a beer, a milkshake—whatever you like to drink?" She paused too long for his liking, and he feared the next words out of her mouth would start with, "I'm sorry, but..."

Instead she smiled, and her brown eyes lit up. "I'd like that."

He let go of the breath he held and smiled, too.

***

Chris couldn't remember the last time he'd been so nervous. He sat at a square table for two in the rear of the coffee shop, his hands tensing every time the bells over the entryway announced the arrival or departure of another customer. He glanced at his watch. Two minutes past seven. She wasn't late yet. Not really. But what if she were? How long should he wait? What if she didn't show? She *had* to show. He felt such an urgency to ask her out. He later wondered if it was some sort of God thing. But what did he know? He hadn't been a Christian long. Why would God prompt him to pursue this girl and then have her not show up?

His rambling thoughts must have distracted him from her approach because when he looked up again, she stood in front of him. Her cheeks were red from the cold air, her brown eyes sparkled, and she rubbed her bare hands together in an apparent effort to warm them up.

"Chris," she said, and he thought he heard a trace of anxiousness in her voice. "Sorry I'm late."

He stood and helped her remove her coat. "No, you're fine. I got here a little early."

"Thank you," she said as he hung her coat on the rack behind the table.

He turned to pull out her chair, but she had already pulled it out and sat down. He took his seat across from her, and tried to get his brain in gear. She looked even cuter than when he had first met her. She obviously had spent more time on her hair and makeup than she did in advance of her trip to the grocery store with her niece and nephew.

"I'm nervous," she admitted before he could think of anything to say. "I thought I'd throw that out there so you don't think I'm a total moron when I spill my drink or say something nonsensical."

"I'm a little nervous, too. First dates are always kind of nerve-wracking."

She picked up the straw wrapper lying on the table and twisted it. "This is my *first*, first date."

Uh-oh. This could be trouble, jailbait even. He had assumed her age ran close to his, but maybe she just appeared older. "How old are you?"

She laughed, a full, but feminine sound. "Don't worry. I'm twenty-three. How old are you?"

"Twenty-four."

"So, how long have you—"

"Wait a second. I'm trying to wrap my mind around the fact that this is your first date. Ever. How is that possible? Surely a pretty girl like you..."

"Well, I've been out with guys before, but I guess I never considered them real dates because my dad had somehow orchestrated them through church. Or at least encouraged them."

Did she say 'church'? He moved his chair in a little closer. The three teens at the next table had gone from giggling to guffawing, and the noise made it hard to hear. Did he happen upon a church-going girl in a supermarket? "So, should I expect your dad to show up here and put an end to this?"

She laughed again, but it sounded hollow. "No. I moved out of his house about six months ago." She fidgeted with the straw wrapper, and her voice lost some of its vigor. "I'm sure he'd have something to say about it, but he no longer has the control he did when I was under his roof."

"How about your mom? Does she need to give your dates a stamp of approval, too?"

The smile left her face, and she looked down at the straw wrapper she had folded accordion-style. "I only have a few memories of my mom. She's deceased, but she had stopped being a part of our lives long before that."

"I'm sorry." Shoot. He wanted to keep things light, not morose, so he steered the conversation in another direction. "You mentioned church. Where do you go?"

"The Free Church."

He knew the one. He'd driven by it thousands of times.

He glanced up at the long line of customers. He should probably order drinks soon, before it grew any longer. "Can I ask you something I've been wondering?"

She set aside the straw wrapper and laid her hands in her lap. "Sure."

"What's your church free from?" He had always taken the name for granted, that is until his conversion. That's when he started to question everything.

Her brow wrinkled, and she looked toward the ceiling. "I think it's just freestanding. You know, not part of some big network or denomination."

Hmm. Uncertain about the appeal of a rogue church, he decided it didn't seem like a topic for a first date.

"Do you go? To church, I mean?" She stared intently, like this was important to her.

"Yes. Just the past couple of years. My parents didn't raise me with any kind of faith, but last year I became Catholic."

Something passed over her expression. Concern? Disappointment? He had been surprised more than once over the past year at the open hostility some people felt for Catholicism. Most Protestant churches weren't anti-Catholic, but he didn't know about her Free Church.

Once he had come to believe in God with certainty, he had followed where he thought he was being led. He hadn't given much thought to anyone else's opinions with the possible exception of his parents. They had met his declaration of faith with confusion and a certain amount of indifference, but never opposition.

"I knew a Catholic boy once. He came to our Bible camp one summer." She gave him a reassuring little smile. She spoke like Catholics were a wild and exotic species she had encountered on an expedition. Maybe he should change the subject.

"What can I get you to drink?"

"A steamed vanilla milk would be great. The regular size, whatever they call it."

He left to get their drinks, looking back at her occasionally. Most everyone else in the place busily tapped on a phone, but she sat comfortably with her hands folded in her lap, people-watching. She saw him looking and gave him a little wave.

He carried their drinks to the table, the heat and scent of his coffee wafting past his nose.

She thanked him for the milk and took a tentative sip.

"So, I assume your sister had the baby."

She set her drink down and reached for her purse. "Yes. He's a handsome little guy. Big, too. Almost nine pounds. They named him Ian." She pulled up a picture on her phone and extended it across the table so he could see.

The ugliest baby he had ever seen lay swaddled in the standard-issue hospital blanket and knit cap. "Congratulations."

"Thank you. I love being an auntie. I get to hone my mothering skills, and if there's any lasting damage it's on my sister, not me." She grinned then, and he smiled. She tucked her phone back into her purse and took another sip of milk. "What about your family? Any nieces or nephews?"

Chris swallowed the scalding coffee and pushed the cup forward on the table. "No. I have one older brother. He's getting married in a few weeks, so no children yet."

"A wedding. Well, that's exciting. I've never been to a wedding."

He leaned back in his chair, turned his head slightly and studied her as if he could tell by looking from that angle if she was for real. "Are you serious? Never?"

"Nope. My dad's side of the family is small, and we're not in touch with my mom's side. I had a couple friends marry. One was a destination wedding, and I couldn't afford the flight or the time off, and the other I had planned on attending until I came down with some kind of stomach bug. My sister, Abby, and her husband eloped."

"Wow." Chris thought about all the family weddings he'd been to throughout the years. He was sorry Rebecca had no happy memories of the dancing, eating, drinking, and general craziness that he carried with him. Being a little boy and trying to wrest a flying garter from the young men. Dancing with his mom while his dad looked on with pride. He remembered last year taking a shot of whiskey with ten of his cousins as they toasted the bride and groom.

As Rebecca finished her milk and stuffed her used napkin into the paperboard cup, the conversation turned to work.

"The yogurt restocking is paying the bills—barely—until I find something else. My degree is in chemistry," Chris said. "In the meantime, I'm trying to keep from getting frostbite on my fingers. So what about you? I have absolutely no idea what you do." If he had to guess, he would have picked something a bit artsy. Maybe music therapy or graphic design. He could easily imagine her creating floral arrangements or working in a museum.

"I'm a payroll administrator," she said with an air of disappointment in her voice. "I work with a handful of vendors to process their payroll and benefits." She poked an unpolished fingernail into her paper cup and studied it for a moment. She looked back up at Chris and shrugged. "Boring."

"What would you like to do, if you could do anything you wanted?"

Looking at her cup again, she opened her mouth as if to say something and then thought better of it. "I try not to think about it. I'm grateful to have a steady job, and I do the best I can at it."

"What about your dreams? Isn't there something you'd want to do if you didn't have to worry about money or education or any of that? If you were free to do what you wanted?"

Her gaze rested on him for a few seconds, and she smiled. "Well, there is one thing. I've never admitted this to anyone."

"What is it?"

"I want a little store where I sell homemade baked goods. Not elaborate cakes, you know, like the ones you see on the Food Network. Just ordinary but delicious cookies. By the dozen. That's what I would do."

"I'd love to see you do that."

She leaned forward in her seat and studied him for a couple of seconds. "I think you mean that."

Chris laughed. "Of course I do. Do you bake much now?"

"Yes. I love to bake. But I just do it for friends and family. Simple stuff like breads and cookies. Nothing too complicated."

"So, why didn't you go to school for that? Why business or whatever got you into payroll?"

"My dad said he would only help pay for college if I studied something practical. He didn't deem baking practical, although he's never refused anything I've baked." She gave him a wry grin. "Anyway, I figured I'd be better off doing things his way and getting out without a mountain of debt. Then I could always go back later and do what I wanted. Only now there are bills to pay, and I can't keep going to school without having some kind of income."

"Would you bake something for me some time? My mom is a good cook, but she doesn't care to bake. My sweet tooth has been sorely neglected." He realized as he said it, he had pretty much just asked for another date. That's what he wanted, but not how he meant to go about it. Rebecca was easy to talk to, easy to look at it, and he wanted to know more about her.

She nodded her agreement, and he realized the other tables had emptied save for two metrosexual-looking men in slim pants and turtle neck sweaters who sat in the leather chairs at the front of the café.

"I think they're getting ready to shut things down here. Can I walk you to your car?"

"Sure." She pushed back her chair before he had a chance to pull it out for her.

He had to get better at this stuff. He grabbed her coat from the hook and held it for her.

"Thank you." She turned into the coat and used her left hand to free the hair that had been caught beneath the collar. When she couldn't get it loose, his hand itched to help her. He let her struggle another second and then gave in, pulling her shiny brown tresses out so that they spilled over her faux fur collar. They were luxurious and tempted him to gather them again in his hands and release them, watching them splay over her coat. Before he could even attempt to do so, she shook her head, letting her hair fall evenly over her shoulders.

They walked outside, and the wind hit them. Rebecca tightened her coat around herself.

He zipped his black leather jacket. "Geez. It hardly feels like May. Where are you parked?"

She pointed to a small, white sedan at the end of the first row of cars. He took her elbow as she stepped off the curb and walked alongside her to her vehicle.

"Where's your car?" she asked as she unlocked her door.

"I don't have a car right now. I ride a motorcycle."

"Are you serious?" Her brows rose and her eyes widened. "I wouldn't have pegged you for a biker dude."

Chris smiled. He loved to see people's reactions when he told them he drove a motorcycle. "Why not?"

She shrugged. "No facial hair. No jewelry. No visible tattoos."

"Stereotypes," he said with a half grin. "Well, I had a nice time this evening, Rebecca. May I call you again?"

"I'd like that," she said, her cheeks growing rosy. "And I'll have some goodies—for your sweet tooth."

"Thank you." Before he could overthink it, he leaned in and brushed his lips against her cheek. She moved toward her car and gave him a nervous smile. "Good night."

He stepped back and allowed her to start her car, watching as she pulled out of the parking space and exited the lot.

2

You and Me

The spring-like weather the following weekend convinced Chris a trip to the zoo would be a safe second date. There would be plenty of opportunity for them to talk, but if the conversation lagged there would be lots to see and do.

Rebecca had brought him chocolate chip banana bread, and he knew it wouldn't last the weekend. It was moist, delicious, and must have smelled like heaven when she'd baked it.

The conversation between them flowed naturally, and the more he got to know Rebecca, the more he liked her. The only awkward moment had come at the mountain lion exhibit. The reason for the female's vocalizations wasn't immediately obvious. The incessant half-moan, half-growl eventually gave it away.

Chris stared for a moment. "Whoa. I think they're...I thought visiting the zoo was a G-rated activity."

Rebecca's eyes widened and her cheeks bloomed an endearing shade of pink as the realization hit her. "Oh my. They are definitely—involved."

The next day, he caught up with his friend Father John Cavanaugh. Chris often joined him in the rectory after the last Sunday Mass. Sometimes they'd watch football, and sometimes they'd just have a beer and talk. Their friendship began when Father John was still Deacon John, and Chris peppered him with an endless series of questions about God, faith, and Catholicism. John wasn't much older than Chris, and they found they had a lot in common.

Chris took a seat across from Father John, who tore the wrapping from his Philadelphia-style hoagie and twisted the cap off of his Yuengling lager. Father John said grace, and before he'd gotten his sandwich to his mouth, Chris blurted, "I met someone."

Father John bit into his hoagie, wiped some stray sauce from his chin with the napkin, and chewed before he spoke. "A woman?"

Chris nodded.

"So spill it. You know you're dying to. Is she from the college or is she a local?"

Chris smiled. Father John knew him as well as his own brother. "Well, her name is Rebecca, and her family lives in Gettysburg, but for the last six months she's had a place up in Harrisburg. She does some kind of payroll administration." *And she's got the most beautiful brown hair and eyes I've ever seen.*

Feeling a bit like a fool, he bit his tongue before he went on to list every one of her positive attributes. He turned his attention back to his sandwich, which was proving to be surprisingly spicy, and waited for Father John's response. His tongue felt like it had caught fire as the jalapenos slid over it, and he began to sweat.

Father John took a swig of beer and smiled. "Sounds like you're enamored with her. So, is she Catholic?"

"No, she's not." He'd hit upon the one reservation he had about pursuing a relationship with Rebecca. Two years ago he couldn't have cared less what kinds of religious beliefs she might have possessed, or if she had any at all. Not anymore. He expected when he found the right woman he'd be united to her in every way—emotionally, physically, intellectually, and now spiritually. The fact that she was a Christian comforted him, but he'd be lying to himself if he claimed he didn't wish she were Catholic.

"Do you know anything about the Free Church?"

"Not much." Father John rolled up his paper wrapper and took it to the trash. "I've met the pastor a couple of times. He seems nice enough. Can't say they're very ecumenical. The church kind of keeps to itself."

"Do you think I should end it before it goes any further?" Chris's heart ached even as he said it. He liked Rebecca way more than he should after only two dates. "Because I felt like the Holy Spirit led me to her."

Father John smiled. "Well, sometimes a pretty face and what I'm guessing is probably an attractive body to match can muddle our discernment." He sat and drummed his fingers on the table a few times.

"Knowing you and your journey and taking into account my admittedly limited experience counseling couples, I'd say it would be better for you if the woman you chose to settle down with was Catholic, and not the kind of Catholic that checks off that box on a census form because she goes to a fish fry with her grandma or hangs rosary beads from her rearview mirror. The kind that knows her faith and lives her life accordingly."

Chris tried to keep the disappointment from his face. He didn't want to hear this. Not when he was near to bursting with the excitement of a fresh, new relationship that had, just a moment ago, held so much potential.

"That said, sometimes God puts people in our path for reasons we don't fully understand. At least at first. And maybe he uses attraction, even sexual attraction, to draw us to them." He stared at a point somewhere on the wall beyond Chris. He wasn't just talking about Rebecca anymore.

"That's clear as mud, Father John."

"Yeah. Just because they gave me this Roman collar doesn't mean I have it all figured out yet. I guess I'd say not to lose your head over this girl. If you're dating because you're looking to get married, then you've got to think about her in the context of marriage and children, not just how she looks when she's seated across the table from you or how much fun you have together."

Father John was right, and Chris knew it. He would just have to find a way to navigate this relationship so that he didn't lose his head—or his heart—until he thought it had a reasonable chance of success.

***

Rebecca sealed the lid on the container of blueberry muffins then rested her elbows on the kitchen counter. She swiped her finger across the phone, opened the contacts app, and scrolled down to R. Reynolds, Chris. She tapped his entry, and her finger hovered over the call button.

Facebook.

She hadn't checked in this morning. Rebecca switched apps and scrolled through her news feed. Cat photos, unfunny memes, and inspirational quotes.

If he didn't want me to call, he wouldn't have given me his phone number, right?

She and Chris had two really good dates, and he said he wanted to see her again soon. Unfortunately, a family dinner on Friday night and an overnight camping trip Saturday left little time for a date. It wouldn't be for long, but this morning he'd be at his parents' house packing for his trip.

When Rebecca baked the muffins, calling and arranging to drop them off seemed easy. Now, it seemed presumptuous.

She thought back to a conversation with Abby a few weeks earlier, just before she met Chris. That conversation later convinced her to accept Chris's offer to meet her for a drink. The first stage of labor removed most of Abby's filters, not that she had many to begin with.

Abby had stopped pacing her dining room and pressed her palm into her back. She breathed heavily through a contraction and then focused on Rebecca, seated at the table. Abby dictated a list of bedtimes and favorite foods for the kids so Rebecca would know what to do while Abby was at the hospital.

"The bottom line is, do you want to spend the rest of your life with one of the Daddy-sanctioned church boys? You know, the ones so socially-backward they can't pry their eyes off their gaming devices? I swear I spotted that last guy—what was his name? Douglas?—at the furry convention. Joel's work banquet was in the same hotel. The guy was dressed like a sexy porcupine puffer fish. Cause, you know, nothing turns a woman on like poisonous tumescence. So, if the answer is no on the Daddy-approved social rejects—and if it's not, I swear I'll disown you—then you need to put yourself out there and meet someone. You can't continue to hide out and think your

Prince Charming is going to sweep you out from under Daddy's overlong nose. You're out of his house now, and that's a good start."

And then her water broke.

For those few seconds in that rainy grocery store parking lot, those words swirled through Rebecca's head. *A good-looking guy had asked her out. Nothing big, just a drink in a public place. She could do this. Abby was right. Nothing good would happen if she didn't take a risk. This was a small one.* So, she had said yes.

And it was a great date. She hadn't even realized until she'd started to drive home that night he had called her pretty—right before she steamrolled over his side of the conversation and blathered on about the dates her dad had set up for her. So, why was this so nerve-wracking?

Rebecca inhaled deeply through her nose and exhaled slowly through her mouth.

You can do this, Rebecca. She tried to steady her finger as it scrolled through her contacts until it landed on Chris's name again and hit 'call.'

***

Hearing from Rebecca had brightened Chris's morning. Was she as eager to see him again as he was to see her? The homemade muffins she made would be an added bonus.

Chris gathered the last of the camping gear from his parents' garage and organized it for packing onto his motorcycle.

Alan emerged from the house where he had been discussing wedding reception details just as Rebecca's car pulled up.

"Who's that?" Alan asked.

Chris hoped he planned on heading home, not staying to find out. Alan's hair hung over one eye, mussed to perfection, and his strong but stocky frame was loose and relaxed in his oversized tee shirt and sloppy cargo shorts. The typical picture of nonchalance.

"Rebecca."

"The brown-eyed beauty you took on two amazing dates, Rebecca?" He made air quotes around the word "amazing," as if he didn't believe Chris's assessment.

"The one and only." Chris set aside the small camp stove he held and headed to the end of the driveway. He opened Rebecca's car door. "Good morning."

"Hey, there." She stepped out carrying a large basket covered with a beige tea towel. It smelled like fresh berries and cinnamon. "For you."

"Thank you. They smell delicious." He took the basket from her and walked her toward Alan. Being that he hardly dated, Chris had never introduced a girl to Alan. He didn't know whether his brother would try to make a fool of him or not. It wouldn't be hard.

"So, Alan, this is Rebecca. Rebecca, my brother, Alan."

"Good to meet you." Alan gestured toward the basket. "Mind if I try one? I haven't had anything homemade since Jamie moved in. These look amazing."

Rebecca thanked him for the compliment and turned back to Chris.

"Jamie's a lousy cook," he offered by way of explanation as the crumbs gathered on his brother's tee shirt.

"Chris." He couldn't miss the gentle scolding in her voice.

"No, it's true," Alan said. "Jamie says it herself. She can't even make pasta. It's either crunchy or gummy. I've got six takeout places on speed dial."

Having exhausted that line of conversation—Chris couldn't disagree since Jamie had more than her fair share of culinary disasters—he hoped Alan would leave and give them a few moments alone. Instead, Alan leaned against his car and crossed his ankles.

Jerking his head toward the street, Chris hoped he'd get the idea. His brother smiled, and Chris knew that he got the message all right, but he refused to comply.

"Get lost," he mouthed, but Alan smiled and didn't budge.

So that's how he wants to play it. Fine.

Scowling at his brother, he placed a hand lightly on

Rebecca's back and guided her into the yard. "Excuse us," he tossed over his shoulder.

Chris glanced down to ensure they didn't step in one of the little "presents" the neighbor's chocolate lab had left in the yard.

"Sorry I'm not going to be around this weekend. I've had this overnight planned for months."

"No problem." She widened the space between them a fraction, and his hand fell away from her back.

Her gaze quickly dropped to her feet. He hoped her disappointment matched his. He had badgered his mom about moving that dinner, but she was adamant.

"Where are you camping?"

"Shenandoah National Park in Virginia. Have you been there?"

She shook her head, a wistful expression on her face. "No, can't say that I have."

He stopped and faced Rebecca. Beyond her Alan gestured to him and made hand signals. Chris squinted and tried to make it out. A little cross sign and then his index finger. Alan said something, too. Not much of a lip reader, Chris needed four tries to get it. Alan was saying, "Plus one."

Chris knew what he was asking. He and Jamie had been hounding him for weeks about whom he was bringing to the wedding. He had thought of asking Rebecca, but they hadn't known each other long, and he didn't know how she'd react. He'd be introducing her for inspection to nearly all his living relatives. Not to mention, as best man he would have to leave her on her own part of the time, which would make him feel guilty, since she wouldn't know another soul there. Still, if he didn't ask her that would mean he wouldn't see her for two weekends in a row. He could try a weeknight, but his schedule varied. Maybe he should ask and let her decide. At least it would get Alan off his back. Chris refocused on Rebecca, who glanced around the yard.

"I want to ask you something. I know we've only been on a couple dates, so I understand if you want to pass on this. No hard feelings. I don't have a date for Alan's wedding. Since you've never been to a wedding and all, would you like to go with me?"

"Yes." No hesitation. That was good.

Movement in the distance drew his attention. Alan walked toward them. Geez, the guy lacked patience.

"Hey, Chris," Alan said, "Have a good trip. I've got to go. I'm heading out of town, too." Then to Rebecca he said, "It was nice meeting you."

Rebecca returned the sentiment, and Alan turned to leave.

"Where are you headed?" Chris called.

"Going to see Dave Matthews in Maryland tonight," he yelled over his shoulder before heading to his car.

Chris took hold of Rebecca's hand, and walked back toward the driveway. Alan better not have run off with his muffins. "Alan follows Dave Matthews all over the country."

"Who's Dave Matthews?"

She never heard of the Dave Matthews Band? They'd been around forever. "You know, 'Tripping Billies,' 'Dancing Nancies,' 'Ants Marching'?"

She arched her brow a bit, squinted, and shook her head. Negative. Did this poor girl live in a cave?

"Well, they're a rock'n'roll band. They have a big following. Lots of people, like Alan, travel all over for their concerts. They're known for their live shows. I'll have to play one of their songs for you some time. You've probably heard them and don't know it." The look on her face made him doubt his last statement.

"Maybe. I don't listen to music much, but when I do it's usually contemporary Christian. Sometimes a little bit of country. Or 'new' country I guess they call it."

They made it back to her car, and Chris was relieved to see the muffins were still alongside his motorcycle where he had left them. Alan had better not have taken any more than the couple he snagged when Rebecca first arrived.

"See you later." He gave her a quick kiss on the cheek. After she left, he texted Alan.

Plus one. Rebecca Rhodes.

His phone buzzed with Alan's response.

Atta boy.

Tucking his phone in his pocket, Chris ambled up the driveway and entered his parents' house through the garage, hoping to snag a bottle of water before he left. He opened the refrigerator and grabbed some spring water from the bottom of the door.

"Hey, honey, who was that out there?"

Chris bit the inside of his cheek to keep from grinning. Mom didn't miss a thing. She had probably been watching him and Rebecca the whole time.

He unscrewed the cap and took a long drink of water as he closed the refrigerator door. "Rebecca Rhodes. We've gone on a couple of dates. She brought me some muffins she baked last night."

"Oh, how nice." She straightened the napkins in their holder on the counter as an obvious pretense for being in the kitchen. "She likes to bake?"

"Yeah, she does. She's good at it, too." He waited for the next question. There *would* be another.

"So, where did you meet?"

"Rieser's Market." He capped the bottle and leaned against the counter. It would be easy to get irritated with her questions, but he reminded himself that she only asked because she cared. The older he got and the more people he met, the more he realized how lucky—no, how blessed—he and Alan were. Their parents had been married nearly three decades.

Mom had a strong will and a short temper, and he'd witnessed plenty of arguments between her and Dad over the years, but just as many heartfelt apologies. Mom and Dad were still very much in love, and his mom wanted that lasting love for her sons.

"When do I get to meet her?" Mom pushed the napkins aside and slid her glasses up into her short hair as she focused on him.

At least he had a firm answer for her. "At Alan's wedding. She just agreed to be my date."

The look of satisfaction on his mother's face amused him. He crossed the room and kissed her on the cheek. "I've got to go. I'm doing an overnight at Shenandoah. I'll see you when I get back."

She pulled him into a hug. "I'll be here assembling table centerpieces. Be careful on that death machine."

Ah, the obligatory swipe at the motorcycle. Now the conversation was complete. "Goodbye, Mom."

***

Chris assembled his backpacking tent in about five minutes. After putting the rest of his belongings in the bear-proof metal box at his campsite, he tightened the laces on his hiking boots and pored over a park map deciding on a hike that would keep him away from the campground most of the day. He settled on a circuit hike that would take him past a couple of old family cemeteries and the remains of a small logging village.

Returning to the campground late in the evening, he grilled some hot dogs he had picked up at the camp store and warmed a can of chili over the fire. Grilling made even the off-brand wieners savory, but the chili was bland with chewy bits of mystery meat that sat in his belly like a brick. Although still early, Chris was ready to call it a night after all the day's exertion. He leaned back in his camp chair and enjoyed the fire while watching the campers around him.

On his right, two young children blew bubbles while their parents grilled dinner. Farther down the hill from them, a middle-aged couple and a teenager gathered around a picnic table playing a card game. Directly downhill from him, a young couple about his age or a few years older talked and laughed. The woman sat on the man's lap, and his arms encircled her. To his left, a large, Mennonite family prepared their dinner. Their constant chatter punctuated with laughter made Chris smile.

Loneliness was something he'd never experienced before

while camping. He nearly always camped alone. He had gone with some buddies a few times, but those were exceptions, not the rule. In fact, he preferred to go alone. The peace, the solitude, and being outside refreshed and invigorated him. For the first time, he didn't relish the solitude. It felt somehow deficient.

Gazing at the lovey-dovey couple still wrapped up in each other's arms, he wondered if Rebecca liked the outdoors. He imagined her sitting in the firelight with him, her hair shining as the flames lit her face. What would it be like to sit here with Rebecca, talking and relaxing?

He inhaled the scent of burning campfires and grilled hamburgers and read through *Day and Overnight Hikes in Shenandoah National Park* until his eyes grew tired. The sun hadn't completely set, but as he watched the couple down the hill retire to their tent, the woman pulling the man by the hand, he thought going to bed might not be a bad idea.

A pair of birds rustling in the leaves woke him at dawn. After a couple of protein bars, juice, and some coffee he picked up at the lodge, he packed his gear and set out on a short summit hike before loading everything back on his bike and heading for home. The next time he came back, he hoped it would be with Rebecca.

***

"I don't know, Abby. It's a little clingy." Rebecca loved the dusty rose-colored, A-line dress Abby had her try on, but it was so different from the plain, serviceable outfits she usually wore that she had a hard time feeling comfortable in it. It was a simple gown, but it did flatter her figure.

"Don't worry. Yes, he will see that you have nice hips for birthing and full breasts for nursing babies, but you're all covered up, nothing's too tight, no bare shoulders. You'll look elegant and sexy but not the least bit trampy."

Rebecca stepped away from the mirrors and back toward the changing room. A pair of giddy teens took her place at the mirror, admiring themselves in prom dresses that clung to them like plastic wrap. Even Abby, who had worn her share of scandalous dresses to college formals, raised a brow at the slit that traveled to the top of the taller girl's thigh. Rebecca blocked out the sound of their giggles and the cloying fragrance of their perfumes and refocused on her task. She'd need to get a pair of matching shoes, too. Being that she was the best man's date, people were going to notice her. She didn't want to embarrass Chris. "Are you sure?"

"Positive. It's perfect, Rebecca. Really. You're going to knock his socks off."

"I really like him, Abby." She didn't know how much she should share with Abby. To call her a loose cannon was an understatement. She could imagine introducing Chris to Abby and her asking him if he had any communicable diseases or mental health disorders. She was that kind of crazy.

"I can tell, and I'm glad. It's about time you met someone normal outside Daddy's web of weirdoes." She took Rebecca's hand in a gentle gesture uncharacteristic of Abby's usual brashness. "Rebecca, relax. The dress is perfect, and even if it weren't, any man should consider himself lucky to have you on his arm."

Abby didn't hug. Rebecca knew that, but she couldn't resist. Her sister had said just the right thing. "I love you, Abby."

"I love you, too, Becca."

3

Good Good Time

Alan, Chris, and the groomsmen stood, and Rebecca realized the wedding was about to begin. Chris's gaze searched the crowd and when it rested on her, he smiled and winked. She smiled in return and then slid down in her seat as three young women with bare shoulders, ample bosoms, and elaborate updos turned to see where he'd directed that smile. Old girlfriends?

Maybe this hadn't been such a good idea. She liked Chris. A lot. But a wedding three dates in may not have been wise. Chris knew everyone here it seemed. And she knew no one but him.

When they arrived at the reception, she stuck close to his side, and thankfully he made every effort to see that she didn't feel out of place. He either held her hand or slipped his arm around her waist. Every time someone stopped to talk to him, Chris introduced her. When the conversation lulled he always had something to add so that she wasn't left standing there like a fool.

Rebecca traced a line in the condensation on her champagne flute while she waited for Chris to rejoin her after some photos. She had never tasted champagne before tonight. Her dad hadn't found much cause for celebration in their home. She felt like celebrating tonight though. Chris liked how she looked in her dress. What word did he use? Exquisite. He said she looked exquisite. She smiled when she remembered the dreamy look on his face as he greeted her in the receiving line after the ceremony and introduced her to his parents.

She took another sip of the champagne. She had learned three things from Chris's toast to Alan and Jamie. First, Alan was considered the fun-loving, wild brother whose engagement last year surprised everyone, while Chris was the shy and steady one. Second, their parents, especially their father, had a tremendous positive influence on both of them, and their sons loved them deeply. Finally, it was obvious to everyone in the room that Chris exuded an irrepressible charm not born of smoothness or sophistication, but derived from sincerity and authenticity.

After their meal and the requisite bridal party dance, she and Chris ended up at a table for ten in the rear of the hotel ballroom. The guests rotated from time to time, but it was a continuous series of cousins and friends of Chris and Alan and their wives or girlfriends. Chris always had a drink in front of him. He threw back the shots with the other guys at the table, maybe three in all, and then switched to beers. He took his time with them, and she guessed he only had a couple over the two hours they sat there.

Just the presence of alcohol made Rebecca nervous, the bubbly champagne she enjoyed notwithstanding. Her dad had never allowed a drop of it in their house. Still, although everyone at the table relaxed and had a good time, no one seemed drunk. They laughed a little harder at the jokes than she did, but not one person had said or done anything inappropriate. Twice Chris had offered to get her a glass of wine or a mixed drink, but when she said, "No, thank you. A ginger ale would be great," he didn't push her the way some people did.

Chris whispered in her ear. "I'm tired of sitting. Are you ready to dance?"

She knew it would come up. It was a wedding after all. She just hadn't decided ahead of time how she would handle it. "I can't dance."

Chris smiled, and she noticed that little dimple in his left cheek. "Neither can I, but it'll be fun. Pretty please. For me."

If she wasn't careful, those blue eyes would have her saying yes to all sorts of things she had no business doing. "I've never danced. My dad discouraged it."

"Well, I'd be honored to be your first partner."

She didn't want to ruin his evening or his memories of his brother's wedding, so at the risk of public humiliation she relented. "Okay. But don't expect much."

He lifted his hand and pinched his thumb and forefinger together, twisting his wrist as if he were turning a dial. "There. My expectations are set to low." He smiled again, sans dimple, and pushed back his chair. Taking her hand, he excused them from the table.

They walked onto the dance floor as an up-tempo seventies song came to a close. The next track started with the twang of a guitar, and Rebecca watched as a crowd of four or five guys headed to the floor. Several girls followed in their stocking feet.

"Dave Matthews?" She gave him a sideways glance as they stopped near the edge of the dance floor.

It took him a second to register her meaning. "No, John Mayer."

"Let's go, Reynolds," one of the guys shouted at Chris. Chris nodded and released her hand for a moment while he took off his jacket and draped it over an empty chair. He took her hand again and looking at her feet said, "You might want to lose the shoes."

Rebecca looked at her dusty rose-colored pumps with the conservative heel and then back at Chris.

"Go ahead. I promise not to step on your toes."

Rebecca slipped them off and placed them beneath the chair where Chris had hung his jacket. The guys were already doing some kind of crazy line dance that morphed into a Rockette-style leg kick while the girls watched and clapped in time to the music. Rebecca was glad to stand aside while Chris joined them. They looked so ridiculous she laughed. As they broke ranks, Chris caught her by the arm and swung her around in a circle.

Alan and Jamie had joined the group and took center floor for their own duet. As they moved off to the side, another couple took their place and then another until Rebecca realized they were taking turns. She and Chris were going to have to do—something. Her throat constricted, and she stood stock-still.

Before she could protest, Chris took her hand and pulled her into the center where he led her into some kind of do-si-do until his foot caught the hem of one of the bridesmaids' dresses and he fell to the floor. The little crowd roared, and Chris got up, made a big show of dusting himself off and took a bow, holding Rebecca's hand out for a curtsy. She laughed and obliged as someone else claimed the spotlight.

She didn't know when it happened, but her apprehension lifted, and she joined in the rowdy silliness for the next couple of minutes.

The next song was a ballad, and Chris took her elbow and pulled her in to face him. She felt a smidgen of discomfort but pushed it aside. She was breathing hard and sweat beaded on her neck, but dancing had been fun, and she wanted to have more of it.

She raised her head to peer up at him. "Dave Matthews?"

He gave her a soft, amused smile. "Nope."

The song began with a few mellow chords and the singer sang with a yearning that pulled at Rebecca's heart.

Bound and battered
I want to loose your shackled heart
Washed and winged
You fly free
Keep circling back to me
Stay with me

The lights had dimmed, and Rebecca tried to relax against Chris. It had been a long day, but she could still smell his aftershave, a clean fragrance that reminded her vaguely of pine. The disco ball hanging above the parquet dance floor created shimmering squares of light around the room.

After a few moments, Chris said, "You know it's not fair to Jamie."

She turned her head slightly and raised an eyebrow. "Not fair?"

"Not fair for you to look so beautiful. How will anyone notice the bride?"

She raised both her eyebrows in question. "That sounds an

awful lot like a bad line to me, Chris. I'm sure everyone noticed Jamie."

He smiled as if to concede, but stared into her eyes. As she relented and averted her gaze, he tucked some stray hairs behind her ear. "It may be a line, but it's also true."

He pulled her in closer so that she could rest her head against his shoulder. He slid one arm around her back while the other one held her hand in his.

After a minute, he pulled back and said, "Thank you for being my date tonight. I hope it wasn't too uncomfortable not knowing anybody."

"Not at all." It was a little lie, but he really had made it almost painless.

***

Chris's pulse raced, and it wasn't just because of the dancing. Being this close to Rebecca overwhelmed him. The mild berry scent that followed her, the way she looked at him, and the feel of her soft, delicate frame in his arms. Had he had too much to drink? No, he was a little buzzed, but nowhere near drunk. He'd be fine to drive her home in an hour or so like he planned.

The music played on, but as they neared the edge of the dance floor, Chris stopped moving. He couldn't take it anymore. Sliding a finger under her chin, he raised her face to his.

"Rebecca, may I kiss you?"

Her eyes widened, but she gave a slight nod of her head, which he took as a 'yes,' and he tilted his head down. The moment his lips met hers he knew. He knew he was falling fast and hard for this beautiful, guileless woman. He had worried she might pull away, but she let him kiss her again and again, gently pressing his lips to hers and tasting her soft champagne sweetness. He knew whatever happened or didn't happen after this, he would never hear this song again without thinking about this night with Rebecca.

He wasn't aware the music had ended until a chorus of cheers and whistles brought him out of the moment. When he lifted his head, he realized what had felt like the most intimate moment of his life was, in fact, a very public display of affection. His cheeks warmed, and he pulled Rebecca snug against his chest, hugging her with both arms. He smiled because he couldn't help it. He couldn't remember ever feeling so elated.

A fierce protective streak rose in him, and he continued to shield Rebecca from the whistles and leers. He lifted his hands to the sides of her face and leaned back, wanting to see what was in her chocolate brown eyes.

"Sorry. I should've waited until we were alone."

"It's okay." Her sweet smile and the sparkle in her eyes said that she meant it.

A hand slapped his back, and he turned around to see Alan, a knowing look on his face.

"Keep that up, and I'll be toasting *you*."

***

Chris took her hand, and they grabbed his jacket and her shoes on the way back to their seats. The faces at the table had changed, but the conversation and drinks continued to flow. Rebecca noticed that Chris had switched to Coca-Cola. The pale, red-headed guy across the table was talking about a golf course he played on in Florida when a slender hand fitted with several gaudy rings burst into her peripheral vision, wrapping itself around Chris's face. He released her hand under the table and tried to dislodge the two that were blocking his line of sight.

At first, Rebecca only saw the woman's fancy up-do with expensive highlights. She cooed into Chris's ear, "Guess who?" What was this, high school?

Chris didn't bother to guess. He removed her hands and shifted in his seat so that he could see her face.

"Megan, I'd like you to meet Rebecca. Rebecca, this is Megan. We went to school together."

It was obvious Megan hadn't been seeking an introduction, but that's what she got and to her credit she extended her hand to Rebecca and said what a pleasure it was to meet her. Rebecca realized hers was one of the heads that had turned to see her at the ceremony and that she was inebriated. Megan turned back to Chris. "It would be a shame if we didn't have at least one dance. For old time's sake."

Chris didn't take the bait. "I just sat down to take a breather, Megan. Maybe later?"

"Oh, come on." If Megan were sober, she probably would be embarrassed by the pleading tone she had used, not to mention the way she ran her perfectly-shaped and polished nails up and down Chris's sleeve. "I'm sure Becky doesn't mind, do you?" Megan's glassy eyes turned back towards her.

Rebecca floundered for an answer. "Uh, no. It's fine."

Megan tried her best to pull Chris out of his seat. "See? She doesn't mind at all."

With Megan pulling him away from the table, Rebecca finally got a good look at Chris and the browbeaten look on his face. Once Megan's back was turned, he leaned down toward Rebecca's ear.

"Thanks. You're a great friend, Rebecca." His tone dripped with sarcasm.

Rebecca smiled. It amused her to see him in such discomfort, in a flirty sort of way. His lack of interest in dancing with Megan also pleased her.

Chris did his best to pry Megan's arms off him in the nicest ways possible. When the music ended, he escorted Megan off the floor and into a gaggle of similarly-coiffed girls, then met Rebecca with an exaggerated sigh of relief.

Rebecca laughed as he sat down next to her, took her hand and placed it back on his leg where it had rested before Megan's interruption. The degree to which she liked the feeling of his warm, strong palm encasing her hand and the smooth texture of his pants and sturdy leg beneath her fingers discomfited her.

"Well, at least that's over." He planted a little kiss on her cheek. "Next time you don't have to be such a good sport, okay? Tell her to leave me alone or you'll scratch her eyes out or something."

Afraid of saying something too catty, Rebecca just smiled.

Chris squeezed her hand, and all of a sudden everyone around her sang. The song was familiar, even to her. By the time they hit the chorus, the dance floor had filled and even the people still sitting were singing along, "What a lady, what a night." Chris sang, too. She stared at him as he watched the dance floor, knee bouncing and head bobbing to the music.

Oh my gosh, he's handsome. What am I getting myself into?

She tapped her knee to the catchy tune, but even when Chris leaned in and sang to her, she merely smiled, refusing to sing along. She hoped he didn't notice.

In another forty-five minutes, the crowd had thinned out considerably, and Chris squeezed her hand and asked if she was ready to go.

"I'm ready any time you are."

"Let's go then." He stood and pulled her chair out for her. No one had done that for her before, and Rebecca feared she might land on the floor. Good thing she was sober.

Chris and Rebecca said their goodbyes to the remaining people at the table. Alan and Jamie were barely holding each other up, glassy-eyed and slurring their words. Why were they still here so late in the evening anyway? What kind of wedding night did that make for?

Chris stopped as they stepped out into the lobby. "I'm going to run to the restroom before we go. I'll be right back."

"Okay." She turned to face the reception ballroom again while toying with the leather strap on her handbag. A door opened and slammed shut behind her. Chris already? She knew guys could get in and out in a hurry, but really, he'd just gone in.

It wasn't Chris, but Megan. She veered to the side either because she had too much to drink or because she was looking down as she adjusted her overflowing cleavage in her royal blue, sequined, strapless gown. When she looked up, she spotted Rebecca and made a beeline for her—the kind a crazy, drunken bee with poor sensory perception would make.

Rebecca tried not to stare at the stream of toilet tissue she dragged on the heel of her right shoe.

"Becky, Becky, Becky." Megan must have enjoyed a few more drinks since her spin on the dance floor with Chris. "So, where did you and Chris meet?"

"The grocery store." She hoped Chris would be out soon. Megan obviously had a thing for Chris, and this could get unpleasant fast.

"How cute." Her voice rose to a tone ordinarily reserved for fawning over baby animals. "We've known each other since we were like, seven."

Rebecca nodded and hoped Megan would get bored and head back into the ballroom. No such luck.

"You know, I always thought I'd be his first." She reeked of alcohol and perfume.

"His first?"

"You know, his first time. Between the sheets." She tried to adopt a whisper for this delicate subject, but it came out more of a hoarse slur. "He was so shy though, and then we went off to college. I didn't see him for years. Time has been really good to him." She exaggerated "really" and leaned into Rebecca as if she were sharing a secret. "But, I guess that ship left the station years ago, so to speak." Her flimsy metaphor struck her as funny, and she snorted and held onto Rebecca's arm for support. "You take good care of him tonight. For me."

Should she let that comment slide or correct her? Megan probably wouldn't remember the conversation in the morning, but Rebecca didn't want her assuming she and Chris were sexually involved.

"Oh, we're not, uh, we haven't known each other all that long."

Megan leaned back in an exaggerated fashion. Fearing Megan might lose her balance, Rebecca grabbed hold of her wrist, pulling her upright.

"Doesn't matter." Then she stilled and wagged her long finger at Rebecca—the index finger that brandished a shiny bauble. "I saw you kiss him, you know. You don't kiss a man like that and then refuse him. Not after a wedding of all things. Everyone knows if you leave a wedding with someone, well, you'd better be ready to set sail to the train."

Her metaphor wasn't working anymore, but Rebecca got her meaning. Mercifully, she stopped speaking then, and Rebecca heard one of the restroom doors open and close again. This time, thank God, it was Chris.

He smiled at Rebecca and put his arm around her waist. She felt him tense when he recognized Megan, but seeing her condition, he softened.

"Megan, do you have a ride home?

"Are you offering to take me home, Chris?" She swayed in his direction, and he steadied her.

"Sorry. I've got to get Rebecca back to her place, but I could call you a cab or see if someone else here can give you a ride."

"That's what I thought. Don't worry about me. Brittany's the designated driver." She motioned to a raven-haired beauty in a skin-tight sheath dress pressed up against one of Alan's coworkers.

"Okay then," Chris said and nudged Rebecca toward the door. "Good night."

They began to move before Megan could protest. As they reached the double doors at the exit, Chris removed his jacket and put it around Rebecca's shoulders. "It's gotten a lot cooler out since we came in."

After he closed the rental car door behind her and got behind the wheel, he rested his hand on her lap. "Sorry about Megan. That was probably an uncomfortable, if not painful, conversation. I don't know how she managed to get on the guest list. Her brother, Tim, is a buddy of Alan's, but I didn't see him here tonight." He gave her a sheepish smile. "Megan's always had kind of a crush on me."

"Really? I hadn't noticed." Rebecca tried to keep a straight face. When Chris gave her a curious look, she laughed.

"You had me there. I started to think you were hitting the bottle in there when I wasn't looking." He smiled, removed his hand from her lap, and turned the key in the ignition.

She thought he would put the car into gear, but he paused and looked at her again.

"Megan's always liked attention, especially from guys. She's a flirt, no doubt about it, but it wasn't until her oldest brother was killed by an IED in Afghanistan that she dove headlong into the party scene."

Rebecca felt a stab of guilt. She had judged Megan unfairly. She looked down and straightened the fabric in her gown before she had the nerve to look at Chris. "I'm sorry to hear that."

Chris nodded once and backed out of the parking space. A comfortable silence ensued, and Rebecca relaxed into her seat. When Chris passed her exit, a worried shudder ran through her. Where was he taking her? Was Megan, for all her drunken stupor, right? Did leaving a wedding with a guy mean you were going to sleep with him?

"Chris, you are taking me home, right?"

"Shoot, I missed your exit, didn't I? Sorry. I'm tired, and I'm driving on autopilot I guess. I'll get off up here and go around."

She hadn't realized the sigh of relief she let out was audible until Chris looked her way.

"What's the matter?" He glanced between her and the road. "Did you think I was kidnapping you?"

She laughed, but she could tell by Chris's wary look that he didn't buy her attempt to laugh it off.

When they reached her apartment, Chris got out of the car and then let Rebecca out. He offered his hand, and she took it, holding on as she gathered her handbag and dress in her other hand and stepped onto the curb. He held onto her as they walked up the steps and to her door. They slowed to a stop, and he drew his tux jacket in around her shoulders.

"Thank you, again, for coming with me. I know weddings can be—" He searched for the right word and hadn't yet found it when she finished the sentence for him.

"Beautiful. Magical."

Chris smiled. "That wasn't what I was going for."

"I know, but being there was a blessing. Really."

"I'm feeling pretty blessed myself." He inched closer to her. "So, first taste of champagne and first dance. Could I be lucky enough to have claimed a first kiss, too?"

Suddenly shy, Rebecca looked down and twisted her hands. "Unfortunately, no. You're about eight years too late on that one." She looked up again, touched that Chris was grateful to have shared these special 'firsts' with her. "But it was *our* first kiss."

"Yes, it was." Chris slid his hand along her neck, resting his fingers beneath her ear and stroking her cheek with his thumb. His gaze bored into her, and she thought at first he would kiss her, but he just stared. She wanted to look away but couldn't. His eyes were there challenging her. Then he smiled like he knew something she didn't. And then she knew, too. This was something real, lasting, and powerful. So powerful it frightened her.

He kissed her cheek, and then stopping as if he hadn't planned to do it until that very second, moved to kiss her on the lips. "That would make this our second kiss." His lips hovered over hers before he pressed them to her mouth in the most delicate, ethereal kiss she could imagine. It was as gentle and nonthreatening a kiss as could be, but Rebecca tensed as she recalled Megan's assessment of Chris's expectations for the night.

Chris released her and gently removed his jacket from her shoulders. "You okay?"

She nodded, feeling silly now. He clearly hadn't intended to do anything but see her to her door.

"I'm going to have to take this back." He lifted the tux on his finger. "You'd better get in there before you get cold."

"Yeah. I've got to get in and get to bed. I told my dad I'd meet him for church in the morning." She switched her handbag to the other hand and pulled out her keys. She realized that Chris was waiting to see that she got in the door, so she fiddled with the key until she turned the dead bolt and unlocked the door. She faced him one last time. "Good night."

"It sure was."

4

Crush

As Chris waited on Rebecca's doorstep the next morning, he thought for the hundredth time of their kiss the night before. Kisses. There were two. He had felt it again just as he had in the grocery store—that pull on his heart almost from outside himself. After the second kiss, he knew it hadn't been the alcohol earlier in the evening. Rebecca herself was intoxicating.

He had slept soundly but woke before dawn. Since then he couldn't get her out of his mind—and not just her kisses. She had tensed several times during the evening. At the time, he couldn't understand why. Thinking back on it, he realized it had been in response to him, as if she couldn't decide whether or not to trust him. He'd swear when he missed her exit last night, she truly feared he'd abscond with her. He needed to reassure her that he wasn't a threat or she'd never let her guard down. The sooner he did that the better. He hoped she hadn't left yet to meet her dad.

The postwar, white vinyl-sided home reminded Chris of the neat little houses used in model train displays. Entrance to Rebecca's first floor apartment was by way of the concrete porch. A red, white, and blue pinwheel rooted in a small, sand-filled terra cotta pot spun in the breeze, and wooden flower boxes lined the ledges. The red geraniums and white petunias were small, but by the end of the summer they'd be spilling out over the sides of the containers. A set of bamboo chimes with a wooden pig carved at the top clattered in the breeze.

In less than a minute, Rebecca answered her door.

"Chris, this is a surprise. I'm about to leave for my dad's." She stepped onto the porch, slung her purse over her shoulder, and closed the door.

What on earth is she wearing? The dowdy dress she wore

diminished her natural beauty. The Mennonite girls on last week's camping trip wore homespun dresses that fit better than that dull sack. Last night she had looked like a veritable Cinderella, and today it looked as if she had sent her fairy godmother packing. Did her father expect her to dress this way for church?

"I'll only take a minute. Something's been bothering me." He stepped closer to her as the screen door swung shut behind her. "Is there anything I said or did that made you think I expected something from you last night?"

"Not at all. You were a perfect gentleman."

He didn't detect anything but sincerity in her answer. "What made you so uncomfortable after we left the wedding?"

Rebecca blew out a breath.

He was right then. She *had* been uncomfortable.

"It was something Megan said. I know I'm naïve, and I thought maybe she knew something I didn't about leaving a wedding with someone. I'm sorry."

Megan. Now it made sense. She had filled Rebecca's head with nonsense that had caused her unnecessary worry.

"No. You don't have anything to apologize for. Let me make this clear. I've never thought casual sex was a good idea. That's not how my parents raised us, Alan's previous behavior notwithstanding. Then when I converted, I couldn't find any wiggle room in the Bible or the *Catechism* for sex being for anyone but a husband and wife. And believe me, I looked." He lifted his eyebrows and sighed, his look of exasperation having the intended effect of making her laugh. Then he smiled, too. "So, you don't need to worry about me expecting something from you or pressuring you or anything like that, okay?"

She nodded. "Thank you."

Chris looked at his wristwatch. "I've got to go, or I'll be late for church myself. I'll call you." He kissed her quickly and walked her to her car before mounting his motorcycle. The unsettled feeling that had weighed on him all morning lifted. In its place, a sense of peace prevailed along with a whole lot of something that felt more and more like burgeoning love.

***

Rebecca didn't expect to see Alan hanging out at his parents' house the week after his wedding, but when she pulled up alongside the curb, he stood in the driveway, his hands in his shorts pockets, while Chris polished the chrome on his motorcycle.

She put the car into park and grabbed the container of fudge-full peanut butter bars that rested in the passenger seat. Having a new outlet for her baking had inspired her. It didn't hurt that Chris showered her with compliments about her muffins a couple weeks ago.

Chris stood and checked his work before buffing a spot near the front fender.

"So, is it ready for a joy ride?" Rebecca asked.

"Almost." He stood again and stuffed his polishing cloth partway into his back pocket. "Want to join me?"

"I'd—"

"Don't let him talk you into taking a ride on that thing," Alan said. By the way he eyed the container under her arm, she knew he'd spotted her cookies. There were plenty for Chris to share.

"Number one, he drives like a madman. And number two, he just wants you to sit close to him."

"I'll keep that in mind," Rebecca said. She smiled and held out the container to Chris. "Surprise inside for you."

Chris accepted the box and popped a corner of the lid. "Mmmm. Smells like peanut butter and chocolate."

"Did I mention I haven't had breakfast yet?" Alan wasn't very subtle.

Chris obliged by opening the container and taking a cookie for himself before extending the box to Alan.

"Don't listen to him," Chris said around mouthfuls of gooey peanut butter. "He knows very well I'm a safe driver."

Alan swallowed and wiped a few crumbs from his mouth before responding. "Notice he didn't refute the other point about sitting close to him." He lifted his eyebrows a couple times before heading toward the house.

Rebecca laughed. She wouldn't mind sitting close to Chris, and although she hadn't considered it until recently, she really did want to ride a motorcycle.

Music suddenly blared from the house.

"Sorry," Alan called from the garage as he adjusted the volume on an old stereo system.

Rebecca listened to the repeated guitar riff, which sounded vaguely familiar. It reminded her of an old song, but she couldn't place it. "This song—is it Dave Matthews?"

Chris stopped gathering his cleaning supplies and listened for several seconds. "No. The Black Keys."

He wiped one more smear from his motorcycle, intent on finishing his job before they left for lunch.

Rebecca knew nothing about motorcycles, but she liked the look of the one in front of her—a black and silver Harley Davidson with burgundy fenders. It emanated a subtle, sleek masculinity that appealed to her nearly as much as the man who rode it.

Chris wore brown leather motorcycle boots with a metal buckle on the side, faded jeans, and a charcoal Henley shirt layered with a white tee shirt. His sleeves were pushed up nearly to his elbows as he crouched to dust something from the wheel and then stood. He was a sight to behold.

"Caught you looking." He let her squirm for a couple seconds before he added, "But I'm not sure if it's at me or my motorcycle."

She couldn't deny she'd been staring. Her cheeks probably flamed red. "Both. With the motorcycle and the music, you've got kind of a bad boy thing going on."

"Are you saying I'm a bad boy? Because I'm pretty sure I've never had that label before. I've always been the dreaded 'nice guy'."

He stepped toward her, placed his hands on her waist, and dragged her body flush against his. "Are you saying you like bad boys?" She could see the teasing in his eyes and the way they crinkled at the corners.

She pressed her hands against his forearms to put a little

distance between them. "No, but I'm not immune to the appeal. Besides, you're just a bad boy poser."

"Poser?" he said with mock indignation. "Poser?"

So quick she couldn't evade him, he captured her again around the waist, spun her around and tickled her sides. *How did he know?* She doubled over laughing and twisted out of his grip but nearly fell on the ground in the process.

Chris relented and helped steady her. He had the advantage now that he knew she was ticklish, and she didn't doubt he'd use it. She could tell by the mischievous gleam in his eyes.

The gleam disappeared, leaving something more earnest in its place. He smoothed her hair back into place where it had come free from her loose ponytail, and his gaze dropped to her lips. He wanted to kiss her.

"Hey, you two. The neighbor's kids are out playing," Alan said from where he emerged from the garage. "Let's keep it clean."

His remark reminded her of what she'd wondered when she had first arrived.

"I'm pretty sure tickling is 'Rated E for Everyone,'" Rebecca said, "but speaking of behavior more suited to privacy, I thought you and Jamie would still be on your honeymoon."

Alan shrugged a shoulder. "Jamie didn't want the hassle of planning a vacation on top of a wedding, so we're taking a vacation later in the summer. We were at Disney a few months ago anyway."

"Oh." Rebecca didn't know what to say. She couldn't imagine being a newlywed and not wanting to get away with her new husband, but it sounded like Alan and Jamie had been living like a married couple for a while and the impetus to go away and get lost in each other in some exotic locale had waned.

Lucky for her, Chris finished with his motorcycle and foisted his dirty rags and supplies onto Alan, effectively ending that line of conversation. She waited while Chris moved the bike into his parents' garage. Apparently he hadn't been serious about taking her for a ride, and they were taking her car to lunch.

Lunch at Neato Burrito was always good—and filling. Someone had a heavy hand with the cilantro in the salsa, and Rebecca loved it. Chris polished off his enormous beef burrito as Rebecca wrapped her leftovers.

The restaurant sported a bohemian atmosphere from the colorful vinyl booth seats to the odd, red lamps that hung over the tables. A few patrons occupied the counter stools, and a couple placed their order at the counter. Occasional remarks shouted between the counter help could be heard over the folk music pumped through the overhead speakers.

Chris rolled up his foil wrapper and used napkin and set them on his paper plate. He folded his hands on the table in front of him. "So, do you have any plans for next weekend?"

"I don't know, do I?" She was flirting. She never flirted. *What has gotten into me?*

"Have you ever been hiking or camping?"

Does crossing the mall parking lot at Christmas or a backyard sleepover in a play tent count? "Just some day hikes. I've always wanted to try camping, but I've never had the opportunity."

"Well, this may be your big chance then." Chris's hands disappeared beneath the table, and he leaned on the padded seat back. "I'm thinking of going back to Shenandoah National Park if you'd like to come."

"I would, but . . ." It sounded good, but there were so many reasons she should say no.

Chris dipped his head and peered up at her, brows raised. "But what?"

"I don't know the first thing about camping. I don't have any gear. And what are the sleeping arrangements?"

Chris rattled off the answers as if he'd already thought it all through. "I know enough about camping for the both of us. I have gear you can use. Separate sleeping bags on opposite sides of the tent. Or I could see if I can borrow a separate tent from someone."

Rebecca wanted to say 'yes.' She loved the outdoors, but neither her dad nor her sister cared for it, so aside from her limited summer camp experience, which included air-conditioned cabins and bunk beds, she had no chance to indulge her interest. A weekend alone with Chris tempted her, but even with separate bags or tents, going away with him overnight might not be a good idea. If her father found out...she didn't want to think about it.

"Can I have a day or two to mull it over? I appreciate the offer; I'm just not sure if...I'm just not sure."

The light went out of Chris's eyes, but he sat forward again and placed his hand over hers where it rested on the table. "Take a couple days to think." His thumb stroked hers. "It's my favorite place in the world, and I want to take you there."

How could she say no to that? He wanted her to be a part of something he loved. Still, it wouldn't hurt to think it over.

That night, once Abby's children were in bed, Rebecca called to ask her opinion.

"Should you go? Heck, yeah. I mean, you're sure he's not a serial killer, chronic nose picker or rapist, right?"

Rebecca giggled. "Yes on all three."

"Then go. What do you have to lose? A weekend of what? Listening to me whine about Ian's explosive diapers or sitting at home watching bad reality TV and eating ice cream from the carton? Go. Live."

Rebecca sighed. She hadn't done much living. Not really. These past months out from under Dad's control made her realize how little she *had* done, seen, or experienced. Travel topped the list of things she'd missed out on. And she did trust Chris, didn't she?

"Thanks, Abby. I'm going to do it."

When she told Chris that, yes, she'd go, she could tell he was elated, even over the phone.

"What do I need?"

"Hiking boots, if you've got them, and your personal stuff. I'll take care of the rest."

She ought to confirm the sleeping arrangements once

more. "Separate sleeping bags, right? No fooling around?"

"No fooling around. I promise."

He didn't try to backpedal. Good. He had even upped the ante with a promise to behave.

"What time do you plan on coming back Sunday? I'd like to go to church."

"It's kind of a haul to get to the Catholic church from the campground. You have to go down the mountain. I figured I'd go here Sunday evening. You're welcome to come with me, or I can find out if there's a nondenominational service at the campground Sunday morning."

"Would you do that for me?" She switched her phone to the other ear and bit her bottom lip.

"Sure. I'd be happy to go with you, too."

Rebecca smiled and squelched her desire to let out an excited squeal. She couldn't wait for the weekend.

5

One Sweet World

Rebecca's stomach lurched to a stop a second after the car as they pulled up to the campground entrance. The winding road through the park, beautiful as it was, had made her a little carsick.

"You okay?" Chris asked.

"I feel better now that we've stopped moving." She laid her hand across her belly, and the nausea subsided.

"I'll reserve us a site. Be right back." Chris hopped out of the car and walked to the window of the small ranger station. The ranger passed some information to him under the glass. Chris pointed at something on the paper and slid it back under.

Rebecca rolled the window down and breathed in the fresh mountain air. Two white-tailed deer, a doe and a fawn, ambled from the campsite on her right toward the road. A pair of robins chased each other across the grass calling to one another. Peaceful. She loved the park immediately.

The slam of the door brought her attention back to the car interior.

Chris held a campground map out to her and pointed to the circled site. "We got a walk-in back in the woods. I love the sites back there. Wooded, level, shady, and private."

She tensed a little at "private." Nothing would be happening between them that required privacy. She reminded herself of Chris's promise to her about "no fooling around" and that he had proven himself to be a gentleman. She would relax and enjoy this weekend.

"There it is." She pointed at the site marker, and Chris backed into the space, giving them easier access to the gear in Alan's trunk.

"Let's check it out." Chris took her hand, and they walked down a narrow, rocky path lined on either side with weeds and wildflowers. A few red and black butterflies flitted above the foliage.

She and Chris passed tents on either side and continued until the path dead-ended into their site. Her gaze followed the trail of light up through the canopy to the sun. Dark clouds moved in from the west, but bright and sunny skies dominated the east.

"What do you think?" Chris rubbed the sole of his hiking boot over some rocks in the tent pad area. He picked a few up and chucked them into the woods.

Rebecca touched the base of her neck. "You're the expert. Looks perfect to me."

He smiled. "You like it here?"

"I love it so far."

His smile grew bigger. "Good. I thought you would."

"Maybe we should put up the tent right away." She inclined her chin overhead, where the dark clouds continued to roll in.

Chris squinted at the sky. "Yeah, we should. Let's get our stuff."

It took three trips, but they managed to get everything Chris had packed out of the trunk and down to the site. They piled everything onto the picnic table, and Chris shuffled things around as he found what he needed first. He glanced at the clouds again. "We're going to have to be quick."

Rebecca nodded but knew she would be little help. She'd never set up a tent in her life. What could she do? She stacked some small containers and put them in the storage box.

"It's nice they provide these big metal boxes to keep stuff dry."

Chris stopped shuffling his gear and stared at her. Then at the metal box. Then back at her and laughed. "They are nice, but they're not there for our convenience. They're bear-proof containers. So bears don't tear into our food and stuff."

"There...are...bears here?" Could he hear the terror in her voice?

He glanced up and gave her a half grin, then grabbed the

tent bag, unzipped it, and removed the poles. "Yep. Black bears. If we're lucky, we'll see some. Last time I stayed back here, a mama bear and her two cubs walked through the woods." He pointed behind their tent through the trees and bushes.

"They won't eat us?"

Chris laughed. "No, but they would eat our food if we left it out." When she didn't respond, he looked up again. He must have seen the worry there because he set down the poles he was assembling and came to the table.

Taking both of her hands in his, he said, "You don't need to worry. The bears don't want to be bothered. We'll steer clear of them. If you make noise, bang some pots or something, it scares them right off."

A bear big enough to maul her with one paw was afraid of a pot lid? It didn't seem right, but Chris had done this many times, so she chose to trust him. She nodded. "Okay. How can I help you?"

He handed her three poles to assemble. "Just finish this."

While she sprung the poles into place, Chris laid out a tarp, arranging it just so, then laid the flattened tent on top of it.

"Okay. Let me see those poles."

Rebecca mostly watched as Chris assembled the tent. She held things steady as he secured the tent to the poles and then handed him stakes as he pounded them into the ground.

"Rebecca, can you hang onto these poles while I tie this?" Chris was holding up the two main poles where they crisscrossed over the tent.

She stepped in front of him onto the tarp, where their toes poked beneath the edge of the tent. Chris had about six inches on her, so when he handed off the poles, she had to stand on her tiptoes to keep hold of them. His body heat warmed her as he reached above her and laced the thin fabric ties. He smelled woodsy and fresh, not at all sweaty like she expected, given that he had just staked a half dozen guy-wires.

She felt rather than saw that the poles were fixed and

rocked back onto her heels. When she turned, her face was nearly up against Chris's chest. She looked up, and he looked down as his hands dropped to her sides. His gaze lowered to her lips, and she remembered their two kisses the night of Alan and Jamie's wedding. She wouldn't mind reliving those moments.

"Thanks. It's nice to have help with this kind of stuff for a change." Then he took a step back, allowing her to move away from the tent.

Chris eyed the mostly gray sky that threatened to empty itself on them. "Let's see if we can get this canopy over the eating area, too." He grabbed a canvas sack and walked toward the picnic table.

They repeated the process with the poles and had the canopy up but not staked when the heavens opened in a downpour. They scrambled underneath the cover, but the rain and the accompanying wind caused it to wobble. Rebecca grabbed a pole to steady it. The tree leaves repeatedly sagged with the weight of the heavy drops and then popped back up. The smell of the fresh rain rejuvenated her, making her smile.

"I'm going to have to finish this." Chris snatched the remaining stakes from her hand, grabbed the mallet, and ducked out into the rain. He had one corner secured before he set down the stakes and mallet, whipped off his shirt in one motion, and tossed it to her under the canopy.

It made sense. Why get his shirt soaking wet? This way he could dry his back and chest with a towel and have something warm and semi-dry to put on. She just wasn't prepared for it.

She realized then how little time she had spent in the company of men other than her father and brother-in-law. Chris didn't bear the six-pack abs of a ripped body builder, the kind that graced the covers of romance novels, but he was masculine, muscled, and she couldn't pull her gaze from him as he worked. He didn't work out at a gym as far as she knew; he lived—biked, hiked, helped care for his parents' yard, and played flag football and whatever other sport was in season with Alan and some other guys. Had she been caught looking, she would have been embarrassed but not guilty. He was almost an innocent curiosity to her, albeit a very attractive one.

In a few minutes, he had finished and darted back under the cover saying something to her.

She blinked and forced herself out of her reverie. "What?"

"The towel?"

"Oh, here." She handed him the towel and forced her attention elsewhere as he dried his hair and arms. "It's not a very big towel."

"No, but it does the job." He ran it over his hair one last time and shrugged. "And at least it's warm out."

Rebecca smiled. Yes, her cheeks did feel a little heated.

The rain eased.

"Just a passing shower, I hope," Chris said. "When it stops, we can go to the camp store down at the entrance and get some supplies."

"Whatever you say. I'm the newbie."

After fifteen minutes, the rain stopped and the sun came out. They drove out of the campground and to the store near Big Meadows, aptly named, she thought. That's all it was—a big, big meadow. When she looked carefully, she noticed more deer nibbling their way around a copse of small trees.

Chris grabbed a basket in the store, and he picked up an extra camp towel, a small whisk broom, and enough food for dinner and breakfast. She left him to finish his shopping while she browsed the tee shirts and typical tourist trap items— Christmas ornaments, magnets, shot glasses, and back scratchers. She meandered into the children's section and perused a variety of bug catchers and magnifying glasses. She selected one of the small bug holders and took it to the cashier.

"Found something you like?" Chris had a bag in each hand.

She held up her own small bag.

"Bug holder. There are lightning bugs down here, aren't there?"

"Yep."

"I kind of never got over catching them." She shrugged and gave him a sheepish smile. She couldn't resist catching as many fireflies as she could every opportunity she got. Silly, but true.

***

Chris planned a day hike for the afternoon. Rebecca knew that he slowed his pace for her, but he didn't seem to mind; they took their time and enjoyed the natural beauty that surrounded them. Chris knew all about the cabin foundations they passed, what kind of trees lined the trail, and even where to find some elusive little salamanders that lived only inside the park. He acted as a personal park guide for her.

Despite their leisurely pace, Rebecca was dog-tired by the time they got back to the campground. When Chris told her he'd handle dinner, she sunk into the hammock with relief. She must have been more tired than she thought, because an hour and a half later, Chris leaned into the hammock, nudged her arm, and summoned her to dinner.

She hadn't counted on more than hot dogs and beans, but Chris had grilled steaks, baked potatoes in the fire, and cooked corn on the cob, too. Between mouthfuls of hot, buttery potato she praised his cooking.

"Thank you. I'm sure I'm not as good a cook as you are a baker. Those peanut butter bars were out of this world. I do think everything tastes better over a campfire though."

"So, do you cook in a kitchen, too, or just over a fire?"

"Uh, let's just say my indoor cuisine is limited to things I can boil and microwave."

Rebecca leaned away from the picnic table and patted her full belly. "I'm stuffed. What's for dessert?"

Chris laughed. "You remind me of Alan. He used to eat about three nibbles of his dinner when we were kids, say he was full, but then tell my mom there was still room in the 'dessert part.' And, I do have a bag of marshmallows."

"Ooh, marshmallows. I can do dessert. You point me in the direction of the marshmallows and the long fork-thingies, and then go put your feet up by the fire."

"The marshmallows are in the bear box, and the 'fork thingies' are on top of it." Chris must have been beat, too, because he went right to his camp chair, unlaced his boots and propped his feet on an old log to the side of the fire pit.

Rebecca came back with the forks and marshmallows and tore open the bag so she could place a couple of marshmallows on each tine. "So, do you like your marshmallows burnt, toasty with a gooey inside, or lightly browned?" She ticked each option off on her fingers.

When he didn't answer right away, she looked over. Chris's hands were behind his head, which he had leaned back as far as he could, and his eyes were closed. "I could go for something hot and luscious."

That had to be a double entendre—one she chose to ignore. He confirmed her suspicions when he sat up and smiled.

"Toasted and gooey sounds perfect."

She shot him a crooked grin. She wished she had a witty retort, but instead her stomach, which she thought had been filled to the max with steak and potatoes, made room for a swarm of butterflies as well. "Excellent choice."

After a few minutes of holding the sweet treats over the hottest part of the fire, Rebecca lifted the fork to examine their toasty perfection before offering one to Chris. When he didn't move from his seat, she took them over to him, slid the gooey, delicious mess off the metal stick and proffered it with her fingers. It smelled so good she couldn't wait to taste her own. Instead of taking it from her fingers, Chris took her hand and guided it to his mouth. Rebecca froze. Chris's lips touched her fingers, but thankfully he didn't do anything suggestive with them.

"No sense getting my fingers sticky, too." His eyes glimmered like they had last week when he had tickled her. He was playing with her again. "Mmmm. Superb." He licked his lips and watched as Rebecca enjoyed her own marshmallow.

***

Chris moved his seat closer and poked at the fire. "Why don't you go to the restroom and brush your teeth and stuff before it gets too late? I'll sit here with the fire."

"Okay."

Rebecca grabbed her things from the bear box. The heavy door clanged shut as she turned and headed up the trail. Chris remembered the soft blush of Rebecca's cheeks and the self-conscious way she smiled when he teased her. He hoped he hadn't gone too far with the marshmallows. He was just trying to play with her.

He stared at the fire a few minutes longer before he noticed the flashes in his peripheral vision. Lightning bugs. He scurried over to the picnic table and took Rebecca's bug container out of the bag. Releasing its Velcro strap, he popped it open and ripped off the tag.

The bugs lit in the dark spots at the edges of the campsite and alongside the larger trees. It was cute that Rebecca still liked to chase the little bugs. In truth, he did, too. He spent the next twenty minutes carefully scooping up as many as he could and filling her little container. Not bad: about fifteen bugs flashed behind the vinyl netting. He set the container in the middle of the table and slid the empty lantern box in front of it so he could surprise her with it.

As he took a seat, he noticed a group hauling their stuff down the trail to the empty campsite nearest theirs. A grown man chasing lightning bugs with nary a child in sight? Embarrassing.

The arrival of new neighbors disappointed but didn't surprise him. It was a weekend, after all, and these were desirable sites. He would miss the peace and the privacy though. He watched for ten minutes or so as five college-aged guys tried to set up their tents using only the light generated by one Coleman lamp. They shouted directions at one another punctuated by insults and raucous laughter. He hoped they wouldn't be loud once they got settled.

A few minutes later, Rebecca came half-running down the trail, her headlamp bobbing as she went. "Where's my bug container? The lightning bugs are everywhere."

"It's there on the table." He pointed in the general direction of her bug holder. He smiled and waited for her to discover his surprise.

She circled the table once before she spotted it. Her chin dropped and her eyes widened as she picked it up by the small handle, looking first at the flashing bugs and then at him. "You've been busy."

He grinned. "I guess you're not the only one who hasn't outgrown catching them."

She smiled. "I'll see how many more I can add." She chased the flashing bugs around the fringes of the campsite while Chris grabbed his things and headed to the restroom. Camping with Rebecca was turning out to be more fun than he'd ever dreamed.

Darkness and quiet had settled over the campsite during the fifteen minutes he had been gone. Their new neighbors had apparently set up and then left. A soft glow from the campfire lit the area around the fire pit, and Chris took the big stick he kept by the campfire and pushed around the ashes until the glow subsided and only a little smoke rose from the heated coals.

He returned his things to the bear box, and as he stepped toward the tent, a light shone through the ceiling.

"Chris?" Rebecca's voice sounded tentative.

"It's just me." He slipped off his boots outside the tent, unzipped the door, and stepped inside.

Rebecca smiled, then bit her lower lip as she sat on top of her bag with her knees bent and her arms wrapped around them.

"Everything okay?"

"Yes. I'm glad you're back."

Had the loud guys setting up their stuff given her a hard time? "Did something happen?"

"No. It got dark. And quiet. And lonely. And I've never been out in the woods alone at night before."

Oh. Just a little scared. He had been camping since he

could walk, and he hadn't thought how it might be frightening to Rebecca. He zipped the door closed and sat on his sleeping bag. He'd play the role of her protector if that's what she wanted.

"There are no locks on this thing." She looked from one side of the tent to the other where Chris had unzipped the windows to let in the cool evening air.

"No, but we won't need them. It's safe. I promise you."

"But anybody could walk up and—"

Before she could dream up some kind of *Blair Witch Project* scenario, he said, "No one has any reason to be back here."

"But you said the Appalachian Trail runs—" She gestured in the opposite direction of the trail, but Chris didn't correct her.

"Rebecca, no one's going to bother us."

"What about bears? Did we leave out any trash?"

"I put it in the dumpster on my way to the restroom. All our food is locked up in the bear box, and we didn't bring anything like that in the tent."

"What about. . .us? Don't we smell like food to bears?"

"We bagged all our toiletries, and you didn't use any perfume or lotion tonight, did you?'

She shook her head. He had told her to leave all that stuff at home.

"Then there's no need to worry." She must have been suffering some serious anxiety while he was gone.

"But what about if I'm...well, if it's that time..." Her cheeks were getting pink.

Chris wrinkled his brow and tried to figure out why she was being so reticent. "What time?"

She let out a breath and allowed her head to fall down against her knees. When she spoke it was no louder than the whisper of the wind through the trees.

"What if I'm menstruating?"

He hadn't seen *that* one coming. "Uh, the bears won't mind." *Awkward.*

She peeked out from under her folded arms. "But I heard

bears were attracted to . . ."

He knew what people said, and he had Googled it once. "No, not black bears, and that's what's here in the park. The research only shows that polar bears may be attracted to...to that scent."

"You're sure?"

She really was scared. He wanted to gather her up in his arms and offer to hold her all night long. "Yes, I'm sure."

After studying his face a few more seconds she dropped her knees and readjusted herself in her bag. "Okay. You're the expert. If you say we're safe, I'm going to trust you."

"Thank you." He switched off his head lamp before breaking into a smile and sliding down into his bag. Rebecca turned her light off, too, and as he lay on his back, he peered through the skylight panel at the top of the tent. There was no moonlight, and the stars shone brilliantly.

A loud screech rang out in the distance and grew louder as it passed directly over their heads.

Rebecca shot up from her bag. "Chris, what was that?"

Talk about bad timing. If she weren't scared she would probably realize how cool that had been. "An owl. Probably a barred owl." As if on cue, a faint hoot sounded in the direction the owl had flown.

"Chris?"

"Yeah?"

"Would you sleep a little closer to me?"

He knew she couldn't see his expression, but he smiled. He hoped she couldn't hear it in his voice. "How close?" He dragged his bag and sleeping pad with him as he scooched across the tent floor towards Rebecca.

"Next to me."

He repositioned his sleeping pad, bag, and pillow alongside hers, lying on his stomach while she remained on her back.

"Still scared?"

"Just a little. I'm not used to this."

Raising himself onto his elbows, he leaned over her and

tenderly kissed her taut lips once and then again before scooting back down into his bag.

"I thought you promised no fooling around." She was smiling. He was sure of it; he *could* hear it in her voice. The kiss he had given her was reserved and controlled. She could not construe that as threatening.

"Kissing's not fooling around. At least not that kind of kissing."

He had been desperate to kiss her earlier when they were setting up the tent but had resisted. She had turned toward him and was tucked perfectly against his chest. His heart rate had sped up and his hands had ached to pull her to him and kiss her like crazy, but he wouldn't break his promise to her. He wanted her to trust him.

"Chris?"

"Yeah."

"Do you pray at night?"

Good—a change of subject. If she could get her mind off of being scared he knew she'd be fine. "I do."

"What do you say?"

"Well, I thank God for the day, and I do an examination of conscience and say an Act of Contrition."

"You do what and say what?"

"I think about the sins I committed that day and ask God to forgive me."

"Oh . . . Can I pray with you tonight?"

"Sure."

The polyester sack crinkled as she shifted onto her belly and folded her hands on her pillow. "I'll start and then you do your act of whatever it was there."

Chris chuckled. "Okay."

Her gaze followed his right hand as he made the sign of the cross. She waited, so he nodded for her to begin.

"Lord, thank you for our safe trip here today. Thank you for the beauty you've created here—the mountains, the trees, the wildflowers, and the animals. Thank you for Chris and for all he's done to make me comfortable here. Please keep us safe from harm."

She looked up, signaling she was done, so he spoke. "Now I take a minute to think about my sins." He bowed his head over his folded hands, so he didn't see if she did the same. Then he thought about his day. How he had been short-tempered with his mom when she pressed him for information about Rebecca. How he had thought himself better than the sloppy obese man at the campsite near the road. And how his eyes and his imagination had lingered a little too long on Rebecca's curves while she helped him put up the tent. He looked back up, and she had an earnest expression on her face. She gave him a small smile, and then he recited an Act of Contrition from memory. She joined him in the "amen" and then watched as he blessed himself again.

"Why do you do that?" she asked, setting off a half hour or more of conversation about the practice of his faith. She was respectful and inquisitive, and her questions were sincere. Chris found that they helped him refine his own thoughts about why he did what he did. Finally, she said, "I like the Act of—what was it?"

"Contrition."

"Yeah. It says it all. I'm sorry, here's why, and this is what I'm going to do about it so it doesn't happen again."

"That's pretty much it."

"Maybe you can teach it to me."

"I'd be happy to."

After that, they must have both drifted off to sleep. The next thing Chris knew he was awakened by an ear-splitting crack of thunder that reverberated in the ground beneath them. Rebecca shrieked and called out to him.

His own heart thundered from the shock of it, but he had been in storms at the park before and knew that this wasn't out of the ordinary. Because of their elevation, the clouds were closer and heightened the storm's intensity.

"It's just a thunderstorm. It'll pass."

Her bag rustled as she shifted onto her side to face him. Despite the fact that it had cooled, even inside the tent, she wrestled her arm out from her twisted sleeping bag and groped for his hand. Lying on his side now, too, he took her hand in his and held it lightly, rubbing the back of her hand with his thumb.

Lightning flashed, followed immediately by another loud crack of thunder. They were right in the thick of it. Her hand tightened around his.

"Are you okay?" he asked.

"Yeah. I like thunderstorms, but this one is fierce, and it caught me off guard."

For a half hour or more they laid awake, their hands squeezed together, talking only about the storm and whether it was letting up. By the time the thunder had stopped and the rain had diminished to a steady patter on the tent, Rebecca's soft, even breaths told him she had fallen asleep.

6

Crash Into Me

Chris didn't know which had woken him—the sunlight streaming through the skylight, the birds chattering in the treetops, or the persistent rustling outside the tent. Maybe it was the faint odor of skunk lingering in the air. After studying the shadows of the leaves, twigs and other debris the night's storm left on the outside of the tent, he looked at Rebecca, who faced away from him now. Sometime during the night their hands must have separated.

He pushed down his sleeping bag and crept to the tent door, careful to make as little noise as possible. After unzipping the door, he slipped into his unlaced boots and stepped around the side of the tent. He discovered the source of the rustling: a fat raccoon. It nudged aside the base of the tent, searching for something.

Chris kept his distance and waved the raccoon off. The last thing he needed was to wake Rebecca and have her pepper him with questions about raccoons, rabies, and God forbid—menstruation.

"Shoo, shoo. Get out of here."

"Chris?"

Uh-oh. "I'm right out here. Just a pesky little varmint." He shooed the masked rodent one more time, and it scurried off into the weeds.

Chris went back into the tent to find Rebecca wide awake. She had rolled back over so that she faced his empty bag.

Sleep had mussed her wavy brown hair, making it look even fuller and giving her a natural, slightly-untamed look. Her wide, brown eyes looked like matching pools of melted milk chocolate. The sleeping bag silhouetted the gentle slope from her feet to her hips, the dramatic dip of her waist, and the rise to her shoulder. She took his breath away and had him rethinking his whole "no fooling around" promise.

What would it be like to wake up to *that* every morning? He doubted he'd ever get to work on time again. Chris didn't know if he could manage a coherent conversation or whether he should even try. It would probably be better if he left.

"Everything okay?" She tilted her head as if it would help her understand, but it just made her hair fall from her shoulder to her bust line.

Sure, everything's fine if you think spontaneous human combustion is okay. "Yep...Just, uh, a..." He jerked his thumb toward the side of the tent. "A, uh, an animal. Got rid of it." He forced himself to look away and slipped back out the door. "I'm going to get some dry wood and start a fire for breakfast."

***

Rebecca shoved down her bag and folded her legs in front of her. She pulled a hair ribbon from the pocket on the tent wall, dragged her fingers through her hair, and pulled it back into a messy ponytail.

Nothing like having a cute guy that you're falling for see you first thing in the morning. That should dispel any illusions he might have about her. With her wild hair, tired eyes, and oily face maybe he wouldn't notice her worn, baggy, makeshift pajamas. She remembered what a scaredy cat she had been the night before, and then that she had basically told him she had her period. She groaned and pushed herself to her feet. There was only one way out of the tent, but maybe she could kill some time by cleaning up inside first.

She fluffed their pillows, rolled the sleeping bags, and let the air seep out of the sleeping mats. She took the little whisk broom and dustpan that sat in the corner and swept the bits of leaves and tree needles they had tracked in on their feet.

After dumping the debris outside of the tent, she slipped her hiking boots onto her bare feet and walked toward the picnic table where the smell of bacon hung in the air.

Chris cracked eggs into a cast iron skillet alongside thick slices of sizzling bacon. If he kept feeding her like this, they'd have to do another hike.

"Smells delicious. Are you sure you only cook in the outdoors?"

"Positive." He smiled, but he didn't look at her. That was odd.

She took a seat in her camp chair next to the fire and pulled her sleeves down over her hands while she listened to the small fire crackle and pop. The sun hung low in the sky, and the air carried a chill. "So, what did you find outside the tent?"

"Just a raccoon." He still didn't look at her. Weird.

"Chris?"

"Yeah?"

She didn't respond, and finally he looked away from the skillet and up at her.

"There. Is something wrong? I didn't think you wanted to look at me."

He laughed, but it didn't sound genuine. "Why wouldn't I want to see you?"

"Well, I know I look ratty in the morning, but I pulled my hair back, and as soon as I can get to the showers, I can make myself presentable."

He shook his head as if he couldn't believe what she said and stood up. He pointed his greasy spatula at her. "You...you look fabulous. Better than anyone has a right to after a restless night in a tent."

He was just trying to make her feel good, and it worked. She smiled. "Is it almost ready? I just realized I'm starving."

"You and me both."

***

Once they finished breakfast, Chris offered to clean the dishes and tear down the tent while she showered.

"You'll need to take the car since the showers are all the way up by the amphitheater. And make sure you have quarters. They're pay showers."

"Please tell me there's hot water."

He smiled. "There is. I'll go when you get back, and by then it will almost be time for the church service."

As Rebecca gathered her things and left the campsite, Chris noticed their neighbors were back and all seated around their fire pit. A heap of wet logs billowed white smoke, and he assumed they were attempting a campfire. Thankfully whenever they had returned to camp last night—and it must have been late—they hadn't made noise. They were a curious bunch. Cheap model tents from a big box store didn't denote serious hikers or campers. Their bulky coolers looked as if they were designed more for holding beer at a tailgate party than efficient packing. Instead of bagged and hanging from a tree limb, their trash was strewn around an overflowing box that, wouldn't you know it, had the name of a major brewery on the side. More than likely they were drinking buddies, not hiking companions.

Chris stopped scraping the bits of egg from his skillet when one of the guys called to Rebecca. Chris couldn't hear what he said, but she responded with a few words and a nervous laugh and continued on her way. He couldn't say the guy had done anything improper, but he had a gut feeling about it, and it wasn't good. He took comfort in the fact that he and Rebecca would be packing up and heading out soon.

After smearing some bacon grease on the skillet and setting it down to season over the coals, he brought all of their gear out of the tent and set it on the picnic table. Then using the metal hook on the back of his mallet, he removed the stakes from the tent fly and then the tent. Once the ends of the tent poles were lifted from their pockets, the tent collapsed in front of him. Chris grabbed a wad of paper towels and dried some of the parts that were still wet and dirty from last night's storm. He nearly jumped when a man's voice rumbled no more than a yard over his left shoulder.

"You packin' up?"

The guy who had spoken to Rebecca stood behind him. He wore a white undershirt and dirty jeans with a threadbare red plaid flannel shirt. He looked more like a man coming off a bender than someone who had spent the night in a tent.

"Yep. We're heading out this morning."

"You mind if we take whatever wood you have left?"

There wouldn't be much left, but he wasn't hauling the cheap pine out of the park in Alan's car.

"No problem. There's a little left under the table. I can't say it's completely dry, but I did have a tarp over it last night."

"Thanks, man."

Chris turned over his damp wad of paper towels and wiped the tent in preparation for folding it. He figured the guy would leave, but apparently he had more to say.

"That was some storm." He motioned back to the guys still circling the stinky, white cloud emanating from the fire pit at his site. "We decided to ride it out at the bar up at the lodge."

Lifting his chin in acknowledgement, Chris didn't want to encourage more conversation. Something about this dude unsettled him.

"'Course if there had been something to interest me back at the tent, that would be a different story."

Chris spared him a glance. He didn't know what that remark meant, but from the tone of his voice and the lascivious look in his eye, he guessed it had to do with a woman.

"The chick you brought. She's hot."

So, his instincts were right. This guy was a dirt bag, and he had an interest in Rebecca. "She's beautiful."

"Nothing' like getting laid in the fresh mountain air, is there?"

Whoa. Where did that come from? Chris's uneasy feeling ratcheted up to mild fear. "It's not like that. We just shared the tent. She's a really nice girl."

The next thing that came out of the guy's mouth made Chris's blood boil. A stream of crude words and implications made him fear for Rebecca's safety. Had he put her in danger? He'd camped here himself at least a dozen times and never had a problem with other campers. If anything, they were decent and polite. Not this guy. When his filthy words ended with a lightly-veiled threat of bodily harm if Chris didn't "share" Rebecca with him, all his internal alarms went off. He hoped there was a long line at the showers, and Rebecca wouldn't come strolling into this. It might be five on one, but Chris wouldn't let them harm Rebecca. He brought her here, and he felt responsible for her safety.

Chris stood and realized with dismay that the guy had a good three inches on him, not to mention being just plain bigger. *Lord, give me strength. And wisdom.*

He looked into the slightly-dilated eyes that were now trained on him. "How about you take the wood and go back to your campsite? We're going to pack and leave. And you're not going to say a word to my friend. In fact, I don't even want to see you or your buddies looking at her."

Not much of a threat, but he didn't have anything to back it up with, so it would have to suffice. He hoped.

The guy laughed—a mocking snort that made a knot twist in Chris's stomach and his fists clench at his sides. The damp towels he held dripped as he inadvertently squeezed the excess rainwater from them.

"What's the matter? Afraid she might realize you're a lousy lay?"

When that didn't provoke the response the guy wanted, he took a swing at Chris.

Chris darted to his right, missing the hit by inches.

He had never hit anyone in his life, not even Alan when he deserved it, but in that instant a surge of adrenaline rushed through his veins, and he punched the guy in the jaw. His knuckles felt more like they had slammed into a brick wall than a face, and they hurt so badly his instinct was to pace and try rubbing out the pain. Instead, he shook out his hand and waited for the retaliation.

The guy fell back a step, rubbing his bloodied lip and cheek. Chris spied movement in the distance. One of his buddies leapt to his feet.

"Darryl, you need a hand?"

Darryl didn't turn or answer. He waved his buddy off and gave Chris a slow, seedy smile before he hauled off and took a swing.

Chris darted to the right again, effectively dodging the fist aimed at his face but, in stepping to the side, he twisted his ankle on the tent pole lying at his feet.

He broke his fall with his right hand, but he lacked the agility to avoid the boot that landed in his side. Darryl could've pummeled him, but for some reason he allowed Chris to get back on his feet before he took another swing.

This one hit its intended target, and Chris winced at the flash of pain in his left cheek and behind his eye.

He cursed as the metallic taste of blood reached his tongue, then he steadied himself.

Weaker and less skilled, Chris's only advantage was his desperate desire to defend Rebecca, and that wasn't turning out to be an advantage at all. With a guttural growl, he charged at Darryl's middle and hoped he could at least knock him off balance. Darryl's meaty hands gripped his waist, and Chris tried to get better purchase on the wet ground as a yell came from the trail.

"Hey, break it up!"

Darryl's hands fell away, and when Chris lifted his head, he glimpsed a park ranger jogging toward them. *Thank you, Lord.* He didn't know who had alerted the rangers, but he'd be forever grateful to whoever did. Now he had to convince the ranger he hadn't instigated this; he wanted to safeguard Rebecca.

***

Rebecca ran her fingers over her damp braid as she walked from the showers to the car. The warm water soothed her aching muscles; she only wished it weren't a race against an invisible clock before the water stopped. She rubbed a hand over the prickly stubble on her left shin. She had been afraid to even try shaving her legs; she hoped Chris wouldn't get too close.

She kept the car at fifteen miles an hour as she drove the short distance to the campsite. A ranger's vehicle and a golf cart idled in their parking area. She didn't bother attempting to back Alan's car in since she knew Chris would be heading to the showers next. As she closed the door, she noticed a couple of rangers at the empty walk-in site closest to the parking lot. Chris sat on a stump next to the ranger. A first aid kit lay open on the ground next to him, and he held an ice pack to the left side of his face.

Her breath caught. She jogged over to the site and stopped short of the fire pit in front of Chris. Had there been some kind of accident? "What happened?"

Chris lifted the pack from his face and raised his gaze to her, but before he could say anything, the ranger asked, "Is this her?"

Rebecca's eyes widened as she scanned Chris's face. The left side of his lips swelled, and it looked as if his upper lip had been bleeding. The eye on the same side was nearly swollen shut.

"Yes, this is Rebecca," Chris said. His voice sounded slurred either from the swelling around his lips or the numbness caused by the ice pack.

The ranger spoke again, this time to her. "Your friend here took a little heat for defending your virtue."

Rebecca looked from the ranger to Chris and back to the ranger again. "My virtue?"

"Apparently your neighbor took a less-than-wholesome interest in you. Your boyfriend took a blow to the face defending you."

Her boyfriend? She squelched her desire to quibble with the ranger over terminology and turned back to Chris. "Someone hit you? Who? Why?"

Again before Chris could answer, the ranger spoke, and she started to get perturbed.

"Excuse me," the ranger said, "I'm going to escort our unwelcome guests out of the park."

Finally. Maybe now she could get some answers. For the first time, Rebecca noticed the men who had been camping in the walk-in site closest to them hauling out their gear while another park ranger kept close tabs on their progress. One of them, the big guy that had leered at her and made some dumb remark on her way to the showers this morning, glared at her.

Rebecca stepped around the fire pit and sunk to the ground in front of Chris. She ignored the muddy earth sticking to her knees. "Was it one of them?"

Chris removed the ice pack again, and she saw that his skin had bruised already.

"Yeah. The big dude with the flannel shirt. Darryl."

"Why? And what did this have to do with me?"

Chris shifted on the log and leaned his elbows on his knees.

Why did he seem reluctant to tell her?

"After you left, he came over to ask if he could have our extra wood. I said yes. Then he...he said some things...some disrespectful things about you." He looked up at her then, and his blue eyes held a fierce determination. "I told him to take the wood and leave, and he wouldn't. He didn't back off, and then it degenerated into a fight."

"Did you hurt him?"

Chris attempted a smile. "He's got a matching fat lip. I did a little damage, but I think he got the better of me. Or he would have if the ranger hadn't broken it up."

She folded her hands over his and turned them over, opening them so she could press her palms against his.

"Thank you. I hate to break it to you, but I'm not the kind of girl guys throw fists over." She tried not to get emotional, but tears stung her eyes, and her voice quavered. No one ever came to her defense. Not since John, the first boy who had ever kissed her.

"My face, fist, and ribs beg to differ." Somehow he smiled about it.

"Your ribs?"

"He kicked me when I fell."

"Oh, Chris. I'm so sorry." He was hurting because of her. Bleeding. Her heart ached for him, and she wished she could take away his pain. How could this have happened?

"Hey, not your boot in my side."

She let her hands fall away from his, stood up and turned toward the fire pit. She brushed at the dirt and dried grass caked to her knees. "No, but this is my fault. Obviously I did something or, I don't know, somehow I gave them the impression that..."

She heard Chris stand, and one of his hands slid into hers while he used the other to angle her shoulder back toward him. His brow pinched, and his eyes had that determined look again.

"Hey—none of this is your fault. You understand that, don't you? There's nothing you said or did—there's nothing you *could* say or do—that would justify that jerk's behavior."

It was sweet that he didn't want her to feel responsible. She may not have intended it, but there had to have been something. She tried to think of what she had worn, what she had said this morning. She realized Chris still stared at her.

"You really think you provoked this somehow, don't you?" He wanted her to say no and mean it. She knew that, but she couldn't deny she felt responsible. Somehow, some way she had given Daryl the wrong idea. Her silence turned out to be all the answer Chris needed.

Chris captured her face between both his hands, and she couldn't avoid the earnest intensity in his eyes. He spoke each word slowly and with emphasis as if it could make them true.

"You . . . are not . . . responsible for this. Okay?"

She nodded her head. She wanted to believe him.

His hands fells from her face. "Our stuff is all on the table. I'm going to go take a shower, and then we can pack it into the car." He glanced at his wristwatch. "I'm sorry, but I don't think we're going to make the church service now."

She waved her hand in front of him. "Don't worry about that. Go get cleaned up. I'll make sure everything is ready to go in the car."

Nodding, he grabbed his bag of toiletries and some clean clothes she hadn't noticed were resting beside the log, and headed for the parking lot. For the next half hour, Rebecca stacked their gear on the table and bear box, leaving only their camp chairs out in case they wanted to sit. Now that they'd missed the church service, she didn't know what they would do for the remainder of the morning. She had an idea though, if Chris was willing.

"Looks like you got everything together," Chris said as he took a seat in the camp chair and tied his boot laces. His wet hair appeared several shades darker—almost black—and made the contrast with his blue eyes more pronounced. Well, it contrasted to the one eye that remained fully opened. The left eye remained shut, but at least his lips looked better.

He grimaced and reached for his side as he stood again. "So, I guess we might as well pack up and head out if you're ready."

She hesitated for a second, not knowing how he would take her request. "I noticed a guitar case in the back of the car. Is it yours?"

Chris shoved his hands in his jeans pockets. "Yep."

He didn't offer any other explanation, so she continued. "Were you going to play it?"

He started smoothing out the dirt with the sole of his boot. "I thought maybe it would be nice to play something around the campfire last night, but then I forgot. I'm not very good anyhow. I've been watching YouTube videos, trying to teach myself to play."

"Would you play something for me? I'd love to hear it."

His foot stopped and his hands came out of his pockets. He flexed and released the fingers on his right hand a few times. That must have been the hand that delivered the blow to Darryl's face.

"You know, I never considered that slugging someone like I did would hurt me as much as him."

"Do you think you could still play?" She had to admit she was enamored with the idea of hearing him sing to her. Didn't every girl dream of being serenaded like that?

Lucky for her he must have found her enthusiasm more charming than annoying, and he agreed to give it a try despite the lingering stiffness in his hand. When he returned from the car with his instrument, he strummed a few minutes and tried to loosen up his fingers.

"Okay, I'm going to give this a go. Like I said, I'm not very good to begin with, but at least now I have an excuse for being mediocre." He looked up from the guitar and grinned. If only she could freeze-frame that moment. With his body angled away from her to accommodate the guitar, his swollen eye was hidden from view. The words "devastatingly handsome" clogged her thinking and made her heart stutter. Thank goodness she needn't speak as he began to play.

Rebecca only caught snippets of what he sang as he moved back and forth from singing to her and watching his hands as they moved over the strings. The chorus consisted mostly of "it's always better when we're together," and she assumed that or something close to it must be the title of the song. His right hand, swollen and stiff, still picked out the appropriate strings with only an occasional sour note finding her ears.

His smooth, resonant voice wouldn't rival any superstar's, but it was good, and it was his, and like everything about Chris, it exuded sincerity.

She thought he must be closing in on the end of the song when he smiled and rested his hand over the strings. He slowed his rhythm and sang *a cappella*, "and when I wake up, you look so pretty sleeping next to me." Her cheeks warmed, and she wondered if he had chosen this song for those lines or whether it had snuck up on him as it had her. She knew she wore a ridiculous, ear-splitting grin, and she didn't care.

Rebecca had no experience with real relationships, but this sure felt like one. Regardless of whether this thing with Chris lasted another week, another month, or the rest of their lives, she knew she would treasure this memory. Chris was attractive in and of himself, but it was the way he made her feel about herself that wowed her.

For most of her life, Rebecca had felt like a millstone dragging people down. Chris buoyed her. He acted as if he didn't even see her rough edges, and she felt for the first time as if she might be worth something, not for what she did—or when it came to sex—*didn't* do, but for who she was.

Chris laid his hand over the strings, and she applauded.

"Thank you so much. That was great."

"You make a good audience." He placed the guitar back in its case.

"I liked the song. By any chance could it be a Dave Matthews song?" This had become their inside joke. She'd almost be sorry when she finally stumbled upon a correct song and guessed right.

"Nope. Jack Johnson." He closed the guitar case and set it on the picnic table. He turned back toward her and looked at his watch. "We should probably get out of here. It's getting close to check-out time. I thought, since we missed the service this morning, maybe you'd like to come to church with me this evening. What do you think?"

She realized saying yes would extend the weekend a little longer and give her a little more time with Chris. Plus, she knew next to nothing about how he worshipped, and attending services with him might help her understand what he believed. It was an easy question to answer. "Sure. That sounds great."

7

Water Into Wine

Rebecca struggled to keep up as Chris led her toward the church with two minutes to spare before Mass began. The classical columns made the building look more like a monument than a place of worship. Like many other buildings in Gettysburg, this one had been used as a field hospital after the battle. They climbed the steps and came to a stop inside the double doors as people made their way into the church. Chris dropped her hand and reached across her to a small bowl of water mounted to the wall. She looked from the bowl to him as he blessed himself with the water. Should she do the same? The exact sequence of touching her head, chest, and shoulders confused her. Chris's hand, with fingers still wet, grasped hers again as he led her along the back of the church and up the aisle to an empty seat.

Chris chose a pew and stepped aside, allowing her to enter first. She started in, but when she turned back to ask him how far in she should go, he was still in the aisle, down on one knee blessing himself again. In a moment, he was beside her. After giving her a quick kiss on the cheek, he reached down and lowered a narrow, padded board behind the pew. She wasn't entirely sure of its purpose until Chris knelt on it, and she noticed others around them kneeling as well.

"Should I—"

"You can sit. Whatever you're comfortable with, Rebecca. There's kind of a lot of up and down. I should've given you a better idea of what to expect." Chris turned back toward the front and bowed his head, letting it rest on his hands.

The humility of his actions struck her. Chris was out of her league. Handsome, intelligent, and capable in every way. To see him here, head bowed and eyes closed in prayer, did funny things to her heart. The juxtaposition of strength and weakness was—she felt guilty even thinking it in church—

downright sexy. Suddenly conscious that she had been staring, she looked away, embarrassed.

A minute later, a pipe organ blared from behind and everyone stood. Chris grabbed a hymnal from the rack on the back of the pew and thumbed through it until he found the song. Holding it out between them, he smiled at Rebecca. She smiled back, then resumed looking forward. She didn't know the hymn, but it must have been familiar to the rest of the congregation because they all sang. She hoped Chris wouldn't notice that her lips remained closed.

She didn't sing as a rule, but her silence had the added advantage of allowing her to hear Chris. He seemed as comfortable singing in church as he did around the fire pit in the morning. She closed her eyes and homed in on his voice—deep and rich. When his hand touched her back, she opened her eyes.

Chris leaned into her, his brow wrinkled, and whispered, "Don't you sing?"

She shook her head, and then turned to watch as the priest and some others adorned with colorful robes processed to the front of the church. She only caught a glimpse, but the priest looked young, and Rebecca thought it must be Chris's friend Father John.

The music stopped, Chris slipped the hymnal back in the rack, and the priest began to speak. They made the sign of the cross again.

She tried to push down the creeping discomfort, but something about all the ritual struck her as cultish. Maybe it was because her experience of worship in a cinder block hall differed drastically from this experience.

Whereas the walls of her father's church were plain and unadorned, here there were murals and statues affixed to every surface. Frescos and stained-glass windows pulled her attention in every direction. She studied a scene from Matthew's Gospel depicted in the window nearest her until the creak of pews groaning under the weight of the congregants jolted her to attention. She sat, too, and Chris took her hand and held it between them, giving it a little squeeze.

Rebecca relaxed as a woman read from the Old Testament. More singing, and again Chris placed the book between them, presumably so she could sing along. She kept a small smile plastered to her face, but she wouldn't be cowed into singing. A reading from the New Testament followed, and then everyone stood again, singing. She focused on the priest for the first time as he read from one of the Gospels.

Her eyes widened and her chin dropped as she took in the familiar features of the priest. Thank God Chris was beside her and couldn't see her reaction.

The priest's short, light brown hair threatened to curl if allowed to grow even a half inch longer. His pointed nose and strong jaw gave him a look of authority despite his age. Although not near enough to see his eyes, she knew they were green, and even reading from a text his sonorous voice charmed her as it had that summer eight years ago. *This* was Father John? Chris's good friend—the man he thought of almost as a brother? What were the odds?

Rebecca reeled in her thoughts and tried to focus on the Bible passage when everyone spoke in unison again and took a seat. Up, down, up, down. She thought she'd never catch up. As if she hadn't had enough time to focus on Father John already, he launched into his sermon. Rebecca had to admit he was a gifted speaker. He had the rapt attention of everyone there—quite a feat considering the mixture of old, young, and in between, men, women, white, Hispanic, Asian. She'd never been amongst such a diverse group of people.

Her mind drifted as Father John wrapped things up. She remembered a seventeen-year-old boy, handsome, smooth, and confident. And herself—a fifteen-year-old girl, plain, awkward, and shy. What that boy saw in her, even for a moment, she didn't know. Then again, she wasn't sure what the man next to her now saw in her either.

Chris gave her palm another little squeeze. "Okay?" he whispered.

As she nodded, everyone rose to their feet again. Still holding Chris's hand, she stood. At least the next part she knew and knew well—the collection basket, apparently the same the world over. More up and down, then the Lord's Prayer, in which she prattled on aloud when everyone else had stopped. She clamped her lips shut as her cheeks heated. If Chris had noticed her faux pas, he didn't let on. The next song's words were indecipherable, and she concluded they were in a foreign language. More kneeling, and then something else familiar: communion.

As the people in front of them rose and got in line, Chris whispered, "Just wait here." He sat back and raised the kneeler.

She put her hand on Chris's arm to keep him from climbing over top of her. "No, I'll go."

Standing now, he leaned down to her, his tone gentle yet adamant. "You can't. You don't believe what we believe."

An elderly lady at the end of the pew pressed towards them, hobbling as she gripped the back of the pew in front of them for support. With no time to discuss, Rebecca relented and twisted her knees to the side, letting Chris and the woman pass, surprised to feel tears stinging her eyes.

She slid forward onto the kneeler not because she wanted to pray, but because there she could better hide her unshed tears behind her hands. She listened as the singing began again, catching an occasional waft of perfume as people passed by her on their way back to their seats. She shouldn't have come. The entire experience made her uncomfortable despite Chris's efforts to set her at ease. His command to stay in the pew only confirmed she did not belong here.

I'm sorry, Lord. This was a mistake. One tear crept from her left eye, and she wiped it away when suddenly a sense of peace washed over her, like a gentle wave receding into the ocean. She heard, not with her ears, but with her heart: *Home.*

She didn't know what to make of it, and in another second, Chris returned and knelt beside her. She didn't raise her head, but he lifted a piece of her hair that had come loose from her braid and tucked it behind her ear. She shivered as his breath caressed her neck. "I'm sorry. I'll explain after Mass."

She gave the slightest nod so he would know she had heard him, not really interested in talking about it later. Home. That was where she wanted to go. Maybe that was what the voice—God?—meant.

The whole weekend had been a mess. Not a bad mess, but the kind of mess that left her out of sorts—scared one second, thrilled the next. Chris's presence amplified every feeling, and all the emotion had worn her out.

They stood a final time, and Father John dismissed them.

Chris ushered her out of the pew, guiding her with his hand to the small of her back as they made their way to the back of the church. As they passed through the double doors, she saw Father John greeting everyone personally. Surely Chris would want to introduce her to him. She needed to tell Chris now how she and Father John were acquainted if she wanted to spare him any awkwardness. She had about five seconds before they would be face to face.

"Chris, do you remember after Alan and Jamie's wedding, when you asked about my first kiss?"

His brow knit together and his eyes narrowed as he struggled to understand why she would bring that up at this moment. "Yeah. You said I was eight years too late."

"Yes. Well, my first kiss . . ." She inhaled deeply and let the rest out in a rush. "I kissed Father John."

8

Dreams of Our Fathers

The torrential rain required Chris's full concentration on the road, forestalling any conversation on the ride from the church to Rebecca's apartment.

The drum of rain on the rooftop created a relentless rhythm. Rebecca's thoughts drifted back to the church as she struggled to see through rain splattering and rolling down the windshield. The scene after Mass turned out not to be a scene at all. She had caught Chris off guard, but being a good-natured guy, she didn't detect even a trace of discomfort in his introduction.

Father John had taken her hand and begun shaking it, saying how pleased he was to meet her when his arm stilled with recognition.

"Rebecca Rhodes? It can't be."

"It is. It's been a long time."

"Too long," he said before he released her hand. "Chris didn't mention your last name."

"He didn't mention yours to me either. I didn't realize until I saw you up front."

"Your first Catholic Mass?"

She nodded. It may have been her last, too.

That's when he caught sight of Chris's bruised face. "What happened to you?"

Chris bit the right side of his bottom lip, the uninjured side, and shrugged. "Ran into a fist."

"Yeah. I bet there's more to the story than that."

Father John had a great smile, which he bestowed on them then as he looked back and forth between her and Chris a couple of times and then at their hands interlocked between them. He shook his head. "I never would have guessed . . . but God never ceases to amaze me."

Chris glanced back at the long line of parishioners waiting

to greet Father John and inched them forward while clapping Father John on the shoulder. "I'll catch up with you later this week," Chris said as they moved toward the exit.

***

Rebecca ran up the three steps to her door, yanked her key off of her wrist and jammed it into the lock. She felt Chris on her heels, the bag he carried for her bumping into her calves. The rain came in blowing sheets now, and when she had managed at last to get it open, the storm door blew out and allowed them quick entry.

She stripped off her sopping hoodie and dropped it on the hook in her entryway. Chris set her bag down on the laminate floor, careful to keep himself dripping on her mat.

"Do you want a towel to dry off?"

"Nah, I'm fine. I'd better get going."

He didn't move to leave then, and her gaze locked on his. She watched as a tiny rivulet ran from his hair down his temple and along his cheekbone, tracing the now-swollen and purple bruise along his jaw. She raised her hand to caress it, but drew it back not so much afraid to hurt him as she was nervous about what seemed like an intimate touch. Before she could pull her hand back to her side, he took hold of it and laid it on his face.

"I'm sorry about this." She brushed the tender skin with her fingertips.

"You have no reason to be sorry. We should have slept in separate tents. I should've thought what it might look like." His blue eyes, lashes still wet with rainwater, focused on her.

"You offered, but if you remember, I was so chicken I could barely sleep with you *inside* the tent."

He smiled until the movement must have caused his cheek some discomfort, and he winced. "Thank you for coming with me. It was like seeing the park for the first time again through your eyes."

She let her hand slide the length of his arm, cool and wet. "It's beautiful. I can see why you love it so much."

He rested his hands on her waist, inching closer to her,

and the smell of campfire and bug spray lingered on him as he leaned in to kiss her. She slid her arms around his neck, pulling him closer. He'd given her no more than a couple of pecks on the lips all weekend, but apparently now all bets were off. The feel of his lips sent a chill through her already cool body, but she warmed quickly—from the inside out—as his lips fused to hers, coaxing her to surrender a little of the feeling simmering in her chest. She felt a deep affection for Chris, even more so after the weekend they'd shared, so why was this so difficult? His kiss was persistent, and eventually her heart capitulated, her fervor overriding her reluctance. She knew the instant he felt the response he sought because his hands tightened on her waist, and he murmured, "I knew you were in there somewhere." He pulled away from her ever so slightly and pressed a final kiss to her lips. "Good night."

"Good night, Chris."

He tugged his collar close around his neck and turned, letting himself out the door and closing it behind him. His feet thudded down the slick wooden steps, the pattering of rain a steady backdrop, and then the engine hummed as he drove away.

Deciding she couldn't stay transfixed in a heady, kiss-induced haze all night, she grabbed her bag and moved away from the door just as someone pounded on the opposite side. At the same time, her cell phone buzzed in her pocket. She slipped the phone out of her shorts and read the one-word text message from Abby. "Sorry."

Rebecca walked back to the door and looked through the peep hole, its bleary view already little better than a funhouse mirror further distorted by moisture. Her breath caught in her throat. She swung the door open and braced herself for a torrent worse than any summer storm.

"Daddy."

"Who was that?" He gestured with his thumb in the direction Chris had headed.

There was no "hello" or "how was your weekend?" He pulled open the storm door, stepped inside, and pushed passed her as his rain jacket dripped onto her floor.

"A friend of mine, Chris." The warm feeling had all but left her body, replaced by a tightening coil in the pit of her stomach and a chill that made her tremble.

"Is that how you say goodnight to all your friends?"

"No. . . No. Of course not. I've been seeing Chris for, uh, a while, and he's very special." She wished she could say her dad would like him, but that wouldn't be true. Almost any other dad would be thrilled with him, but not hers.

"Is this the friend you were camping with overnight?" He spat the last word out, a fine spray mixing with the water splattering her floor as he shrugged out of his jacket. "Abby assured me you were in, and I quote, 'good hands'."

What had Abby told him? If she had intended to rile him—and knowing Abby, she had—it had worked. How could she convince her dad it was perfectly innocent?

She took his jacket from him and hung it alongside her hoodie, then stepped into her living area. "Yes, Daddy, but it's not what you think. He invited me—"

"Did you share a tent?" Her father's gaze drilled hers and without a word demanded the truth.

"Yes, but only because I—"

"I want his full name, Rebecca, and his address. Now." Her father's face reddened, and he dragged a hand over his head, a sure sign he was going to lose it. He paced in small circles, and she followed him.

"No, Daddy. It's not like that. We were in separate sleeping bags. He offered to pitch a tent for me, but I was too scared to sleep alone in the woods."

He stopped then and studied her as if he were trying to decide whether or not to believe her. "Scared? Of what? You weren't afraid of him taking advantage of you. Or ruining you or your reputation."

"He's a good man, Daddy. He's not like that. He respects me, and I trust him."

"Is he a Christian?"

"Yes." It was true, but she knew her dad considered

Catholicism little more than a cult or false religion. Having gone to church with Chris, she could see how others might think it all strange. She certainly did. But she had also heard Scripture sprinkled throughout the whole service. More Scripture than she ever heard on a given Sunday.

"If he's such a respectable Christian man, why are you hiding him from me?"

"I'm not."

"Then bring him over."

"Okay, but he...he works weird hours, and I don't know when..." She didn't like where this was headed.

"I want to meet him." He stared for a moment, then in a gentler tone said, "How about Friday night? My manager Reggie's got a bunch of fresh salmon he's bringing back from Alaska. I'll grill it."

Surprised by her father's sudden reversal, Rebecca didn't know if she wanted to subject Chris to her dad yet. He may decide a relationship with her wasn't worth dealing with her father. She had met Chris's parents though, and if she didn't agree to the dinner invitation, her dad would be suspicious.

"Okay. I'll invite him."

Her dad nodded his approval. "I made a special trip here with that floor lamp from the attic. You acted like you wanted it, and you said you'd be home this evening. I get here, and you're nowhere to be found."

Rebecca twisted her hands, anxious to claim the lamp and bid her dad goodnight. "We got held up by the weather."

Her dad snapped his jacket back off the hook. He reached into the pocket, retrieved a small plastic bag, and tossed it at her. "Here's the hardware for the shade." He glared at her, shrugged into his dripping jacket and zipped it. "Lamp's on the porch, in case you didn't notice."

With that, he flipped up his hood, turned, and walked out into the rain.

***

The invitation to have dinner with Rebecca at her dad's house surprised Chris. She hadn't said much about her father, but he knew that, while they were in regular contact, their relationship was rocky, at best. He also sensed getting her father's approval would be an uphill battle, but one he wanted to win. After last weekend, Chris felt certain he wanted this thing with Rebecca to be long term. The good news he had gotten this morning would be important to their future.

He knocked on the door, and as he waited outside the cream-colored bungalow where Rebecca had grown up, he took in the homey feel. Faded burgundy paint covered the gingerbread on the wooden porch supports and the shutters. White petunias and ivy spilled out of matching flower boxes below the two first-floor windows, and a sturdy wooden porch swing hung from rusted chains.

He straightened his tie and pushed up the knot so that it pressed neatly into his collar. He had offered to bring a bottle of wine, but Rebecca informed him her father did not allow alcohol in the house.

Rebecca swung the door open, and he couldn't stop the smile spreading across his face.

"Hey, you." He stepped inside the door and glanced about to see if they were alone.

She blushed, and it drove him crazy. "Hey yourself."

He pulled her close and kissed her, then whispered in her ear. "I have some good news to share with you, and I'm about ready to burst."

"What is it?"

That smile. Those eyes. This job had suddenly become more important to him than he had ever dreamed. He couldn't rely on his motorcycle anymore. Not while he dated Rebecca. He needed a car. "I got a new—"

Rebecca's father bustled into the foyer. While taller than Rebecca, his eye level reached only to Chris's chin. His narrow face, long nose, and graying hair gave him an authoritative air. Chris couldn't find a whit of family resemblance between him and his daughter.

"Daddy, this is Chris Reynolds. Chris, my dad."

Chris extended his right hand. "Nice to meet you, Mr. Rhodes."

"Likewise," came out of his mouth, but from the way her dad looked him over, he sensed he wasn't pleased. He welcomed Chris in and excused himself to tend to dinner.

Rebecca took hold of Chris's hand, squeezed his fingers, and ushered him to the dining room where her dad set a bowl of boiled potatoes on the table. It looked like how he remembered his great grandmother's dining room.

An antique hutch filled with fancy china sat in the corner. A buffet against the wall topped with a beige doily featured several framed pictures and a tarnished silver platter. Both a fabric tablecloth and a plastic liner covered the oval dining table, which had been set for three with fancy white china plates and real silverware. A cheap print of DaVinci's *Last Supper* in a dingy frame hung on the interior wall.

Rebecca let go of his hand and headed for the kitchen, he presumed to help her dad. He glanced at his watch to make sure he hadn't been late. No, right on time. Apparently, Rebecca's dad didn't waste time socializing.

In a few minutes, the table filled with drinks, dinner rolls, and broccoli, and Rebecca told him to take a seat. Dinner smelled good but more like beef than fish. He pulled her chair out and then sat next to her. Her dad brought in the remaining platter of steaks—beef, not salmon as Rebecca had told him. Chris held his breath knowing that simple menu change could very well cinch her dad's opinion of him.

It was Friday, and like every Friday, Chris abstained from meat. It wasn't Lent, so he wasn't bound by that sacrifice, he could choose another, but no meat on Fridays had become an ingrained habit for him over the past couple of years. He didn't have another second to dwell on it since her dad announced it was time for grace.

Chris shifted in his seat as Rebecca released his hand under the table, and he bowed his head in prayer.

"Dear Lord," her dad began, "Bless this meal and those who eat it. Amen."

Short and sweet. Chris refrained from making the sign of the cross as he was apt to do.

"Chris," her dad said as he reached for the steak platter, "I hope you like sirloin. A friend of mine had promised me Alaskan salmon, but he wasn't able to bring them by this week. Maybe another time."

Her dad stabbed the top steak with a fork. He and Rebecca had talked about whether he should tell her father he was Catholic or save that particular detail for later. They had decided that unless it came up they would avoid the topic. For now. But here they were about thirty seconds into the meal, and it had come up.

"Thank you, sir, I do like sirloin, and those look delicious, but I'm—"

"Fasting." Rebecca sounded breathless as the word erupted from her lips. "Chris fasts on Fridays, Dad."

That caught her dad's attention, and he stopped and studied Chris with a look almost of admiration. "Really? Well, while I find that commendable, I think you can dispense with that this evening."

Chris's instinct was to say that he didn't have the authority to do that, but he reminded himself that it wasn't Lent, therefore it wasn't an obligation. He could and should dispense with it tonight for the sake of harmony. He opened his mouth to say that he'd love a steak when Rebecca, looking anxious and wary blurted out, "Chris is Roman Catholic."

Geez, did she have to add the "Roman?" It made him sound un-American.

Her dad had set the steak on Chris's dish and was in the process of dropping one of the juicy cuts onto his own. It fell to his plate with a thwack, and he looked between the two of them, a steak knife in one hand and a two-tined fork in the other. He smiled, a saccharine smile that left his lower lip twitching.

He glared at Chris. "Rebecca said you were a Christian."

"I am, sir. Catholic Christian."

Her dad let out a little "humph," and began to cut his steak. That set the tone for the entire meal. Rebecca tried to introduce a topic of conversation, Chris tried to find common ground with her father, and her dad responded with a panoply of disgusted noises.

After her dad gave a final swipe to his mouth with the linen napkin, he pushed his plate forward and gave them each a forced smile. Chris was almost finished as well, so he set his hands on the napkin in his lap.

"So, Chris, what is it that you do for a living?"

Finally, an opportunity to salvage things. With the news he had accepted a new job this morning, Chris sat straighter in his chair. He cast a quick glance at Rebecca, glad that he could finally share his good news with her. He turned back to her dad and watched as he rattled the ice cubes in his glass before taking a long drink of his—water.

All at once it hit him. This wasn't going to be his saving grace; it would be more like the nail in his coffin as far as her dad was concerned. There was no avoiding it now, and he was eager to share it with Rebecca anyway. He'd just dive in.

"Well, my degree is in chemistry, sir, but I've been having a hard time finding something that suited me. In the meantime, I've been working at Rieser's Market, restocking and stuff."

Her dad looked into the bottom of his now-empty glass, not impressed.

"I went on an interview last week though, and this morning they offered me a position, and I accepted it." Rebecca's dad had looked up now, anticipating the big announcement.

Chris reached for Rebecca's hand under the table again and holding onto it, let their hands rest on his thigh. He pushed the chair back a little bit so he could angle himself towards her. The smile on her lips and in her eyes gave him the confidence to continue.

"They wanted a chemist. Starting in two weeks, I'll be the yeast manager for Gateway Brewery."

He'd always be grateful to Rebecca for her reaction. She had to have known what her dad would think of him working at a brewery, but she didn't temper her response. She released his hand and threw her arms around his neck, kissing his cheek.

"Chris, it's perfect. I mean, I don't know the first thing about yeast management, but you'll get to use your education, it's close by, and it's probably a cool place to work."

That was all true of course, but the fact that it provided a larger income with benefits was foremost in his mind. A man that wanted to court a woman properly and was thinking seriously for the first time that he wanted to be a husband and father someday needed stability and income. He needed something he could offer Rebecca aside from a ride on the back of his Harley.

Her dad's chair scraped against the wood floor, and they turned to see him push away from the table. "Sometimes I wonder what it is I've done that the women in my life are hell-bent on making me suffer."

The smile on Rebecca's face disintegrated and the color drained from her face.

Chris didn't know where the words came from or how to stop them, but he laid them out on the table as Rebecca's father gathered his plate and turned toward the kitchen.

"Augustine said that suffering is not a punishment, but that God is a physician and suffering is his medicine for salvation."

Rebecca's dad stopped and slowly turned back to them. "Thank you, Mr...."

"Reynolds," Chris supplied.

"Thank you, Mr. Reynolds, but I prefer not to take my religious instruction from a papist. Especially one that works in a brewery."

With that he left the room, and in a minute his feet climbed the creaky stairs.

"Well, I guess I'll clean up," Rebecca said.

He heard it in her unsteady voice and saw it in her watery eyes. She was trying to hold back tears. He grabbed onto her arm as she stood.

"Rebecca, it's okay. I tried, but somewhere through the

course of the meal I realized I can't be something I'm not, even if it means I don't gain your father's approval. I'm Catholic now, and I don't foresee that ever changing. And I'm excited about my job. Very excited. Not because it's a brewery, but because it's work. And it's a bigger salary with benefits. It'll open up new doors for me. And for us."

She finally looked at him, her eyes moist and almost sable. "I'm happy for you Chris, truly. The tears are just...I'm just sorry. He was so unkind to you."

Chris stood, too, and began helping her clear the table. "It's okay. I'd like your dad to like me, but I'm more concerned about earning *your* affection, trust, and respect than his."

Rebecca smiled. "Well, your odds of success are definitely better with me."

Chris motioned toward the front door. "I noticed a porch swing out there. Maybe after we clear the table we could sit outside? It's a nice evening."

"I haven't sat on that swing in ages. It sounds nice."

***

Rebecca relaxed for the first time that evening as she sat on the porch swing and touched her toes to the floor to steady it for Chris. He sat beside her and rested his arm on the seat behind her as he pushed off. They swung in silence for a couple of minutes. Rebecca noted how quiet the neighborhood had become. When she and Abby were little there had been a dozen kids running up and down the sidewalks, cutting through yards, and skipping rope at this time of day.

She turned to face Chris. "Your face looks a lot better. The bruising's almost gone."

He rubbed a hand over his cheek and lip. "Yeah. It should be gone by Monday. I hope."

She nodded in agreement. "So, why didn't you tell me about your interview?"

"I didn't know if I had any chance of getting the job."

They swung in silence for a few more beats.

Rebecca twisted her hands in her lap. "You fascinate me."

Chris leaned away so he could see her face. "How so?"

"You quote Augustine, *and* you make an awesome campfire. You carry a rosary in your pocket, *and* you're going to work at a brewery. You're a virgin, *and* you ride a Harley."

They swung back and forth two more times.

"I never said I was a virgin."

Rebecca's cheeks heated instantaneously, and she started to stammer something she realized must be incoherent before Chris's hand squeezed her shoulder.

She looked over at him and her cheeks cooled. She had come to recognize the look in his eyes when he was messing with her.

He smiled. "But your assumption is correct."

She smacked his arm with her hand, and he shrunk away from her, rubbing his bicep. "Ow!"

"You deserve it. You're terrible."

He laughed. "So, none of those things you mentioned are mutually exclusive."

"No, but they are unusual combinations. I think it's part of what makes you so attractive. You're not afraid to be exactly who you are. You'll follow the truth wherever it leads you."

The teasing vanished from his eyes. "I think that's the nicest compliment anyone's ever given me."

Rebecca stared at her hands as she twisted them in her lap. "Well, it's just pointing out the obvious. You're infinitely more interesting than I am. I'll admit I can't quite figure out why you want to hang out with me."

The swing came to a stop as Chris's feet dragged over the wooden plank floor, and she looked at him in question.

"I'm not coordinated enough to kiss you and swing at the same time. Something had to go."

He slid nearer to her on the swing and pulled her close to him with the arm that still rested behind her. His other hand moved over her hands in her lap before he leaned forward and pressed his lips to hers. How many times had he kissed her like this? Twice the night of Alan's wedding, once after their camping trip. Was it possible she'd get used to it and her heart wouldn't feel like it was going to explode out of her chest every time his lips touched hers? She hoped not.

Chris pulled away only enough to speak. "Is there a twelve-step program for this?"

Rebecca placed another light kiss to his lips. "What?"

"Your kisses are addictive."

She smiled. "I don't want you to get help. Ever."

His hand massaged the back of her head and his fingers pulled slowly through her hair. "That means I might be hanging around for a while."

"Is that a promise?"

"Do you need a promise?"

The screen door flew open with such force it slammed against the wall, and her dad emerged. He had changed into his workpants and a matching shirt with the local gas company emblem emblazoned over his left pocket. Rebecca shifted away from Chris in the swing and his arm lifted from behind her as her dad adjusted his fat leather belt around his waist.

"Rebecca, I've been called out on an emergency. Lock up before you go."

"Yes, Daddy."

"Mr. Reynolds, I assume you'll be going."

Chris straightened in the swing. "Yes, sir. As soon as I help Rebecca with the dishes."

His gaze lingered on Chris as if he was trying to decide whether or not to believe him, and then he hurried down the steps and to his car.

She watched him go, and then turned back to Chris. Her heart did that little flutter thing. Dinner had been a bust, but the evening wasn't.

9
Broken Things

Chris couldn't limit his dates with Rebecca to the weekends anymore. He didn't care what his schedule looked like; he had to see her midweek. He'd only be working at Rieser's Market another week anyway, and then he'd enjoy normal working hours except for some special events here and there.

He spotted Rebecca right away. She leaned against the parking garage railing overlooking the amusement park. A long ponytail hung almost halfway down her back, and she wore a white, knee-length skirt that flared around her in the breeze. The roller coaster noise and the accompanying screams reached a crescendo, so when he'd coasted his motorcycle into a parking spot on the opposite side of the garage, she hadn't noticed.

It was like someone had tethered helium balloons to his limbs, and he could glide across the lot to her. Just seeing her made his spirits rise. He smiled as he thought how he could have a little fun with her.

He walked up behind her noiselessly. Then he reached forward and tugged her ponytail before wrapping his arms around her waist. He opened his mouth to say, "Surprise," when she let out a blood-curdling scream. Her elbows simultaneously jabbed into his midsection.

"Rebecca, Rebecca, it's me. It's me—Chris." Finally, he was able to grasp her wrists and get her turned around. "See? It's just me."

She breathed heavily for a few seconds as the terror in her eyes faded. "Chris, you scared me."

"No kidding." Were they taking nominations for the understatement of the century?

A large, muscular guy in a ribbed, white, tank shirt approached from off to their right. "Excuse me, miss. Are you okay?"

Rebecca wrapped her arms around her waist. "Yes. I'm fine."

The man looked back across the lot to a woman standing alongside a stroller holding the hand of a preschool-aged boy. He turned back to Rebecca. "Do you know this man?"

"Yes. He's...a friend." She laid a hand on Chris's arm. "He just scared me coming up behind me like that is all."

"All right then," he said before giving Chris a once over and then heading back to his family.

The tension in Rebecca's face eased, and color flooded back into her cheeks. She moved her hand from his arm to his side. "I didn't hurt you, did I?"

Chris shook his head. "Nah. The new bruises will just blend in with the others."

Rebecca jerked her hand away as if she still might be hurting him. "Oh, my gosh. Your ribs. I'm so sorry, Chris."

"Just kidding. I'm good. If I had known it would upset you like that, I never would've snuck up on you." He took her hand and held it. "Are *you* okay?"

Rebecca nodded. "Fine. You didn't do anything wrong. I overreacted."

Eager to distance them from that awkward scene, Chris asked, "Are you still up for dinner?"

"Of course." Her tone sounded less confident than her words.

The hostess seated them on the terrace of the restaurant and bar under a large orange umbrella. The waitress brought them two tall glasses of water with a small dish of lemon wedges. Chris smiled at the short-haired, middle-aged woman.

"Can I get you something from the bar?" she asked.

"Do you have any Gateway beers on tap?"

She named a summer lager and an India Pale Ale.

"I'll try the summer lager. I start work there soon, so I'd better get familiar with their product." He smiled across the table at Rebecca.

Her breathing rate and color appeared normal. She leaned

forward and asked, "Do you think a glass of wine would help settle my nerves?" Her voice sounded calm.

"I don't think it would hurt."

Her hair was still secured in that long ponytail with a few wisps grazing her neck. Beautiful.

"Would you pick something for me?"

He looked back at the waitress. "What kind of red wine do you have?"

"We have a pinot noir, a merlot, a shiraz, and a cabernet sauvignon."

"A glass of merlot, please."

The waitress left, giving them a few minutes to look at the dinner selections. In less than a minute, Rebecca laid down her menu.

"Whatever they're grilling smells fantastic. I think I'll have the mushroom burger."

Chris made his choice and set his menu down as well. A large truck rumbled past. In the opposite direction, a train whistle sounded, momentarily forestalling conversation.

"So, do you want to talk about why my sneaking up on you freaked you out like that?"

Rebecca leaned back in her chair and sighed. "Not really, but I guess you deserve an explanation."

He waited for her to begin.

"There's not much to it. Just a bad memory." She fiddled with her napkin and pressed it into her lap as the waitress brought their drinks.

They placed their orders, and Chris watched as she sipped her wine. "Do you like it?"

"I do." She took another sip, and he waited for her to pick up the conversation where they had left off.

"Anyway, the summer camp—Bible camp—that I went to in high school—"

"The one where you met someone Catholic?"

She giggled. "Yes. I didn't connect the dots for you. That *someone* was John. Father John. I don't know if I can get used to calling him 'Father.' I think he'll always be John to me."

"We could call him 'First Kiss John.'" She was so easy to tease.

"Ha. Anyway, there was a guy there. Older than both of us. He just...he came on really strong."

Her pause didn't inspire confidence in her story. "What do you mean by 'he came on really strong'?"

"He came up behind me like that and caught me off guard."

That couldn't be all. "And?"

"And he had me sort of trapped, and I got scared. That's it."

He'd have to take her at her word. He sensed that was all he was going to get on that matter.

"If we're done discussing my neuroses, can I ask you a question?"

Chris tasted his beer. It was good; not too hoppy. "Shoot."

Rebecca pushed a loose strand of hair behind her ear. "Well, at Alan's wedding, Megan said you were shy—at least in high school, and I don't think you have a shy bone in your body, so was she out-of-her-mind drunk or have you changed?"

This must have been part of the uncomfortable conversation with Megan he had walked in on when he came out of the restroom. "She said that, huh?"

"Among other things." She gave him a little teasing smile, as if Megan had shared some other secrets about him with her. Maybe she had, but considering he had no real personal history with Megan, it couldn't be too bad.

"She was drunk all right, but she was right about me being shy. I guess from about the time I started school, I remember trying to avoid attention. I was the kid who knew the answers but never raised his hand. When I got to be twelve or thirteen it kind of spread to my social life, too. I didn't speak unless spoken to, and when it came to girls—forget it. I couldn't even string two or three words together."

Her eyes never left his as she twisted her wine glass on its napkin. "Why?"

"Good question. I've thought a lot about that, and the best I can come up with is the typical story of a boy who lived in his big brother's shadow. There were only the two of us, so comparisons were inevitable. Alan was larger than life. He was good at everything. Not great, but good enough to be noticed. He's a people person, an extrovert. And girls—to this day I don't know what his secret was, but girls were drawn to him like flies to honey. So, by being shy, I took myself out of the equation. There was no comparison. No competition."

Rebecca took it all in, but didn't say a word.

"What?"

"Nothing." She pushed her glass forward on the table and rested her hands in her lap. "I'm just trying to square that with the outgoing, confident man I'm looking at now."

The waitress brought their meals and after saying grace and enjoying a few bites of their food, Rebecca picked up the conversation.

"What happened? How did you go from that to this? There must have been some catalyst."

"There was." He finished chewing and took another drink of his beer. "My college roommate and I were polar opposites. I don't know how we got matched up, but we couldn't have been more different. We got along okay, but we had nothing in common. He reminded me of Alan in some ways, but he had a mean streak. You didn't want to cross him.

"So, one Friday night he didn't come home. It wasn't the first time. I figured he met a girl, and frankly, better her place than mine. But the next morning, one of his friends dropped by and told me he'd been killed. I figured he'd been driving drunk or he overdosed or something. . ." He shook his head. "Total freak accident."

Rebecca set her sandwich down. "What happened?"

"He was driving home and whether he was under the influence or not, I never heard, but it didn't matter. Just as he was about to pass over a sewer cover in the road, it burst off and flew right through his windshield."

Rebecca's hand clamped over her mouth. "Oh, my gosh.

I'm so sorry. Even if you weren't close…that's horrible."

Chris sat very still, recalling the days following his roommate's death. "It was harder on his friends and family, but it really made me think about life and how nothing's guaranteed. Here today, gone tomorrow. I decided I wanted to live my life and find meaning in it, not just watch it whizz by from the sidelines."

"And that's it? You were able to change your personality like that?"

"It was more of a gradual process. I had to keep pushing myself beyond my comfort zone, but eventually it came naturally, and I started to feel more like me than I ever had, if that makes any sense."

Chris lifted his burger again, and Rebecca finished off her wine.

"I'm not sure. I don't know if I've ever felt free to be me." Her downcast eyes and fragile tone made Chris's heart ache.

"Why not?"

Rebecca pushed the remainder of her burger around the plate then peered up at him. "Could we save that for another time?"

"Sure. I guess the conversation got kind of heavy."

"That's my fault. You were trying to play with me, and I went all loco on you."

"Please don't apologize, Rebecca." He reached across the table and grasped her fingers. "I want to have fun with you, but I want to get to know you, too. Even your heartaches and your problems."

She smiled, and they finished their meal in silence.

Everyone suffered in this life, Rebecca included. Chris knew that, but if he could, he would take up every one of her crosses for her. He just wondered how many there were.

***

By Saturday evening, Chris longed for a low-key date alone with Rebecca. That wasn't on the agenda. He stared out the car window at a two-story, brick, Tudor-style home as Rebecca gathered her keys and cell phone and dropped them into her purse.

"Is your dad coming tonight?"

"No."

He felt a little guilty at the amount of relief that one word generated. If he was going to keep seeing Rebecca, he'd have to find a way to coexist with her father, but not tonight.

"Abby will complain that he doesn't care enough to come to his own granddaughter's party, but she set the date before she ever asked him which weekends he was working." They exited the car, and she continued. "She resents that he doesn't make a big fuss over her kids but refuses to see how much he dotes on them. I called him last night, and all he talked about was Ricky starting baseball, Emma singing the ABC song, and Ian rolling over."

He had to give Rebecca credit. It would be easy to paint her dad as evil incarnate, but like everyone else he, too, was surely a mixture of good and bad, virtue and vice.

"So, what does one do at a birthday party for a three-year-old?" Chris asked as they walked from her car to her sister's house.

"Well, Emma loves Dora the Explorer, so I'm guessing there will be Dora balloons and a Dora piñata. There's going to be a couple girls from her tumbling class and their moms. Not a big deal. Just pizza, cake, and ice cream. Nothing you can't handle."

She shot him a saucy grin, and all he could think of was what he'd really like to handle. He needed to rein himself in; he was going to a toddler's birthday party.

Chris glanced at the various toys scattered around the yard as evidence that children lived there. Fingerprints smeared the storm door about six inches lower than the door handle.

Rebecca shifted the large present she'd been carrying, wrapped of course in Dora the Explorer paper, and knocked on her sister's front door.

"So, what did you tell your sister about me?"

"Enough." There was the saucy grin again.

She's killing me.

A squeal emanated from behind the door followed by an

infant's cry, and then a young woman answered the door, bouncing Emma on her hip.

Chris remembered the little girl from when he'd first met Rebecca at Rieser's Market.

"Hi, sweetie," he said as Abby motioned them in.

"I love terms of endearment, but you should probably call me by my given name when my sister's in the room."

Chris jerked his head back. Did she really think he was talking to her and not the little girl in her arms?

"Abby, this is Chris. Chris, my sister, Abby. She's truly one of a kind."

Okay. Rebecca did say Abby was offbeat. "Nice to finally meet you, Abby."

She looked him up and down in a way that made him feel uncomfortable. Or undressed. "Likewise."

Abby couldn't be more different than Rebecca. Short, blond, spiky hair topped a narrow face and long features. The combination was different, but not unattractive. The contrast with Rebecca wasn't limited to appearance either. Her no-nonsense manner differed drastically from her younger sister's almost genteel propriety.

As he stepped further into a foyer cluttered with children's shoes, stuffed animals, and Nerf darts, the smell of pizza wafted from somewhere in the back of the house.

Abby had gone ahead with Emma, leaving him and Rebecca to follow. "Is your brother-in-law here?"

"Joel? I would think so. He's probably out back with Ricky."

They made their way to a dining room festooned with crepe paper streamers, Hello Kitty balloons and a Hello Kitty piñata.

"What happened to Dora?" Rebecca asked as she set her present on the buffet alongside a half dozen presents wrapped in Hello Kitty paper.

"She hates Dora," Abby answered as she set Emma down and tucked a blanket around Ian in his bouncy seat.

If the baby picture Rebecca had shown him was a good

representation, Ian had morphed from ugly, wrinkly newborn to adorable, pudgy infant.

"Since when?"

"Last week. A good auntie would keep up with these things."

Rebecca glared at her sister. The irritation didn't last though. "Anything I can do to help?"

"Nope. Got it all under control."

And she did. Joel and Ricky only emerged for the cake and presents. The rest of the time, Abby handled the baby, the food, and Emma and her little friends. She rolled with the state of near-constant chaos.

The party wound down and Joel and Ricky retreated to the basement for a movie.

Emma hugged Chris's leg. "Thank you," she said. The poor little girl looked so sleepy he doubted she knew whom she thanked or why.

"You're welcome, Emma," he said, careful not to toss around any terms of endearment.

Emma released him and leaned against Rebecca. "I sleepy, Aunt Becca."

Rebecca ran her hands over the little girl's silky hair. "Aw, Emmy. Can I put you to bed?" Emma nodded her head, and Rebecca lifted her over her shoulder.

"Abby, I'll take her up if that's okay."

"Okay? I think it earns you the 'Aunt of the Year' award."

Rebecca turned back to Chris. "I'll get her to sleep and then we can go, okay?"

"Sure." Chris sat at the dining room table while Abby took a few remaining paper plates to the kitchen. "Anything I can do to help?" he called after her.

Her reply came back through the archway that separated the rooms. "No, this is the last of it."

Chris glanced around the room. Other than a couple of sconces, only two decorations hung on the walls. An orange and yellow abstract print on a large canvas square hung on one wall, and a Star of David on the opposite wall.

Abby returned from the kitchen and sat across from him. She let out a deep sigh. "Children are exhausting. Would you like a beer?"

"No, thanks."

"I'm going to get one for myself then." She went back into the kitchen. Bottles clanged and a lid snapped before she emerged. Just as she sat and tilted the bottle to her lips, the baby cried out.

"Figures," Abby said. She set down her beer and gathered Ian out of his bouncy seat.

"I noticed the Star of David on the wall. . . Is Joel Jewish?"

Abby looked at the baby and made silly noises in an attempt to settle him down. "Yes, he is. He's not what you'd call observant though."

"And your dad was okay with the marriage?"

"My dad?" She laughed. "He wasn't okay with it, but what could he do? We eloped."

"I hope you don't mind my asking, but, does your dad get along with Joel?"

She looked away from the baby and toward him. "My dad doesn't like you, does he?"

Chris gave her a grim smile. "I don't think so."

"Well, for what it's worth, I think he only tolerates Joel."

The baby fussed again, and Abby laid him on her lap, snapped something under her shirt, and then lifted the hem for the baby to nurse.

Chris didn't know which way to look. He didn't want to stare at Abby's exposed breast, but she was hardly discreet.

"You don't have a problem with me feeding my baby in my own home, do you?"

Geez, she came on strong. "Of course not. Breastfeeding is great. Best for the baby and all that. I guess I've just never been around a woman while she's nursing."

"Well, you might as well take a good look. This is the closest you're going to get to a woman's breasts while you're dating my sister."

Her blunt manner stunned Chris into silence. "I, uh, I

wasn't trying to see...." His cheeks burned. How was he supposed to respond to that? Good grief, how long did it take to put a little girl to bed? Emma was half asleep when Rebecca left the room with her.

The baby continued to suckle, making the occasional gulping sound.

"Abby, there's something I've wondered about Rebecca."

At the sound of his voice, Ian popped off of his mother's nipple and turned to look at him. He smiled at the baby, and when Ian turned his attention back to his meal, Chris continued. "Why doesn't Rebecca sing?"

"What makes you think she doesn't sing?"

"Well, every time it comes up she changes the subject. Or she gets this look, like she closes up and shuts down. When she came to church with me, she opened the hymnal but not her mouth. She didn't even sing 'Happy Birthday' to Emma tonight."

Abby fidgeted with Ian's toes. "She does sing. When she's alone." She glanced up the stairs. "Rebecca's singing voice is amazing. It's a gift. When our Sunday school teachers heard her they encouraged her to sing. So, she'd sing for the little services our class had. Then, when she was thirteen, they asked her to sing a solo for Christmas Eve.

"I can still picture her in my hand-me-down, red-velvet gown with the fur trim and the silver sparkles. She was going to sing 'O Holy Night,' and she was so nervous. She practiced and practiced. Couldn't have been more prepared. And then she got the words all balled up.

"It started beautifully. Her voice moved people to tears. Then somewhere around that really high note, she looked at us. Our Sunday school teachers smiled; I beamed. And then, she looked at Dad. I couldn't see his face, but that's when she tripped on the words. She didn't even finish it. She ran to the back of the church."

Ian had dozed off in her arms, and after she pulled down her shirt, she shifted him over her shoulder and patted his back.

"Everyone was so kind and understanding and told her how beautifully she'd sung. Dad didn't speak the whole way home. When we got inside, he blew up. He called her a disgrace and said she'd embarrassed us all. That she shamed him."

Abby's eyes glistened and her features softened. "I'm not sentimental, but my heart broke for her. The life leached out of her. He crushed her spirit so thoroughly that night. She hasn't been the same since."

Chris imagined the hurt Rebecca felt, and his chest ached.

"We never spoke about it. And she stopped singing. She took D's in music class because she wouldn't sing. Cost her being valedictorian. The director of our high school musicals begged her to be in the plays, and she wouldn't."

"And she hasn't sung since?"

Abby rubbed circles on Ian's tiny back as he emitted a soft snore.

"I heard her sing once since then. When Ricky was a few months old I got the flu, and Rebecca, God bless her, stayed with me while Joel worked. She took care of Ricky, and she'd bring him to me to feed him. One afternoon, he fussed and cried nonstop, and I heard her comforting him. She probably thought I couldn't hear, but she sang a lullaby. 'Down In the Valley.'"

She closed her eyes as if she were transported back to the memory. "Sweet, soft, and almost haunting. He quieted right down."

Chris seethed. How could a man treat his daughter like that? Especially a sweet, obedient girl like Rebecca must have been.

"Abby, I've never hated another person. But your dad...I am so...so close." He shook his head and then rested his forehead against his palms.

"Yeah. He really has a way of bringing out the best in people, doesn't he?"

He raised his head and rested his chin in his hand. "How do we get her to sing again?"

"We don't. She doesn't want to."

How could Abby just accept that? He wanted Rebecca to sing, and not only for the selfish interest he had in hearing her voice, but also for her own sake. She had a God-given talent hidden under a mountain of fear and shame.

Abby cradled Ian again and stroked his fuzzy head. "I swear they get high off breast milk. Doesn't he look high?"

Chuckling, he leaned back in his seat. "Yeah, he does look sort of mellowed out."

Finally, he heard Rebecca descending the steps. Thank God.

"She's out like a light," Rebecca said to Abby. She rubbed her hand on Chris's shoulder and bent to his ear, the sensation of her lips sending a shiver down his spine. "Are you ready, handsome?"

Handsome? That was a first. "I sure am."

They rode back to Rebecca's apartment, where Chris had left his motorcycle. He didn't want the night to end, but it was late, so he walked her to her door.

Taking both of her hands in his, he lifted her right hand to his lips. "How is it that time goes so fast when we're together and so slow when we're apart?"

"You've noticed that, too, huh?"

Not ready to let go yet, he swung their hands back and forth between them.

"So, Monday's the big day, huh?" she said.

Their arms slowed, and he inched closer to her. "Yeah. First day on the job. I'm a little nervous."

"I'll pray for you."

"Thanks. If after a few weeks things seem like they're going to work out, I'm going to buy a car. Or maybe a truck. I haven't decided yet. Something I can use to take you out on dates."

"You don't have to buy a vehicle on my account." She slipped her hands out of his and slid her arms up around his neck. She flattened the collar of his wrinkled, cotton shirt.

"It's time. I love the Harley, and I'm going to keep it, but I need something more practical, too." The thread of conversation slowly unraveled as he stepped closer and looked deeper into her eyes.

"I suppose something with doors and a roof would be better in inclement weather." Her hands left his collar and clasped behind his neck.

"Uh-huh." He couldn't manage anything more coherent before he bent his head towards her and kissed her. She unclasped her hands and played with his hair. She pressed her body closer to him and when she parted her lips, he took it as an invitation. The instant he tilted his head and tried to deepen the kiss, she jerked back like she'd been slapped.

Chris' gaze dropped to his hands, which still held tight to her waist despite the fact she had wrenched her whole upper body away from him. "I'm sorry. I'm so attracted to you, and I thought you wanted me to—"

He looked up and into her eyes—wide and frightened, and she shook her head furiously.

"No. I didn't."

She was like a rabbit. Contented until you got too close, then wary and skittish. He half-feared she'd bolt every time he kissed her.

"Again, I'm sorry. I'm good with taking things slow, but..." What could he say? Any slower and they'd be going backwards. By next month he'd be blowing her kisses from across the room. They had been having a good evening, and she hadn't hesitated to kiss him. Not at first. He tried to make sense of it.

"Rebecca, has someone hurt you or taken advantage of you in the past?"

She pried his hands from her waist. "You mean sexually? No. Gosh, no, not at all."

"Good. I thought maybe—"

She rubbed a hand over her eyes and dropped her head. "I'm sorry I'm being such a baby. I don't know why you're so patient with me."

"I can be patient. I'm having a little trouble understanding is all. You seemed like you wanted me to kiss you and then..."

"Can we save this conversation for later?"

Whatever it was that made her so guarded ran deep, and he wondered if she had avoided confronting it altogether. Reluctant to push her, he decided it could wait.

10

The Idea of You

"Geez, Abby. Can you wait up?" Rebecca jogged a few steps to catch up with Abby as they made their way through the sporting goods section of Target toward the infant clothing.

"I'm a nursing mother. At this time of day I've got two hours max to get back home, and it took twenty minutes for me to get here. Then you were five minutes late. You're going to have to keep up."

Grabbing onto the shopping cart handle, something sticky adhered to her palm. Lollipop residue. Yuck. She wiped her hand on her pants. "Okay, okay. I'll hustle. Sorry I was late. So, what did you think?"

"About?"

She let out a deep sigh. "Like you don't know. About Chris?"

"Oh. I think he's hot, but I don't think Joel's into sharing."

The cart rolled to a stop and Rebecca waited as Abby rummaged through a rack of baby boy onesies. "I swear, if you weren't my sister, I wouldn't even speak to you."

Abby tossed a three-pack of the onesies into the cart. "Lucky for you then that I am."

"I want to know what you thought of him. Besides that he's hot, which I already knew."

Abby continued moving the cart down the aisle. "I think he's smitten with you."

"Smitten?"

"Yes, he's infatuated."

Rebecca stopped. "I was hoping for something a little deeper than infatuation."

"Infatuation doesn't preclude love. They work in tandem—at least at the beginning."

Abby was moving again, and Rebecca caught up. "So that's it? Hot and smitten?"

"Hey, hot and smitten is nothing to sneeze at. I could use more of both in my marriage."

"Point taken." They stopped and Rebecca fingered some bath towels that Abby was examining. She patted the scratchy nubs and turned back to her sister. "I just want to know if you liked him."

Abby tossed some olive green hand towels and wash cloths into the cart. "I didn't spend a lot of time with him, but I didn't get any bad vibes. He didn't freak when I nursed Ian, and he wasn't horribly awkward around the kids. He didn't even try to escape to the basement with Joel and Ricky, so I give him points there, too, but I think that goes back to the whole smitten thing. He can't stand to have you out of his sight."

"You really think so?" Rebecca couldn't suppress the little rush it gave her to think that Chris was as into her as she was to him.

Sparing her no more than a quick glance, Abby pushed off toward the housewares. "I think you've both got it bad."

"Did I tell you he got a new job?"

Abby grabbed a Hello Kitty bowl and plate set from the shelf and examined the back. "No. Where at?"

"Starting tomorrow he's the yeast manager at Gateway Brewery."

"Wow. He's running the whole microbial gamut, isn't he? From yogurt to yeast. I guess it's a good thing you're not gettin' busy with your yeastie boy or we'd have to slather you with Monistat before you—"

"Abby!"

"Two words, Rebecca. Cotton panties. I'm just sayin' . . ."

Abby was nearly past the women's clothing when she stopped abruptly. Rebecca hadn't been paying attention, and the cart rammed into Abby's heel.

"Ouch! Geez, Becca, you're worse than Ricky."

"Sorry."

Rubbing her heel, she gave Rebecca a once over.

"What?"

"You need a makeover. I don't have time to take you to my favorite stores, so this is going to have to do."

What's wrong with what I have on? Pleated jeans and a pink button-down blouse. The sound of metal hangers smacking against one another drew her attention back to Abby, who was rifling through a rack of skirts.

"How do you get off wearing mom jeans anyway when you're not even a mom?"

Rebecca thought she was immune to Abby's criticism, but today it made her squirm. Why? Was it because of Chris? She had to admit she'd been thinking more about her appearance lately, especially when she knew she'd be seeing him.

Abby held up a short, turquoise, flared skirt and a fuchsia camisole. She twisted her wrist to show Rebecca the front and the back and then thrust them at her. "Here, try these on."

"Abby, that skirt is too short, and how do I wear a bra with ...with *that*?" She looked with disdain at the clothes Abby had piled into her arms.

"That skirt is no more than two inches above your knees, and you don't need a bra with the cami; it's got an underwire."

Shoving the individual plastic hangers backward on the rack, Rebecca looked at the clothes with exaggerated horror. The colors were pretty, but she'd feel nearly naked in that outfit.

Abby huffed out a sigh and threw another article onto her pile. "There. Matching shrug. Go try it on."

She turned to survey the racks around her, biting her bottom lip. Surely there was something else here that would please her *and* satisfy Abby. Her eye caught on a pale yellow dress with eyelet trim and a Peter Pan collar. She grabbed the hanger with her free hand and held it up. "Only if I get to try this on, too."

Abby wrinkled her nose. "Fine, but make it snappy."

Rebecca hurried to the changing room and latched the half-door behind her. Forgettable soft rock music hummed through the overhead speaker as she hung the garments on the hooks and decided to start with the yellow dress she'd picked out. She removed it from the hanger and held it against her as she looked in the full-length mirror. It was simple but pretty. She pulled it on and turned back and forth in front of the mirror. Abby rapped on the door three times.

"Coming." Rebecca unlatched the door, and Abby greeted her with a frown. "What? I think it's very nice."

"That's the problem, Becca. It's 'nice.' It's also pale and shapeless, and you're not, yet somehow it makes you look that way." She looked her up and down. "You look like a boy."

Glancing at her chest and back up, Rebecca lifted her chin. "I do not." Abby could say what she wanted, but Rebecca was better endowed than Abby, nursing or not, something that irritated Abby to no end when they were teens.

Abby glared at her and conceded. "Except for your boobs."

Her jaw tensed and Rebecca gritted her teeth. "Breasts. They are breasts. You know I hate that word."

Abby muttered several more crass synonyms for breasts but ignored Rebecca, who had to bite her lower lip to keep from snapping at her sister.

Stepping away from the changing rooms, Abby's eyes darted back and forth, as if she were looking for something. Her gaze locked onto the rack of cheap sunglasses, and she grabbed a pair with mirrored lenses and handed them to Rebecca. Rebecca didn't know they even *made* mirrored lenses anymore. "Here. Put these on."

Doing as she was told, Rebecca slipped them on, and then Abby grabbed her hand and walked several yards to the main aisle. They stood for only a second before Abby stopped a college-aged man. He had short, black, spiky hair, sleeve tattoos on both arms, and at least three piercings on his face.

Abby stepped forward. "Excuse me. Can I get your opinion on something?"

If only the floor would open and swallow her whole.

Abby tugged Rebecca's hand, dragging her closer. "My sister is blind, and she doesn't trust my judgment." She waved her hand up and down the length of Rebecca's torso. "What do you think? Spinster or siren?"

He let out a laugh that could only be described as a guffaw before he said, "No offense to your sister. She's cute...in a conventional sort of way, but even my *mom* wouldn't wear that dress. Definitely spinster."

Abby had said she was blind, not deaf. Abby thanked the jerk before she led her back to the changing room.

"See? Spinster. All you need is a pair of granny glasses and half a dozen cats."

Rebecca took off the glasses and planted her foot into the floor. Hard. "His opinion does not count. I'm obviously not his type."

"He's a man. That's all that's required for this little experiment. Now, go try on the outfit I picked out."

Rebecca twisted her lips. "Don't you have a nursing baby to get home to?"

Abby looked down at her watch. "Joel can deal for ten more minutes. Go." She swished her hand at the changing room, and Rebecca relented.

A few minutes later she emerged, tugging at the hem of the skirt and straightening the camisole where it tucked into the waistband. This time Abby smiled and gave a low whistle. She grabbed Rebecca's hand again and marched her to the aisle while pushing the sunglasses onto her face.

A balding, middle-aged man approached with a boy she guessed was his teenage son.

Rebecca leaned into Abby. "This skirt is too short."

Abby looked her over again. "Maybe for an Amazonian queen, but not for a near-midget like you. Becca, you can show a little leg and not have people mistake your boyfriend for your pimp."

"Huh?" What on earth was she talking about?

"Chris could wear a pinstripe suit with a fedora and carry a pimp cane, and no one would mistake you for a floozy in this. I'll prove it to you."

The last of the wind left Rebecca's sails, and she fixed her face straight ahead while she listened to Abby go through her spiel about her blind sister ending with "Classy or trashy? Babe or bimbo?"

Where was that hole in the floor? *Lord, take me now.*

Rebecca watched the boy's cheeks redden, but he didn't speak. It smelled like either he or his dad had bathed in cheap cologne, and Rebecca suppressed a cough. Apparently being blind *did* sharpen your other senses.

The dad gave her a warm, appreciative smile and said, "Classy babe. I wish my own daughter would dress a little more like that. Everything she wears is black and skintight. Leaves nothing to the imagination."

Abby had issued an invitation to ogle, and the adolescent boy's gaze roamed up and down Rebecca's body and snagged on her bust. Heat blazed her cheeks, and not caring if she spoiled Abby's blind sister ruse or not, she pulled the top of the camisole to obscure any possible glimpse of exposed cleavage.

The dad elbowed his son in the side and murmured something in his ear that made the kid's cheeks redden even more. He cleared his throat. "Definitely babe."

Abby thanked them and, placing her hands on Rebecca's shoulders, turned her around and walked her back to the changing room. "Now you have something to wear on your next date. My treat."

Rebecca knew Abby expected a thank you, but she wasn't going to get one. At least not yet. Of all people, Abby should understand how difficult it was for her to wear anything that could possibly attract what their dad called, "the wrong kind of attention." After all, it was Abby's hand-me-downs that had filled her drawers and closet. Still, she knew Abby meant to help. Maybe Rebecca could loosen up a little when it came to her wardrobe.

***

As she waited outside Chris's apartment on Tuesday night, Rebecca recalled Abby's insistence that she wear her new outfit on her next date. At the last minute, her nerves got the better of her, and she decided to save the skirt and camisole for the weekend.

She hadn't been to Chris's place before, but he'd invited

her over for dinner. He had the front half of the first floor of an older home that had been split into three apartments. The smell of basil and oregano wafted out through the screen door. There was no door bell, so she tapped her hand against the door frame and called, "Knock, knock." She turned back toward the street as a pair of boys whizzed by her on their bikes, nearly knocking her over. "Sorry, lady," a chubby kid on a banana seat bike yelled.

Reckless bike-riding kids aside, Chris's street seemed peaceful compared to hers. At home, honking horns and squealing tires startled her multiple times a day. So far, a week hadn't passed without a fender bender.

When she faced the door again, Chris stood inside, wiping his hands on a dishcloth.

"Sorry. I was making the salads. Come on in." He rushed toward the countertop apparently intent on finishing his task. "I'm almost done with this."

She set her purse on the narrow counter lining the interior wall that extended into a short hallway and surveyed the small kitchen and round table set for two. The smell of tomatoes drew her to the stovetop where the red sauce simmered and the pasta boiled. "Do you need any help?"

"Nope. Got it all under control."

Rebecca bit back a grin. The meal looked under control all right, but her host—not so much. Tidbits of baby carrots flew off the cutting board and landed with tiny plunks on the tile floor. Without so much as a glance at the renegade carrots, he continued chopping until he cursed and swung away from the counter holding his left index finger in his right hand.

"Here, run it under cold water." Rebecca walked to the sink and turned on the faucet for him. "Where can I find a Band-Aid?"

Chris stuck his hand under the water and cursed again as a red stream swirled into the drain. "Medicine cabinet in the bathroom. Down the hall on the right."

She had thought the bathroom would be behind the closed door on her right, but apparently not. It must be his bedroom.

How odd to have a bedroom attached to a kitchen. She walked the short hall to the bathroom, which was small and smelled of Lysol. He had probably just cleaned it. The box of Band-Aids was right where he had said. She pulled one from its box, removed the wrapper and took it back to the kitchen. "SpongeBob Squarepants Band-Aids?"

Chris had a paper towel wrapped around his finger and was scouring his sink with his non-injured hand. "They were on sale."

Peeling back the adhesive ends of the Squidward bandage, she wrapped it around his finger and placed a kiss on it. "There. All better."

"You don't need to patronize me."

Did she hear irritation in his voice? Chris was always so even-keeled. She didn't think she'd ever heard that tone from him.

"Sorry. I'm a little stressed. I rushed home from work, and I wanted this to be perfect for you. Now do you believe my culinary skills are limited to cooking over a campfire?"

Her tummy growled and she placed her hand over it. "It all looks good to me, and I think it's ready." The microwave timer beeped, confirming her assessment, and Rebecca washed her hands and sat while Chris drained the pasta and filled their plates.

The oven had been hiding warm rolls that he placed in a basket on the table alongside a stick of butter and their salads. He opened the refrigerator and stared blankly before he murmured, "Cheese and salad dressing."

"I've found it's not the cooking that's so hard, it's timing everything to hit the table at the right time. That's another reason I like baking. It's done when it's done. Less stress." She started to sip the water Chris had set out when she remembered dessert. "Oh, my gosh, I almost forgot the pie. It's in the car." She leapt up and grabbed the keys from her purse before heading outside.

When she returned with a small peach pie covered in aluminum foil, Chris stood alongside the table filled with steaming spaghetti and sauce. A single red rose, its petals perfectly opened, laid across her napkin.

She placed her purse and the pie on the counter and walked to the table where Chris held out her chair. "Thank you," she said, but before she could sit, Chris took her face in his hands and kissed her.

"I didn't even greet you when you came in."

When his hands dropped back to her chair, she sat, and he pushed her closer to the table. The chair legs dragged on the floor, and she sat too far from her food, but it was the thought that counted.

Dinner was delicious, and he had obviously thought a lot about making their meal as perfect as possible. Could Abby's assessment be right? Could he be smitten with her?

When their plates had been emptied and Rebecca had put the leftover pie in the refrigerator, Chris insisted she allow him to do the cleanup.

He returned the cheese, butter, and salad dressing to the refrigerator. "I'll rinse these dishes off and be right in. Make yourself comfortable in the living room."

Rebecca walked down a short hallway to a small but homey room not equipped for a whole lot of living. A sofa, end table and floor lamp lined one wall, and a flat-screen TV hung from the opposite wall. Against a third wall stood the only interesting thing in the room—a large, oak bookcase.

Board games and puzzles filled the top shelf. The second shelf held books, a mixture of history and thrillers. The bottom two shelves held books as well. The shelf in the middle caught her eye.

On the left stood a framed, five-by-seven photo of Chris and his family. Chris wore a black cap and gown, and she assumed the photo memorialized his college graduation. He had one arm around Alan and one around his father. His mother stood on the end, next to her husband. The photo next to it made her heart stop before it started up again at a rapid clip.

Oh my. How can I get a copy of this, and would it be

considered obsessive if I had it blown up to poster size?

The burnished silver frame surrounded a black and white picture of Chris wearing boots, jeans, a leather jacket, and sunglasses while straddling his Harley. The barest hint of a smile graced his lips. A small piece of folded cardstock adhered to the upper right corner of the frame. Rebecca lifted it to reveal a feminine handwriting in red ink. Her heart seized a little until she saw the signature. It read, "If you're not careful on that thing, I'll kill you. Love, Mom." She smiled. She'd only met Chris's mother briefly at Alan's wedding, but she knew he got his sense of humor from her.

An older photo showed two young boys with an elderly couple. Chris and Alan with their grandparents? She picked it up to take a closer look at the young faces and noticed it had been resting on a couple of identical three-by-five prints.

She picked up the prints and set the picture of the boys back down. As she peered at the photos, a smile spread across her face. She hadn't heard him coming in from the kitchen, but suddenly Chris stood beside her.

"Jamie gave me those. Apparently someone caught us on one of those disposable wedding cameras."

She looked down again at the photo of them kissing and then up at Chris to see if the fact that someone had immortalized that moment pleased or bothered him.

He shrugged. "I'm kind of glad. It's a good shot for those cheap cameras. I only wish I had thought to have someone take a picture of us that actually showed our faces."

Rebecca thought she'd like one of those, too, but the one she held was invaluable. "Maybe the photographer got a shot of us, and we didn't even realize."

"Maybe. One of those is yours if you want it."

"Oh, I want it." Should she ask for a copy of the one with the motorcycle? She was torn between her desire to keep that picture close to her at all times and the fear of looking like a besotted twit. Her pride won out, and she kept her request to herself.

Chris laid a hand on the top shelf. "Want to play a game?"

"Sure." She loved board games, but like outdoor activities,

neither her father nor her sister was keen on them.

"Yahtzee?"

"Okay." Less chance to make a fool of herself playing that than, say, Trivial Pursuit.

Chris removed the box from the shelf and set it in the middle of the floor before sitting down alongside it. "Care to make it interesting?" That wicked look shone in his eyes again.

"As long as the stakes aren't too high. I don't get paid until next week."

"I wasn't thinking in terms of money." He paused and let her squirm for a few seconds. Did Strip Yahtzee exist?

"Best of five. Winner gets to choose his or her bounty."

"Bounty?" Rebecca kicked off her flat shoes, folded her legs beneath her and smoothed out her linen slacks. "You make it sound like someone's going to get his head lopped off."

"Only if *she* loses." He grinned as he opened the box and removed the score sheets, pen, dice, and cup. "Okay. Winner decides on the loser's punishment."

It took less than three seconds for Rebecca to decide. "I'm in."

"Okay." He smiled as if he had pulled something over on her. Well, wait until he heard what he'd have to do when he lost. "You first then."

"If I win, you have to take me for a ride on your motorcycle."

The smile left his face in an instant.

She anticipated him being hesitant. Since he hadn't taken her out already, she assumed there was some reason for his reluctance, but she didn't know what. The surprised—or alarmed?—look on his face had her wondering.

In a flash he recovered.

"Okay. A motorcycle ride. And if I win . . ."

He made a show of scrunching up his face and looking up at the ceiling as he puzzled over what would be an appropriate "punishment" for her. She doubted he needed any time to come up with something. After all, this had been his idea.

"If I win, you have to kiss me."

"Kiss you?" Rebecca gave him a sideways glance meant to question his sanity. "That's it? It's not like I've been playing hard to get in that regard."

"Well, this would be different."

"Oh, I think I see." Her cheeks grew warm. "This is about Saturday and how I—"

"This is about my desire for you. And how maybe it would be better...be easier for you...if you knew what to expect without me barreling ahead, not being sure if that's what you want."

She swallowed hard. Had he just said he desired her? She tried to refocus on the second half of what he had said. She had thought a lot about why she had reacted the way she did on Saturday. She had emotional baggage stored in compartments Chris didn't even know existed. He didn't deserve her lack of trust. On the contrary, he'd done about everything he could to earn it, including having this awkward conversation.

"If you win, and that's a big *if*, I can abide by my so-called 'punishment.'" She said it with a smile that hid the twinge of anxiety she still felt. In truth, kissing Chris was no hardship, but she had made something out of nothing.

Rebecca won the first two games by a wide margin, but Chris rolled double Yahtzees in the next two. Then he edged her out in the final game by using sixes in his four-of-a-kind.

They compared their tallies, and Chris pumped his fist in the air. "Victory!"

Rebecca slumped back against his couch. She didn't consider herself very competitive, but the final game had been intense. Well, for Yahtzee anyway.

"You won fair and square." She straightened her legs out and crossed them at the ankles now that Chris had cleared the game pieces away.

"That I did," Chris said. He closed the box and slid it toward the book case before he positioned himself next to her against the couch.

She already missed that motorcycle ride. So much so that she might challenge him to a rematch.

He rested his arm on the back of her shoulders, and she turned into him. His eyes were all light and heat. She lowered her lids and savored the sweet anticipation of feeling his lips, but they never materialized, and she reopened her eyes.

"It doesn't have to be tonight. I don't want it to feel forced."

Rebecca pushed away a smattering of disappointment and rested her head against him. She had never known the contentment she felt in Chris's arms. He was her Teflon-proofing for life. None of the bad stuff stuck when his arms encircled her.

"Can I get you anything to drink?"

"A glass of water would be great. Thanks."

Slipping his arms from around her, he stood and went to the kitchen. The cupboard clicked open, then the freezer. Ice cubes rattled, and water ran from the faucet.

Again the picture of Chris on his motorcycle captivated her. She needed to get one to put on her desk at work. Her gaze strayed down the bookcase to the bottom two shelves. She shifted onto her knees and studied the titles.

It looked like these shelves were all religious books—Bibles, books about saints and theology. He said he'd read his way into the Catholic Church, and the evidence in front of her confirmed it. She had to admit it intimidated her. Her dad had a Bible, and that was it. She continued to peruse the titles until the ones on the right side of the bottom shelf made her stop and examine them more closely. Some of the titles were loftier than others, but they all looked to be books about sex.

"Here you go." Chris handed down her water. He had a bottle of beer for himself in his other hand.

"See anything that interests you?"

"Well, I'm kind of curious about these books down here." She waved her index finger towards the books she had been looking at. "I don't think I've ever seen books about sex and religion before."

Crouching alongside her, he reached forward and ran his finger along the spines until he found the one he searched for. He slid the slim purple book from the shelf and handed it to her. "Most of these books have to do with the Theology of the Body. This one's an easy read—all Q & A. Why don't you take it home and check it out? You might find it interesting."

She loathed saying goodnight, and if they didn't have to work the next day, she could have envisioned them staying up all night talking. It was well after midnight already, and they would both be tired in the morning. It took three kisses until she got out the door and into her car. She piled a couple of pieces of leftover pie on the seat beside her along with the purple book Chris had loaned her and two others. He watched her pull out and remained standing on his stoop until her car turned out of view.

She was amazed that Chris never found fault with her and never made her feel stupid, despite her naiveté or ignorance. They had spent a lot of time flipping through his books and talking about "Catholic stuff" without him ever pushing her or belittling her. One of the books he loaned her was about Mary, the mother of God. She would have thought that book would have made her uneasy, even more than what he called the Theology of the Body books, but it didn't. Chris had talked about Mary being a mother to everyone, and since she had few memories of her own mother, that idea appealed to her.

Out of nowhere, tears came. *Thank you, Lord, for sending Chris into my life. Please let me be worthy of his*—dare she even think it?—*his love.*

***

Whistling as he went, Chris walked through his apartment gathering dirty socks, unopened mail, and other debris that had accumulated since Rebecca's visit a couple of nights earlier. Father John had called while Chris was on his way home from work, offering to bring a pizza. Father John didn't have a free night often, and he said he wanted to spend it watching a Pirates baseball game over beer and a meat-lover's deluxe.

Particles of food dotted the kitchen table and counters. Chris wiped the surfaces with a damp cloth and took a big sniff as he shook the crumbs into the trash can. Something stank. He yanked the plastic bag out by the straps, tightened, and took it to the door where he nearly bumped into Father John. He'd raised his hand to knock below the screen.

"Hey, come on in. I'm just taking this out." Chris went out, and Father John went in. In a couple minutes, he returned to find Father John slinging large slices of greasy pizza onto paper plates. The aroma of oregano and sausage filled the air. Chris washed his hands and grabbed a couple of bottles of beer from the fridge and removed their caps.

"What time does the game start?"

Father John glanced at his watch. "Five minutes. Let's say grace here, and then we can take this in the other room."

After they prayed, they headed back to the living room, and Chris turned on the game while Father John took a seat on the sofa. "How are things with Rebecca?"

"Good." He spared Father John a big smile before he bit into his pizza.

"It still blows my mind that you two even met, let alone that you're dating."

"She left here Tuesday night with two Theology of the Body books and one about Mary."

"Really?" Father John stopped mid-chew to assess Chris's veracity.

Chris nodded while he downed the pizza. He recalled the flicker of excitement he felt when she had accepted his offer to lend her the books.

"I'm not pushing. If she takes an interest in it I want it to be genuine and not something she does to please me. She noticed the books and asked me some questions, and I answered them the best I could. When I said she could borrow them, she said she would."

"Hmmm."

He had expected a more encouraging response than the noncommittal noise. "What's that supposed to mean?"

"I'm a little surprised is all, but I only knew her for a short time a long time ago."

"Why does it surprise you?"

"Let's just say the Bible camp wasn't the most Catholic-friendly thing I ever attended."

Chris was momentarily distracted by a line drive over second base. Once the runners slid safely into second and third bases he spoke. "How so?"

Father John interlocked his fingers behind his head. "I think six people informed me I wasn't saved."

"Was Rebecca one of them?"

"No." His hands dropped back to his lap. "She heard someone say it though and told them only God knows our hearts."

Taking the final bite of his crust, Chris chewed and swallowed. "Sounds like her. I'm praying she keeps an open mind and heart about it."

"I'll join you in that prayer, then."

After using a paper napkin to wipe the grease from his fingers, Chris set aside his plate and took a sip of his beer. "I'm anxious to see what she thinks of the Theology of the Body ones."

"Why's that?"

He let out a sigh. How much of this did he want to share? His thoughts were based only on his impressions, not something Rebecca had actually said, but Father John would be his best sounding board on something like this. Having this conversation with Alan would be like trying to discuss wine pairings with a teetotaler. Except in reverse. Whatever. Alan wasn't the one to talk to about this. "We haven't spoken about it directly, but I suspect her thinking's kind of messed up when it comes to sex."

"What makes you say that?"

"Well, we agree about sex being for marriage, but I'm coming at it from 'sex is such a great thing we've got to save it for marriage,' and I think she's more like, 'sex is so unholy we've got to confine it to marriage.'"

Father John nodded in understanding as if he'd heard that

a couple dozen times before. "Did you ever talk to her about what kind of sex ed she had? Did she get it from her dad or church or what?"

The thought of her dad talking to Rebecca about the joys of marital intimacy made him laugh. "Somehow I can't imagine her dad delicately explaining the birds and bees to her. How the man single-handedly raised two daughters, I have no idea. I don't think I've ever met a man I've liked less."

"That doesn't bode well, Chris."

"No, it doesn't, but I can't see breaking things off with Rebecca because of it."

Father John had finished both his pizza and beer and leaned back on the couch and stretched his legs out. He folded his hands behind his head. "I'm not saying you should, just that you ought to think long and hard about what it would be like to have him as your father-in-law."

A shudder rippled through him. "He called me a papist over dinner."

Father John laughed and leaned forward to rest his elbows on his knees. "Oh, man. You must have really lost your heart to put up with that garbage."

The blunt truth of that statement struck him. It looked more and more like his heart was a goner as far as Rebecca was concerned. "Maybe his bark is worse than his bite. I guess time will tell."

He thought back to their game of Yahtzee the other night. "You know, I thought I had her all figured out."

Laughing, Father John shook his head. "Never. I may be celibate, but I have five sisters. Just when you think you've figured them out, you realize you don't know a thing."

"I guess so. I've wanted to take her for a ride on my motorcycle, but I thought for sure she'd resist and claim it was unsafe and all that crap I have to hear from my mother all the time. So, I thought of a way to get her out there."

"Oh yeah?" Father John glanced at the TV screen before turning his attention back to Chris. The Bucs had a man in scoring position with no outs.

"How?"

"I thought I was so clever. I challenged her to best of five in Yahtzee. Winner gets to choose the loser's punishment. So, if I won, I'd make her ride with me, but I let her go first, and she said—get this—'if you lose, you have to take me for a ride on your motorcycle.' I couldn't believe it. I had to scramble to come up with something else in case she lost."

"Who won?"

"I did. I almost threw the game, but now that I know she wants to go, I guess I can just ask her."

"What did you come up with for her to do instead?"

Darn it. He'd walked into that one. "There are some things a man doesn't share, even with his closest friends." Chris's lips twitched as he crumpled his napkin, laid it on his plate, and set it on the end table.

"How about with his confessor?" Father John smirked.

"No need for confession."

"Good."

"So what's up with you? All we've talked about is me and Rebecca."

Father John leaned back into the couch again and rubbed his hands over his eyes and face then gave an audible sigh. "You know, I used to think everything was black and white. Now that I see all these shades of gray, it's not so simple anymore."

"Care to be a little less cryptic?"

"I'm not talking about sin or anything, just that even with prayer and trying to discern God's will, sometimes it's hard to decide on the most prudent course of action. I'm drowning in freedom." He stood and started pacing Chris's small room, betraying his Italian heritage by waving his hands this way and that as he spoke. "I mean, freedom is being free to do the right thing, right? But what if you're not sure what the right thing is, or maybe there's more than one right thing? Maybe there *isn't* any right thing—only different choices with different consequences."

Something sure had him worked up. Usually Chris came to

Father John with his dilemmas, but it seemed the tables had turned, and Chris wanted to offer his friend some kind of wisdom. Too bad he didn't have much to offer.

"Well, you've studied a lot more philosophy and theology than me, but in homage to the great Stan Lee, I would say, 'with great power comes great responsibility.' Whatever this is you're talking about, your free will, your ability to choose the good, is your power. Whatever you choose, you need to own what happens as a result. I guarantee no matter what you choose, it won't be perfect, but God will work with that, right? It's all raw material for him."

Father John stopped pacing and stared at the television. He was looking through the screen more than at it while he digested the wisdom Chris had gleaned from his childhood obsession with Marvel superheroes.

"Maybe I'm overanalyzing or making the decision too personal."

Chris scratched his cheek. "Hard to say. Do you want to tell me any more about it?"

Father John shook his head and reclaimed his place on the couch. "Not yet. Pizza, beer, and baseball with a friend. That's what I came over here for."

***

"So, explain to me again why you're staying with your dad tonight," Chris said.

"The girls that live in the other apartment claim they have bed bugs. So, the landlord is having the whole building sprayed or bombed or whatever it is they do. I would stay with Abby and Joel and the kids, but Joel's mom is coming in from New York City for a visit. It's been on the calendar for months, and I don't want to intrude or disrupt their plans."

Rebecca didn't mention that it wasn't mandatory that she leave or that in spite of her mother-in-law's visit, Abby offered her Emma's bed. While she didn't relish staying with her dad, she did still have a bed made up there, and it was only one night. Her dad's proximity to Chris was the real draw. Harrisburg to Gettysburg didn't constitute a long distance relationship, but a forty-five-minute drive each way on weeknights was plenty.

"So, I can thank the bed bugs for the pleasure of your company tonight."

"I guess you could say that."

Chris had taken her to Mister G's for homemade ice cream so good it made waiting alongside a crush of summer tourists worth it. Afterwards, they had walked hand-in-hand around her old neighborhood. Their pace had slowed considerably as they got closer to her dad's house. She didn't want their evening to end, and she guessed Chris didn't either.

"If I didn't tell you earlier, you look great tonight." His glance flitted up and down her new ensemble, courtesy of Abby.

Rebecca ducked her head but couldn't stop the smile spreading on her face. She tugged the lacy shrug across her chest with her free hand. "Thank you."

"You're a babe, Rebecca. I'm a lucky guy."

She stopped moving and peered up at him. "What did you say?"

"I'm a lucky guy."

"No, before that." It couldn't be a coincidence. He had used the same word as Abby.

"You're a babe?" His eyes shone as he studied her face and then her shoulders and on down her body.

A chill pricked her forearms and ran up her spine. "Have you spoken to my sister?"

He wrinkled his brow, puzzled. "No. I wouldn't even know how to get in touch with Abby. Why?"

She started walking again and shook her head. "I thought maybe she put you up to saying that, but I guess not."

"Nope. I came to the conclusion you're a babe all on my own."

As the sky turned a dusky pink in the west, they mounted the steps to her dad's porch. It was hot, but the humidity seemed to be dropping. The fragrance of the neighbor's rose bushes wafted on a light breeze, and she also caught a whiff of someone grilling—probably hamburgers. "Do you smell that?"

Chris stopped and sniffed. "What?"

She smiled. "Summer."

"So that's what summer smells like to you, beef and flowers?"

Rebecca laughed. "Yeah, I guess so."

He stopped, and so did she, and he put his hands on her shoulders and turned her to face him. He stepped closer. "And what does summer sound like to you?"

"Hmm." She took a couple seconds to listen and think. "Kids playing outside, water splashing, and cicadas humming—but that's later in the summer."

"So, screaming, water and bugs?"

She laughed again. "Yep. So, tell me, what does summer *feel* like to you, Chris?"

He inched closer so that their bodies nearly touched. "It feels like the wind in my hair when I ride on my Harley. It feels like soft, warm skin coated in sunscreen." He rubbed his hands over the sides of her shoulders where her tanned skin was exposed at the edge of the shrug, and her arms tingled beneath his touch. Then his voice went down a notch and turned languid. His eyes were almost imperceptibly darker. "It feels like kissing a beautiful girl on her daddy's porch."

"Beautiful?" She smiled, but then it faded as she remembered her lost bet. Her heart pounded in her chest when she realized what came next.

As if reading her mind, he gently rubbed her shoulders saying, "Relax. It's a kiss. Nothing more."

She accepted his reassurance with a nod and leaned into him. She had expected to feel uncomfortable, maybe even to dislike it despite her attraction to Chris. What she didn't count on was the longing that ripped through her like a brush fire on a windy day. She wrapped her arms around Chris's neck and drew him closer.

He smiled against her lips. "Okay?"

Okay? She'd never been more okay in her life. Desperate for more but too embarrassed to open her eyes, she said, "Is it over?"

"It doesn't have to be," Chris chuckled as his lips met hers again.

***

Chris' lips brushed hers a final time, and he leaned his forehead against Rebecca's. His heart drummed against his ribs. "Rebecca, I want to live with you."

The sweet smile fell from her face, and her eyes widened. She misunderstood him.

He slid his hands down her arms to grasp her hands and looked down at their fingers entangled between them. "I don't mean I want to cohabit with you. I'm not expressing myself well." He bit his lower lip in frustration. Translating his feelings for her into words had become more and more difficult.

"My brain doesn't seem to fire on all cylinders when I've been kissing you. I think all the blood is rushing..." Geez. Did he almost say that out loud? It wouldn't be a good idea to follow that line of thinking. He stopped, took a quick breath and tried to explain. "The best comparison I can make is when I converted, my family couldn't understand it—well, for a lot of reasons—but mostly they didn't get why I wanted to subject myself to all these rules. And I couldn't make them understand. But those rules, Rebecca, they make me feel free. Free to become the man I'm meant to be." Her eyes weren't so wide now, and they held a tender expression that made his heart ache.

"You make me feel free. I know now what it is to really be alive. So, when I say 'I want to live with you,' I mean it in the best way. I want to experience everything with you."

Tears filled her eyes and threatened to overflow. She opened her mouth as if to say something and then closed it. Instead she reached up, slid her hands around his neck and pulled his head down to hers where she planted on his lips what was possibly the sweetest kiss he could imagine. After several seconds, she pulled away from him enough to breathe his name, his full name—Christopher. Could she possibly feel the same way he did?

His chest burned. The words pounded against his rib cage and his heart felt like a balloon filled to near capacity. "I love you," threatened to burst out of him, the three little syllables sliding over his tongue and through his lips as he pressed them gently along her neck. He took a deep breath and bit back the words knowing somehow that like fruit ripening on the tree, he just needed to be patient. Those words would be sweeter to her ears if he let them mature.

Her gravelly voice murmured in his ear. "Do you want to come in? My dad said he wouldn't be home until after midnight."

As much as he didn't like it, he knew what his answer had to be, but, man, that tempted him. *She* tempted him even if she didn't mean to, and he knew she didn't. If someday she did, well, heaven help him. Even now, that doe-eyed look she gave him weakened his resolve. "I don't think that would be wise."

"Oh." Her disappointment passed quickly. "Are we still on for breakfast tomorrow?"

"Absolutely. I'll be back here at nine o'clock." He kissed her one last time and left her there on the porch. He put on his helmet and started his motorcycle. Hearing and feeling it roar and rumble to life beneath him never failed to bring him satisfaction. Given the time, he ought to go home and straight to bed; then tomorrow would seem to arrive faster. He didn't feel like sleeping though. His mind was too full of Rebecca.

A hazy moon hung above the houses and trees silhouetted in darkness. As the distance between houses grew and fenced-in yards morphed into fields of corn and soybeans, fireflies danced above roadside gullies. They flashed and drew his attention in every direction the way that ever-present thoughts of Rebecca flitted on the periphery of his imagination. Seduced by their alluring magic, he took the long way home.

11

Mercy

The rising sun broke through the clouds as Chris pulled up outside of Rebecca's dad's house. He killed the engine and checked his watch. Five minutes early. He sat looking blankly at the house and thinking about kissing Rebecca on that porch less than twelve hours ago. She had needed a little reassurance, but once she got going—wow. He hadn't kissed a girl like that in a long time, but he knew somehow it had never been like that. So, so—explosive. Somewhere behind all that hesitancy was a passionate woman waiting to come out. He hoped he'd be on the receiving end of all that heat when she finally let loose.

Chris broke free of his daydream when a movement in the living room window caught his eye. The sheer curtain obstructed his view, but a figure moved across the room. By the ponytail he now saw in silhouette, he knew it was Rebecca. He heard her voice through the open window. It was muffled but raised and carried a strident tone he had never heard from her before. A second of silence followed, and then he heard her father, loud and clear.

"Damn you to hell. Out whoring around with that...that... lowlife last night. How dare you come back here, having done only God knows what with that boy and then run off with him again, not even sticking around here long enough to make me a decent breakfast. Get out!"

That wasn't the end of it. The rest included several words that would've been bleeped out even in the most vulgar of reality shows. When the stream of profanity ended, Chris realized his jaw clenched and his fists tightened at his sides. He heard a clatter and then the sound of something shattering—something glass or ceramic maybe. If Rebecca were hurt, he didn't know what he'd do.

He dismounted his bike, jammed his keys in his pocket,

and tore the helmet from his head before he raced toward her dad's door.

Just as he reached the point where the sidewalk met her dad's walk, Rebecca burst through the front door. In less than two steps, she adopted a normal pace as she came down the stairs with her ponytail bouncing on her shoulders. As soon as she caught sight of him, she smiled and hurried her pace to meet him. Or keep him from going any further; he wasn't sure which.

Without a word, he grabbed her arm and steered her toward her car. When they reached the driver's side door, he stopped and bit out, "Give me your keys."

The relaxed, happy demeanor she wore vanished, and a worried frown formed in its place as she fished her keys from her purse and handed them over.

"Chris, what's the matter?" She sounded as if she didn't know. Unreal.

He took her arm again and guided her to the passenger side. He waited as she slid into the front seat, then slammed the door behind her. He returned to the driver's side, got in, and turned the key in the ignition.

"Chris, you're scaring me. What's wrong?"

He was scaring *her*? He couldn't fathom the complete disconnect between her behavior and what he had witnessed. He gave her a cursory once over and didn't see any bruises, cuts, or other signs that she'd been manhandled. His shoulders relaxed in relief. "Not here. We're going to talk, but not here."

A tense silence filled the car for the next few minutes until Chris pulled into a restaurant parking lot. He could see Rebecca twisting the rings on her fingers and bouncing her knee in his peripheral vision. He finally jerked her car into park, turned the engine off and faced her.

She fidgeted with the drawstring on her shorts.

All the tension and irritation he felt moments before melted in an instant.

He took her soft, cool hand in his, and she stiffened.

"Are you okay?" He searched her face for some indication that she really was okay despite what he'd seen and heard.

"Sure." She acted like she didn't understand the reason for his question.

He stared at her, not knowing what to say. Finally realizing that she really didn't know why he asked, he explained.

"I got to your dad's a few minutes early and thought I'd wait." Something flickered behind her eyes, but she said nothing. "The window was open. I heard your dad."

Her eyes turned glassy, and she looked away.

Her fingers pulled away, and he grasped them tighter. No way would he let her dodge this. Not after what he'd heard. "I take it that's not the first time your dad has spoken to you that way."

Her ponytail swung away from him as she turned from the passenger window and looked down into her lap. "No."

"How often does that happen?"

She bit her lower lip and shook her head.

"Rebecca? How often?" He didn't want to seem dispassionate about it, but right now that demeanor tempered all the anger and fear that was roiling inside of him, threatening to explode.

"Just when he's stressed out about work or something sets him off. Maybe a couple times a month when I lived at home. I'm not around for it so much now."

"Does he talk to Abby that way?"

She looked him in the eye for the first time since they'd gotten in the car. "Sometimes. She never stuck around long enough to hear all of it. She'd take off. She's always been his favorite anyhow."

Strange. How could her dad favor Abby, who rejected every one of his rules and principles and then be so hard on Rebecca, who bent over backward to please him?

He didn't even want to think what he had to say next, but he had to know. "Has he ever hit you?"

"No. Of course not." The way she rushed to answer, you'd

think his question was absurd instead of the next logical assumption. "He may be a little rough some times, but he's never hit me."

"Define 'rough'."

"Grabbing me by the arm or something."

"Does it leave a mark?"

"No. Never."

"Has he hit Abby?"

"No."

"Your mom?"

She paused for a few seconds. "I'm not sure. I've always kind of thought that was it—that's why she finally left. I don't know for sure."

What kind of mother leaves her two daughters in a situation like that?

"I don't think it's a good idea for you to stay there. Ever. If something else comes up, I'm sure Abby could accommodate you somehow. If not, you'll stay with me."

"It's okay, Chris. Really." Her features softened, and she looked as if *she* felt sorry for *him*. Was she serious?

"No, it's not." He was about to lose his temper, something he wasn't prone to, not unless pushed to his limit. "Nothing about that adds up to okay. No one deserves to be treated that way, especially you. And for a man to say those things to his own daughter...Rebecca, why?"

She shrugged. "He's always had anger issues. It's like he blows up, and it's bad, but then he's sorry. He really does feel bad about it. And he tries not to get upset."

"Has he had counseling or anything?"

"My dad?" She laughed. "Uh, no. That's not his thing."

"It should be his thing. Rebecca, you are the sweetest, most innocent girl I've ever met. You are decent and modest and for the life of me I don't know how he could call you a whore, of all things."

The silence between them became uncomfortable, but he waited for her to respond. Finally, she pulled her hand out of his and laid it in her lap. "He saw us last night. He saw us kiss."

"How? I thought he worked last night?"

"Apparently while we were out walking, he came home."

"But you didn't see his car."

"No, he didn't bring it home. He didn't tell me how, but he injured his right leg, and he couldn't drive. Someone brought him home. When he got there he took some painkillers and laid down in his easy chair to rest. He saw us through the window."

It had been a heck of a kiss, but there wouldn't have been much to see. No inappropriate touching. Nothing. And she was a grown woman living on her own for cripes sake. It started to make sense though. Her reluctance to kiss him had nothing to do with him. Or her for that matter. It had everything to do with her dad.

He shook his head and then let it fall on the headrest. "I had no idea. No idea. Or I would not have done that there, in front of his house."

She refocused his attention with the gentle touch of her finger to his cheek. "Please don't be sorry. I'm not. That kiss…I don't regret it. I get breathless just thinking about it, so don't you dare try to take it back."

"Well, next time we'll be more discreet. I won't be the reason for him speaking to you like that. Not ever again." He sat forward again and looked at her. "I want you to promise me something."

She lifted her chin. "What?"

"Promise that if this happens again you'll tell me."

She nodded. "Okay, but you need to promise me something, too."

"What's that?"

"That you won't go pussyfooting around me like I'm some kind of victim. I can't bear it if you pity me. I'm the same person today as I was yesterday. I'm sorry about all this, and I'm embarrassed, and the last thing I want is for you to be mad at me."

"You think I'm mad at you?" He *had* been short with her. "I'm not mad at you. I'm mad at your dad. I'm mad at myself.

I'm frustrated with the situation, maybe a little irritated that you never told me about this, but mad at you? How could I be mad at you?" *I love you.*

 For the first time since she'd practically skipped out of her father's house her eyes welled up. Her chest rose and fell in quick succession, and she hiccupped.

"Why are you crying now when you didn't so much as bat an eye at how your dad treated you?"

The tears ran over the rims of her lids and streaked her cheeks. "I stopped crying over my dad years ago." She shrugged. "I guess I got used to it. I'm crying now because of you. Because you care."

"Of course I care."

She broke into a sob, and he tried to pull her into his arms, but the cup holder, a box of tissues, and the other stuff stored between the front seats blocked his way.

"Hold on."

He shoved open the car door and came around to her side. When he yanked open her door, she stood and nearly fell into his arms.

She sobbed into his shoulder while he stroked her soft, smooth hair and tried to soothe her. After a few minutes, she pulled away and dried her eyes with her fingertips, trying to erase the smudged makeup.

"Are you hungry?"

She nodded and smiled.

"Let's go eat." He put his arm around her and walked her into the restaurant. He tried, but nothing about the meal seemed normal, and more silence hung over their waffles than talking or laughter. When they finished, he decided to take her home rather than finding some way to spend more of the day with her.

He parked her car around the corner from her dad's house and walked her to the door.

"I'm coming in with you." He didn't phrase it as a question, and she didn't argue. He wasn't about to let her alone with her father. He waited in the entryway while she went upstairs to grab her things. Chris thanked God her dad didn't show his face—if he was even there. Rebecca had begged him not to confront her dad, and although not certain it was the right decision, he had agreed.

He walked Rebecca to her car, kissed her forehead, and held her tight for as long as she let him. The whole morning left him drained and confused.

Once Rebecca's car pulled safely away from the curb, he got back on his motorcycle and rode. He rode over two-lane country roads and four-lane highways. Miles of corn, now tall and green, but not yet tasseled, whizzed by him. The sun, the wind, the freedom of the open road all soothed his soul.

Two hours later, he pulled in at a beer distributor. In the cooler, he found a couple of chilled bottles of Gateway's latest brew. He bought them, stowed them on his bike and found himself travelling the familiar roads to home—his parents' home.

After a moment's hesitation, Chris knocked on the front door and waited. His mom insisted that he and Alan walk right in, and while Alan did that, Chris disliked barging in on his parents. In less than a minute, his dad answered the door.

"Chris, I'm surprised to see you here. Nice day for a ride, isn't it?"

He followed Dad down the hallway to the kitchen. "Yeah. I've been riding for a couple hours at least. Time for a break."

With a glance, his dad assessed him and probably the reason for his visit. A sharp guy by nature, twenty-five years in sales had left him with people-reading skills any psychologist or police detective would envy.

The morning newspaper was spread over the kitchen island. His dad climbed onto the stool in front of it. His seat faced the recently-updated cooking area and new cherry wood cabinetry. To the right, a pair of French doors opened onto the deck that descended to his parents' in-ground swimming pool and three acres of land. Chris raised the two bottles of beer he had brought and set them in the center of the counter.

"Brought you a beer."

Lifting the bottle to eye level, his dad glanced at it and wrinkled his nose. He read the label aloud. "Bare Ass Ale. There weren't any bare asses involved in the brewing, were there?"

"Not a one. It's good, despite the name." Chris pulled a bottle opener from the drawer in front of him, popped off the caps and passed a bottle to his dad.

"Thanks, then. So, how's it going?"

"Good."

His dad let his glasses slide down his nose and studied him. Now that Dad had turned sixty, Chris recognized the signs of aging. His salt and pepper hair had become nearly all salt. The lines in his face had deepened, but his eyes and demeanor still exuded the same strength and comfort Chris had found there his whole life.

"Where's Mom?"

"Grocery store."

Good. Chris hadn't planned this visit, but right now he needed the calm assurance of his father not the emotional refuge of his mother.

"Are you still seeing Rebecca?"

"Yep." He wanted the conversation to go in this direction, but letting his dad steer it in that way felt easier. Chris continued to look straight ahead.

His dad took a swig and set the bottle on the counter with a clunk. "She's a beautiful young woman, but I'm sure you noticed that."

Chris saw him grin from the corner of his eye.

"Your mom and I haven't gotten to spend much time with her, but from what we know, we like her."

"Yeah. Maybe I should talk to Mom about having her over for dinner or something."

"Your mom would be all over that."

Chris laughed. He took a sip of his beer and finally looked at his dad. "I'm falling in love with her."

Nodding slowly, his dad's mouth stretched to a grin.

Chris smiled, too. "I know it hasn't been that long, but I can't help myself."

"Does she feel the same way?"

He pursed his lips together for a second, thinking. "She hasn't said, but she hasn't turned down a date or refused a kiss, so I'm hopeful." He let a couple beats pass and then finally got to what he came to talk about. "I'm worried about her, Dad."

The newspaper rustled as his dad folded it and pushed it away. "Why?"

"Her father's abusive. She says he's never hit her, but I overheard him yelling at her this morning." He paused again, taking a deep breath before he continued. "Dad, he cursed, and he called her a whore. Something shattered, and she came out the door, got in her car, and tried to act like nothing happened. It breaks my heart. She's the sweetest girl. She doesn't deserve to be treated like that."

"Does she live with her parents?"

"No. She has her own apartment in Harrisburg. At home, it's just her dad. Her mom is dead, and she was gone long before that." He sighed and continued. "It does explain some things though."

"Like what?"

"I think she's afraid of physical intimacy. The fact that I'm a man, and I desire her threatens her. Some women eat that up, they use it, and they manipulate you with it. It scares her to death."

His dad took a drink of his beer, set it down, and then took off his glasses and set them on the newspaper. "Chris, she's probably never experienced the kind of love you can offer her. That doesn't mean it isn't what she wants or needs, but it's going to require some patience on your part."

Chris folded both hands around his bottle and nodded. He was learning all about patience, but he and Rebecca hadn't dated that long; there was no rush. Still, her reluctance made him feel like he dragged her along—not unwilling, but hesitant. His dad's voice brought him out of his thoughts again.

"For years I watched your brother bring home a different girl for every homecoming, every prom. Summer crushes. He must have fallen in and out of love a hundred times. And you were forever wandering through the woods out here or home with your nose in a book or your ear buds in, listening to music. I knew it would take a special young woman to turn your head."

"It's not that I didn't notice girls, believe me. The shyness paralyzed me."

"In retrospect, I don't think that was such a bad thing. You were being shaped and molded for this young woman so that you could be what she needs to help her overcome her situation. Maybe to be the woman you need *her* to be."

Chris smirked as he raised his bottle a last time. "Careful, Dad, it almost sounds like you're acknowledging a deity there."

"I never said I didn't believe in God. I just don't see the use for religion in my life." He stood, but kept his gaze fixed on Chris. "But, you've given me a lot to think about in that regard the last couple of years."

Huh? Dad thought about God? Chris had been praying for a long time that his family would take an interest in God, but this was the first indication that the little seeds he'd been sowing may someday take root. Before he could say anything in response, the garage door opened and his mother called out.

"A little help here?"

"I'll go get the groceries." Chris ambled to the door off the kitchen that led to the two-car garage. He paused as he grabbed the doorknob. "Thanks, Dad, and if you like that ale, I'll get you a case." Then turning into the garage, he grabbed the plastic bags hanging from his mother's wrists. "I'll get this stuff, Mom."

"Thanks, honey." She pushed her purse back up her shoulder and headed into the kitchen. Her hair, always cut in a simple, elegant style, looked a shade darker blonde than he had seen on her before. It looked good with her glasses.

He slung the bags onto the floor next to the island. "Hey, Mom. Dad and I were talking, and we thought it might be good if I could bring Rebecca over so you could get to know her better."

"Well," his mom huffed. "It's about time."

12

Joy Ride

Chris specified what to wear: long pants, long sleeves, and sturdy shoes—no open toes. She tried coaxing the reason out of him, but he wouldn't budge. Did his parents keep their house unusually cold or something?

Her nerves jangled as she pulled into Chris's parents' driveway. She had only met them briefly at Alan and Jamie's wedding. That being only their third date, she hadn't been very concerned about the impression she made.

They had a beautiful home, which his family had built. Its value had to be nearly double that of her dad's place. Chris said his father sold medical devices, and apparently he excelled at it. His mom had only started working part time when Chris and Alan had gone to college.

Chris's motorcycle was parked in the driveway, and Rebecca thought back to the picture of him that sat on his bookshelf. She noticed the bike faced the road, which was unusual, but maybe he had been cleaning it again. The chrome shone.

She exited the car and went around to the passenger side where she had laid the dessert on the floor in a small cardboard box. She lifted out the bowl and closed her door as Chris walked toward her from the open garage.

"Hey, you're here. What's this?"

"I offered to bring dessert." She lifted the glass bowl filled with cubed cake, whipped cream, and fresh berries. "Berry trifle."

"It looks great." He took it from her and walked with her to the garage. "Wait here while I put this inside." He said something to his mom and then he returned.

"So, let's see how well you follow directions." He stopped a few feet from her and crossed his arms in front of his chest while he looked over her attire. "Very good. Mom said we have at least an hour until dinner."

"Am I too early?" She could've sworn his mom had told her 4:30 p.m. when they talked on the phone.

"Nope. I have something else planned for us first."

She slid her hands into her back pockets and shifted her weight from her heels to her toes and back again. "Okay. Care to tell me what?"

"Despite the fact that I trounced you at Yahtzee—"

She held up a hand. "Wait a minute, buddy, that was not a trouncing. That was a skin-of-your-teeth kind of win."

He smiled. "Okay. Despite the fact that I *beat* you at Yahtzee, I thought I'd make your wish come true and take you for a ride."

"Seriously?" She sounded overeager even to her own ears, but every time she laid eyes on that motorcycle, she became more enamored with the idea of riding on it.

"Why not? To be honest, that's the whole reason I challenged you to the game in the first place." His cheeks pinked a little with his admission.

"What do you mean?"

"Hang on." Chris pulled his helmet off of the wooden shelf, grabbed a large plastic bag from the floor, and walked with Rebecca toward the bike. "I mean, I've wanted to get you out on this bike with me in the worst way for weeks, but I didn't think you'd want to try it. So, I came up with that idea to force your hand."

"What made you think I didn't want to go for a ride?" She circled to the other side of the motorcycle and waited on his answer.

Raising his arm, he lifted his palm in uncertainty. "You don't seem like the adventurous type, I guess."

"Maybe not, but this thing has me hooked. I couldn't figure out why you hadn't offered to take me out on it. I thought you didn't want to, and I had to force *your* hand."

"Well, since we're both in agreement here, let's do this." He handed her the large plastic bag. "This is for you."

Accepting the bag, she reached inside. "A helmet? Chris,

this was probably expensive. I can pay you for this."

"Get out of here. It's a gift, and there's no way I'm taking you out on this without a helmet."

She pulled out the helmet and turned it around, examining the pink trim decorating the sides. "Do you wear a helmet all the time?"

He shrugged one shoulder. "Not all the time. I make exceptions for perfect weather conditions and the irrepressible desire to feel the wind in my hair, but not for you." He flashed a grin. "Double standard, I know, but you're going to have to live with it." He gave her a minute more to look over the mostly-black helmet. "I'm not used to riding two-up, so we're going to take it easy."

Chris spent the next ten minutes or so going over instructions with her—how to get on and off of the bike, where to keep her feet, which parts were hot and how to lean when they accelerated.

"You need to sit close to me and hold onto either my waist or my hips. Don't grab onto me any higher." He pointed to her legs. "You're going to want to squeeze your legs together as close around the bike as you can get. It'll feel more stable."

"Will you be able to hear me if I say something to you?"

"Maybe not. That's a good point. If you need me to stop or slow down tap my right thigh. If you're doing good or you want to go faster, tap my left thigh." He gave her a roguish smile that made her cheeks heat. "Can you see now why I've wanted to get you out on this thing with me?"

"Why do you think I'm so eager?"

He grabbed her around the waist and pulled her towards him. "You know, I would kiss you right now, but my mom is watching. She doesn't think I know she's there, but I can see her rummaging through something in the garage. Spying."

Rebecca snuck a peak. His mom riffled through a cardboard box.

"Hi, Mrs. Reynolds." She made a move toward the garage, but Chris held her back.

"Sorry, Mom, but time's ticking. You can chat at dinner."

He helped Rebecca get her helmet on and tighten the strap. Then he straddled the motorcycle and steadied it. "Okay, get on."

Rebecca grabbed onto his arm and swung her leg over the seat behind him, putting her feet on the pegs the way he had instructed. She scooted closer to him, and when she wrapped her hands around his waist, her heart fluttered. Yes, she was going to enjoy this.

"Okay. Hold on tight and lean with me. You ready?"

"Ready."

He started the engine and with the first lurch forward Rebecca gripped him tighter, not easing up until he stopped at the end of the driveway.

"I've got the perfect song." He picked something out using his audio system, turned it up, and eased out onto the road. They coasted to the stop sign at the end of his parents' street. By then the song's chorus had repeated. If she had to guess, she'd say it was called, "Hold On."

"Is this the Dave Matthews Band?" She didn't want to yell, but she realized now how important the nonverbal communication would be. Even sitting still, she thought he might not be able to hear her.

"No. Alabama Shakes. And that's a woman singing."

She didn't get a chance to respond because he turned left onto the main road. If pressed on it, Rebecca would admit that the first ten minutes scared her to death, especially when they accelerated or turned. Poor Chris would probably have a bruised middle from the death grip she had on him at the beginning. After that, she loosened up and even tapped his left thigh a couple of times when they got out on the highway, signaling that she wanted to go faster.

When they finally pulled back into the driveway nearly an hour later, Rebecca was exhilarated. Riding itself was a blast, but riding with Chris was over the top. He let her dismount and then swung his leg over the seat and stood beside her. She undid the strap, pulled her helmet off, and ran her fingers through her hair to get rid of any possible helmet-head.

Chris took off his helmet, too, took hers from her, and set them both inside the garage. His cheeks were still red from the wind when he came back to her.

"Well?"

"Oh, my gosh. What a rush! It took me a little while to get used to the feel of it, but then I loved it."

"I'm glad to hear you say that." His eyes were all smoky looking, barely even blue anymore.

Her heart started pounding faster, which said something because it already beat at a good clip from the ride. He stepped closer to her and used his fingers to comb through some of the tangles in her hair.

"Would it be too soon to tell you I've fallen in love with you?"

Rebecca didn't breathe for a full three seconds. When she found her voice again, she said, "Kind of a moot question now, isn't it?"

"I guess so." His chin dipped down, and his ears reddened, but his voice was steady. "I love you, Rebecca."

And before she had a chance to say those three lovely words back to him, he kissed her. She thought it was intentional—that he didn't want her to feel pressure to reciprocate the feeling now if she wasn't ready. She was grateful because as much as it thrilled her to hear him say it, she didn't know if she could return his affection. At least not with those three words.

***

Chris considered the meal a success. Of course, compared to dinner with Rebecca's dad, anything short of a fistfight at the table could be considered an improvement. After dinner, dessert, coffee, and the requisite display of Chris's childhood photos, he walked Rebecca out to her car. As they reached her door she stopped. "My trifle bowl. I forgot all about it."

"I'll get it," Chris offered and jogged back to the house. He slipped into the kitchen through the garage and scanned the countertops for the glass bowl. He could hear his parents in the living room. His dad spoke first.

"Well, what do you think?"

"What's not to like? She's charming, wholesome, and pretty."

Peering around the corner, Chris saw his mom relaxing in her favorite overstuffed chair while his dad massaged her shoulders.

"He loves her."

His mom made a waving motion with her hand. "It's written all over his face. And hers."

That last statement pleased him. She thought Rebecca loved him, too.

"There's something I couldn't put my finger on at first," Mom said, "but I think she's scared of something, and she's skittish."

Agreed. She was skittish like a foal. Wobbly, unsteady, uneasy, quick to frighten. He wanted to see her steady, strong, galloping free.

"She's scared, and she's going to bolt," Mom said. "Mark my words."

Chris finally spotted the bowl next to the dish washer. He picked it up and stood still, curious to hear Dad's response.

"Could be. Could be he gives her a reason to stop being scared, too. Either way, he's old enough to make up his own mind about it."

"It's not his mind I'm worried about, it's his heart. That boy has never done anything half way. I don't expect him to be any different when it comes to loving a woman."

Taking the bowl, Chris closed the door without making a sound and slipped back out through the garage. His mom's comment had hit a nerve. Yes, he could definitely see Rebecca's skittishness, but she was neither fickle nor flighty. He hoped with all his heart his mom was wrong, because if she was right, he didn't know what he'd do without Rebecca. He caught sight of her leaning against her car, thought of their ride this afternoon, and knew that he wanted her with him for the long haul.

"Your bowl," he said and handed it to her.

"Thank you, kind sir."

In the moonlight, her face glowed—irresistibly so.

"Give me that bowl back." It came out more a growl than a request. He opened her car door and thrust the bowl onto the seat inside. "Come here." He took her in his arms and pressed a kiss to her hair. "Mmm . . . you smell so good."

Rebecca laughed. "I probably smell like the barbecued pork your mom made."

"No, you smell like you." He nuzzled her ear and whispered, "I love you." He hadn't realized that saying it out loud would be such a relief. He hadn't planned on telling her today; he was waiting—for *what* he didn't know, but it wasn't supposed to be today. Yet, he had gotten off that motorcycle, and he couldn't help himself. The words had bubbled right out of him.

"You're making it hard for me to leave."

He grinned. "Am I?"

She nodded.

"I wish I could take you home. Soon. I'm car shopping next weekend." Then he remembered work. "Shoot. Not next weekend. The week after. I have to go to a craft beer festival at the shore in Delaware next weekend."

"All weekend?" She drew her lips up into a pout.

"Friday night to Sunday night."

"Oh."

His mom called from the front door. "Chris, Alan's on the phone. He wants to talk to you. Says your cell keeps rolling to voice mail."

Chris sighed. "Okay. Tell him to hang on a minute," he called back to her. Once his mom had retreated into the house, he kissed Rebecca goodnight. If only Alan weren't waiting on him.

"Let me know when you want to go for another ride."

"I will. Thank you for taking me."

Once she got into her car, he jogged back to the house. Alan's timing sucked.

13
Ants Marching

The craft beer festival ran for two days at the convention center near one of the most popular beaches along the Delaware Coast. Manning Gateway Brewery's booth left Chris with mixed feelings. On the one hand, it would probably be fun and give him a chance to learn more about the industry. On the other hand, it would be another weekend he couldn't spend any time with Rebecca. By the end of the festival hours Saturday, Chris missed her. Every time booth traffic lulled, his mind wandered. He imagined running his hands through Rebecca's hair and pulling it behind her so he could kiss her cheek, her ear, her neck....

His co-worker Ned, a guy in his early forties who had been with the brewery almost since its beginning, had brought his own car and headed out by himself. Chris stayed behind at the exhibit while the other guys used the restroom. He and his co-workers Tom, Eric, and Scott had ridden together, and they had decided to grab dinner at a restaurant a couple of miles from the hotel. The crowd had thinned to a few stragglers, and the people from most of the other exhibits had already left.

He probably had a few minutes to call Rebecca. He knew he would miss her on this trip, but not to the extent he did. Thoughts of her preoccupied him, making him fidgety and anxious as he continually recalculated how long it would be until he could see her. She picked up on the second ring.

"Hey, how's it going?" The sound of her voice brought him the first peace he'd felt all day.

"I miss you." Geez. He hadn't meant to blurt that out right off the bat, but there it was.

"That's sweet. I miss you, too. A whole lot."

Chris sagged against a cinder block pillar. At least it wasn't a one-sided affair. Maybe a little distance would be good for them. Absence makes the heart grow fonder and all that. "Any plans for tonight?"

Her laugh tinkled like a spoon against a full champagne glass. "Oh, yeah. First a gourmet meal consisting of a frozen burrito with jarred salsa. Then maybe a walk around the neighborhood before I kick back with whatever I've got on the DVR. And, if I can stand the excitement, one of those little containers of ice cream. Portion control, you know. What are you doing tonight?"

"We wrapped up here at the convention center, so as soon as a few of the guys get back from the men's room we're going to have dinner at an Italian place near the hotel."

"That's it? No happy hour or a movie or anything?"

"Nah. No one's mentioned anything. My feet are kind of tired from standing on concrete all day. I'm good with going back to the hotel and crashing." Looking up, he noticed the other guys making their way back to the display. "Looks like everyone's back. I'd better go. I'll call you later, okay?"

"Okay. Enjoy your dinner."

Scott and Eric laughed hard about something. Tom wore an uncomfortable smile, like he didn't find it funny but didn't want to say so.

"Talking to your girlfriend?" Scott asked.

"Just checking in," Chris said and slid the phone back into its holster.

"Don't you have to check in, Tom? You're the newlywed," Scott said.

"Nah," Tom said as he rubbed his palms up and down the sides of his jeans. "Ashley's cool about things. I'll call her tonight."

"Let's go then," Eric said and pulled his keys from his pocket.

The restaurant served authentic Italian, and Chris couldn't help thinking Rebecca would like the place. He tuned in and out of the table conversation. A lot of it centered on some mutual friends he didn't know, and the rest revolved around a videogame he'd never played. He hadn't used his Xbox in months. There didn't seem to be time for that stuff anymore, and he didn't miss it. The sound of his name brought him back to attention.

"How about it, Chris? You up for some fun tonight?" Scott asked.

"Maybe. What do you have in mind?"

"There's a gentleman's club about twenty minutes from here," Eric said. "Thought we'd stop by and pay a visit to Miss Savannah Sexton."

"Gentleman's club? As in strip joint?" Chris's muscles tensed. Not this. Not yet. He'd only been working with these guys a few weeks.

"No, gentleman's club. It's classy," Eric said.

"But there are still strippers, right?"

"You got a problem with that?" Scott said in that Mafia don voice everyone imitated.

A dry laugh came from Chris's throat. "Uh...let's just say you can drop me off at the hotel. It's been a long day."

"C'mon. The girlfriend's got you on a short leash, doesn't she?" Eric asked.

"No, I just don't go for that stuff."

"Or...do you play for the other team?" Scott asked.

Chris wouldn't even dignify that with a response. Tom had been quiet. "Are you going, Tom?"

Sounding less confident than he looked, Tom said, "Sure, why not?"

Maybe because you've been married all of about three months, and your wife wouldn't be happy to know that the first time you're apart, you run out to ogle other women.

Scott jumped back in. Scott, the guy he reported to. The same one that had a hand in hiring him. "Come on, man. Everyone else is going. It's like a work bonding thing."

Three weeks into the new job, and he had to choose between violating his conscience and making nice with his co-workers. There had to be a way out of this.

"Everyone? I don't see Ned here."

"Ned doesn't count," Eric said. "He's been married like, forever, and has half a dozen kids. There's a lesson there. If you don't do this stuff now, your old lady's never going to let you do it later."

Scott's head bobbed up and down in agreement. Tom had a weak smile pasted on. He wondered if these guys, two of whom were divorced, had ever thought that maybe the fact that Ned didn't participate in these extracurricular activities had something to do with the stable marriage and houseful of kids.

He knew he was going to have to give them some kind of firm answer or explanation or they were going to badger him and drag him along. His parents may have not raised him to have faith, but they did teach him to respect women. His mother told him never to forget that the girls in those clubs were someone's daughter or sister or mother. For that reason, he'd stayed out of those places in the past, and he didn't intend to patronize one now.

"Do what you want to do, but I'm out." He hoped his tone would put an end to the coercion.

"You'll change your mind when you get a glimpse of the girls," Eric said, elbowing Scott.

"Whatever," Scott said, "but we're not taking you back to the hotel. It's in the opposite direction. You can come in and live a little with us or you can stick your head in the sand and wait in the car. It's up to you." He pulled a credit card from his wallet and laid it on the table alongside the check as he motioned for the waitress.

Chris couldn't believe this. They were going to hold him hostage in a strange town. He could call a cab, but maybe if he went along he could at least talk Tom out of going in. Tom looked pasty, and Chris knew he didn't want to go.

They rumbled into the gravel lot and parked. It looked as if someone had assembled several adjoining shacks, slapped some paint on and gone into business. Garish colors covered the windowless walls, some hot pink, and some sea foam green. The sign above the tallest roof flashed "Live girls." As opposed to dead ones? A poster next to the front door advertised the presence of the voluptuous Savannah Sexton, whose seductive eyes beckoned passersby to come see what she could do with that red cherry that dangled from her tongue. It was so cheesy it bordered on laughable. Chris thought it appeared more like a strip joint than a so-called gentleman's club.

Eric shifted the car into park.

"Last chance, Reynolds," Scott said and turned toward Chris in the back seat.

"Thanks. I'll pass. I've got my iPhone to occupy me."

"You just became the designated driver, too," Eric said as he opened the car door. Scott exited as well. As Tom moved to get out of the back seat, Chris put a hand on his arm.

"I wouldn't mind the company." He gave Tom one last opportunity to go home to his new wife without a bunch of uncomfortable secrets.

"Sorry, man. I wouldn't have picked this place, but I'm not going to screw with them. I want to keep my job. Besides, what Ashley doesn't know won't hurt her."

Chris looked away. What could he say that wouldn't make him look like an obnoxious moralizer? Tom obviously cared more about being one of the guys than being a proper husband. "Your decision," was all he got out before Tom slammed the car door behind him, leaving Chris in a dark parking lot where he'd get to watch the seedy comings and goings all night long.

He slid down into the seat, pulled out his phone, and called Rebecca. She picked up right away this time. He pictured her on her couch watching TV, her phone nearby waiting for his call. Maybe that's not how it was, but he liked the idea anyway.

"Hello, Chris."

"Hey, how was that burrito?"

"To die for. And your Italian food?"

"Very good. You'll never guess where I am." He watched as an older man, who looked to be in his seventies, exited his Oldsmobile and headed for the door. Chris shook his head in disbelief.

"Where?"

"The parking lot of..." He looked up at the sign. "Rocky's Roadside Lounge."

"What's that?"

"Strip club, or as the other guys prefer to call it, a gentleman's club." He didn't know how that line was going to go over.

"What are you doing there?" At least she sounded confused, not angry.

"Sitting in the car talking to you while my co-workers get drunk and stuff dollar bills into scantily-clad women's cleavage." Let her chew on *that* a minute.

"Did they give you a hard time about not going in?'

"Not too bad." He guessed that was true. It could have been worse. The real test would come when they went back to work. "Would you mind keeping me company for a while?"

"Not at all. You're a good man, Chris Reynolds, you know that?"

Chris rubbed the back of his neck. Hearing her say that almost made up for this lousy situation. "You make it easy for me to be that way."

"Don't try to give me credit. Doing the right thing is seldom easy. I wish you had at least one ally there with you."

"Well, the one guy who I think would agree with me was smart enough to bring his own wheels. I had no idea they were going to pull a stunt like this."

A comfortable silence hung between them for a few seconds. A group of six thirty-something guys entered Rocky's. Bachelor party maybe?

"Chris, would you still feel the same way about me if I had, you know, done stuff in the past?"

"What kind of stuff?"

"Worked in a place like you're at or slept with other guys."

Why was she asking? Was there something she wanted to confess or was she just insecure about his feelings for her?

"That's a tough question. I love who you are right now. I don't think anything in the past would change that. It all made you who you are today."

"You wouldn't see me differently?" She tried to pin him down, but he didn't know why or if he had walked into a trap.

"I don't know. This is all hypothetical. Care to tell me why you're asking?"

She sighed. "It's nothing bad. I just...I've been reading the books you loaned me, and it's got me thinking."

"About what?"

"Well, our church was big on abstinence pledges and purity and all that, and I'm grateful for that, really. I mean, my dad wasn't exactly a fount of information on that kind of stuff. He laid down the rules, and if you broke them you were in big trouble, but he never explained what the rules were for or made any allowance for mistakes."

"Uh-huh." Chris didn't want to say much; he wanted her to continue.

"The message I got was that if you sinned, if you had sex before you married, you were worthless. They even gave examples like used tissues, chewed up food, and all kinds of stuff to show us how our lives would be ruined. Don't get me wrong, I'm glad it kept me on the straight and narrow, but talk about harsh. Didn't they tell us we had to forgive one another and that God forgave us? So, why was that like, the unforgivable sin that would ruin your entire life and make you unlovable?"

"That's what you were taught?"

"More or less. I think that's why my dad dressed us like extras from 'Little House on the Prairie.' For the longest time, if I wore anything more revealing than a burlap sack, I felt dirty."

Well, that would explain that hideous whatever-it-was she wore that morning for church with her dad.

"To be honest, Chris, I never heard anything good about Catholics. John, I mean Father John—I'm never going to get used to that—he totally confounded me, I guess because he didn't have seven heads and horns or something. And I kind of had mixed feelings about going to Mass with you. But what I'm reading in your books makes so much sense, and it's really . . . some of it's beautiful about sex and the meaning of our bodies."

Chris couldn't get his mind and his mouth to work in

tandem to formulate words. He'd prayed for this, but he didn't realize until that moment its importance to him. He repositioned himself in the seat and cleared his throat. He wanted her to come to her own conclusions, not scare her off. "Well, when you're done, there's plenty more on my bookshelf if you're interested."

"Thanks." He heard a bag rustle on her end and then the sound of running water before she spoke again.

The odor of cheap cigarettes drifted into the car as a balding, middle-aged man made his way to his truck. Chris wrinkled his nose. "So, what do you want to talk about?"

Without anything in particular they wanted to discuss, they filled the better part of three hours talking about everything and nothing before Rebecca yawned.

"I'm going to let you go. Thanks for keeping me from getting bored out here."

"How long are they going to be?"

Chris started to say he didn't know when Scott pushed open the door followed by Eric and then Tom. Tom immediately took off for the side of the building where he vomited behind an outdoor ashtray. *Great. Should be a fun ride.*

"They're here now, and I'm the designated driver, so I'll talk to you tomorrow." Tom was standing upright now and caught up to Eric and Scott where they waited for him at the corner of the building. "Rebecca?"

"Yeah."

"I love you." A pause followed, and he dared to hope.

"Good night, Chris." His name on her lips felt like a tender caress. He tried not to let it bother him that she still hadn't said it. He slipped the phone back in its holster, got out of the car, and walked around to the driver's seat.

"Ready to go?" he asked.

"You missed a good time," Scott said, "Aside from lightweight here tossing his cookies a couple times."

A couple times? Yeesh. Why didn't they bring some kind of bucket for him or something? Oh well. Not his car.

"Yeah," Eric said, slurring his words. "Savannah got her—"

"I don't need a play-by-play. Let's get Tom back before he pukes again."

No one could argue with that, and the ride back to the hotel was quiet.

***

Chris wanted to bring a souvenir back for Rebecca, but new clothes for a new job and coming up with a down payment for a car had left him strapped for cash. He had his eye on one small thing at another vendor's booth, but it needed something else to go with it. Today would be his last chance.

He had borrowed Eric's car to go to church. Since he had already been pegged as a square for not going along with the previous night's activity, why not go all the way and be tagged a holy roller as well?

As he walked through the hotel lobby, a noxious floral scent assaulted him. The desk clerk smiled, and he silently commended her bravery for opening her mouth to those fumes. He spotted the culprit: a jar candle that burned on the desk. Thank God the wick burnt low, which gave him an idea.

"Could I have that jar when the candle burns out?"

"Sure. In fact, you can take it now if you want." She blew out the flame and handed it to Chris. "Lid, too?"

"Yes, please."

"Careful, it's still hot." She handed the empty jar to him from across the desk.

"Thanks." He took the candle back to the room, wiped it out with some paper towels, and then used hot water to get out the remaining wax. The clerk had kept the wick short, and few black marks lined the rim.

Figuring Eric and the others were still sleeping off last night, he hurried to the car for a quick trip to the beach and back before breakfast.

***

Chris called about nine o'clock at night from somewhere east of Lancaster and asked if he could stop by. He had to get his motorcycle at work, and he'd be passing through Harrisburg on his way home. Did he think she'd say no? She considered leaving her pajamas on, but then decided she ought to get dressed. She wouldn't bother with makeup though; he'd seen her look worse when they were camping.

The mere knock on the door filled her heart near to exploding. She opened it, and before she could even get out a "hello," his palms squeezed her cheeks and his mouth crushed hers.

"See how much I missed you?" he breathed against her lips.

"Wow, that much?" She took a step back to let him through the door.

"More. I was holding back."

Her heart thudded. *That* was restrained? What would it be like if he *weren't* holding back? "Is it safe to let you in?"

"I'll behave, I promise. I just missed you like crazy, and I've got a caffeine buzz. The other guys weren't up to driving, so I got to man the wheel while they slept. I needed some high test java to keep me going." He picked up a small gift bag from the floor and walked in.

"Can I get you something? A mild sedative maybe?" She took a seat on the couch next to him, smiled, and took hold of his hand.

"I'm good. Thanks." His left knee bounced up and down, and he took the brown paper shopping bag from the coffee table where he had set it and handed it to her. "This is for you."

She let go of his hand and set the bag in her lap. Reaching inside, she discovered a heavy jar. She held it above the bag and turned it in the light. "Sand?"

"I couldn't bring you to the beach, so, I brought a little of the beach to you."

"So sweet." She leaned over and kissed his cheek.

"There's something else in there, too." His knee slowed and stopped as he leaned toward her to peer into the bag, too.

Rebecca lifted white tissue paper out of the bag and held it in her lap. She unfolded the paper and pulled out—well, she wasn't sure what. It was beaded and silver and beautiful, but she didn't know how to wear it. Judging by the size and placement of the loops and the lack of a clasp, it wasn't a necklace, and as one slipped onto the floor, she realized there were two of them.

"Chris, it's very pretty, but I have to be honest. I have no idea what these are." She feared she'd hurt his feelings by not recognizing his gift, but he must not have expected her to know.

His eyes teased her, and he grinned. "Give me your foot."

"Excuse me?"

"Your foot, please."

Rebecca lifted her bare left foot and rested it on the edge of the coffee table in front of him. She never paid her feet much attention. She knew Abby and everyone else got pedicures all the time, but she had never had one, didn't care to have one, and couldn't justify the expense anyway. Her nails were clean, short, and unadorned.

"Give me one of those," he said and gestured to her mystery jewelry. She handed one to him and he slid the large loop over her foot and around her ankle. Then he stretched the small loop at the other end and fitted it around her second toe. "Other foot."

She lifted her right foot, handed him the other piece of jewelry, and he slid it into place as well. She loved the sensuous feel of his hands moving over her feet. When he was finished, she placed her feet side-by-side on the edge of the coffee table.

"There," he said. "What do you think?"

"They're beautiful. The make my feet look pretty and exotic."

"Sexy."

She cast a sideways glance at him. He meant it. Her cheeks warmed, and she wondered how two little syllables from his mouth did that to her.

"What do you call them?"

"Barefoot sandals. They're handmade. I hope you like them."

"I do. You didn't have to get me anything, but these are so feminine. I love them."

"A woman should have some frivolous, pretty things, and I get the sense you don't buy those kinds of things for yourself."

She shook her head and continued to look at the way the sandals made the curves of her feet look so delicate and alluring.

"Let me see." He sat back on the couch. "Lie down and put your feet in my lap."

Rebecca scooted back onto the couch and propped a pillow against the arm so she could lean against it. Chris took her feet and laid them on his legs. His fingers traced the line of beads and caressed the arch on each foot. She leaned her head back, closed her eyes, and in a matter of minutes found herself drifting off to sleep.

His voice roused her. "I should go home and let you get to bed, but I can't figure out how I'm going to be able to sleep."

"The caffeine will wear off eventually. Abby and I used to sneak downstairs and drink milk and eat graham crackers when we couldn't sleep. It always seemed to help."

"Worth a try, I guess. I know—why don't you sing me a lullaby?"

Suddenly his hands on her feet felt more irritating than relaxing.

"You know I don't sing."

"Aw, come on, Rebecca. I bet you have a beautiful singing voice. Please."

"No."

"You don't want me to be so tired I can't get up in the morning, do you?"

Seriously? He'd send her on a guilt trip over this? "Try the milk and graham crackers."

"Please, Rebecca. I love you."

He had just moved from irritating and pesky to hurtful. Was his love conditional on her singing? "That's not fair."

He raised his palms in a gesture of surrender. "Okay, okay. I love you whether you sing or not, but I'd really like to hear you sing."

Chris Reynolds made Rebecca want to sing, maybe like no one or no thing ever had before. She remembered singing praise songs as a little girl for the simple pleasure of singing and for the love of God. Chris made her want to sing like that again, out of sheer joy, but now singing was a sad reminder. A reminder that she didn't measure up. That in her father's eyes, the thing she did best was disappoint. That even when she hadn't failed *per se*, her femininity—the very thing that Chris seemed to foster and treasure—caused sin and shame. She curled her toes, and pulled her feet from his lap, hugging her knees to her chest.

"I'm sorry," Chris said as he reached for her. "I pushed too hard."

"You talked to Abby about it, didn't you? My singing." Oh, no. The tears. Where were the tears coming from? She had been a child. Why did it still hurt?

"I'm sorry, Rebecca. I hate to see you bound by a heartless, thoughtless comment made so long ago."

She pushed off the couch and took her jar of sand to the counter that separated her kitchen and living areas. "Please, let it go, Chris. I know you mean well, and I appreciate it. Truly, I do, but I can't sing. I won't."

He was off the couch now, too, and walking toward her. "I won't push again, I promise, but I'm going to keep asking." He pulled a tissue from the box on the counter and wiped her eyes. "I'd better go."

She nodded and walked to the door with him. He stopped before he opened it.

"Alan texted me this afternoon. They want to have us over on Friday. Is that okay?"

"Sure. Your family must think we're serious."

He shrugged. "I think they know you mean the world to me."

The blue intensity of his eyes made her feel small and ashamed. Why did she have to overreact about the singing anyway?

"Thank you for the gifts. It was very thoughtful."

"You're welcome." He smiled and gave her a quick kiss. "Goodnight, Rebecca."

She opened the door and then closed it behind him as a weight settled on her chest the way a mood had settled over her when Chris had asked her to sing. Maybe it was all an illusion. Maybe she'd just drag Chris down, too. Tempt him. Keep him from finding a woman worthy of his love and generosity.

"Goodnight, Chris."

14

I'll Back You Up

Rebecca inhaled the smell of scorched food as it wafted through the screen door. Apparently Chris and Alan hadn't been exaggerating when they said Jamie couldn't cook. The shrill and incessant beep of a smoke detector punctuated the continuous clattering of pans culminating in a loud curse that included the Lord's name.

Chris winced. "Everything okay in there?" he yelled through the front door of Alan and Jamie's gray-brick ranch house. He slid his arm around Rebecca as she clutched her homemade cheesecake to her chest.

"Should we go in?" She didn't want to intrude, but she thought maybe Jamie could use her help.

"Let's give them a minute."

In less than ten seconds, Alan strode toward the door with his phone in hand. "Hey, guys. How does Italian sound? I'm going to order some cheese-stuffed shells, salad, rolls. Sound good?"

"Sounds great," Chris said, sharing a look with Rebecca. "And Rebecca made a cheesecake for dessert."

"Awesome," Alan said as he let them in and then adjusted the screen to bring more fresh air into the house, which smelled like burnt pasta. There was another curse from the direction Rebecca assumed was the kitchen, followed by a choked sob.

"Maybe I can help. Is the kitchen this way?" She pointed down a hallway with gleaming hardwood floors.

"Yeah," Alan said. "I can't seem to do anything right for her. Maybe she'll be more receptive to another woman."

Rebecca found the kitchen and Jamie on the floor in front of a cupboard. Her face was hidden by her hands and her red hair hung like a long, straight curtain at her shoulder. Above her, the countertop was cluttered with pots and pans, the sink was near to overflowing, and the vent above the oven whirred at high speed.

"Jamie? Is everything okay?"

Jamie wiped her face with her hands and clambered to her feet. "Rebecca. I'm so embarrassed. I'm an utter failure in the kitchen. It's pasta for crying out loud. I had to boil the noodles and heat the sauce, and I nearly burned down the house."

"If it makes you feel any better, I once turned a dozen Ziploc bags into a molten pile of goo while trying to make toast."

Jamie smiled, but it didn't reach her eyes. "That's the worst you've got?"

Rebecca didn't know what to say. "So, cooking's not your thing. You're good at lots of other things I'm sure."

"Yeah, but it would be nice to be good at something we have to do three times a day every day of our freakin' lives."

Rubbing Jamie's shoulder, Rebecca spoke softly. "I think Alan ordered dinner. Why don't you let me help you clean up?"

"Thank you. I just wanted us to have a nice evening together. Can I get you a glass of wine?"

"Water or iced tea would be great. Thanks." Rebecca loaded what she could into the dish washer and then started filling one side of the sink with warm, soapy water.

"You don't drink, do you?"

"Not much." Rebecca hoped Jamie would leave it alone.

"Do you like chocolate?"

Maybe there was something they could bond over after all. "It's my favorite food group."

"Then you've got to try some chocolate liqueur. Next time I pick some up, I'll get a little sample bottle for you. You'll love it."

Jamie placed a glass of water next to Rebecca on the counter as she took a long drink from her wine goblet. "Thank you for bringing the cheesecake."

"Oh, you're welcome. I hope it turned out okay."

"The way Alan raves about your baking, if Chris weren't so far gone over you, I think he would make a move."

Chris stood in the living room, where Alan showed him a Blu-Ray movie he'd pulled from a bookcase filled to capacity with them. He glanced up and gave her a wink and a little wave.

When Jamie spoke again, Rebecca turned to find her staring at her and Chris in the background behind her. "I've never seen him happier," Jamie said. "You're good for him."

Her heart fluttered. She flattened her breezy summer skirt with her hands. Another new skirt and top. She was worried the dressy tee shirt hugged her chest too tightly, but Chris had said he liked it.

"He's...he's more than I ever dared to dream." She didn't mean to share something so heartfelt, but with him standing there so handsome in his khaki pants and Polo-style shirt with eyes only for her, she didn't even think before she spoke.

"I kept trying to set him up, but it never took. Alan's friend has a sister who's had a thing for him since they were kids. I gave them every opportunity, but Chris would rebuff her every time." Jamie swiped at the counters with a wet dishcloth, occasionally shaking it out over the trash can. "When he brought you to our wedding and you two shared that, uh, soul-melding kiss on the dance floor, I think she finally conceded."

Megan. It had to be Megan. Did Chris even know they had been trying to set him up? And did she just hear a hint of disappointment in Jamie's voice?

"Anyway," Jamie continued, "I'm glad he has you. I mean, not only is he great eye candy, he's a great guy. Great husband material. Even if he is a little loopy about the God stuff. But I suspect you already know all of that."

The God stuff?

The doorbell rang, and Alan headed for the door while Jamie searched through her purse looking for cash. When they both went to meet the delivery man, Chris came into the kitchen and put his arm around her and kissed her temple. She felt a twinge there just as she had earlier in the day. Over the past hour, a mild headache had crept up on her. It might be tension or maybe a change in the weather. Sometimes barometric pressure changes gave her headaches.

The shells were rich and filling, but by the time Alan sliced the cheesecake for them, both Rebecca's temple and her jaw on her right side were aching. No, throbbing.

When Chris had finished his dessert and coffee, she leaned into him and whispered, "I'm not feeling well. Would you take me home?"

Chris's brow creased, and the worry in his voice touched her. She laid her hand on his leg. "I'm okay. I think it's my tooth, but the pain is in my jaw and my cheek and my whole head."

"I'm sure Alan has some ibuprofen or something."

"I've got some in my purse. I'll take a couple, and then maybe I can call my dentist on the way home. He said he thought this molar was trouble."

Chris made apologies for them and made sure she was seated comfortably in her car while he said a final thanks to Alan and Jamie. Alan joked that it was the first time someone left their home sick and not from Jamie's cooking. Rebecca felt sorry for her; she had really tried. So she couldn't cook; maybe Alan should give it a try if home-cooked meals were that important to him.

Rebecca's jaw pounded and pain shot through her temple by the time she got a hold of her dentist through his answering service. After describing the situation and reminding him of the warning he had given her about that tooth, he told her he'd call in a prescription and ordered her to see him first thing Monday morning.

She leaned against the headrest and closed her eyes, grateful that she could count on Chris to see that she got home safely.

She kept her head as still as possible while he drove and tried to focus on anything other than the pain. What had Chris told her dad about suffering? He called it medicine for salvation. Well, then this was some strong medicine.

Through her conversations with Chris and reading the

books he had loaned her, she knew that Catholics didn't dismiss suffering as something to be avoided at all costs. If she understood things correctly, his faith valued suffering if it was united to Jesus' pain at the crucifixion.

In fact, it seemed like his church placed considerable value on the body itself. She'd always felt like having a body held her back. The way her head throbbed now, she still couldn't disagree. After all the sermons she'd heard about the temptations of the flesh, she couldn't help but wonder what good a body was. But in Chris's church, the body freed you to experience God in a tangible, corporal way, through the sacraments and even more so through communion. Even through making love to her husband some day, if she could believe that.

They hit a bump and the car jolted, sending pain shooting through the side of her face. She groaned.

"Sorry. I couldn't see that pothole until I was on top of it."

She let out a deep breath. "It's all right." When the pain receded, she thought once more about lending meaning to suffering and said a silent prayer. *Lord, if you can make something good of this pain, then do it, because otherwise this is a whole lot of misery for nothing*.

***

Chris pulled into the pharmacy and looked over at Rebecca. Was she asleep or resting with her eyes closed? He touched her leg. "Rebecca, honey, we're at the drug store. I'm going to run in and get your prescription."

She rolled her head slowly to face him and opened her eyes. She grimaced and then answered. "There's cash in my purse."

He fished her wallet out of the purse at her feet and removed some bills. "Hey, it's going to get better once you get this antibiotic, okay?"

She nodded her head, but the unshed tears in her eyes made his heart ache. She must be in a heck of a lot of pain.

After they got to her apartment and she took the penicillin, Chris asked what he could do for her. "Make the pain go away," was all she said before she buried her head—very gently—in his chest. He wished more than anything he could do that for her, but they would have to wait until the medicine got into her system.

"Do you think you could sleep?"

"I don't know. Maybe you could knock me unconscious."

At least her sense of humor was intact. "Why don't you try?"

"You don't have to stay, you know."

No, he didn't, but she wasn't well, and he didn't like the idea of leaving her alone. "I could spend the night on your couch if it's okay with you. That way if you need anything, I'm right here."

"I'll be okay, but I do like the idea of you staying."

"Then I'll stay. I'm supposed to help Tom and his wife move tomorrow, but I can go straight from here."

He kissed her goodnight on her pain-free cheek, and she retreated to her bedroom. After a few quiet moments of prayer that Rebecca's pain would go away, he made himself comfortable on the couch. Thinking he wouldn't be able to sleep for at least another hour or two, he found a decent B movie to watch on TV. When the credits rolled, he took the quilt off the back of the couch, wrapped it around himself, and got as comfortable as he could.

Despite its small size, she had made her apartment homey with only sparse furnishings. All the colors went together and she had arranged pictures of Abby's kids and landscapes artfully on the walls. Potted plants filled every window sill, and two large containers near the front window held more greenery. He'd have plenty of oxygen.

Chris slept and didn't budge until he heard Rebecca up and moving around. A glance at her wall clock told him it was half past four. He sat up and rubbed the sleep from his eyes. Rebecca stood in the kitchen drinking a tall glass of water.

"Hey, how are you feeling?"

"Much, much better. It's a mild ache around my tooth now. I took more penicillin and a couple more ibuprofen. I'm not used to going to bed so early though, and now I can't fall back to sleep."

"Come here," he said as he rearranged himself and the quilt on the couch so that she could sit between his legs and lean back against him. She settled in there with her head nestled under his chin, her breathing soft and steady, and he felt himself drift off again almost immediately.

Chris woke again when the sunlight peeked through her drapes, the warm beam hitting him in the eyes. The wall clock said six o'clock. He reached over the back of the couch, careful to move only his arm and not his upper body, where Rebecca still slept with her back to him and her head leaning on his chest. He yanked one drape so that it overlapped the other, blocking the light.

He glanced down at Rebecca's head, tracing the trail of her hair as it fell over her shoulder. With a lone finger, he carefully lifted a section of hair and pushed it so that the tangled, wavy softness rested on her right shoulder, leaving the left side of her neck exposed.

He couldn't resist. Didn't even want to. He leaned down and pressed his lips to the tender skin of her neck where he had cleared away her hair. No reaction. He did it again, exerting a little more pressure. This time she let out a breathy sound somewhere between a sigh and a moan.

"Mmmmm."

A tingling sensation raced through every nerve ending in his body. "Good morning," he whispered into her ear.

Again with that sound, "Mmmmm."

When he'd said he would spend the night in case she needed him, he hadn't counted on this. Waking up with her warm and soft against him was courting danger. Still, if he could get her to make that lovesick sigh again...

With both arms wrapped around her waist, he pulled her back to him so that their bodies were pressed against one another from stem to stern. After two full seconds of bliss, every muscle in her body grew rigid.

She straightened and started to pull away from him,

struggling against his arms at her waist.

He released her, utterly confused. What had happened? Yes, he was behind her, but he hadn't snuck up. She had been pleased if those delicious sounds she made were any indication. It must have been when he had pressed himself against her. *Oh*. She *would* be able to feel everything through those thin cotton pajamas.

He got up and followed her across the room to the table where she mindlessly shuffled a few envelopes and papers left there. "I'm sorry, Rebecca. If I get in that kind of proximity to you, especially first thing in the morning, it's, uh…"—*man, this is awkward*—"…uh, all systems are go. I don't think I can help it." He paused, and then to reassure her added, "It doesn't mean I'm going to do anything about it."

Standing with her back toward him, she didn't acknowledge what he said. He used both hands on her upper arms to turn her toward him.

She was pale, but that could have been due to the fact she had just awoken. The pain and tears in her eyes couldn't be dismissed so easily.

Her shoulders went limp. "I'm sorry. I know you're not. It was fine when you kissed my neck." She shook her head again and wiped a single tear from her eye. "Better than fine. I thought I'd died and gone to heaven…but then, when you pulled me tighter, and I could feel you…it just triggered a bad memory."

A bad memory? Chris tensed. What hadn't she told him? Did this have to do with the guy at Bible camp when she was a teenager? She had only said that he came on a little strong. It didn't sound like the kind of thing that could generate tears years later, but if feeling him against her like that triggered a memory then the incident wasn't as innocent as she had led him to believe.

"Is this about this guy from Bible camp? Cause if it is, it sounds like he did a lot more than come on too strong." He framed her still-pale face in his hands, and her chin quivered. "Rebecca, what did he do to you?"

She jerked out of his grasp and turned again to the table although this time she pressed her hands into the boards. "Nothing more, really. He couldn't. John stopped him."

"Wait a second." Chris walked to the other side of the table so he could see her face again. "John? As in Father John?"

"Mm-hmm."

"And what do you think would have happened if Father John hadn't been there?"

Her mouth opened and closed. "I...I don't. I can't. I don't think about it. Nothing *did* happen. Jeremy grabbed me from behind and pinned me against a wall with his body. Then John came and confronted him, and he left."

She crossed her arms in front of her. He could tell from her posture she wouldn't say any more. He sighed and rubbed his fingers over his eyes and brows. Then he grabbed his phone off the counter and sent a quick text message.

"Who are you texting?" She sounded anxious, and he'd bet she feared he had texted Father John, which made Chris certain something more happened that she hadn't yet told him.

"I texted my mom. I'm going to make you pancakes, and I need her recipe. Do you have syrup?"

Wiping her eyes once more, she straightened her shoulders. "I think so." She opened the refrigerator and rearranged several bottles before she located a small jug of maple syrup and set it on the counter.

"Go ahead and get dressed if you want. I think I can find what I need. I can't stay long after breakfast though."

"Why not?"

"Remember? I'm helping Tom and his wife move today."

"Oh, that's right."

Once they had finished their breakfast, and Rebecca assured him that her pain was almost gone, Chris kissed her and left. He had to hurry if he wanted to fit in a stop before he got to Tom's apartment.

***

Father John told Chris he could find him in the school

gym. The lingering odor of stale sweat and the sound of a ball bouncing on a wooden floor led Chris right to him. He walked through the double doors as Father John dribbled a basketball with one hand and then the other before landing a three-point shot from the edge of the court. Ordinarily, Chris would have joined him, but he figured he'd be getting enough of a workout hauling boxes and furniture the rest of the day. Father John held onto the ball as Chris crossed the gym and once he was within earshot called, "So, what's on your mind?"

"Rebecca."

Father John smiled as he dribbled the ball. "Is there ever anything *else* on your mind these days?"

The dribbling slowed as Chris approached. "I want to know about something that happened when you and Rebecca first met at summer camp."

Father John put the ball under his arm and ambled over to Chris. "What do you want to know?"

Chris took a breath. "I know that some creep named Jeremy tried something with her, and you stopped it, but she won't say much more." He snatched the ball from Father John and spun it around between his hands, trying to use up some of his nervous energy. "All I know is that the one time I tried to come up behind her and surprise her, she lost it. Let out an ear-piercing scream and seemed not to even recognize me at first. Then this morning she freaked out when I held her really close, again from behind. The only thing she'd say was that he grabbed her from behind and pinned her to a wall. Then you came and confronted him."

Father John ran a hand over his hair. "I haven't thought about this in years, Chris."

"She said he didn't hurt her. Is she telling me the truth?"

Father John hesitated, and Chris tensed.

"Yes, she is. He didn't physically hurt her. From what you're saying, she must have been more emotionally bothered by it than she let on at the time."

"So she was okay after it happened?"

"She seemed to be, but . . ."

"But what?"

"Does she know you're talking to me about this?"

Chris didn't want to play these games. He needed answers, and if Rebecca wouldn't supply them, Father John would. "I asked, but she clammed up."

"Then it sounds like she's not ready to talk about it with you."

"Listen, if she's going to wig out every time I come up behind her, then I need to know what happened to her."

"I think you should tell her that."

Chris groaned. He wanted to take the basketball and slam it into the floor so hard it would bounce up and hit the ceiling.

Father John sighed. "I think this would be better coming from her, but I'll tell you what I know. It's not much."

"Thank you." He ran his hand through his hair and waited.

"Rebecca and I became friends over the first week of camp. We seemed to click. We were going to meet and go over to the rec room to play video games or something. I said I'd meet her at the first-aid office since it was midway between our cabins and the rec room. It started to rain, so when I got there and didn't see her outside it didn't surprise me. When I stepped in, Jeremy had her pinned to the wall like she said. He was big enough that his sheer size and body weight were enough to keep her from escaping." He stopped speaking for a second, and Chris sensed this part would be news to him.

"He had his hands around her waist, and he was struggling to get her shorts off. Actually, they weren't shorts. We laughed about it later, but she said those ugly, modest 'skort' things her dad made her wear saved her. Apparently they had a clip, a button, and a zipper, and that's why Jeremy fumbled with them for so long."

"He didn't get them off?"

"No."

Chris let go of the breath he held. "Thank God for skorts."

"I yelled for him to stop, and he did. He could've easily taken me out, but he didn't. He sort of shoved her at me and left."

"What happened? Was he disciplined? Did you call the police?"

"We walked over to the camp office and told the counselors what happened. They questioned Jeremy, and his parents came and got him the next day. I never saw him again."

"The police?"

"If charges were filed, that would've been up to Rebecca's father."

"You sound doubtful."

Father John twisted his lips. "All I know is her dad didn't come and get her. She stayed the week. And honestly, she seemed okay. We hung out a couple of times after that. Then I didn't see her again until you brought her to Mass."

This made sense. An aggressive guy didn't affect your behavior eight years later. An attempted rape—and that's sure what this sounded like—that did.

"That explains her behavior. I don't know why she didn't tell me."

"Maybe it embarrasses her? Makes her feel like a victim? Maybe it dredges it all up again. I don't know."

Chris glanced at his watch. He had to leave now if he wanted to get to Tom's place on time. He tossed the basketball back to Father John. "I've got to go. Thanks for filling me in. She hasn't come to terms with this. It's obviously still an issue."

Pausing at the gym exit, Chris turned around and yelled over the sound of the bouncing basketball. "Hey, Father John!"

The dribbling stopped, and Father John lifted his chin and met his gaze.

"Thanks for keeping Rebecca safe."

Father John raised his hand.

Pushing through the gym doors and down the stairs, Chris jogged to the school exit. One side of his mouth lifted in a grin. Father John had told him what he needed to know, but funny how he left out at least one detail from the weeks at camp—that he'd kissed Rebecca before it was all over.

15

A Dream So Real

Rebecca stared at her reflection in Abby's living room window. "Abby, what's wrong with me?"

"I thought you'd never ask. I keep a list. Can you hang on while I grab it?"

Rebecca flopped backwards on the loveseat and rolled her eyes. "Come on, Abby. I'm being serious. I'm messed up. Why is that?"

"Mom left, and Dad stayed. They screwed us up royally." She continued folding baby blankets and burp pads from the heap beside her on the couch. "Is there a particular deficiency you'd like to focus on today?"

"I'm in love with Chris. I wasn't sure, and then yesterday morning he was holding me close, and I knew. I think I've been in denial for weeks. I've got it so bad for him I feel like I'm going to crawl out of my skin when I'm close to him. And I can't say it to him. I don't know why. I want to. I tried to. The words won't come out of my mouth. He's been so patient with me, but I know he wants to hear me say it. He needs to hear it...he deserves to hear it."

"Does he know, even though you haven't said it?"

"How could he?"

"I know Mom left a lot unsaid when she left, but really, Rebecca. When a man and a woman love each other, they—"

"Stop it, Abby. You and I both made promises about sex before marriage." Couldn't Abby be serious for once? And she'd about had it with her treating her like she was some kind of simpleton because she actually lived what they were taught.

"Oh, your issues go *way* deeper than that. Do you let him touch you? Kiss you?"

"Of course I do."

"Then he probably knows."

"What do you mean about 'my issues'?

Ian let out a cry over the baby monitor.

"It's as plain as the nose on Daddy's face. Hold on."

Abby pushed a baby towel she had been folding back onto the pile and walked out of the room. Abby cooed at the baby over the monitor, and it clicked off. Rebecca shut off the companion speaker on the end table next to her. In a few seconds, Abby strolled in with Ian. His pink lips opened in a huge yawn that made him shudder. He looked so cute in his baseball onesie, Rebecca could eat him up.

"Here," Rebecca said, holding out her hands, "I'll take the little butterball."

Abby handed the baby over and returned to the couch. She held something that Rebecca hadn't noticed at first. Abby held it up so she could see it—a picture frame. "Ever seen this?"

Ian squirmed and fussed in her lap. She bounced him on her knee and squinted at the photo. It looked like a picture of her, only she didn't remember it being taken or recognize the clothes she wore.

"It's Mom," Abby said.

Rebecca's eyes darted back and forth between the picture and her sister, stunned. "I look just like her."

"Identical. This was taken when she was twenty-three years old."

"Where did you get that?"

Abby lifted her chin. "I found it in the top of Dad's closet."

"You took it?"

"Years ago. I wanted a picture of Mom, and he never put any out, so I took this one." She paused for a few seconds. "Do you get it now, Rebecca? This is why you've got a hot guy who's falling-all-over-himself in love with you, and he's not getting as much action as Ian is right now."

Ian grabbed onto her breast with his hand and tried to latch onto her through her blouse.

"He wants you," she told Abby and handed him over.

"Yeah, and Chris wants *you*. I'm sure of it. Becca, have you looked at your boyfriend? Because he could probably have any woman he wants. If he rides in on that Harley of his, he could probably have two—at the same time."

Why did Abby think this was all about sex? Sex played a part, but not in the way Abby thought. "Abby, us having sex is not the issue. Chris wants to wait as much as I do."

"You're kidding, right? I thought he was Catholic."

"He is." Where was she going with this? Didn't all Christians believe sex was for marriage?

"I've never met a Catholic yet that had a problem with sex before marriage, living together, birth control or any of it."

Her mouth hung open, then closed. "Uh...I don't know what to say. Chris would take issue with all of that, and from what I've read, he's toeing the line on everything the Catholic Church says."

Abby got Ian situated at her breast and sighed. "Okay, so you're both freaks, which I of course mean in the best, most loving way. You've still got issues. Look at that picture again."

The frame sat on the pile of unfolded laundry. Rebecca lifted it and stared at the image.

"What—or rather who—do you think Dad sees when he looks at you?"

Where was Abby going with this? Of course he'd see her mother, but—

"How much do you know about Mom? Did you know she flirted with anyone with a y chromosome? Did you know that Dad caught her meeting another guy?"

Her mouth went dry, and Rebecca swallowed hard. "How do you know all this?"

"Mom kept a journal."

"You took that, too?"

"No, but I read it."

The revelations were coming too fast for Rebecca now, and her head spun. "She cheated on Dad?"

"No, never, but she craved the attention she got from other men. Maybe because Dad didn't give her any of his. I don't know. But do you see why Dad has said and done the things he has with you? I mean, besides the fact he's a mean—" Abby looked at Emma and Ricky, who were both assembling wooden blocks within hearing range, and amended her statement. "Besides the fact he's a big meanie, do you understand now why he's had it out for you? And why when that douche bag assaulted you at camp he came down even harder?"

So much made sense now. "He thinks I'm like her.'"

"Bingo." Abby said it like everything was solved. Now that the universe had been explained, Rebecca could run across a flowery summer meadow into Chris's outstretched arms and everything would be okay. Except it was *not* okay. What if she *were* like her mother? Nature versus nurture. Rebecca was a loser on both counts.

***

What did her dad expect her to do? He had called at the crack of dawn complaining that he'd thrown out his back, which wasn't out of the ordinary. Even the simplest movements could on occasion leave him laid up with an ice pack and unable to manage the simplest chores for the better part of a week. There wasn't much she could do about his back. He knew that.

Her dad explained that after twenty-five years with the same company, he had switched home insurance last month to get a better rate. The new insurer sent out an inspector, who noted that a few boards on the front porch were rotted and must be replaced before the new coverage would go into effect. They gave her dad thirty days to make the correction. Thirty days just so happened to be Monday, and he needed to have photographic proof of the project's completion emailed to the insurance company by Monday at noon. He hadn't even begun. His back rendered him incapable of completing his weekend project.

Not knowing how to handle tools, there was no way she could tackle this job on her own. Her dad knew that, too. She could only conclude that he wanted Chris's help. He wouldn't know if Chris was handy—neither did she really, but since he maintained a motorcycle and his job was somewhat mechanical in nature, it wasn't a bad bet.

The whole thing made Rebecca's blood boil. It took a helluva lot of nerve for him to even think he could count on Chris's help after the way he'd treated him. Well, if he wanted Chris's help, he'd have to swallow his pride and ask for it.

To her surprise, he did. When for the third time Rebecca told him she didn't know what she could do, he finally said, "If that boyfriend of yours is the Christian he says he is, maybe he's willing to come over here and give me a hand."

Well, gee, since you asked so nicely...

Not wanting to commit Chris to anything, she told her dad she'd talk to Chris and let him know. And then she had to follow through, despite the fact she didn't want to bother Chris with this. She knew what his plans were. He and three friends were going on a motorcycle ride as long as the weather held out. He had wanted her to come along, but since none of the other guys were bringing a girlfriend, she had declined. Chris planned to stop by early in the evening, and they would do something together.

"Hey, is your ride still on?"

"Absolutely. Change your mind about coming?" He sounded hopeful.

"No. Actually, I'm calling to ask for a favor."

"What do you need?"

"Well, it's not for me. It's for my dad."

Silence. She explained the situation and ended with, "So, he's in a bind, and he's hoping you might be able to help him out." More silence.

Chris sighed. "I've been looking forward to this ride for weeks."

"I know."

"But, if I can build some goodwill with your dad, I guess it's worth it."

"This is my dad, Chris. I'm not promising goodwill."

"Well, then I'll have to think of it as doing a good deed and expecting nothing in return. You'd better tell him though, that

I've never done this before. I mean, it seems straightforward, but sometimes when you start a project you run into unexpected problems. I'll do my best, but I can almost guarantee it won't be a perfect job."

"Well, seeing as though he's in no condition to do *any* job, I don't think he can be too fussy about it."

"Okay. I'll be there in a half hour. Where are you at?"

"My apartment. I'll meet you at my dad's. And, Chris—I owe you one."

***

When Rebecca arrived, she found Chris on the porch in old jeans and a tee shirt, a pencil behind his ear, squatting to measure the length of the tongue and groove floorboards.

"Do you want to be my 'Tool Time Girl'?"

"Huh?"

"My lovely assistant."

She didn't know how lovely she appeared in a long, baggy, tee shirt and Capri-length leggings, but it would have to suffice. "Oh. Sure."

He extended the tape measure to her. "Grab this end and pull." Chris scribbled the length on a small piece of bare two-by-four lumber. "I brought what tools I have, but it's not much. I could borrow some of my dad's stuff, but if your dad's got what we need that would be better."

"I'll show you where he keeps stuff."

She and Chris walked to the detached garage at the rear of the yard, and they came out with two sawhorses, a band saw, a sander, a crow bar, and a hammer and nails.

"So, why didn't your dad have Joel come over here and help?"

Rebecca laughed. "Uh, Joel can't even work a screwdriver. He's a good lawyer, but he has no practical skills. Abby takes care of all that stuff, and what she can't do, she hires someone else to do. Here's an analogy—as Jamie is to cooking, so Joel is to carpentry."

"That makes it crystal clear."

"Dad's not exactly Joel's biggest fan anyway. Dad kind of ignores him."

"Oh." His lips set in a thin line, as if he'd just glimpsed his own fate.

Chris made steady progress all morning as the day grew warmer and more humid. By noon he and his sweat-soaked shirt had made two trips to Lowe's, and by the way he grumbled about the rotted support beams he discovered, she'd bet another trip was in the offing.

Rebecca did whatever he asked, which wasn't much and consisted mainly of holding boards steady while he sawed, handing him tools, and talking to him while he did something that didn't require much concentration. She brought him lots of water and a sandwich for lunch. When dinner time came, she got Chinese takeout for them and her dad, who had yet to emerge from his bedroom.

She didn't mind watching Chris work. The back of his neck and arms had reddened in the day's sun even though they had set the sawhorses up in the shade of the elm tree in the front yard. She watched as he finished sanding the boards, and it reminded her of their weekend camping trip when she had been bowled over by his masculinity. He had said this job wouldn't be perfect, but near as she could tell, it was.

By early evening, he had finished replacing and sanding the boards. Rebecca brought him a big glass of strawberry lemonade as he took a break before painting. She sat beside him on the porch steps, but when she touched his leg and leaned in to kiss his cheek, he pushed her hand back and stood.

"Thanks for the lemonade. It hit the spot."

She didn't even try to hide the hurt on her face. "Did I do something wrong?"

Chris stopped. "No, of course not." He lowered his voice so only she could hear him. "Part of the reason I'm here busting my you-know-what is to score points with your dad. If he looks out and sees us canoodling, I can kiss that goodwill goodbye. When I said I wouldn't be the cause of him going off on you again, I meant it." He took a breath and lightened his tone. "So, save your tokens of affection for later. I promise you

I'll cash them in."

The screen door creaked, and Rebecca's dad stepped out. His gait was stilted and awkward as he moved toward the end of the porch where Chris had been working.

"How's your back?" Rebecca gathered up their empty lemonade glasses and napkins.

"Still hurts like hell, but I need to move around." He looked at the boards and then over at Chris, who had opened a paint can and was stirring the contents with a stick.

"What grit sandpaper did you use on that?"

Chris nodded toward the garage. "Whatever you had out there. Looked like a medium grit to me." Chris scraped the excess paint off the stick and grabbed the brush he was going to use. "Some of the two-by-fours underneath were rotted so I replaced them."

Her dad nodded and rubbed a hand over his lower back. "Looks like I might have to go back over some things later, but it'll do for tomorrow. I appreciate it."

Rebecca raised her brows and smiled from where she stood behind her dad. Chris was careful not to change his expression.

"Dad, there's some wonton soup and a couple egg rolls if you'd like them. I can warm them up for you."

"Sounds good, Rebecca. I'm going to try sitting in my chair for a little bit and watching some TV."

He turned and hobbled back into the house with Rebecca behind him. Chris hadn't exactly won him over, but at least her dad had been civil. Chris would be able to see he wasn't an ogre *all* the time. And maybe Dad would see what a great guy Chris was - generous, hard-working, and kind.

Chris was hammering the lid back on the paint can as she stepped back out on the porch. The paint fumes dissipated in the breeze. The sun had begun to set, and had he not been finished, he would have had to rely on artificial light from here on out.

"Done." He sighed and leaned against the porch rail.

"You must be beat."

"I am." He walked over to where she stood at the foot of the steps looking over his work. "Do you have your helmet?"

Rebecca turned to him. "Hmm? Oh, yeah, in my car. Why?"

"What do you say we put things away here, I change out of this shirt so I don't smell quite so bad, and I take you home?"

"What about my car?"

"I'll pick you up in the morning, we'll go to church, and then I'll bring you back here to get your car."

He had it all worked out. Going to Mass with him would mean that she couldn't go to a service at her own church, which made her a little uncomfortable. It would be a church though, and she remembered how much Scripture was incorporated into the Mass the last time. Plus, she wondered if her impression would be different now that she understood things a little better. She had already traded in the three books Chris had loaned her for some more, and one of them was all about the Mass. It would be okay.

"All right. Let's put this stuff away, and I'll tell my dad we're going. You did a good job, by the way. It looks great." She moved her gaze from the gleaming porch floor to the sweaty, sawdust-covered, sexy guy next to her. She wished she could kiss him, but she remembered what he'd said before. He was right, too. Her dad seeing them kiss would be counterproductive. "Is there anything you can't do?"

"Plenty, including getting your dad to like me."

She tilted her head. "Maybe he'll come around. Today was a good start."

"I hope so. I want to make one stop on the way to your place, okay?"

"Where?"

"Let me surprise you."

***

Rebecca hadn't anticipated anything more than a stop at a frozen yogurt shop. Chris killed the motorcycle's engine in Harrisburg's Reservoir Park where the view of the capital city was spectacular from the overlook even with the haze brought on by the hot summer day. Other than some sirens off in the distance and a few kids laughing and hollering as they cut across the parking lot, it was more peaceful than she would have expected. Rebecca grabbed hold of Chris's arm and swung her leg over the seat while he steadied the bike. She dismounted, took a step back and removed her helmet.

He got off the bike only to turn around and swing his opposite leg over the seat so that he straddled the bike again—backward. He motioned for her to come back toward him.

"Get back on the bike."

"What for?"

"You'll see." He motioned again. She caught a slight quirk of his lips that looked a lot like a suppressed grin. "Come on."

Rebecca did as he asked, and again using his arm for balance, got back on the bike, now facing Chris.

Inching first his left and then his right foot forward, he moved closer to her and settled his hands on her waist.

Gravel crunched beneath his boots as he shifted into a comfortable position. When he spoke, his voice was as smooth and rich as honey, but his eyes spoke the loudest, so filled with love and desire. "I can't ask you to fulfill all my fantasies ...yet. But I thought maybe you'd indulge me just one as thanks for today. You *did* say you owed me one."

He had alluded to a future with her, and the only context for her fulfilling his every fantasy would be in marriage. All the air left her lungs in a whoosh.

His brow creased. "Nothing kinky. I promise." He gave her a reassuring smile and his right hand combed through her hair, which was all knotted from their ride. Holding the back of her head, he lowered his lips to hers. He tasted like the strawberry lemonade she had served him. His kiss was all sweetness and hinted at a promise he hadn't yet made but she was now fairly certain he wanted to. One that would keep her encircled in his arms forever.

She gripped the sides of his cotton shirt and pulled him closer although it didn't feel nearly close enough. Why on earth had she ever been nervous about kissing him like this?

It was a foretaste of heaven.

His hand let go of her waist and slid up her side until it moved dangerously close to a place it shouldn't be. What could have been a clumsy grope was a gentle and loving touch, and she hated the fact that she had to squelch it. Without breaking the connection to his lips, she laid her hand atop his and slid it across her tee shirt where she flattened it, sure that he could feel the pounding of her heart.

He ended the kiss, but neither one of them moved their hands folded over her heart.

"Thank you," he said, his breathing ragged and irregular. "Now I don't have to imagine it; I can remember it."

Rebecca smiled. "My pleasure."

"I hope so." Chris grabbed her around the waist and tickled her until she fell against him laughing. "Okay. Let's get you home."

16

Say Goodbye

Usually Chris waited until Rebecca got into her car or her apartment before he left, but this afternoon he had to hurry. They were already cutting things close between 10:30 a.m. Mass in Harrisburg and his 1:00 p.m. tee time with Alan in Gettysburg. Factor in the ten minutes they'd spent saying goodbye, otherwise known as kissing, in a private spot on the edge of the battlefield boundaries, and Rebecca knew he had to go if he didn't want to keep Alan waiting.

Her experience at Mass had been positive this time around. Part of that she attributed to the fact that she knew better what to expect. It also helped that she now had an inkling what was going on. She was more at ease with Chris now, too, and felt comfortable whispering a question to him when she had trouble following along.

She unlocked and opened the back door of her car and laid her helmet on the floor. After closing the rear door, she lifted the handle on the front door, then decided she ought to check on her dad. Chris didn't like her spending time alone with him, but he *was* her dad after all, and the least she could do was check in on him to see if his back had improved this morning.

The car door clicked shut and, hoisting her purse onto her shoulder, she turned up the walk to her dad's house. Chris's job on the porch floor looked good even in the daylight, although she noticed a small spot where the boards met the wall that could use a little dab of paint. It had been a long day for him yesterday, and while he didn't complain, she could tell by the way he moved in church that the work he'd done had left him sore.

Rebecca knocked on her dad's door, then opened it and called to him. When he didn't answer right away she went in.

"Dad? You upstairs?"

"I'm right here," her dad said as he descended the stairs, taking each one like a man twenty years his senior so as not to jar his back. "Chris isn't with you?"

"No. He had to meet his brother for a game of golf."

Her dad walked to his favorite leather chair and sat with a groan.

The smell of bacon lingered in the air.

"I guess you managed breakfast okay?"

"Yes. Bacon and eggs."

"Good. Do you need anything, Dad? Otherwise, I'm going to get home. I haven't done any laundry yet this weekend, and I need to run to the grocery store."

"One thing. Can you put the cast iron skillet back in the drawer under the oven? I can't bend while holding something that heavy."

"Sure." Rebecca tossed her purse onto the coffee table in front of her dad and went into the kitchen to put away the heavy pan for him. When she returned to the living room a couple of minutes later, her dad held a small booklet in one hand that he smacked against his other hand. She recognized it right away.

After Mass, while Chris talked to someone he knew from work, she had browsed the rack of pamphlets at the rear of the church. She picked up one with a picture of a statue of Jesus' mother on the front entitled, "Mary, Our Mother." What she thought of as the Catholic Church's preoccupation with Mary confounded her. Chris said it was simply honoring Jesus' mother. She thought maybe the booklet would help her understand why Catholics placed her in such high esteem. She took the pamphlet and stuffed it in her purse to read later. It must have slid out of the open pouch when she tossed it onto the table.

"What's this?"

She hoped that her dad wouldn't make too much out of it, so she tried to convey an air of nonchalance. "Oh, I picked that up in the back of church. I thought maybe it would help me understand why Catholics think Jesus' mother is so important."

Her dad winced as he leaned forward in his chair and rubbed his hand over his face. His voice took on a tension she hadn't heard in it before. "Rebecca, I have to admit that Chris seems like a decent young man despite my reservations about him. I *am* grateful for what he did yesterday—but, and this is a big but, I cannot abide with you attending that heathen church with him. I'm sorry to say this, but I will never, ever accept him nor give my blessing should things become more serious between you two."

"Dad, I'm trying to understand what he believes, that's all."

"Rebecca, I see how he looks at you. I remember that feeling. Your mother and I were in love once—back in the beginning. Trust me when I tell you it would be easier for both of you if you ended it now. You are unequally yoked. There is nowhere for the relationship to go. Whatever you *think* you have in common, you're wrong. It's not enough. You're a physical temptation to him and nothing more. Better to end it now."

She walked to the window and stared blankly at the street. Why hadn't she just gone home? She didn't want to hear his ridiculous opinion. A physical temptation and nothing more? What did her dad know about what they had in common?

"Rebecca, honey." He waited until she looked at him again. "All I want is your happiness. I know you girls think I'm a cruel, old man, but it breaks my heart to say these things."

Maybe if he had made the slightest effort to get to know Chris as a person that would mean something to her, but he had prejudged him, plain and simple. Lost in her thoughts and the battle to restrain her tears, Rebecca hadn't noticed her dad heave himself out of his chair and over to the end table. He opened a drawer and pulled out several small pamphlets. He flipped through them, assessing whether they were the right ones, then took them to the coffee table and pushed them into Rebecca's purse.

"Read those if you want the truth," he barked. Then, taking the pamphlet about Mary, he opened it up and ripped it down the center, letting the pieces fall on the floor. "Then end it, Rebecca, before it's too late."

***

Something was bothering Rebecca, but so far she hadn't said what. For the past few days she'd seemed reticent. She talked to Chris, laughed with him, even flirted with him, but her heart wasn't engaged. This evening as they'd walked around City Island, past the mini golf, the baseball field, and the kids' train, she'd been unusually quiet, her mind elsewhere.

She walked toward him from the restroom, drying her hands on her shorts the whole way. He admired her top, a sort of frilly blouse that was cut to fit a woman's body. Now that he thought about it, she'd been wearing more of that kind of thing lately. Her clothes were still modest, but they were more fashionable and accentuated her curves more than the subdued, shapeless clothes she had worn when they first met.

"Yuck. This weather and public restrooms don't mix." She was right. They had endured a week-long streak of hot and humid days. That's why he had suggested they stop and have a snow cone before leaving. Rebecca ordered a blue raspberry, and Chris chose root beer.

Only one picnic table was vacant—the one closest to the trash. They sat at the end farthest from the offensive container. Chris finished his snow cone first and dropped the paper wrapper into the can. Several bees buzzed around the receptacle. He swatted at one as it tried to land on his forearm. The persistent bug circled around and came back, determined to land. Chris swatted again and twisted away from the can. He slammed right into Rebecca as she threw away her cone and napkins.

"Ouch!"

"I'm sorry. It's that darn bee. I'm trying to get away from it."

"Yeah, well, I think it stung me." She held her hand over her upper arm.

"Are you allergic?"

"No, but it sure hurts."

"Let me see." He lifted her hand revealing a red, swollen blotch. "The stinger's stuck. Hold still." He pinched the stinger, pulled it out, and showed it to her. "Nasty little thing."

"You're telling me. I never had one hurt like this."

Chris's eyes darted left and right as he looked for something to ease her pain. "I'll get a little ice from the snow cone vendor." In a couple of minutes, he had a small cup of shaved ice to put over her sting.

"I just remembered I've got some kind of sting wipes in my purse. Abby gave me some to keep on hand for when I'm out with Ricky and Emma. It's in the inside pocket of my purse. Can you get it?"

"Sure." He handed her the ice, and they sat back down at the table. He rummaged through her purse pushing aside tissues, lip gloss, and her change purse until he found the little packet labeled "Sting Relief Wipe." He tore open the packaging with his teeth, unfolded the wipe and handed it to Rebecca.

She laid it over her sting and sighed. "Feels better already. Thank you."

Chris couldn't get over how much it bothered him when she hurt. Could he sign up for a whole lifetime of this? Absolutely, he could. It was crazy, but to get to be with her all the time would be worth it.

Now that she was feeling better, he started to gather the contents of her purse and put them back inside. He grabbed a handful of small pamphlets. They were plain on the back, and he flipped them over to see the covers. The one on top was called, "Are Roman Catholics Christians?" and had a picture of a rosary. The one beneath was called "Why is Mary Crying?" and showed a weeping statue. The third and final one was called "The Death Cookie" and featured what looked like a small, round wafer with skull and crossbones imprinted on it. He flipped through this last one, his gaze running over the black and white comic strip images. His eyes caught on words here and there: "idolatry," "religious con job," "hocus pocus."

A sick feeling grew in the pit of his stomach.

Rebecca held the wipe to her arm, but her face was ashen. "I-I, uh—"

"Where did you get these?"

Her eyes grew watery and her lower lip quivered. He hoped she wouldn't cry. He was angry, and if she were going to go all weepy on him, they wouldn't be able to have this conversation. And they needed to have this conversation.

"My dad. When you dropped me off at my car on Sunday, I stopped in to make sure he was okay. I didn't stay long, maybe ten minutes. He said he was grateful for what you had done for him, but he could never approve of my being with you, and he shoved those into my purse."

He sensed there was probably a little more to the story than that. "Have you read them?"

She nodded. "Yes. I read them the next day. I thought I should know why he's so against us."

"Me, you mean. He's against me." He held the tracts up, waving them. "Do you believe this stuff? Do you think this is what I believe—that priests, that Father John, has magical powers and that we bow down and worship little wafers? Is this what you saw when you came to Mass with me? What you read in the books I lent you? You knelt with me on Sunday, Rebecca, I thought...I don't know what I thought."

She lifted her hand from her arm and transferred the wipe to the other hand. Palm up, she reached her free hand out across the table, waiting for him to take it.

He hesitated, but then couldn't resist.

"Chris, those pamphlets are hateful. You have to know I don't feel that way about you. Or Father John. I wanted to know what my dad thought. I'll admit I don't understand it all yet, what you believe and how you worship, but believe me when I tell you I liked being at Mass with you on Sunday. I felt, I don't know, at home. I started to see a rhythm to what was going on."

She seemed sincere. Thank God she held the tears at bay.

"Why did you keep these?"

"I don't know. I...I guess my gut tells me that stuff isn't

true, but I'm not sure how to refute it. I don't know everything you do. And I...."

She was having trouble getting this part out. This must have been what had been bothering her these last few days. "You what?

She let out a breath. "I have doubts, okay? Isn't there maybe a grain of truth in there?" She gestured toward the tract still in his hand.

He threw them on the table with more force than was necessary and let go of her hand.

"So you think these are right? They're crude and mean-spirited maybe, but they're right? Do you think your dad's right about me, too? About us?"

Now the tears fell, and it *was* his fault. In his anger and defensiveness, he'd made her cry. "I don't know. I don't know anything." She wiped her eyes and glanced about, obviously conscious they were in a public place.

Clambering to his feet, he blew out a breath. He'd handled this poorly. "Rebecca, there's nothing wrong with you having questions. I went through all kinds of doubts when I was trying to figure out where I belonged, spiritually-speaking. I'm not threatened by you looking at these. I think they're trash, and it doesn't do much for my opinion of your dad, but I guess you owe him at least as much consideration as you do me."

He moved to her side of the table and straddled the bench, facing her. He pulled her towards him. "I love you," he whispered against her hair. "I only wish you had brought these to me instead of me finding them like this. It caught me off guard. I felt like I was being ambushed. I'm sorry I got defensive."

She sniffed and dabbed at the corner of her eye. "I'm sorry, too. You're right. I should've told you about them and asked you to help me understand why they're wrong."

"We can do that if you want. Go through them one by one and look at what's true and what's not. It would be good for me, too. I don't want to worry about that now though." He lifted her chin. "I want to enjoy the rest of the evening with you, okay?"

"Okay." The tears had stopped. Gosh, she was beautiful. Her brown eyes shuttered closed as he kissed her lips. Then he pulled back. "How can I have an argument with you when you have those ridiculous blue lips?"

She slipped a hand over her mouth. "I forgot. How bad is it?"

"Oh, it's bad. Let's see if we can get it to wear off faster." Her hand fell and one side of her mouth rose in a grin before he smothered it with another kiss.

***

Thank God it's Friday. Truer words were never spoken as far as Chris was concerned. It had been a long week fraught with unexpected problems. Problems with people, machinery, and just about everything else. He had a two-day reprieve, and this evening he had a date with Rebecca. If anything or anyone could make him forget about his lousy week, it was her. Just the thought of her had him smiling as he tugged at his necktie, loosening it so it hung around his collar.

He unbuttoned his wrinkled white dress shirt with one hand while he opened the refrigerator with the other. He pushed aside the milk and the juice, and then crouched to move a bag of wilted lettuce and some mysterious leftovers.

I work in a brewery, and I don't have a single beer in this place? He discovered a lone bottle on the door's bottom shelf. Not the best place for a beer, but it was all he had. He grabbed the bottle opener from the counter, opened it, and took a long drink as he fished the tails of his shirt out of his pants.

A knock sounded. He didn't expect Rebecca for another hour.

Despite his surprise, a smile broke free when he saw Rebecca standing on the other side of his door. "Hey, I thought you were coming at seven o'clock." He stepped back to let her in, and she walked into the kitchen, waiting for him to join her. Her eyes darted to his open bedroom door. Thank goodness he had made the bed this morning.

They had planned on a casual dinner and a movie, but it didn't look like she had changed her clothes after work. How could she? There wouldn't have been time. She wore a long crinkled skirt that reached her ankles and a snug-fitting tee with a silver bangle belt. She twisted her fingers and let her left ankle tilt, the low-heeled shoe falling on its side. Rebecca seemed almost nervous to him.

"I didn't want to wait to see you," she said in a rush.

He smiled and took her hand in his. Her palm seemed a little sweaty, and he wondered what had made her so anxious that she rushed to seem him straight from work.

"Rough day?"

She shook her head, and her gaze locked onto the half-empty bottle of beer still in his hand. "Do you have another one of those?"

He lifted the bottle and glanced at it, holding it up. "This? I didn't think you liked beer."

"I haven't given it a fair try. It looks good to me today."

He turned his head slightly and narrowed his eye at her. "Really? This is all I've got, but the rest is yours if you want it."

She took it, and her hand shook a little as she raised it to her lips. "Mmm."

He laughed.

She wrinkled her brow and glared at him. "What?"

"You're a horrible actress. You can say, 'mmm' all you want, but that look on your face tells me you haven't acquired a taste for beer yet."

"I guess not." Despite her admission, she proceeded to take another swig. What on earth was going on?

"So, not that I'm not happy to see you, but do you want to tell me why you're here straight from work chugging a half-drunk beer you don't like?"

Her gaze met his for a half second, and then she turned and walked into his living area. "I wanted to see you. To be with you." Her voice dropped until it was low and husky, but still unsure. "Alone."

She set the empty beer bottle on his end table and turned back to him. While her hands still twisted with nervousness, clear affection sparkled in her eyes. She stepped toward him and pressed her hands against his chest. He had forgotten until he felt her hands through the thin cotton of his undershirt that he had been about to get undressed when she arrived.

She tilted her head up to him, and he happily obliged her with what she sought. He let his hands fall to her waist and leaned down to kiss her. Even though it ran contrary to everything he felt, he kissed her as he always did with a gentle ease. When he touched her lips, the pressure he felt returned was anything but gentle. It was hard, greedy, demanding, and wholly unlike Rebecca.

Sweet mother of mercy! She pulled at his shirt, yanking the tails out where they remained trapped by his belt. It sent a thrill through him that had him returning her kiss with an equal amount of intensity, but it also set off a silent alarm. Something about this whole situation wasn't right.

He had almost convinced himself to back off from the kiss when he felt her hands at his waist struggling with his belt buckle. He pulled away, grasping her wrists tight in his hands and pushing them away from his pants. He let out a breathy moan before he took a small step backward and said, "Whoa. As much as I'm enjoying this—and God help me, I'm enjoying this—I'm not daft enough to think you were suddenly overcome by your passion for me and drove over here to seduce me. So, what's this about?"

"You know how I feel about you." He could tell she was off script now. She had planned on him succumbing to her unspoken offer and wasn't prepared to answer his question. If she was nervous before, she bordered on panic now. Her breaths came quick and rapid, and he couldn't attribute it all to their kiss.

"Well, Rebecca, I think I do, although you haven't really told me." Heck, if she wanted to get in his pants, she should at least be prepared to tell him she loved him. He could see already by the way she looked at anything in the room but him that he wasn't going to hear it now. He couldn't for the life of him figure what had turned his demure beauty into a brazen temptress, but he knew now why she wanted that beer.

"Maybe not in so many words, but—"

"Words are good, Rebecca." He loosened his hands on her wrists and slid them along her palms until they were holding hands. He waited for her response, but she turned it back on him.

"You say you love me. Don't you want me?"

She had to be kidding. *I want you so badly I can't sleep at night or think straight all day.* He wasn't about to say that out loud, not when she would use it to justify doing something rash and foolish.

"I do love you, but this isn't about how I feel about you. I *get* going too far in the heat of the moment. I pull myself back from that ledge every time I kiss you, but this is premeditated. You want to use me for something, and I'd like to know why."

That stopped her, like she hadn't considered this wasn't what he wanted. When she didn't respond, he cocked an eyebrow in question.

It took a full five seconds, but her whole veneer collapsed as if she finally realized that she had in fact been using him to suit her own purpose.

"I'm so sorry." She clapped her hand to her mouth. Her eyes took on a wet, shiny appearance that soon left tears rolling down her cheeks.

Her tears caused an ache in his heart, and he pulled her to him. "Shhh. It's okay."

She cried into his shirt for a minute or two before she lifted her head. "I'm so sorry. Can you forgive me?"

"Of course, but you still haven't told me what this is about." She stilled as he stroked her hair, but she acted as if he hadn't even spoken.

"I didn't think of it that way. I was so selfish."

His heart still pounded from that kiss, and the way she looked so broken and vulnerable tempted him to kiss her again.

"If you give me a minute I'll get changed, and we can go get something to eat and talk through this. Just sit tight."

He headed to his bedroom, and closed the door behind him. With a couple breaths, he tried to stop thinking about that kiss and where it would've gone if he would've let it happen. He changed his clothes, then glanced in the mirror as he ran his fingers through his hair. When he opened the door, Rebecca stood with her back to him. By the way her slim shoulders shook, he knew that she was crying.

He came up behind her and cleared his throat to make sure she knew he was there before he folded her into his arms. "Hey, it's okay."

"No, it's not." Tears choked her words. She turned to face him, and her eyes were red-rimmed and teary. "I've made a complete fool of myself."

"What are you talking about?" He could see where she would feel bad about it, but he couldn't understand what would make her feel foolish.

"I threw myself at you, and...and..." The tears came in heavy waves now. "And I'm such an idiot. You don't even want me. No one ever has, and no one ever will."

At first she resisted, but then she let him pull her into his arms so that she could relax against his chest. "You think I don't want you?"

She didn't answer.

"Rebecca, why do you think I had to leave this room? Why do you think I suggested we go out? Because I *do* want you, and while I like to think I have a fair amount of self-control, I have limits. And I really don't want to test them tonight." Her gaze dropped to her feet, and he took her hand again. "You ready?"

Breathing deeply, her eyes finally met his. "I have some clothes in the car. Do you mind if I change?"

"Of course not."

She retrieved her clothes from the car and changed into shorts and a shirt in Chris's bathroom.

Chris didn't like the unnatural silence, but he figured they could wait until they got to the restaurant to sort things out. The little sandwich shop in town would be perfect—large enough to afford them some privacy but busy enough to keep the drama to a minimum. It had the added advantage of being devoid of comfy horizontal surfaces. Considering how he still didn't know if he deserved a pat on the back or a kick in the rear for putting a stop to her advances, that was a plus.

They ordered soup, sandwiches, and iced teas, and the waitress brought the order to their table in the corner. Chris said the blessing, and they ate—or in Rebecca's case, picked more than ate.

When they were done, Chris stacked the dirty plates and pushed them aside. He reached across the table for her hand, but Rebecca merely looked at it and settled her hands in her lap. Chris tried to pretend that simple action didn't feel like a knife to his heart. This rift that erupted in his apartment seemed more serious than he had first thought, and his heart seized a little. "Do you want to tell me what's happened?"

***

Rebecca stared at her hands and began. "I overheard some people talking about me in the break room."

Chris nodded, waiting for her to elaborate. "I take it what they were saying wasn't kind."

She shook her head. "I'm a joke."

She could hear every word of the conversation in her head. Neal, that little weasel in human resources, talked to Marcus, the frat boy in the cubicle behind hers.

"I heard she's got a boyfriend."

"Poor jerk. Either he's as much of a prudish prig as she is or he's gettin' some on the side."

The next voice belonged to Angela, the receptionist. "You guys are mean. Have you ever even spoken to her? She's sweet, even if she is a little straight-laced. I think you're spiteful because she's too smart to give either of you reprobates a second look." Angela's heels clicked on the tiled floor, and Rebecca knew that she had left the room. It was the last comment that Marcus made that cut her deepest.

Repeating it to Chris embarrassed her, but was also somehow cathartic.

"He said that he bet it was all a farce. That I might *act* like I wouldn't know what to do with...with ... a, uh, certain part of the male anatomy if I held it in my hand, but that I *had* probably slept with every guy dumb enough to give me a second look. "

The muscles in Chris's jaw tensed and then relaxed. He leaned forward on the table with his hands folded in front of him and kept his voice low.

"You're innocent. I love that about you, Rebecca."

She leaned back in her seat, not wanting the intimacy he was trying to create. She didn't want his pity. *Poor little Rebecca. We mustn't corrupt her delicate sensibilities.*

"I'm either a prude or a slut depending on whom you ask. But you know what I really am? I'm a freak. Abby even said so."

Chris rubbed his fingers over his brows and down his temples and cheeks. "Abby's one to talk. You're not a freak. You're beautiful. Inside and out. And if you're a freak, so am I. Maybe not freaks. Fools. Fools for Christ."

She rolled her eyes. "Don't throw Scripture at me. I'm not in the mood."

"So, what happened at my place—you were trying to prove you aren't who they say you are? They're jackasses, Rebecca, and I'd like to beat the crap out of them for hurting you, but they're so, I don't know, misled, confused, degraded, that they see virtue as some kind of albatross. That's not how I see you."

She lowered her head, not wanting to glimpse the pity on his face.

"Hey. Look at me."

His stern tone sent a chill up her spine. When she didn't look at him he softened his tone. "Rebecca, please."

She didn't lift her head, only her eyes.

"I love you, Rebecca. I don't say that lightly. I've never said those words to anyone other than a blood relation. I love who you are, right now, and who you will be for the rest of your life."

He meant it, and that's what made this so hard. She looked away and watched as the busboy cleared the table next to them. Could someone do that with her life? Sweep away the trash and the clutter and the dirtiness and make her free and clean?

God could.

She pushed the thought from her mind and focused on Chris. She expected him to be angry with her. She wanted him to be angry with her. She'd used him, and now she half-ignored him, but he didn't seem mad, only sad and hurt.

"What is it that scares you so much about caring about me? Because for the life of me, I can't figure it out."

He nailed it. He knew, even when she didn't.

"I'm afraid of this." She motioned to the space between them with her index finger. "I'm afraid of the heat and the chemistry and the fact that you love me. I'm afraid I'm not who you think I am. Why you, Chris? If I'm so special and wonderful, why are you the only one that sees it?"

"Rebecca, I can't account for the stupidity of other males. I can only be grateful for it because it gave me a chance with you."

Then all at once she knew what she had to do, just like her dad had told her.

"No. You need to go find someone who's not so messed up."

"Rebecca, we're all messed up in one way or another. If I've gone too fast or pushed too hard, I can wait for you. I haven't hidden how I feel about you, but I didn't mean to pressure you."

His eyes were wide and plaintive and little lines creased his brow. "God can fix this. He can heal all your hurts. Have you prayed about it? Maybe this is an opportunity."

There it was again. God can fix it. Well, He hadn't done much fixing yet.

"There's nothing to fix. We're different. Too different. I'm sorry, Chris." She pushed away from the table, grabbed her purse and fled.

"Rebecca, wait!"

She didn't respond and didn't slow down. She had an advantage because he was too upstanding a guy to walk out without paying the bill short of it being a true emergency. She'd have enough of a head start on him that she could beat him back to her car and be gone. Gone from his street and gone from his life.

17

The Space Between

Chris parked his bicycle in his parents' driveway, hung his helmet on the handlebar, and walked around the house to their deck. Not wanting to wake his parents, he used his key to slip in the sliding glass door to their kitchen and helped himself to a cup of coffee from their single-cup coffee maker. He grabbed the steaming mug, slipped back outside, and took a seat on top of the wooden picnic table where they often ate during the summer months.

He breathed deeply, inhaling the scent of freshly-mowed lawn, and looked out over their property where the yard gently sloped toward a line of trees. Birds twittered as they alternately hopped and pecked at the clumps of grass clippings scattered across the hillside. He set the still-hot coffee next to him and let his head fall into his hands.

The bike ride was supposed to help him get his mind off of Rebecca, but it had merely postponed the inevitable. Without work to distract him today, he knew he'd be hard pressed to think of anything but her. For the entire week, Chris's chest felt like it had collided with a fast-moving train—one he hadn't seen coming. But he *had* known he was on the tracks. There were signs. She had been uneasy from the start. She bristled when he pestered her to sing. Then there were the anti-Catholic tracts from her dad. Her attempt to seduce him. Next thing he knew she insisted they were too different and ran away.

He'd grown to love her so much, indulging in foolish dreams: dreams of marrying her and starting a family. Finally giving in to a week's worth of sadness and the relentless tears he kept pushing back to the point it left him with a dull headache, he let go and cried.

His tears were far from spent when the sliding door hissed

as it opened and shut. Footsteps sounded on the deck, moving in his direction. He dried his face with his hands, sniffling and clearing his throat as he tried to pull himself together. He recognized Alan's voice as he boosted himself onto the table alongside him.

"Hey," Alan said, not bothering to look at him. "I've got an early tee time with Dad. Saw your bicycle in the driveway. Did you take it out on the trail this morning?"

He was grateful that Alan didn't point out the obvious—that he had been blubbering like a baby a minute ago. "Yeah. I couldn't sleep, so I decided to get out there early and get in ten miles before the trail got overrun with dog walkers."

A half-minute of silence passed between them before Alan asked, "You okay?"

"Yeah." Then he figured he would have to tell Alan about Rebecca at some point anyway. "No. Actually, my life sucks lately."

Alan arched a brow.

Chris took a breath and exhaled. "Rebecca won't return my calls or texts. She walked out on me last weekend, and I haven't heard from her since."

"You had a fight?" Alan asked, looking forward again and stretching his legs out in front of him.

"That's just it. We didn't. She was upset, but not with me. She's got some baggage, a lot of insecurities, and some major daddy issues. She embarrassed herself in front of me, and now she's got it in her head that we're never going to work. It's messed up."

"Sounds like it." Another half minute passed. "I'm not blind. I could tell you loved her almost from the beginning. Does she feel the same way?"

"If she does, she's never said."

"Not even when you're in bed?"

And, here we go. It was amazing they had avoided this topic up to now. "We've never slept together."

Chris had never had a conversation filled with so many dramatic pauses. A full ten seconds passed, and Chris knew when the realization hit Alan because he turned to face him.

"You're not still a..."

He couldn't get the word out, as if it were obscene, so Chris responded. "Yep."

Alan dropped his head and cursed, and despite his lingering sadness, Chris laughed.

"What the heck are you waiting for?"

"Marriage."

"Man, you take the whole God-religion thing seriously, don't you?"

"I guess so."

"Rebecca, too?"

"Yep."

Alan must have figured there wasn't much point in pursuing that line of conversation, which filled Chris with relief. He didn't feel like explaining premarital chastity when that was the least of his present concerns.

"So that's it? You're going to let her go?"

"What am I supposed to do?"

"Get her back. Convince her that what you have is worth working through whatever bug it is she's got up her butt."

"How am I supposed to do that? And why should I? *She* doesn't think we're worth fighting for."

"You do though, or we wouldn't be here trying to pretend you weren't just wiping the tears and snot off your face."

Chris shot him a look that said he ought not to have brought that up. "I get your point. What do you think I should do?"

"That's up to you, but I would think the usual would be a start. An extravagant bouquet sent to where she works."

"And what if after all that she still doesn't want to talk to me?"

"Well, you're no worse off than you are right now except that you don't have to wonder if you did everything you could."

***

Rebecca shifted in her seat, leaned her head back and

stretched her legs. She had been looking at the same spreadsheet for an hour, and her eyes were dry and her vision blurred. She pushed back her seat and rose to fill up her water bottle from the cooler when the phone on her desk buzzed. She reached across the desk and pressed the button next to the flashing line.

"Yes?" A couple seconds of silence followed before she heard Angela adjust her headset.

"There's a delivery out here for you, Rebecca. And if you don't come claim it, I will." Angela sounded excited, typical since she was bubbly almost to the point of obnoxiousness. Day in and day out she plastered a smile on her face. It would be intolerable were it not genuine.

"What is it?"

"You've got to come see it for yourself."

"Okay. I'll be right out." Angela's exuberance piqued her curiosity. She left her water bottle behind, walked through the line of cubicles, and opened the glass door that separated the staff from the reception area. She had no sooner swung the door open than the largest bouquet of roses she had ever seen nearly bowled her over.

"This?"

Angela sat behind the high desk, and her ever-present smile loomed larger than ever.

"These are for me?"

"Yes," Angela said. "They're gorgeous."

They were. There must have been three dozen red, long-stemmed roses, some budding, but most fully-opened with some baby's breath scattered in between. They sat in a large, clear vase encircled with a gigantic red bow.

Rebecca's mouth opened, but no sound came out. She looked back at Angela.

"Some guy named Chris has the hots for you. And bad. I mean, three dozen roses? A guy only sends something that expensive for one of two reasons. Either he's a guilty cheat or he wants you to have his babies."

Rebecca's cheeks warmed, and she shot Angela a look that said, "Don't go there."

Ignoring her, Angela proceeded. "So, which is it? Is he a cheat or does he want you to produce an heir?"

The thought of mothering Chris's baby set her heart aflutter, and her cheeks grew warmer. "Angela," she pleaded as several accountants opened the glass door and crossed the reception area to the exit. Their conversation faded as the door clicked shut behind them.

"So, tell me, Rebecca. What's he like?"

Perfect. Beyond my wildest dreams. "Just a guy."

"Nice try, but those rosy cheeks and the way you're wringing your hands make me think he's more than that."

"Okay. He's gorgeous, smart, funny, considerate...." She let the words trail off before she added, "And I told him I didn't want to see him anymore."

"You're crazy, girl. Cra-zy." She shook her head a few times for emphasis. Then she reached up into the enormous bouquet whose fragrance permeated the room, pulled out a small envelope, and extended her hand to Rebecca. "There's a card."

Rebecca stepped forward and took the envelope. She slid her fingernail under the flap and opened it. She recognized Chris's handwriting on the small card dotted with hearts. There was no signature, only a message. "Did you think I'd make it easy for you?"

Not the tears. She had cried so much over the past week there couldn't be any left. She bit her lip hard and pushed them back, refusing to lose control at work. The glass door swung open again, and Marcus breezed in. He leaned against Angela's high desk and lifted his chin toward the ostentatious display.

"So, Angela, reeling one in, huh?"

Angela gave him an icy smile. "Oh, they're not for me. They came for Rebecca."

Marcus's eyebrows shot up. "Huh." And he breezed out as easily as he'd breezed in.

***

By midweek, the slightest provocation sent Rebecca into a

fit of tears. She suspected that if she Googled "emotional wreck," it would turn up her picture. Despite the heat, she decided that a long, late lunch hour walk would give her some perspective. With no destination in mind, she didn't realize until she arrived that she stood in front of the cathedral where she and Chris had gone to Mass. Had it only been a couple of weeks ago? It felt like a lifetime.

She walked up the steps and into the dark, cavernous church. Noon Mass had long since ended, and people had gone back to work, leaving the sacred space cool, quiet, and empty. Even if people did come through at this hour, she hoped they would leave her be. She took a seat near the front and stared, not knowing why she had come. She didn't feel as if she could pray. Maybe if she were silent, God would speak to her. People claimed He did that, right? How long had it been since she'd even listened for His voice?

She sat in silence for at least ten minutes before a familiar figure moving across the altar caught her eye. Father John. He belonged at Chris's church in Gettysburg, not here. He crossed the altar, genuflecting midway, then glanced her way without stopping. He took care of something at the side altar where a couple dozen candles burned in red glass jars beneath a statue of some saint. When he was done there, he came toward her.

Her furtive glances to the side and rear turned up no possibility of escape.

He slid into the pew beside her. "Hey, how's it going?"

Chris hadn't told him? "Oh, you know, it's going. What are you doing here?"

"I filled in at noon Mass for a friend who's on retreat." His smile seemed forced. "Chris is hurting."

He knew.

Father John's gaze slipped to his hands folded in his lap, then he looked back up for her reaction.

No, not the tears again. Would they never stop? She nodded because she knew if she spoke, the dam would break. A single tear escaped. She hoped Father John wouldn't notice, but he did.

"You're hurting, too."

She looked away.

"Can I say something as Chris's friend? And maybe yours?"

"Of course." Her voice came out thin and broken.

"I want you to think a minute about all the voices in your life. Your dad's. Your co-workers'. Chris's voice." He paused for a couple seconds. "God's voice. Who has spoken to you in love and truth? Whose words make you free to love and whose words hold you back?"

Chris *had* told him everything. Had he told him she tried to seduce him, too?

"I'll think about that, John. I mean, Father John." She made a show of looking at her wristwatch as if she were in a hurry.

"Rebecca." He waited until she looked at him again. "You came to the right place. You can leave all your burdens here." He inclined his head toward the crucifix suspended above the altar. "All the pain. All the guilt. All the stuff that's holding you back. He can take it."

She nodded quickly. "Yeah. Um, I'm on my lunch hour. I've got to get back to work. It was good seeing you." She didn't even wait for him to let her out of the pew. Instead she darted out the other side. When she pushed open the heavy doors, the afternoon sunshine blinded her, and it took a moment for her eyes to adjust. She wished her heart could adjust to change as easily. She would think about what Father John had said though. Later. Maybe God had spoken to her after all.

***

She survived another weekend, though Rebecca wasn't sure how. The distraction of babysitting her niece and nephews helped. Abby and Joel needed a date night anyway, and Abby had told her she could nurse her broken heart by watching her kids anytime.

Monday morning came again, and her giant rose bouquet still filled most of her cubicle although some of the blooms had begun to brown and droop.

She hadn't been at her desk more than five minutes when her phone buzzed in her purse. She used to reach for it right away, expecting a short but sweet text message from Chris. "Thinking of you," "Can't wait for tonight," or a simple "I love you." She had ignored the messages since their breakup. In a couple of days they'd stopped, and except for an occasional message from Abby with something like, "Help! These little people are killing me," her phone had been silent. It was kind of early for a message from Abby, but who else could it be?

She swiped across the phone and glanced at the screen. Her breath froze.

A message from Chris read simply, "Take as long as you need. I will wait." She opened the attached file in her music app, tapped "play," and a song called "I Will Wait" blasted.

Marcus's head popped above the cubicle, a scowl on his face.

She quickly turned down the volume. "Sorry, Marcus." Like the near-constant noise coming from his side of the prefab wall didn't disturb her.

Marcus made a snarling noise and disappeared again.

Rebecca read the artist's name, which appeared directly below the song title, but she couldn't resist. She texted back, "Dave Matthews?"

A minute or more after she'd played back the song twice, the response came. "Mumford & Sons." A few seconds more, and another message followed.

"You're the one. I know it as sure as I know the sun rises in the east and sets in the west. I will wait."

The tightness in her chest or the inevitable tears—which was worse? At least no one could see the chest pain. She'd had enough of displaying her dysfunction for the whole world. She couldn't think about this now. Not at work. She'd think about Chris's text and what Father John had said later.

***

Another week passed. "Later" hadn't arrived, but Labor Day Weekend did. There were no cookouts or picnics nor anything else on Rebecca's social calendar. She'd spend the last Sunday night of summer having her own personal Hitchcock movie fest.

She paused "Vertigo" and set the remote control on the couch's armrest. She headed for the kitchen, dragging her soft, cotton blanket with her. It fell to the floor as she lifted her arms to find the ice cream carton in the rear of her freezer. Rebecca grabbed a spoon from the drawer and bumped it closed with her hip. Clutching her ice cream and spoon in one hand, she scooped up her blanket with the other and headed back to the couch.

Only five minutes further into the movie, her cell phone ringtone sounded. "I Will Wait," was a masochistic choice, but she'd grown to like the song and, she had to admit, the idea behind it. The notion that Chris loved her enough to wait until she worked through her issues gave her hope. Pausing the movie again, she reached for the phone and wondered who would call her after ten o'clock at night. She didn't recognize the number.

"Hi. This is Rebecca."

"Rebecca, don't hang up."

She knew that voice. Using her legs, she pushed the blanket onto the couch, dropped the carton of ice cream onto the coffee table, and stood. She paced around the room vacillating between hanging up and listening to what Chris had to say.

"I just wanted to hear your voice. I knew if you saw my number on the caller I.D. you wouldn't answer, so I borrowed someone's phone."

A loud clatter in the background melded with laughter and what sounded like banging pots. A shrill voice whined above the ambient noise. "Chris Reynolds, you get back here. I won fair and square. And bring my phone."

She knew *that* voice, too. Megan. Three sheets to the wind again, or so it sounded. She could imagine her falling all over Chris. The thought of it turned Rebecca's ice cream-laden stomach. Oh well. Chris was a big boy. He'd fended off Megan before. He could do it again—if he wanted.

"Sorry. It's getting a little loud. I'll step outside."

The background noise faded and the line grew quiet.

"Where are you?" Rebecca asked.

"My parents' place for Alan and Jamie's First Annual End-of-Summer Barbecue and Pool Party. My parents are out of town, and they said Alan could host the party here. They're throwing quite a bash. I'm glad I'm not on cleanup duty."

A pool party. Rebecca's mind conjured an image of Megan lounging in a string bikini by his parents' pool. Maybe in her naiveté Rebecca had overlooked an unwritten rule about poolside kisses, too. Maybe a kiss tonight would earn Megan that place between Chris's sheets that she coveted.

Rebecca dug her fingertips into her brow. That wasn't fair, and she knew it. Chris didn't sleep around.

The silence lingered between them, and then his voice came across the line, barely above a whisper. "I wish you were here."

Rebecca's eyes filled with tears, and the lump in her throat grew. He sounded sincere, but she could imagine the party atmosphere at his parents' place. She remembered all the free-flowing alcohol at the wedding. Steeling her heart, she dismissed the call for what it was—a sentimental moment brought on by too much booze.

"This isn't a drunk dial, if that's what you're thinking. I've been getting over some kind of virus, and the strongest drink I've had tonight is Coca-Cola."

Could he read her mind?

"I guess I shouldn't have called. Maybe it's the change of seasons and all, but I had a lot of hopes for what the coming year would look like for us, and I'm having a hard time letting go of them."

Rebecca had hopes, too. Ridiculous, fantastical hopes that would never be. Hopes that involved diamonds, a gown with a fabulous train, satin sheets, sleepless nights, the soft glow of a Noah's ark nursery lamp, and a minivan full of blue-eyed children. If she tried to speak, her voice would break.

"I'll let you go. It's late, and I'm sure you want to get back to whatever you were doing." His voice didn't sound so steady itself, and when it got quiet, she thought he had ended the call. She pulled the phone away from her ear and was about to hit "end" when he said, "Rebecca, I still love you."

With an unsteady finger, Rebecca pushed the end button and ran her wrist across her mouth, trying to stifle a gasp. She sank back onto the couch, wrapped her arms around her knees, and huddled under her blanket. Then she let the tears come.

She shut the TV and DVD player off and dragged herself to bed, where she stared at the ceiling for forty-five minutes. Had she made a mistake breaking things off with Chris? What was the fruit of that decision? Chris didn't sound any happier than she was. The roses, the calls, and the messages all proved he wanted her back. She wanted him back, too—more than she wanted to admit.

"Later" finally came the next morning, and it stayed all week.

It's all just dragging me down, God. Mom leaving, Dad being the way he is, even what happened at Bible camp. And I can't move forward. I'm stuck.

Oh, He already knew all of it, but she had to say it just the same. And then she listened like she'd never listened before. She recognized that she had sabotaged things with Chris on purpose. Her ridiculous attempt to seduce him was meant to drive a wedge between them. It didn't matter whether she accomplished her goal; it would—and did—drive them apart.

At the end of the week she saw no sign, no message, no bolt of lightning or writing in the sky. There was something better—a peace she hadn't known since she was a little girl and an unflagging confidence in what she needed to do.

18

So Much To Say

On Sunday, a full week after the call from Chris, Rebecca baked a peace offering. She called Chris and left a message three times, then texted him twice. When she hadn't heard from him by late afternoon, she resorted to doing a drive-by. His motorcycle wasn't at his apartment, so she drove by his parents' house. His motorcycle wasn't there either, but Alan spotted her as he slammed the door closed on his car. She caught a glimpse of Jamie as the storm door swung shut behind her.

She pulled into the driveway, parked her car, and took a breath. She wanted to speak to Chris, not Alan, but maybe Alan could help her find him.

"Rebecca, this is a surprise." There wasn't a bit of snark in his comment and for that she was grateful.

"Hi, Alan. I'm looking for Chris. I've been calling and texting him all day, and I haven't heard anything back."

"He went to Shenandoah for the weekend."

That explained it. He probably had no cell phone reception. Maybe he hadn't gotten her messages.

"He has to work tomorrow, though, so I'm sure he'll be home soon. Whether he'll come here or not, I don't know. Ordinarily I'd say he would, but he hasn't been in the mood for company lately."

Rebecca nodded and focused on the pavement, humbled. Alan probably knew everything, too. "I understand."

"He's probably going to end up like one of those mountain men, killing his dinner and growing a long, scraggly beard."

She squinted her left eye and tried to imagine Chris with a big ol' Duck Dynasty beard. She had never seen him anything but clean shaven. Not with more than one night's stubble. "Really?"

Alan looked at the cloudless sky, thinking. "No. He's never

been patient enough to get past the itchy stage." He offered her a smile then jammed his hands into his pockets and took a few steps toward her, lowering his voice. "I don't want to butt into my brother's business, but I thought you weren't seeing each other anymore."

"No, we haven't been." Rebecca twisted her hands in front of her. "I really need to speak to him, though. I want to apologize for some things."

"Would you do me a favor?"

She nodded. "Sure."

Alan's gaze met hers, and no trace of levity marked his face or his stance. He meant business. "Be straight with him. He would hate me for saying this, but he's insanely idealistic and romantic." Alan set his mouth in a grim line, and he paused as if he were measuring his words carefully. "I saw my brother cry for the first time since we were kids. He's not taking this well. Hence the road trip." He paused again for a second and sighed before he continued. "He's a good guy. Better than most. He's in love with you, and he doesn't deserve to be strung along."

"I understand. I'm so sorry I've hurt him." Sorry didn't even cover it. Hearing how he was hurting scorched her insides, caused her chest to ache, and stung her eyes with tears she refused to spill in front of Alan. Alan was a good guy, too, and he obviously had his brother's back. She didn't deserve the decency he treated her with now, not blaming or accusing when he knew she'd inflicted such pain on Chris.

She gave Alan a final nod and turned to walk back to her car. By the time she had slid behind the steering wheel, he had gone into the house. Rebecca let loose the fresh tears she'd been holding back. What if she had screwed things up beyond repair? What if Chris decided he didn't want her back? Could she blame him?

After a minute, she grabbed a tissue from her purse, dabbed her already puffy eyes, then put the car into reverse. As she looked behind her and released her foot from the brake, the familiar rumble of a motorcycle grew louder and then came to a stop as Chris's Harley pulled in alongside her. She put the car back into park and hung onto the steering wheel, breathing deeply.

At first Chris didn't acknowledge her. He parked the bike, removed his helmet, and ran his hand through his hair. Such a simple, familiar motion, but it set Rebecca's heart racing. He placed the helmet on the rear of his bike and then taking a step toward her car, he bent down and knocked on her passenger-side window with his gloved hand. After a second, he opened the door and slid in.

"Looking for me, I presume? I can't imagine what there is left to say. You've made it clear you're through with me." The humorless tone was so unlike him.

"There's plenty to say...if you'll let me."

"Go ahead."

Please, Lord, give me the words. "First, thank you for the beautiful roses. They were perfect, and every woman in the office envied me."

"You're welcome."

He still seemed so cold, so distant.

"Second—I'm sorry. I let all my own insecurities and everyone else's opinions get the best of me. Everyone's but yours, anyway. You've been nothing but good to me and good for me, and I was careless with you and your feelings." Her heart pumped wildly, afraid of how he might answer her question. "Can you find it in your heart to forgive me?"

"Yes."

She blinked. It shouldn't be that easy. "That's it? Yes? Just like that?"

"Just like that." Finally she saw a hint of a smile.

"You don't even want to tell me how horrible I was to you?"

"Nope." He shrugged. "It sounds like you already know." He tugged off his gloves one finger at a time and laid them in his lap. "I went away to get some perspective. The road and being outdoors do that for me. I had a lot of time to think and to pray, and I had already decided that I would forgive you whether you asked me to or not. Am I still hurt? Yes. Am I a little angry? Definitely. But those feelings are nothing compared to the love I have for you. Four weeks, four months, four years can't change the way I feel about you."

"But I hurt you—really hurt you." Couldn't he yell at her? Sting her with a biting remark?

"I'm not going to argue with you. Ask Alan. I was a wreck for a while. But I seem to recall you hurting, too, and instead of letting me comfort you, you used the pain to push me away. To divide us. You walked out on me—in a public place, I might add—and it wasn't really about us. Or even me. It was a bunch of boneheaded co-workers and the ghosts of every person who ever dissed you. And I'm sure a healthy dose of daddy issues entered into the mix, too."

Rebecca stared out the windshield, not really focusing on anything. He had forgiven her, he still loved her, but did he want her back?

"Do you...do you still want to see me?" A few tense seconds passed in which Rebecca felt as if her whole life were hanging in the balance, and, in fact, it was.

"I'm seeing you right now." He smiled so big his dimple showed. He was playing with her—definitely a good sign.

"You know what I mean."

"I think you know what I mean, too."

She did. She sunk back into her seat and felt her heartbeat start to slow. Before she had a chance to gush about her gratitude and happiness, he opened the door and stepped out of the car.

He leaned back in and said, "I want to go in and let my parents know I got back okay. Then, do you want to take a little ride with me? Go someplace we can talk?"

"Sure. My helmet's still in the back."

His eyes darted to her back seat, and he sniffed a couple of times. "Your car smells like gingerbread."

"It's a cake." She had baked it as a peace offering, but now she feared he would think she was trying to buy back his love with food. His smile let her know he hadn't taken it the wrong way.

"Sweet. I'm starving. I'll be right back."

Chris drove them to the battlefield. His knowledge of its topography and history impressed Rebecca. No matter how many times she'd been there, she'd get all balled up not knowing which way to the Peach Orchard, Devil's Den, or anything else. The narrow, one-way lanes always made her feel like a rat in a maze. Chris knew every entrance and exit, where the major monuments were located, which roads went which directions, and where you could find a quiet spot away from all the tourists. That's where he took her. They sat in the high grass beneath a smallish monument topped by an eagle, frozen in its majesty, and spent the next two hours mending their hearts.

The late summer moon loomed large and orange over the horizon. Wisps of smoky clouds floated above and beneath the giant, luminous orb. Crickets and katydids hummed and chirped from the thickets and trees, their chorus lending a soothing undercurrent to the heartfelt whispers and professions that passed between them like a zephyr snaking a path through the wild grasses and sedges.

Rebecca plucked a long blade of grass from the hard earth and slid her fingers up its length. The sharp edge caught the tender skin of her fingertip, and it bled. She pressed her finger to her lips, and the pain subsided. She didn't think she'd ever forget the aching, bone-deep hurt she'd felt since she'd walked out on Chris. In some ways, she didn't want to. He was a precious gift to her, and she never wanted to take him for granted.

She had feared that even if they reconciled, that hurt would never fully heal; it would fester beneath the surface. But when they climbed back onto his bike and she wrapped her arms around his waist, she realized the fissure was already being soothed and filled, that love was spilling into all the brittle cracks and crevices that the pain had etched. Love really did cover all offenses. It was okay. *They* would be okay.

She would have been elated save for one thing—he hadn't touched her yet. His hand never held hers, his thumb never caressed the back of her hand. His fingers never dug into her hair or stroked her cheek. There was no tickling. No playful swats to her backside. His hands never grazed her arms. And his lips—they never touched hers.

***

In addition to their sporadic texts throughout the day, Rebecca looked forward to Chris's call every evening, and they spent hours catching each other up on their lives. She told him about Ian's latest feats and the fudge recipe she perfected. He talked about the scratch brew they were bottling and the used car he had bought. By the end of the work week, they had re-established their rapport, and when Rebecca invited him for dinner at her apartment on Saturday, he readily accepted.

After they had eaten, Chris took their dirty plates to the counter. She smiled as he eyed the decadent-looking chocolate cake she left cooling on a metal rack.

"You've been holding out on me. You're as good a cook as you are a baker." He looked again at the cake. "Alan is so jealous."

"I don't know about that. Are you sure Alan doesn't hate me?" She stood and gathered the remaining silverware from the table.

"Hate you? Why would Alan hate you?" Chris ran some water in her sink and turned his back to it, leaning against the counter.

"Because of how I hurt you." Despite the assurances of Chris's forgiveness, Rebecca had a hard time forgiving herself. Her ridiculous behavior led, in the end, to many good things— her restored faith and their reconciliation being the most important. Still, it shamed her.

"If I don't hate you for that — and I don't — then I can't see how he could." He turned and squirted dishwashing detergent into the sink, then shut off the water.

She set the utensils in the sink, shook out the damp dishrag, and laid it over the ridge between the basins. She stood motionless, watching the suds pop and struggling to overcome the embarrassment she still felt when she thought of Alan or Father John.

Chris gently held her by the arms and pulled her in front of him. Finally, he touched her, and his eyes filled with compassion. She feared she might collapse as if she were a fragile, nineteenth century damsel or do something equally embarrassing. His eyes staring into hers kept her grounded.

"Thank you," he said, his voice soft and tender.

"For what?" It was no more than a breath. Her ability to converse had an inverse relation to his nearness.

"Dinner, dessert. This night. We needed this. We need to reconnect. Emotionally." He traced the frame of her face with his index finger, his skin barely grazing hers. "Physically." Her heart thudded to a dead stop. At least that's how it felt. His lips were not more than a hair from hers when she said, "Chris." Only one word spilled over the dam, but a reservoir of worry swelled behind it.

"Trust me," he said against her lips before he silenced her. His kiss transported her back to Alan and Jamie's wedding, to the first time she'd tasted his lips. He'd been assured and confident, a stark contrast to how she'd felt—uncertain and hesitant.

Every bit as sweet, this kiss held no trace of that uncertainty. For whatever reason he had withheld his touch until this moment, and it gladdened her because everything about this felt right. Emboldened, she reached for him, gripping his shoulders as if her life depended on it.

Leaving behind the dirty dishes and the untouched cake, he led her to her couch. Worry tried to creep in, but she reminded herself of his words, "Trust me." She could. From the moment they met, he had done nothing but earn her trust.

They spent the remainder of the evening on her couch, not a word passing between them, *just* kissing. No urgency, no compulsion drove them to do anything more than savor every second, every sensation for its own worth. When finally Rebecca nestled her head on his chest, and he circled her in his arms, he breathed one word: "Heaven."

She couldn't agree more.

19
What Will Become of Me?

A month or more of Saturday nights passed with motorcycle rides, dinners, long walks, and a few movies sprinkled in between. Their relationship had developed a sense of inevitability that Rebecca delighted in. Just one thing bothered her, niggling at her conscience, irritating it like a rough tag on the inside of a shirt. While she realized she loved Chris long before their breakup, she still hadn't told him.

If she blurted it out in the heat of the moment, it would seem insincere. If she said it in response to his declaration, it would be anti-climactic. She kept waiting for the *right* time until she realized there could never be a *wrong* time to tell the man who loves you that you love him, too. Chris had been so patient. Even now he hadn't pressed her, asked her, or even hinted at it.

They had cut the evening short since Rebecca had to work early in the morning. Closing the door behind him, after another long goodbye, she decided she would tell him the next time they were together.

She tidied the room, put the remote control back on the shelf, and placed an empty glass in the sink. As she padded toward the bathroom in her stocking feet, she slid the elastic band from her ponytail and freed her hair.

With a flip of a switch, the bathroom light flickered to life. She slid her hand through her hair surveying herself in the mirror. Squealing brakes resounded from outside her window. Screeching tires were followed by the sickening thud of crunching metal.

Until recently, the intersection of Orchard Spring and Wood roads had stop signs only along Wood Road. Stop signs had been added to Orchard Spring Road in order to reduce accidents. It worked when people actually stopped at the new signs, but drivers accustomed to blowing through the intersection as they descended Orchard Spring Hill were known to ignore the signs out of sheer habit. The number of accidents had actually increased.

In a minute or so she'd hear the sirens. She turned on the tub faucet, and her heart lurched. Chris. He couldn't be much farther than the intersection.

She turned the water off and didn't bother with the light. She grabbed her cell phone and house keys, slipped on her ratty sandals, and took off out the door. Her hair, freed from its band, whipped behind her as she raced down the stairs and out toward the sidewalk. As she reached the street, she noticed cars stopped in either direction. Acrid smoke rose from two vehicles whose fluids leached out into the street. Although no precipitation had been forecast, the ground was wet, so there had been a rain shower. She ran faster and tried to see around the large, black SUV in the middle of the road. Cloud cover blocked the moonlight, but the intersection was fairly well lit.

As she neared, she spotted it—Chris's motorcycle lying on its side.

Where was Chris?

She slowed to a jog as she scanned the area for him.

The wail of emergency vehicle sirens pierced the air, growing incrementally louder. Thunder cracked overhead, and in seconds, a deluge ensued.

Her heels slid on the wet leather soles of her sandals, and she fell. She brushed the gravel from her skinned knee with her fingertips and ignored the blood running down her leg.

Her pulse raced and tears formed in her eyes. Had Chris worn his helmet today? She never saw him ride without it, but he told her that on particularly nice days he left it at home and enjoyed the feel of the sun on his face and the wind in his hair. He had it at her apartment, didn't he? She berated herself for not paying closer attention. It had been overcast when he arrived, and she hoped he had worn it. She couldn't form a thought other than the prayer she repeated in a continuous loop, "Please, Lord. Let him be okay."

A sick feeling settled in her gut. Chris had been hurt, maybe worse. Her heart pounded, and a sob burst from her lips as she quickened her pace.

Where is he? Tears and rainwater blurred her vision.

When she came on the scene, the paramedics hadn't arrived yet, and Chris lay on his back, half on the berm, half in the street. A bearded, middle-aged man sat next to him, his lips moving.

She pushed the wet hair away from her face wanting nothing to obstruct her view of Chris. Eyes closed and motionless, he appeared unconscious. His left arm curled protectively around his midsection. His helmet lay on the ground by itself, but his face and head appeared unharmed save for some abrasions on his right cheek. Rainwater streaked the dirt and blood on his face, and she wished she could shield him from the storm.

Rebecca dropped to her knees alongside Chris, opposite the man, and her pantyhose ripped and ran up her uninjured leg. The fresh brush burns and rough gravel stung her knees. Her discomfort was nothing compared to the pain Chris must have felt when his body slid across the road.

The smell of burnt rubber, oil, and antifreeze filled her nostrils. She reached to touch Chris then withdrew her hand for fear of hurting him.

"Is he alive?"

The man looked up at her, his face blank with shock as water dripped from his nose and beard. "He's breathing, but I think he's unconscious. I've tried talking to him, but he doesn't respond. Do you know him?"

"He's my boyfriend. He left my apartment five minutes ago." Her *boyfriend*. Had she ever called him that before? He loved her, and he reminded her of that at every opportunity, and she hadn't even been able to call him what he was to her.

Flickering red and blue emergency lights reflected in an oily puddle on the side of the road. In seconds, the emergency personnel descended and jostled her out of the way. An EMT removed Chris's boot and cut away the bottom of his jeans.

How hadn't she noticed that they were soaked in blood? Another EMT worked near his head. A third prepared to transfer him to the ambulance.

The police diverted traffic around the accident, which seemed to involve Chris's motorcycle, the bulky, black SUV, and a maroon Dodge Ram. Several people—the other drivers or witnesses?—surrounded one of the police officers.

Rebecca turned her attention back to Chris. The EMTs got in position to lift him into the ambulance.

"I want to go with him." She didn't know what protocol existed or if she had to be family, so she said it with as much determination as she could muster through her tears. She would not leave him.

"Sorry, miss. Only patients in the ambulance."

She needed to be with Chris when he arrived at the hospital. She wrung her hands and swallowed back a fresh round of tears.

"Miss?" The bearded man who had sat with Chris touched her arm. "I can drive you."

"Can you? Thank you so much." It crossed her mind that she had just agreed to get in a car with a strange man, but she dismissed her worries. She'd just have to trust that this guy really was a Good Samaritan.

When she arrived at the hospital, they took Chris from her again. They had to treat him, of course, but it frustrated her nonetheless. She provided the admissions desk with all of the information she could. She hadn't even thought about searching for any of his belongings at the scene and assumed the police would take care of that. He kept his identification and insurance cards in his wallet, which he tucked in his back pocket.

Contacting Chris's family concerned her most. She didn't have his parents' phone numbers, but Chris texted Alan from her phone once when his battery died, so she had his number. Her call rolled directly to voicemail. After three attempts, she remembered they were out of the country. Before their breakup, Chris had mentioned something about them all going on a European vacation to celebrate his parents' wedding anniversary. He said he couldn't go because of work.

Rebecca couldn't remember when they had left or when they'd return, and she didn't know what to do besides leave messages. She spent an hour pacing the waiting room, praying and texting Abby when Alan finally called.

"Rebecca, what happened?" His voice was deep and raspy. What time was it where he was at?

She told him everything she could about the accident and Chris's condition, which wasn't much. Alan put his end on mute for a couple of minutes to talk with his family and then told her they'd be on the first flight home in the morning. "Alan, I don't think his life's in danger although they haven't told me much, but if there are any decisions to make..."

"Call me, okay? We had our phones off and were checking messages periodically, but as of now the phones stay on. It's the middle of the night here. I couldn't sleep, so I decided to check my messages. I'm glad I did."

"Me, too."

"Tell him to hang in there, we love him, and we're on our way."

"I will." Tears filled her eyes again, and she swallowed the lump in her throat.

"Rebecca, we're glad you're there with him, especially my mom. You hang in there, too. We'll be there as soon as possible."

It seemed like hours until they finally updated her on Chris's condition and moved him to a private room. Abrasions covered most of the right side of his body, particularly his leg. He had been knocked unconscious, so they weren't certain of the extent of his injuries, but it appeared he had neither broken bones nor any internal damage. They suspected a certain amount of head trauma in spite of the fact that he *had* been wearing a helmet, although it was unclear how it had been removed after impact. Most likely Chris had taken it off himself before he lost consciousness.

Rebecca sat in the chair and stared at Chris as if in a

trance. The nurse finished adjusting the IV pole and slid the wheeled tray from the foot of the bed to the side. She closed the window blinds, blocking the glare of headlights as they passed. On her way out, the nurse gently squeezed Rebecca's shoulder, a simple gesture that pushed her over the edge. As soon as the door closed behind the nurse, all the pent-up tears flowed in a torrent while Rebecca buried her head in the sheet covering Chris's lower body.

After a few minutes, she lifted her head and slowed her tears enough to let her hand grope around for his. Finding it, she pulled his cool hand out of the covers and lay it on top of the sheet. His gloves had done their job in protecting his hands. She rubbed her hand over his, trying to warm it before grasping it firmly in her own.

She stared at it, remembering all the ways she'd touched and been touched by his hands. She pictured his hand in those fingerless gloves he wore when she first met him at the dairy case. Those strong hands staked their canopy in the rain. That hand had been bruised when he tried to take down a man who dared say something bad about her in his presence. Later that hand strummed the guitar. That hand gripped a hammer as he pounded nails into her dad's porch floor. They were the same hands that so tenderly touched her face and wove themselves through her hair. She'd seen them gloved and gripping the handlebars of his motorcycle and bare, folded in prayer as they rested on the back of a pew. She loved those hands just as she loved the man they belonged to.

"I love you." She sobbed and then reached for a tissue on the table next to his bed, wiping her nose before she dared try to continue. "I don't know why it's taken me so long to say it. I wasn't sure at first. I've never been in love before. And then I was afraid. I might have to really think about my faith or take a stand with my dad. And all this time I've been a coward and wouldn't say it. And yet you stayed with me. And now I'm afraid I won't get the chance to tell you."

Chris lay perfectly still on the bed. She pushed his hair back at his temple. How many times had his mother done that when he was a little boy? Her chest tightened and her stomach knotted at the thought of Chris's family not being there. *They should be here.*

Loathe to admit it, Rebecca envied Chris when it came to family. His parents provided a stable, loving presence in his life, and even as an adult, their love and protection surrounded him.

Chris's life, even his faith life, had a richness and depth she'd never experienced. Jesus remained at the center, but Jesus' parents, especially his mother Mary and mother Church played an integral role, too. A whole communion of saints in heaven as well as brothers and sisters in Christ on earth stood side-by-side as extended family.

Her dad's church boasted a tight-knit community, but in Chris's parish, though they seemed less personally demonstrative — maybe less effusive and less apt to share Sunday potlucks — they seemed somehow connected. Chris attributed it to their being physically bound by the Eucharist, the sharing of Christ's body and blood.

Her hand covered Chris's and she rubbed her thumb over his, smoothing his skin. She felt compelled to pray, but she wasn't sure how. Her gaze drifted from his serene face to his personal items in a plastic bag on the table next to the bed. She gently lifted her hand, stepped over to the table, and opened the bag. She carefully pulled out Chris's rosary beads—round, smooth, wooden beads strung together and knotted with brown cord. Simple and masculine.

Rebecca had never thought to ask him how to pray on the beads, and now she wished she had. She wrapped them around Chris's hand and let the crucifix lay on the sheet beneath his hand. Where had she seen that before? She remembered being a little girl and visiting the funeral parlor and seeing her elderly neighbor, Mrs. Kennedy, lying in the casket, her hand wrapped in pearlescent beads with a silver crucifix. She had never known Mrs. Kennedy to go to church, but looking back now, she realized she must have considered herself a Catholic.

Chris was *not* going to die.

Rebecca unwound the beads wrapped around Chris's hand then pressed them into his palm, closing his fingers around them.

She knew only one prayer they shared in common—the Lord's Prayer, so she said it, first slowly and then at a more normal pace, at least a dozen times in all. Then she sang it. From there she moved on to "Amazing Grace," repeating all the verses she knew three times. She thought she'd had enough of her own voice until she thought of another song. One that she hadn't sung before and one to which she didn't know more than a few words.

Her voice sounded high and fragile, even to her own ears. "Keep circling back to me. Stay with me."

***

He hurt. His head. His chest. Chris opened his eyes, blinking a few times as he adjusted to the light in the room. A hospital room. It took him a few seconds to process, and then he remembered the accident. How badly was he hurt? Everything looked okay from this vantage point, but his feet— he couldn't move them. Couldn't move his legs. Couldn't even feel them. That couldn't be good.

Silence filled the room. It must be night. He raised his head off the pillow, and then he saw Rebecca. Her head lay on his legs, but he couldn't feel it. Her hair fanned out on the sheets, and he lifted his hand to stroke it, releasing the rosary beads that he'd unknowingly held. He ran his hand over her head once, twice, and then whispered her name as he did it again. She lifted her head, and her eyes appeared tired and bloodshot. She blessed him with the most beautiful, joy-filled smile in spite of the puffy, red splotches that dotted her face and the tangled, matted mess of her hair.

"You're awake."

He nodded. *Ouch.* Everything hurt.

"Thank God. How do you feel?"

"Sore. Tired."

"I should call the nurse, and tell her you're conscious." She had pushed her chair away from the bed, but Chris's next words stopped her from getting up.

"Rebecca, stay with me a minute. I'm scared. I can't feel my legs."

"Are you sure? Maybe they're stiff or—"

"No. I can't move my toes."

"Let me get a nurse."

"In a minute. Can you tell me what happened? How did they find you?"

"I heard the crash." She told him how she'd found a bystander with him, then recounted what they thought were his injuries. "Your family will be on a plane home as soon as they can. They might already be in the air."

Rebecca called for the nurse, who came immediately, followed in a short while by a doctor. After evaluating Chris again, they took him for an MRI. The doctor suspected that Chris's paralysis was temporary due to swelling around his spinal cord, but time would tell.

When Chris was returned to the room it was nearly four o'clock in the morning. He held his eyes open, but just barely, and no sooner had they gotten him settled in bed than he closed them again. Rebecca scooted next to the bed and fished for his hand that had been buried beneath the covers.

"I'm glad you're here," he said before he fell asleep again.

***

The sun slid under the window blinds and right onto Rebecca's face as she slept in the pull-out chair. It took her a few seconds to register where she was. Although the quiet of early morning offered no clues, the smell of antiseptic cleaners gave away her location—the hospital.

Pushing out of the makeshift bed, she shuffled to Chris's side. He hadn't woken up yet this morning. Again, she nudged back the hair hanging on his forehead and ran her hand along his face, feeling a day's growth of beard beneath her fingertips. A small bandage stuck to his right cheek where he had an abrasion.

She reached then for his hand, squeezing his fingers between hers. His warm skin sent a wave of relief through her. He wasn't in danger of dying, she knew, but seeing him lying so still unnerved her. She wished he would squeeze her hand, whisper her name, open his eyes—anything that would offer a connection to him. She stood there for a few minutes, and as she studied his face, the familiar rush of attraction came over her just as it had the first time they met and he expounded on the bountiful varieties of yogurt available.

She smiled and then prayed for him with as much deliberate thought as she could muster. Then she prayed that his family would have a safe return trip.

Unlike her relationship with her dad, Chris's family was supportive and nurturing. He would need them here, particularly if...she didn't want to think it, but it was a possibility. If he didn't regain feeling in his lower body. The thought of Chris being paraplegic made her chest physically ache, and again she pushed the thought aside, not ready to deal with it. A sob choked her, and she breathed deeply, trying to expunge thoughts of Chris never again hiking a mountain trail.

The door opened behind her letting in the noise of a young family passing through the hall. She stepped back expecting to see a nurse returning to check Chris's vital signs. Instead, Father John entered wearing his freshly-pressed, black dress-thingy. She'd have to find out the proper name for it. If it weren't for the worry on his face, she'd have thought him a man ready to conquer the day.

He touched her arm. "Rebecca, I saw your message first thing this morning and got here as soon as I could. You could've called the emergency number."

"He wasn't in imminent danger. I didn't want to wake you."

"Your message said he was in an accident. What happened?"

Rebecca stepped back, letting Father John approach the bed. She told him as much as she knew about the accident and Chris's condition.

"When he woke up, he couldn't...couldn't move his legs."

He winced. "Where are his parents and brother?"

"They're on their way. They were on vacation in Europe. A family trip celebrating his parent's thirtieth wedding anniversary. Chris begged off because he was starting a new job."

"I remember now. He did tell me about the trip, but he didn't name work as his reason for not going."

Rebecca cocked her head. "He didn't?"

"He told me he didn't want to be away from you for that long. He knew he couldn't take you along for a whole host of reasons, so he decided he'd rather stay here."

Tears stung her eyes again. He passed up an opportunity to see Europe with his family because he wanted to be close to her. That was crazy.

She hadn't thought until then what a wreck she must seem. She had fled her apartment before she'd taken her shower last night. Then she had gotten dirty and rain-soaked and spent the night alternately crying and sleeping in a sorry excuse for a bed. She'd have to clean up as best she could after Father John left.

"I think Chris is probably the kind of guy that tells you all the time, but in case he's not, he loves you."

"He is that kind of guy." And what had she given him in return? Not once had he heard the words "I love you" fall from her lips. Father John didn't know how she had failed Chris, never once assuring him of her devotion. Her body crumpled over Chris's where he lay on the bed. Her head rested on his legs, the legs that hadn't moved at his command since he was thrown from his motorcycle. The way she collapsed reminded her of a tent whose poles were pulled out from the pockets. Like a billowing heap, she hit bottom.

A choked cough that could only have come from Father John reminded her she was not alone. She turned to see him losing his own battle with his emotions. His eyes were moist, and he cleared his throat as if by doing so he could swallow away the grief threatening to overcome him.

In an instant, he pulled her into his arms, and she felt

more than heard him succumb to the sobs trying to escape their prison. She squeezed him tighter, ceding whatever strength she had left to him. His visit seemed less like the simple duty of a parish priest, and more like a man scared that his friend's life may have been drastically and irreversibly altered.

After a minute his breaths steadied, and he rubbed soothing circles on her back.

"He's going to be okay, Rebecca. Whatever happens, we have to trust God."

Those words transported her back eight years to a moonless, muggy night alongside a bug-ridden lake. Her legs dangled off the dock, inches above the murky, algae-covered water. Another pair of legs hung next to hers—older, hairier, and decidedly more masculine. He put his arm gently around her and said those same words. "I know it's unfair, Rebecca, and it seems like he's getting off scot-free, but we have to trust God." When she looked into his green eyes, nearly obscured by the darkness of night, she was too inexperienced to recognize what she saw there.

A mosquito landed on her calf and she swatted it. A second later he did the same to a mosquito on his arm. They laughed, and then the hum of the cicadas seemed to swell to a roar as he leaned slowly into her and placed a gentle kiss on her lips.

That memory had lain dormant, lost in her subconscious for years. Despite the sweetness of that kiss, there would be no others, and the summer crush that formed during camp fizzled by the time school resumed less than a month later.

She was grateful for the innocent moment they had shared because it bonded her, however subtly, to the man whose black clothing she now drenched with tears.

"I think God sent you back into my life at just the right time, John."

"He's good at that." This time a little laugh escaped his lips instead of a sob.

Being with someone else who cared about Chris eased Rebecca's tension. She sensed the man who was still holding her up felt it, too.

She backed out of his arms, suddenly aware of how it might look if someone were to come into the room. She wiped her eyes and accepted a Kleenex from the box Father John held out to her. He pulled a couple of the flimsy hospital tissues for himself and set the box back on the tray at the foot of Chris's bed.

After wiping her eyes and nose a few times, Rebecca had an idea. "Chris had his rosary on him. I took it out of the bag last night, and I wanted to pray on it for him, but I don't know how. Maybe you could teach me?"

Father John smiled and dug into his pocket. He pulled a small plastic card out of his wallet and handed it to Rebecca. It had a drawing of a rosary and all the beads labeled with the appropriate prayers. He turned it over in her hand and pointed to the back. "This side lists all the mysteries."

Mysteries? The whole thing was a mystery to her. She'd have to ask Chris for a more thorough explanation later.

"Here, why don't you use Chris's beads?" He took the beads that were lying on the nightstand and handed them to Rebecca. "Start here," he said, grabbing the crucifix, "and we'll work our way up and around. One bead for each prayer. Just follow my lead."

For nearly twenty minutes, Rebecca stumbled her way through the repetitious prayers, at last learning most of the words to the "Hail Mary." She hadn't known what it was all about, but by the end she felt a sense of peace she hadn't before.

Just as they finished and Father John tucked his beads back in his pocket, Chris opened his eyes. "Hey. Two of my favorite people."

Rebecca took his hand and scooted by Father John to the side of the bed. "That timing is too perfect. How long were you lying there awake faking us out?"

Chris gave a weak smile. "Last two decades."

Father John moved closer to the bed. "How are you feeling?"

"Tired, achy, out of it."

"The nurse gave you something for pain last night,"

Rebecca said, stroking the back of his hand. "She said it might make you a little groggy."

"Still can't move my legs."

Rebecca willed herself not to break down again. "It might take a while."

"I'm going to let you two have some time alone," Father John said, looking at his watch. "I've got a couple appointments this morning. Can I anoint you before I go?"

"Is it that bad?" Chris asked.

"It's a sacrament of healing. Doesn't mean you're on death's door. I'd say the severity of your injuries warrants it."

Rebecca's head moved back and forth between them as if she were watching a tennis match. She had no idea what 'anointing' was and why Chris thought it meant he was near death.

"Okay," Chris said. "Please do it then."

For the first time, Rebecca noticed that Father John had brought a small, black case with him. He opened it and withdrew a small vial, a leather-bound book, and a white cloth.

"Latin?" Father John asked, and a little sparkle glimmered in his eye.

"Go for it," Chris said with a weak smile.

Rebecca followed along as best she could, but when Father John switched to Latin, she got lost. He laid his hands on Chris's head and then put oil on his forehead and his hands—those hands she loved so well—and prayed over him. They said the Lord's Prayer—finally, something she knew—another prayer, and then it was over.

Father John left, and she and Chris were alone again. She held his hand, inhaling the fragrant scent of oil as she rubbed it into his skin, and not a word passed between them. Chris seemed calmed by Father John's prayers, and she didn't want to disrupt his peace. The quietude didn't last more than five minutes before Chris's mother burst through the door followed by his father, Alan, and Jamie.

***

Chris felt like he had been hit by a bus although they told him it was only an SUV. Watching his mom and Rebecca worrying about him felt like being hit again from the other direction. After his family had fussed over him for a couple hours and he had coaxed out some of the details from their trip, he insisted they get something to eat and take Rebecca with them. She hadn't eaten the whole time she'd been there. They all needed food and rest, and he needed time alone.

So far he'd been successful at holding himself together. Only pride prevented him from dissolving into a puddle of tears in front of all of them. Finally alone, he felt like he could cry, but he didn't. The tears were frozen by fear, and he entertained all the "what ifs" he'd pushed to the back of his mind. What if I can't walk? What if I can't work? What if I'm impotent and can't marry? What if I never have children? What if Rebecca leaves? What if I need a caregiver?

He knew, given what the doctor had said, that his paralysis was likely temporary. He would probably be fine, but he couldn't dismiss the possibility, however slim, that he wouldn't.

Being left alone to wallow probably hadn't been such a good idea after all. When Rebecca eventually returned, his mood lifted immeasurably.

She kissed the cheek that wasn't covered by a bandage.

"Where's the rest of the gang?"

"I made them go home and sleep. They're exhausted. I told them now that they've seen you're okay they should go home, rest, and get cleaned up so they can come back refreshed tomorrow."

"And they listened?" He couldn't imagine Rebecca giving orders and his family obeying.

"I told you they were exhausted. Alan said something about coming back after he took a shower, but I tried to discourage him."

Chris leaned back into his pillow. His worrying had worn him out nearly as much as his family had, and he wanted to relax with Rebecca for a while before falling sleep.

He sat straight again. "Wait—do you even have your car here?" She said she had walked to the scene of the accident and then hitched a ride behind the ambulance.

"No, Abby and Joel are going to swing by with it this evening."

He nodded. It hurt less now. "Good."

When he tried unsuccessfully to get into a comfortable position, Rebecca leaned in and gently pressed her hand to his back, sliding the pillow up behind his head.

"Thank you," he said and sighed. "Happy as I was to see them, it's kind of a relief now that they're gone."

"I know what you mean. I'm so glad they're back, though. All through the night I was wishing your mom here for you." She settled back in the chair, the legs squealing as she pulled it forward alongside his bed again and took hold of his hand.

They sat in silence for a while before Chris thought he could speak without tearing up too much. "Rebecca, I want you to go home tonight and rest."

"I can stay, Chris. It's more important that your family gets a good night's rest after all their traveling."

"No, it's important you all rest. You, too. I'll be fine here tonight."

Her eyes narrowed and a slight scowl twisted her lips.

"Really, Rebecca. I want you to go home and sleep in your own bed. You can come back in the morning."

"I hate to think of you here all alone."

"I'll hardly be alone. There will be people in and out of here all night long checking on me and everything else. Please. I want you to take care of yourself."

Finally she sighed and relented. "Okay."

Now the hard part. "There's something else I want to talk to you about."

She didn't respond, but she scooted her chair forward another inch and squeezed his hand.

"I appreciate all your prayers, and I think we should pray and hope for the best as far as me getting the feeling back in my legs." He paused, and she gave a little nod while he readied himself for her objections. "But I think we should prepare for the worst."

"No, Chris. You're going to walk. I know it. I can feel it somehow."

"I hope you're right, but just in case, you should think about how it might be... if I don't get that ability back."

He didn't want to make her cry, but the tears fell from her still-red eyes.

"Chris, it's too soon to—"

"Please, Rebecca. I'm not giving up hope, and I don't want you to either. I just want you to think about the fact that things may be different. I may not walk. I may not be able to do a lot of the things I've always taken for granted . . . My future, our future, may look a lot different than either of us imagined." He used her hand to pull her closer. She didn't say anything, but tears rolled down her cheeks, one then the other. "I know we haven't talked about marriage, but I've thought about it. A lot. And I thought if maybe you had, too, well, you should be prepared."

She pulled her hand away and sat back in the chair, folding her arms against her chest. "Fine. You said what you wanted to say, but I don't think we should go borrowing troubles from tomorrow when today has enough of its own. When and if a doctor says with certainty that you won't regain use of your lower body, then we'll deal with it. Even then I would have a hard time believing it. People defy doctors' expectations all the time."

He closed his eyes. That went about the way he expected. At least he planted the seed. He looked at her again, and she unfolded her arms and scooted herself onto the side of his bed. He thought he felt her body press against his thigh, but it must have been the shift of the elevated mattress that he felt behind his back. On instinct, he tried to move over for her, and while his legs didn't move, again, he felt what he thought might be some kind of muscle reaction. It was so slight he dismissed it as wishful thinking. She had placed one of her hands across his lap, and he hadn't felt that at all.

Her other hand stroked his face from his temple to his chin, and he felt that to the core. Her eyes registered affection and thankfully not pity. After a few seconds she leaned in farther and pressed a kiss to his lips.

Except for the seductive kiss that spiraled into their breakup—and even then she'd let him lead—Rebecca had never initiated a kiss between them. That she chose this moment to do so spoke volumes to Chris. Her kiss was as loving as he could imagine, a gentle caress, but he couldn't miss the undercurrent that said, 'I want you' in the most primal, elemental way possible. For the first time since he opened his eyes to the harsh fluorescent lights of his hospital room, Chris felt fully alive. More than that, he felt hopeful. He couldn't help but respond to the balm her kiss spread through his soul and into his body, reviving him, setting his heart to race, and...

"Rebecca," he rasped, breaking off what he would call nothing short of a life-changing kiss, "call the nurse."

20

Hunger for the Great Light

Rebecca paced the hospital hallway from Chris's room to the nurses' station.

An abrasive nurse shot her a look and quipped, "If you want to walk the hallways, you'll have more company up on four at labor and delivery."

Stopping, Rebecca planted her feet against the wall several feet from Chris's room. She had summoned a nurse as soon as Chris had asked. While they waited for the nurse to arrive, he told her he felt some movement.

A glimmer of hope sprouted in her heart, unfurling and blossoming to life. When the nurse arrived, Chris asked if she'd mind stepping outside. She complied and waited outside the room, watching as the nurse left without so much as looking her way. In a few minutes she came back with a young doctor in tow.

Fifteen minutes later, the doctor emerged smiling. He nodded at her but did not invite her back into the room. Nor did the door reopen.

Realizing she could use something to drink, Rebecca decided to visit the cafeteria and get herself an iced tea. She stopped at the chapel on the way back. The nurse would surely be done by then.

When she returned, she heard a man's voice in Chris's room and hesitated until she identified it as Alan's. He sounded tired, but whatever he said was punctuated with laughter—not only his but a woman's. She would recognize that laugh anywhere.

If Alan and Abby were in the room, Chris's need for privacy must have ended. She pressed her palm onto the door, pushed, and stepped inside.

Chris's gaze met hers immediately, and by the dimpled smile on his face, he was happy. Very happy.

"I was ready to send out a search party for you. Good news." His eyes lit with glee. "The doctor expects me to regain all feeling in the next day or so."

Tears flowed again, but these were happy tears, and she squeezed past her sister and moved to the bed to hug Chris and press a kiss to his cheek. Well aware of the company in the room, she stepped back but held onto his hand.

"So, how did it happen?" Rebecca squeezed his hand. "All at once you could move again or is it little by little? Can you move your legs?"

Alan leaned toward Abby, turned his head, and said something in a hoarse whisper just below Rebecca's range of hearing.

Never one to be bothered with decorum, Abby blurted out, "That must've been one helluva a kiss. No man has probably ever been so happy to get an —"

"I really appreciate you seeing Rebecca home, Abby." Chris's words came out rushed and loud in an obvious attempt to shut Abby up. *Good luck with that.*

It was a nice try, but Rebecca was naïve, not stupid. The uninjured side of Chris's face reddened, and he looked like he'd be grateful if his hospital bed swallowed him up then and there. Alan broke the tension with a laugh, and Abby, oblivious to her *faux pas*, said, "What?"

Rebecca felt three sets of eyes on her. They must have seen the irritation on her face because Alan starting making excuses for himself, saying he needed to get some sleep. Abby said she would go get her parking validated and then meet Rebecca in the hall.

"Alan, please don't tell Mom how—"

Alan shook his head. "Don't worry. I still have nightmares that involve her having 'the talk' with me and saying the words 'wet dream.'" He shuddered. "Catch you in the morning."

Alone again, Rebecca pointed a stern glance at Chris. "Why didn't you tell me?" She didn't give him a chance to answer. "Please don't coddle me. I'm not a child. I know how a man's body works."

He tilted his head and cocked an eyebrow. She heard his unspoken question loud and clear. *Then what about that morning on your couch?*

"That had more to do with you being behind me and that whole thing with Jeremy. You know, I'm not as naive as you think I am. It's not like these are the only two times that has happened."

His eyes widened, but he didn't say anything right away. What *could* he say?

"When you sat next to me on the bed, I thought I felt some movement, but I wasn't sure. Then when you kissed me, well, I definitely felt movement, but everywhere at once. I could move my feet, toes and everything. The way Abby put it, well, that's only part of it. I thought it might embarrass you if you were here when I talked to the doctor. To be honest, it embarrassed me. I told Alan because he's a guy, and he's my brother. I thought he had more sense than to tell Abby."

Rebecca took a second to get over herself and realized her initial reaction had been crazy. The man would walk and have full use of his body again. They should be celebrating, not bickering about inconsequential stuff. Maybe all the stress and lack of sleep were catching up with her.

"Listen to me going on about nothing. This conversation is ridiculous." She didn't have to force her smile; she was elated. "You've gotten the best news in the world."

Chris smiled, too. "It is. A slight concussion, a few abrasions, and some temporary paralysis aren't bad considering that I could be dead. God's been good to me."

"Me, too." She sat back down on the bed and gave him a quick kiss. She didn't want to leave him. Not ever.

"Rebecca, last night, my memory is hazy—did you sing to me?"

She stiffened her posture but hoped he didn't notice. "You know I don't sing."

"I do." His disappointment was palpable, and she wished she could tell him something different, but some hurts were too deep. Their roots were long and the tendrils wrapped around every hidey hole where they could get a footing. Someday she hoped that somehow she could get in there and snap the root tips. Today wasn't that day.

"Hey, Abby's waiting. You'd better go."

She nodded but didn't move from the bed.

"They're going to discharge me tomorrow, so go home and sleep, and I'll see you in the morning, okay? At least it'll be Saturday, and I won't feel so bad about you missing work."

"Do you think *I* feel bad about missing work?" She rolled her eyes and then kissed him a final time before heading for the door, where she'd have to endure Abby's inevitable jabs about the miracle kiss that spurred Chris's recovery.

Abby leaned against the wall in the hallway. "There she is, the lady with the lips that make the lame walk again."

Ugh. She wished she'd called a cab.

***

It had only been a week since his accident, but Chris felt as good as ever. The headaches and dizziness caused by the concussion had worn off midweek. There were no lingering effects from the paralysis. The only physical reminder of his accident was the road rash that lined nearly the entire right side of his body: his face, arm, side, and leg. It wasn't pretty, but it was healing.

Rebecca hesitated to accept his offer when he invited her to have dinner with him at his parents' house, but he assured her that the doctors had given him the all-clear. He was more than capable of serving her dinner.

Since their anniversary trip had been interrupted, Chris's parents had decided to spend the weekend at the Spa at the Hotel Hershey. They said they didn't mind him having Rebecca over at their place for dinner. It would be nice to hang out in a real house instead of his shabby apartment.

He heated their whole meal "to go" in the oven and watched the clock, waiting for Rebecca to arrive. He couldn't put his finger on it, but something about the evening had him anxious—in a good way. Of course, he had taken on everything with a new vigor this week. It probably had something to do with the greater appreciation he had for his blessings, especially the pretty brunette one who hadn't wanted to leave his side in the hospital.

When they had finished dinner and the sun began to set, Chris pulled a large, plaid blanket from the cedar chest where his parents kept all the quilts and comforters.

The sun began to go down, and he thought they could lie on the west-facing hillside, watch it set, then stay to watch the stars come out. He knew it was cliché and sounded like a teenage boy's scheme to get lucky, but he didn't care. Watching sunsets and stars held universal appeal for a reason: it was romantic.

Somewhere between the setting of the sun and the rising of the stars, they became distracted by less celestial matters.

"Chris ... Chris. Stop ... Please." The breathy sound of her voice didn't lend much urgency to her command.

"I'm sorry, Rebecca. It's just—I'm crazy in love with you. You're all I think about. And since my accident, well, I'm more conscious of how precious everything is. How precious you are to me and how quickly things can change."

Smiling, she pressed a finger to his lips. "It's okay. Really. You can resume what you were doing in a minute, but there's something I have to say to you, and it can't wait."

Okay. Now she had his attention.

"I've been doing a lot of soul-searching. And I've been praying, like you suggested way back when. I prayed for clarity on a lot of things, and I found it. When you were lying unconscious in the hospital, a lot of things came into focus for me. That first night, when we were alone..." She pursed her lips and closed her eyes for a moment. "I said some things to you that I know you can't recall. I was going to tell you when you woke up, but it didn't seem right to burden you with all that when you had enough on your mind already. And now I need to say these things again, because I want you to remember them."

His heart seized, but he tried to keep his expression neutral. He failed if the look of compassion in her eyes was any indication.

She touched his face. "It's all good. I promise."

Rebecca took a deep breath. "You are without a doubt the best thing that has ever happened to me. You are such a gift from God. And you're all I can think about, too."

There was a pause, and again he dared to hope what she would say next.

"I love you, Christopher."

It was like a long-burning fuse had just burned itself out, and all that was left was the boom. He didn't hear it, but he sure enough felt it. His mouth closed over hers in a kiss, long and intimate. He laid a trail of kisses down from the base of her throat to the top of her chest while his right hand slid under the hem of her skirt. He knew he needed to back off soon, but he allowed himself one more minute. One became two, and two became five.

"What was that light?"

His fuzzy brain barely registered her question.

"Chris?"

He raised himself up on his arms as if doing a push-up. "I don't see anything. Probably the headlights from a car up on the main road." He lowered himself carefully back down alongside her, kissed her neck and relished the feel of her hand running the length of his bare chest. This time the light caught *his* eye, and he raised himself up again.

"Oh, crap."

"What?" Rebecca propped herself up on her elbows, craning her neck to see.

"My dad. With a flashlight." He rocked back onto the balls of his feet and smoothed down Rebecca's skirt. He stood and called to his dad.

"Dad, can you turn that thing off?"

The light bobbed up and down as it grew closer.

"Chris, is that you? What are you doing out here?"

"Looking at the stars."

"What the heck? Why don't you mount your telescope on the deck?"

"Dad . . . I'm, uh, I'm not alone. Rebecca's with me."

"Oh." Then after a beat, a knowing, two-syllable "O-oh. Sorry to intrude. We didn't see your car. Your mother thought she saw something out here, and she wanted me to check it out. I didn't mean to—"

"It's all right, Mr. Reynolds. It's time we went inside anyhow." Rebecca stood and mouthed "button your shirt," to Chris as he grabbed the blanket and shook it out.

He looked down, gave the blanket a final shake and folded it. After tucking it under his arm, he buttoned his shirt one-handed as they crossed the yard toward his dad and the still-glowing beacon.

"I thought they were gone until tomorrow," Rebecca whispered.

"So did I."

"You don't think he saw anything, do you?"

He stopped then and turned to admire how her gauzy white skirt almost glowed in what little light was left. "What was there to see?"

"Well, your hand was edging under my skirt."

"Barely. I'm sure he didn't see anything. Besides, I don't think he cares." He started moving toward the house again, and Rebecca kept pace with him.

"What do you mean?"

"I'm sure he assumes we were having sex and we have been for months."

This time Rebecca stopped. "You let him think that?"

He smoothed out her hair and pushed it behind her ear. "It's not like he thinks there's anything wrong with it. It seems like a lot to get into with him when it's none of his business anyway." If it were *her* dad instead of his, it would be a whole different story, but it wasn't a conversation he wanted to have with his parents right now.

They sat inside and talked with his mom and dad for more than an hour, and he could tell Rebecca was uncomfortable at first by the way she sat ramrod straight and gave terse answers, but before long she had relaxed. His mom, in particular, had seemed to gain a new respect and deeper affection for Rebecca after she'd stayed with him faithfully in the hospital. He hoped it had assuaged any lingering concerns she had about Rebecca being a flight risk. Those days were over. She had found a peace that would keep her anchored to God and, he hoped, to him.

He walked her out to her car where he sat with her while they said goodnight.

"I had a wonderful evening. Dinner was delicious, and I liked looking at the stars with you." She laughed, and he did, too, knowing there had been little stargazing.

"Yeah, I'm sorry if maybe I was a little too aggressive tonight."

She shrugged. "I don't know. It felt right."

He rubbed his hand up and down her arm. "I just...I don't want to put us in the 'occasion of sin,' as they call it."

A trace of guilt nagged his conscience. They *had* already crossed that line.

"I trust us," Rebecca said. "We're not teenagers, and this isn't our first date. I know we wouldn't have let it go any farther."

"No, I don't think we would have. It's just...well, when I converted and started learning right from wrong about a lot of things for the first time, I had some bad habits to break. I don't want to stir up things that create too much temptation for me or for us. I don't want to get in the habit of thinking about you in ways I shouldn't."

He took hold of her hand, and they interlocked their fingers. He hoped she understood. He didn't want to say it out loud. Masturbation was an ugly-sounding word. Thankfully, she seemed to get his meaning. He expected her to minimize the issue or quickly change subjects, but she smiled.

"What are you smiling about?"

"I admire you so much." The squeeze she gave his hand comforted him.

"I admitted how weak I am, and you admire me?"

"You admitted you're human. And you showed me your heart."

"How can I *not* show you? It belongs to you."

Her eyes grew watery. "That's sweet." She ran a finger along his sideburn and down his cheek. "I didn't get to tell you everything I wanted to tonight before you smothered me. There was one more thing." She grinned and her eyes cleared.

"I'm listening now. No smothering."

She reached into the back seat and retrieved a small stack of books, which she placed in his lap. "I'm returning your books, but I have a favor to ask of you."

"Yeah?"

"I thought you could help me. I want to become Catholic, and I don't know how."

"Really?"

"Yes, really." She giggled.

They hadn't even discussed it. Sure, she had taken his books, and they'd had some interesting conversations, but he didn't realize she was even thinking along those lines. "Why?"

"Why?" she echoed.

"Yes, why? Is it because of something you read or something you felt or is it because of me?" If she was doing it just to please him, it wasn't likely to last. He wanted her to want it for herself, to feel that God was calling *her* to it.

That's how it had been for him. What the Church taught about marriage and family appealed to him — it rang true. Despite its unpopularity, it drew him in. He studied various religions, but ultimately he felt *called* to become Catholic.

"All of the above," she said. "The reading has done a good job convincing my head, and you've done a good job on my heart. Even from the first time I went to Mass with you, and I hadn't a clue what was going on, I felt this sense of being at home. I didn't quite understand it like that at the time, but..." She laid a hand on top of his and squeezed. "It's where I belong, which not-so coincidentally, is with you."

That was good enough for him. She'd just mowed over the last roadblock in his heart.

21

Build You A House

"I'm going to run to the ladies' room. If the waitress comes, would you order me a root beer, please?"

Rebecca kissed Chris's cheek, and he and Father John took their seats as she headed for the rest rooms. They had told Father John after Mass about Rebecca's decision to convert, and he had insisted on taking them out to lunch to celebrate.

"You two aren't going to be so sickeningly sweet that I'm going to need a root canal?"

Chris grinned. "Maybe. We're pretty stinkin' happy."

Father John smiled, too. "Good. So, how was your date last night?"

"Excellent. I served Rebecca dinner at my parents' house, and then we sat on a blanket in the backyard for some stargazing."

"So that's what the kids are calling it these days." Father John grabbed the menus from where they were leaning behind the ketchup bottle and handed Chris two.

"That's my story, and I'm sticking to it. Hey, can I ask you something quick before Rebecca gets back?"

"Shoot."

Rebecca was nowhere in sight, but Chris lowered his voice anyway. "I'm going to ask Rebecca to marry me."

"I thought that might be happening soon. Good for you. When are you going to ask her?"

"I'm not sure yet, but there's something I'd like your opinion on. I asked Alan, but I don't know if I agree with him."

"Uh, marriage proposals aren't my area of expertise, but I'll give it a shot."

"It's not that. I'd never given it a whole lot of thought, but I always figured that when I asked a girl to marry me, I'd ask for her father's blessing first. I don't even have a relationship with Rebecca's dad. Frankly, I can't stand him, and I don't think I'm overstating things by saying he hates me. My first inclination was to bypass him completely, but then I thought maybe I could engender some good feelings between us by asking."

Father John stared a couple seconds, tapping his fingers lightly on the menu. "No. Don't ask him. It's a nice enough custom if you want to ingratiate yourself with your future father-in-law, but I wouldn't put it past him to withhold his blessing. Then you're in the position of defying him, which would make matters worse, not better."

"Alan said the same thing. I guess I'm trying to hold onto the hope that he might reconsider his opinion of me."

"Here's the other thing. If this guy is abusive, you don't want him to think he has more power than he does. Rebecca is a grown woman. It's her decision to marry you or not. He has no say in the matter. Don't let him think he does. He's her dad, and he can offer her counsel, for whatever that's worth, but that's about it."

"Okay. I agree. It's between me and her. Thank you."

"Glad to help."

Rebecca walked back to the table, and Chris rose to let her slide into the booth next to him. "Miss me?"

"Always." Chris swung his arm around her shoulders and pulled her closer to him.

Father John rolled his eyes. "I've got my dentist on speed dial."

Chris laughed.

"Your dentist?" Rebecca's eyes darted back and forth between them.

"Never mind," Chris and Father John answered in unison.

"I think for Father John's sake we might want to dial down the syrupy sweetness a notch."

"If I remember correctly, Father John, you actually had a thing for sweets. I seem to remember you with an ever-present package of Swedish Fish on you."

Father John smiled. "That was that summer, huh? I do still like those."

"Good to know." Rebecca smiled and then stopped as she listened intently to the music coming from the overhead speaker. "This song—is it Dave Matthews?"

Father John listened to a few bars. "Isn't this one of those American Idol guys? He had one of those redundant names. Chuck Charles or William Williams?"

Chris laughed. "Phillip Phillips. He's been compared to Dave Matthews a lot." He turned to Rebecca and patted her leg. "You're getting warmer."

Finally the waitress arrived and took their orders for drinks and lunch.

"Hey, Father John, how did it turn out with that tough decision you were telling me about?" Chris didn't want to say too much since he didn't know how much Father John would want to share with Rebecca. The last time they had spoken it had seemed like it was weighing heavily on him, and he didn't want Father John to think he had forgotten.

"Hmmm? Oh—that." He looked at Rebecca and explained in a way that wouldn't exclude her from the conversation. "I had someone come to me for pastoral counseling, but what she really needed was professional counseling." He turned to Chris. "I steered her in the right direction."

It seemed like an awfully pat answer to a problem that vexed him and had him philosophizing about the nature of right and wrong. Before Chris could follow it up with a question, Father John changed the subject.

"So, I've been charged with doing the preliminary interviews for a new youth minister. What do you think I should be looking for?"

And just like that they were on to something else. Either he had worked it all out, or he didn't want to talk about it. If Chris had to guess, he'd say it was the latter.

***

The fall weather had been perfect for day hikes, and that's what Rebecca and Chris had been doing every Saturday for the past month. Chris knew where all the good trails were, and they had hiked through Saint Anthony's Wilderness, a couple of state parks, and even some sections of the Appalachian Trail. After a few rugged climbs, Rebecca realized falling in love with Chris had the unexpected result of getting her in the best shape of her life.

To her surprise, Chris had sold his newly-repaired motorcycle several weeks earlier, so the time they would have spent on the back of his bike cruising two-lane roads along corn fields and apple orchards was freed up for hiking. Today's hike had a steep incline with a series of switchbacks that Chris promised would pay off with a spectacular view of the Susquehanna River north of Harrisburg.

He wasn't lying.

When they reached the top, Rebecca flopped onto a big, cold rock and stared out at the wide, shallow river as it snaked through the valley. Tiny islands dotted the center of the river, and mild riffles created small patches of white in the green water. Jagged rocks jutted from the shores. The trees covering the mountain on the western side of the river were magnificent in their fall brilliance. Reds, oranges, and yellows melded into a pageantry of all that was autumn. As if it knew it couldn't compete with the trees' opulent display, the sky filled with bleak, billowing clouds characteristic of November, a patch of denim-colored sky exposed here and there. Rebecca inhaled the musty fragrance of decaying leaves and savored the unique bittersweet beauty that was fall.

She pulled her water bottle out of her small pack and drank half of it in seconds. Chris took a seat next to her as she pulled her legs up in front of her on the rock. He bumped her playfully with his shoulder. Well, she assumed he meant to be playful, but it left her teetering on the edge of the rock and putting a hand out for balance.

"Can I ask you something?"

"Sure," she said, bumping him back. It didn't have the same effect. He didn't budge. She raised her water bottle to her lips as she continued to look out over the river.

"Will you marry me?"

She did a spit take, coughing and sputtering as Chris's

palm smacked her firmly on the back. "You okay?"

Rebecca nodded and wiped her mouth on her sleeve. He had her full attention now. "Come again?"

His eyes weren't kidding; they were dead serious, and he stretched a hand out and stroked her cheek.

"Will you be my wife?" Seconds passed. His voice grew softer. "Bear my children?" More seconds, and this time his voice cracked. "Grow old with me?"

Blinking slowly, she stared. If he was trying to surprise her, he had succeeded. "How can you be so nonchalant?"

He withdrew his hand and rubbed it on his pants. "Is that how it's coming off? Because I'm dying inside."

After a few seconds to process what was happening, she recognized his apprehension. His brows knit in worry and his eyes searched her face, looking for some indication of which way this was going to go. "If you need some time to think about it . . ."

Her answer tumbled out over his words. "No."

His expression didn't change. "No, you don't need time to think or no, you won't marry me?"

Poor Chris. She needed to think straight and make sense. "No, I don't need time. Yes, I'll marry you."

He relaxed his posture and let out a breath. He smiled at her then, enough for his dimples to show. "Let's make it official."

He slid off the rock and dug in his pants pocket, then knelt on one knee in front of her. Taking her left hand, he slid a white gold band with a huge princess cut diamond onto her ring finger. She covered her mouth with her free hand as she continued to stare at the ring that was so obviously bigger than his salary would allow.

"Do you like it?"

"It's beautiful, but it must have cost—"

"Uh-uh." He shook his head as he took a seat beside her on the rock again. "It's taken care of, and I'm not bringing debt into our marriage."

Our marriage. Her heart skipped. "But Chris—"

It dawned on her then—the only way he could come up with the cash. "You sold your motorcycle for this ring." He didn't deny it, and she knew it was true. "You loved that bike."

He shook his head again. "I love *you.*" He slid his hand along her neck, behind her ear and wound his fingers through her hair.

She closed the small distance between them and kissed her fiancé for the first time. After a couple of minutes, the fiery kiss that started to burn out of control was interrupted by a "Who Let the Dogs Out" ringtone in the distance followed by the sounds of boys' laughter. Chris ended the kiss and looked behind them.

"Cub scouts," he grumbled. "I know their motto is 'be prepared,' but I doubt they have a contingency for finding a couple making out at their hiking vista."

"Probably not." Rebecca grabbed her bottle that had rolled to the ground and stuffed it into her pack. It didn't matter if they headed back down. Whatever the elevation, she knew her head would be in the clouds for days, maybe weeks.

Eight boys in matching orange tee shirts mounted the summit and streamed around the large rock, exclaiming at the view. As Chris and Rebecca vacated the boulder, the boys climbed atop it and hurled small rocks and twigs ahead of them over the mountainside. A couple of haggard-looking middle-aged guys finally caught up with the boys, quickly dropping their packs and their bottoms onto a log. The boys discussed which bones were likely to break if a person fell from the overlook onto the ledge. One of them pointed skyward and yelled, "Look—it's a bald eagle."

Rebecca thought they had most likely mistaken a red-tailed hawk for an eagle, but sure enough, a bald eagle circled the sky above them.

Chris adjusted his pack at the shoulders. "*That* is cool," he said in her ear.

"Maybe it's an omen."

"About what?"

He nuzzled her neck, and she had trouble thinking. "Our marriage."

"Well, it symbolizes courage, strength, faith in God. I guess we'll need all those things."

Before she could respond, a small voice said, "Lady, your boot is untied."

A boy about Ricky's age, thin and tow-headed, pointed at her boot.

"Oh, thank you." She stepped out from under Chris's arm and walked over to a small rock where she could prop her foot while she re-tied her laces. It took her three tries because she kept being distracted by the rock on her ring finger sparkling in a sunbeam that poked through the trees behind her.

Chris spoke to another boy a couple of yards away just loud enough for her to overhear.

"See that pretty girl over there tying her boot? I just asked her to marry me."

"Did she say yes?"

"She did." She could feel the happiness radiating from him when he said it, and she couldn't keep the smile from her face.

"Are you going to kiss her?"

Rebecca glanced over and saw the boy looking up at Chris. The boy scrunched up his face as if it were the most repulsive idea imaginable.

"She might have cooties. Should I?" Chris darted a look her way and winked.

"Yeah!" So much for the revulsion; his head bobbed up and down and his little face lit.

"Is that a dare?" Chris asked.

"Yeah. *Double*-dare."

Chris made an exaggerated sigh. "Okay, but only because it's a dare. A guy can't be too careful about cooties, you know."

She stood and waited for Chris to reach her.

He grabbed her fingertips and squeezed. "I *have* to kiss you. I was dared."

"Double-dared." The kid meant business.

"Oh, well, if it was a dare . . ."

Chris leaned in, and just before his lips touched hers, he pulled back.

"You don't have cooties, do you?"

By now four or five of the boys were gathered around, and the tow-headed kid whispered, "He's going to kiss her."

"No. No, cooties. But I have been bitten by a bug. The love bug."

The boys groaned at her corny joke, and she laughed.

"I'll take my chances," Chris said, before pressing a soft, sweet, and chaste kiss on her lips. Then he whispered in her ear. "It's hard for me to stop at that anymore. We'd better go before we get in trouble."

Then he turned to the boys, stepped in front of Rebecca and waved his hands. "Show's over, boys. No cooties here. Have a good hike."

They smiled at the scout leaders as they headed toward the trail that would take them over the other side of the mountain.

"Did you really just get engaged?" the shorter, stockier of the two men asked.

"Yes, we did," Chris answered him.

They both offered their congratulations, and the taller guy apologized if the boys had ruined their celebration. "Not at all," Chris said, "they made it even more memorable."

He and Rebecca got back on the trail, and when they reached the switchbacks, they took a break. Rebecca leant against a big oak tree and admired the light playing off her diamond.

Chris held her hand. "It looks a lot better on your finger than it looked in the case."

She smiled and then felt it fade as she remembered. "Chris, your motorcycle. I don't need a big ring. Something small and simple would have been fine."

Chris dropped her hand and rested his arm against the tree. "It's not just the ring, Rebecca. It wasn't cheap, but it's not worth as much as the motorcycle. I don't expect your dad to foot the bill for our wedding when he likely won't even approve of it. I'm sure my parents will want to help out, but I still probably can't give you the wedding of your dreams. I'd at least like it to resemble that though. Not to mention I want a long honeymoon with you. At least ten days."

"But Chris, I don't need—"

He stopped her with a hand laid gently over her mouth. "It's not up for discussion. I will happily go along with almost anything for the wedding and the reception, but what's done is done. I'm not willing to reconsider."

When she nodded, he grinned and took his hand away. "Now that you've said 'yes,' which I hoped you would, I have something else I want you to consider."

"What's that?"

"Once we get married, whether we live at my apartment or your apartment or somewhere else, our expenses shouldn't go up much. Rent and utilities are about the same for one or two; I can support us on my income. You don't have to decide now, but I'd like you to think about quitting your job and going back to school. Culinary school or pastry chef school— wherever it is people learn to bake fancy desserts."

Her heart swelled with love for him. "You would do that for me?" Her eyes grew all watery again.

His hand stroked her cheek. "Yes. Rebecca, I want to make all your dreams come true."

"You already have. And I don't need time to think about it. I'll do it. I want to make you proud of me. Baking is something I can do as much or as little as we want when we have children." She threw both arms around his neck and squeezed him tightly. "I love you."

"I love you, too....hey, let's get down this mountain so we can go tell our families."

"Okay." She wiped a few tears from her eyes with her fingertips. "Abby is going to be so excited."

"That reminds me. I do have one non-negotiable stipulation about the wedding and reception."

"What's that?"

"At no time is your sister to have access to a live microphone."

Rebecca laughed. "No argument there."

22

Some Devil

"Dammit, Rebecca. Why did you have to get so good at that?" Chris paced her apartment, alternately running his hands through his hair and drying his palms on his jeans.

"Maybe kissing is one of my hidden talents," she said from the corner of the couch where she fluffed the cushion and rearranged the pillows they had squashed.

Chris stopped and sighed. "I may as well take my pillow and sleep in the confessional for all the time I spend there."

"I thought I was the one with hang-ups. You don't have to run off to confession every time we kiss."

"No," he said on another sigh. "I don't. It's just—" What could he say? She would be his wife in less than two months. He could say the truth.

"There's a certain amount of lust tangled up in my love for you. And, well, I need the extra shot of grace." There. That was most of the truth. Getting so turned on he couldn't see straight and then going home to an empty apartment. She got that, didn't she? He didn't need to elaborate.

He turned back toward her and saw that she got it—if not all the details, she got that despite the fact that they had each committed to the idea before they met, waiting had become difficult for him.

"I'm sorry." Rebecca uncurled her legs, rose from the couch, and placed a hand on each of his arms. "It's not that this doesn't get me going. Believe me, if we were already married, I would have already torn every inch of fabric—"

"Not helping, Rebecca."

"Sorry. Again. I was trying to say I understand. It's not easy for me either." She paused a second and spoke with obvious reluctance in her tone. "Maybe we need to lay off a little bit. No more marathon kissing sessions. We should go out and do something instead of hanging around one of our apartments with nothing to entertain us but each other."

"That's probably a good idea."

She lowered her head until she was in his field of vision again. "It's only seven weeks, Chris. And then we can entertain each other all we want."

"Promise? All day, all night?"

"That's a promise I'll be happy to keep."

***

Chris sat in the retro-looking upholstered green chair alongside Father John's desk. He clasped his hands together and bounced his left knee at a rhythm wildly out of sync with the soothing chant that Father played from his iPod.

"You want a cup of coffee?" Father John already carried two steaming mugs, which he placed on his desk.

"Yeah. Thanks." The coffee was too hot to drink, so Chris inhaled the pungent aroma and clutched the mug between his hands, more to keep them busy than anything else.

"I was surprised to see you at Mass this morning. I thought you were on your way to work this time of day."

"I usually am. I told my boss I needed a couple of hours to take care of some things this morning. He's cool with that kind of thing as long as you don't abuse his generosity."

"Hey, is that Limberlost Lager on tap yet?"

"Another week, I think."

"I need to get a growler of that."

Chris tried a sip of the coffee, burnt his tongue, and set it back on the desk. He stretched his legs out in front of him for a second, crossed them, uncrossed them, and resumed bouncing his leg.

"So," Father John said, his gaze surveying Chris's bouncing leg and nervous fidgeting, "what's up?"

"Can you hear my confession?"

"Sure. Do you want to talk about this first or in confession?" He wagged a finger at Chris's still bouncing knee.

Chris stilled his leg with the palm of his hand and sat straight in his seat. "Doesn't matter."

"So, how many weeks until the wedding?"

"Six. Six weeks, one day, seven hours." He looked down at his wristwatch. "Twenty-one minutes."

"A little anxious, huh?"

"You could say that."

"'What have I gotten myself into' anxious or 'I think I'll go crazy if I have to wait that much longer' anxious?"

"The latter. Definitely." Chris repositioned himself in the chair for the umpteenth time and took a calming sip of his coffee, letting the sounds of chanting monks soothe him before he spoke.

"It's the 'goodnights' and 'goodbyes.' They're killing me. Us. It's like everything has been ratcheted up a notch. Or ten. The goodnight kisses are really...hard."

"That's the word you're going to go with? 'Hard'?"

Chris let out a humorless laugh. "That would be the most accurate I suppose, but maybe 'difficult' would be a better word choice."

"What's changed?"

"It's not enough anymore. The hand holding, the chaste kisses. Even the not-so-chaste ones. They're going on longer. Hands are straying places they haven't wandered before. I don't want to let her go, and we've still got six weeks left."

"I can't help think sometimes that things were simpler when people got married without these long engagements. Not that yours is long by comparison. Unfortunately, most people are so ill-prepared for what marriage means that it's best that we give them a little time to stop and think."

"Believe me, we're not into long engagements. We're making this as short as the Church will let us."

Laughter and loud conversation from people passing by Father John's office momentarily distracted Chris. Maybe this visit was a waste of time. He didn't know what he expected to get out of it, but there had to be something he could do to bolster his restraint and self-control.

"It was easy to say we wanted to wait until we were married when we were getting to know each other, but it's something else altogether to feel the love of my life lying in my bed, nestled in my arms at two o'clock in the morning and resist showing her how much I love her in every way possible."

Father John held a hand up. "Back up. You're sleeping together?"

"A couple of times. Like Monday night. She stopped by my apartment after work. We had dinner, worked on some wedding stuff, watched TV, and then when it was time for her to go that nasty thunderstorm with the tornado warning hit. I insisted that she stay."

"I'm guessing she didn't object to that."

Chris gave a rueful smile. "Not much."

"Okay. I get the storm. It was a bad one, but sharing a bed? You're asking for trouble."

"It didn't start out that way. I took the couch, but then sometime during the night, the lightning or something woke me. I went to check on her. I just wanted to see her sleeping in my bed. She was so beautiful. So peaceful. Somehow I must have woken her, because she opened her eyes, and then she lifted the covers for me to climb into bed with her. I didn't have the will to refuse."

"All right. No more of that." Father John set his coffee down and wiped his hand over his face. "But you knew that already. No more spending the night together short of an emergency, and then not in the same bed. Pray together every time you're together. Pray for your marriage. Pray for the grace to resist temptation. If it comes down to it, one of you may just need to leave. And last, come to confession. Once a week until the wedding doesn't seem like too much to me. Both of you. You need the sacramental grace."

Chris glanced at his watch again and rubbed his palms over his thighs. "I have to get to work. Those are good suggestions. Rebecca won't go to confession to you though. She says it feels weird."

"Go wherever you want, just go."

Rebecca had a lot fewer issues with sacramental

confession prior to converting than he did. Chris had nearly driven Father John crazy with his objections before he realized it was his pride standing in the way. Since she entered the Church at Easter, Rebecca seemed to have taken to confessing her sins aloud with ease. Her only reservation was Father John hearing her confession.

"Yeah, okay." Chris kneaded his hands together, and frowned at the amused look on Father John's face. "Are you laughing at my predicament?"

"No, not at all." Father John suppressed his grin and leaned back in his leather chair. "Just thinking about something an old monsignor once said to me. Holiest man I've ever met, bar none. He told me this before I entered the seminary, while I was still trying to ignore God's call."

Father John leaned his arms on his desk and adopted the manner and voice of a crotchety old man. "He said, 'Son, don't start the engine if you're not going to bring the car out of the garage'."

Chris bit the inside of his cheek to hide his grin as he imagined a young Father John being chastised by the old priest.

"I know there are different considerations for casually dating teens as opposed to two adults whose marriage is imminent, but I think it's still good advice. It sounds to me like you two are not only starting the car, you're revving the engine and then slamming on the brakes. One of two things is going to happen. Either the brakes are going to fail and you're going to burst right through the garage door or you're going to asphyxiate in the garage... maybe blow out your engine...kill the transmission?"

"Okay, okay. I get it. No more car metaphors."

"Chris, it will all work out. Really. You're in the home stretch now, so to speak."

A buzz came over the intercom on Father John's phone followed by the voice of the secretary, Erica.

"Father John, there's a call for you on line two. Kimberly Mitchell's mother, Myrna. Says it's urgent."

"Okay," Father John answered. Then to Chris, "Hang on a second. I should take this."

Chris checked his watch again and leaned back in his chair. He really did need to get going soon. He was glad he came, though. Father John gave him concrete things they could do that would help keep them from going too far. Outside the window, the morning clouds dissipated, and the sun broke through. He wondered what weather was forecast for the weekend.

The urgency in Father John's voice tore Chris out of his own thoughts.

Father John rattled off a stream of questions: "Is she conscious? Do they think she's suffered any brain damage?"

Given the conversation Chris overheard, he felt increasingly awkward. He stood and moved to leave, but Father John motioned him back to his seat.

"Okay. I'll be there shortly. Thank you, Myrna."

Father John hung up the phone and dropped his head into his hands. "This is my fault."

"What happened?"

Father John looked up, the strain in his face evident. "I need you to keep this confidential. Between you and me."

"Of course." Chris had never seen Father John this unnerved. He was remarkably even-tempered despite the wild ups and downs of his days. He could leave a wedding to go to a funeral home, counsel a couple on the brink of divorce and baptize a baby the next morning. He seemed to take it all in stride. Something about this was personal, and it ate at him.

"A young woman, married less than a year, came to see me. She wanted to talk to me about her marriage—specifically her abusive husband." He sighed and shook his head. "Chris, I notice beautiful women all the time. They come up in the communion line for goodness sake, but never since the day I accepted God's call to the priesthood have I felt any real attraction to a woman. I figured it was all part of the honeymoon phase of my priesthood. There was no attraction, no temptation. I saw a beautiful woman and admired her as

God's handiwork with not an iota of desire. I knew it wouldn't last, and it didn't. It was over the day this woman, Kimberly, came to see me."

What was Father John saying? He wouldn't have broken his vows. *Chris* needed help resisting temptation, not Father John. "I know you know this, but there's nothing wrong in being tempted. Jesus was tempted."

"It's not that. It's how I reacted to the temptation."

Father John stood and walked to the window. Several seconds passed before he tucked his hands into his pants pockets beneath his cassock and turned back to Chris. "Because it hadn't happened in so long, what I felt for her caught me off guard. She's beautiful, Chris. Blond hair, blue eyes, the sweetest, softest smile. Long legs. The whole package."

Chris had only heard Father John talk about a woman in that way once when he had casually mentioned an old girlfriend.

"She's a lovely person, too. Comes to Mass every Sunday and volunteers at a crisis pregnancy center. She gets married, and this guy does a total one-eighty. He started smacking her around, keeping her from her family and friends. She confided in a couple of people, friends, and they didn't believe her. They insisted she misinterpreted things, that her husband would never do that."

"So what happened?"

"She wanted to talk to me. Now, ordinarily, I would refer someone like that to Catholic Charities for professional counseling, but she insisted she didn't want to go there. She couldn't see herself as some kind of victim. She didn't think she needed professional help; she was adamant she wouldn't go there. She just wanted some pastoral advice."

So, this was the dilemma that had been brewing for months. So far it sounded like Father John had done everything right.

"Instead of meeting with her and encouraging her to see a professional counselor as well, because of my attraction to her, I cut her loose. I told her I couldn't help her and refused to schedule another appointment with her.

"Chris, the look on her face. I may as well have slapped her myself. I didn't even think of how that kind of rejection might harm her relationship with the Church. I tried to soothe my conscience by telling myself I fled temptation, but in truth I was selfish. I wasn't going to act on what I felt. Not in a million years. Nor was it some kind of mutual thing. She came to me for guidance, but because of my discomfort, she went back home to her husband with no more support than she had come in here with."

"What happened? What was the call about?"

"Her mother found Kimberly this morning beaten so badly that she's in a coma."

Chris let out a breath and shook his head. He'd never understand how a man could do that to a woman he supposedly loved. "I'm so sorry. I get how you feel like it's your fault. I really do. But you can't do that. Maybe you could have handled it better, but the only one responsible for her condition is the man who hit her."

Father John nodded, but Chris doubted he agreed.

"Listen, I want to go to the hospital. At least maybe I can offer some comfort to her mother. Before I go, let me get my stole, and I'll hear your confession."

"No, that's okay. Go. I've got to get to work anyhow. I'll come by tomorrow morning during the scheduled hours."

"Thanks. And I appreciate you listening. Father Richard's a good enough guy, but I don't have much of a connection with him like I do with you or some of my other brother priests."

"No problem. I'll see you tomorrow morning. And I'll pray for Kimberly."

For her sake and for Father John's, he hoped she'd make it. Because if she didn't, he had a feeling Father John would blame himself.

23

Lover Lay Down

With less than a month to go before the wedding, Chris's stress level ratcheted through the roof. He pulled up outside the neat split-level home with white siding and brown shutters and rubbed his hand over his forehead. He could use a beer. Because of a tank problem, he had been called in to work, and it had thrown off his whole day. He missed confession, and there hadn't been time to clean his apartment or stop at the tuxedo shop like he'd planned.

He looked again at the house and didn't see any movement. It belonged to Craig, a childhood friend of both his and Alan's. He and his wife bought the home three months ago, and this was the first he'd seen it. He noticed Alan's car in the driveway, along with three others, two of which he recognized. He hoped Alan hadn't overdone it or gone against his wishes. While Chris would have preferred something small, low key, and memorable like camping, a rafting trip or even a night out at a couple of bars, Alan insisted he had to have a bachelor party, so he relented.

A month before Alan's wedding, Chris had spoken to him about what he'd like to do to celebrate, and Jamie had given him a list of the local men invited to the wedding. Chris rented a room at a restaurant and bar. It was simple, but it served its purpose.

Three hours into the festivities, when everyone was feeling good, a blond girl appeared at the entrance to the room asking for the Reynolds party. They summoned Chris since he was the best man. The young—*very young*—woman identified herself as the hired entertainment for the evening and asked him to point out the groom. It caught Chris completely off guard. He didn't know who had enlisted her or what exactly she would do, but apparently it had been prearranged and paid for by someone, so he let her proceed.

She looked like she might be pretty if she hadn't had on so much makeup. Instead she looked a little skanky, but that didn't prevent her from getting the men's attention when she removed her coat and revealed a skimpy black teddy with black fishnet stockings. Chris hung around for half of her "performance," but when she proceeded to give his brother a lap dance, he left the room.

Chris didn't go for that kind of thing. *Nothing says "I'm about to make a lifelong commitment to love and honor" like letting a nearly-naked, possibly underage girl that you've never met before rub herself all over your genitals, right?* Then there was the fact that when Jamie found out and everything hit the fan, he didn't want to be held responsible. The more he could do to distance himself from the debacle, the better. Or so he thought.

The kicker had come the next day when he sat at Alan and Jamie's kitchen table and learned that Jamie had hired the girl as her wedding gift. And Alan had sure enjoyed it. Chris didn't know if their mother ever got wind of it, but if she had, she would've given Alan the tongue-lashing of his life.

The whole thing struck him as supremely messed up, and tonight it made him nervous. He had been clear with Alan that he didn't want anything like that. Just the guys and some drinks. A pool table or a dart board would be good, too.

Chris saw no sign of Craig, but a sign next to the door said, "Party downstairs." He let himself into the split entry, and laughter and heavy metal music billowed up from below. The place already reeked of beer and cigars. Craig's wife was going to love this. At the bottom of the stairs he crossed the hall to a wide-open family room with a humongous flat screen TV, a couple of couches and an entertainment center on his right. On the opposite side of the room stood a bar.

From the first call of "Get the groom a beer," Chris never saw the bottom of his cup. Once the party was in full swing, about twenty guys were evenly split between a Stanley Cup playoff game on the TV and the keg next to the bar. Chris gave them a hard time about not having any Gateway beer, but even aside from the keg, someone had purchased a nice selection of bottled beers, not to mention hard liquor.

As he tilted the first full SOLO cup to his lips, Chris thought of Rebecca. He remembered how uncomfortable she'd seemed about the alcohol consumed at Alan and Jamie's wedding. She had loosened up a lot since then, and they would be serving alcohol at their own wedding reception in a few weeks, but he thought she would still feel tense if she were with him.

In the beginning, even his drinking a couple of beers made her uneasy, but she needn't have worried. Chris didn't get drunk.

Twice in his life he drank enough to be considered inebriated. He celebrated his twenty-first birthday by consuming so much alcohol he vowed to never drink near that much again. Only two weeks later, Jamie drove him home from a party at Alan's apartment while he vomited into a bag on his lap. He had no intention of overindulging that night, but every time he refused a drink or said he'd had enough, his "friends" doubled their efforts to get him to drink.

After that he got smart. He liked being in control of himself and not having to worry about saying or doing something stupid or dangerous while under the influence. His strategy included never turning down a drink. Instead he held onto a cup. No one noticed if he nursed two or three beers or a couple of ginger ales the entire night. As long as he imbibed they were happy, and they left him alone. That had served him well in the past, but not tonight.

They were all adults now, and no one really cared what or how much he drank, with one exception: Megan's brother, Tim. Chris knew he was not on the wedding guest list, but Alan must have invited him to the bachelor party anyway. It seemed that neither he nor Megan could pass up free booze.

Chris didn't know if Alan had tipped him off, but Tim actually looked in Chris's cup and sniffed it to see how much and what he drank. If beer didn't fill the cup to the brim, he topped it off. The one time Chris had covered his cup with his hand, Tim poured a beer right over it, letting it splash over his fingers and onto the carpet. The guy was so intent on seeing him sloshed, he wondered if it had something to do with Megan and the fact that despite her interest, she and Chris had never gotten together.

To make matters worse, if someone made a toast, he foisted a shot on Chris. He found it difficult to say no when the toast honored him. Even so, a few hours into the party Chris had sipped so slowly, filled enough glasses with ginger ale, and thrown enough shots into houseplants that he was by no means drunk. Still, enough alcohol had passed his lips that he knew he shouldn't drive home. He could stay longer while the alcohol wore off, but Tim would be there forcing more on him. Around midnight, he called Rebecca and asked her to come get him. Given the hour, he hated to ask her, but she didn't live far away. Besides, he hadn't seen her in three days, and he missed her.

A half hour later her car pulled up outside. He had already said his thanks and goodbyes even though only about half the guys had left. It had been a good chance to catch up with some friends that he probably wouldn't have time to talk to at the wedding, and at least no stripper or lap dancer had shown up. He was grateful Alan had honored his wishes.

Chris rushed out the door to meet Rebecca so she wouldn't have to come in. He had told her it was smoky, and she wouldn't like it, but he also didn't want his fiancée in a room of drunken men. They were decent guys, but why invite trouble?

She stood outside of her car under the diffused light of the street lamp. He could see only her silhouette. Every last curve looked like it was carved in relief. From across the yard he couldn't make out what she was wearing, but whatever it was, it looked tight and clingy and unlike anything he had ever seen her in before. Before his imagination had a chance to take over where his eyes had left off, she reached into the open window of her back seat and pulled out a long, sleeveless shirt, which she stretched over her head and then pulled down over her hips. *Drat.*

"Hey, there," she said. "How bad off are you?"

At that point, he had come under the soft light of the street lamp, too, and could see she wore some kind of stretchy black exercise clothes under the shirt. He thought she must be cold, given the cool spring night.

"Not so bad. I just don't want to take any chances by driving." He couldn't take his eyes off her. "You look like you've been exercising." Maybe that's why she didn't appear to be cold.

She looked down at her clothes and her long ponytail bobbed up and down. "Oh, yeah."

"Isn't it kind of late?"

"It's never too late to exercise when you're having your wedding dress altered the next day."

He shook his head. What was she worried about? She was perfect, and the dress would look perfect, too.

"I stayed late at work trying to get things organized for when we're on our honeymoon, which made my dinner really late. I wanted to let my food digest, and so, I was exercising at midnight. At least until you called."

"Sorry I interrupted you." He moved in close to her, bent his head and kissed her. Wow. Maybe it was the buzz he had going or maybe it was the feel of the slippery spandex pants his hands grazed on the way to her waist, but only one word described that kiss: hot.

She pulled away and laughed. At him? "Let's go. You can hang out at my apartment until this stuff wears off. You smell like a distillery, by the way."

"Does it turn you on?" He was joking. Sort of.

She let out a sharp laugh. "Hardly. I call first dibs on the shower because it's mine, and I'm sweaty, but you're up next."

She opened her apartment door with her key, and they stepped into the dark entryway. Rebecca kicked off her shoes, and turned on a lamp. Her apartment smelled fresh and clean, and he sniffed the cheap cigar smoke clinging to his clothes and skin. He still couldn't keep his eyes off her and wished she had never thrown that shirt on over those slinky clothes. The loose-fitting shirt had arm holes so large that when she sat in the car, the insubstantial fabric couldn't hide the sports tank she had on underneath. He bet it felt as smooth as her pants. He tried to shove his hands in his pockets to keep them out of trouble, but they were full.

He lifted a small sample bottle of liquor out of each pocket. "I almost forgot. Alan gave me these. He said Jamie promised them to you."

She took one of the small dark bottles from his hand and read the label. Then she laughed. "I forgot all about these. Jamie promised me I would love chocolate liqueur." She screwed the top off one and sniffed it. "Do I drink it straight?"

"You can. Or you can mix it."

"I'll try it straight." She lifted the little bottle to her lips and winced as if she were anticipating an awful taste. A couple seconds later, she lowered the bottle and said, "That's not bad. It's smooth and yummy."

Chris grinned.

"Do you want a sip?"

"No thanks, I've had enough, remember?"

"Oh yeah." She finished off the small bottle herself. "I'll save the other one." She set it on the counter.

She undid her ponytail and ran her hand through her hair as she sauntered toward the bathroom.

"I'll be out in a few minutes." She gave him a devastating smile.

Maybe it was the racing of his heart interacting with the depressant quality of the alcohol, but he felt almost woozy.

The water in the bathroom ran and the door shut. He walked over to her small computer desk and shook the mouse. Selecting the music playback app, he logged himself in and selected one of his favorite playlists. Some soft rock music played. He took a seat on the couch, leaned his head back, and closed his eyes. Three weeks from tonight, he would be a married man. The wedding and the reception would be over, and they'd be on their way.

He started to drift off when she called to him from the shower.

"Chris, could you put out a towel for me? I forgot."

"Sure." His voice sounded a little groggy and raspy. *Darn cheap cigars.* He entered the bathroom, the steam hitting him in the face, and retrieved a towel from the cabinet beneath the sink.

"So, do you sing in the shower?"

She hesitated and then said, "I guess that's for me to know and you to find out."

He grinned. Coy. He liked it, and it was the closest he'd gotten so far to getting her to sing. He looked down and noticed Rebecca's clothes laid on the floor—a pile of spandex pants, athletic socks, and a sports tank topped with discarded lace and satin strung together with bits of red fabric. He'd bet those panties were the product of this morning's lingerie shopping with Abby. He had a hard time not envisioning Rebecca modeling it all for him.

He flung a clean towel over the rail outside the shower.

"Thanks." Her voice was muffled by the running water.

Inches away from him on the other side of the curtain, Rebecca was naked. He imagined her pulling her fingers through her wet hair as she rinsed it, water running down her ...he cleared his throat and gave his head a little shake. He should leave. He had put out the towel like she'd asked. He should leave, but he didn't have the will to do it.

"You're right about me needing a shower, too. Craig passed around these stinky, cheap cigars."

"Well, it's all yours as soon as I'm done."

He didn't know where the next words came from. He didn't even think them; they just flew out of his mouth. "I have a better idea. And it will save water and time." He yanked his shirt over his head, and added it, his jeans, socks, and underwear to the pile on the floor.

"What's that?"

He peeled back the shower curtain and stepped into the shower with her.

Stunned. That was the only word for her reaction. Her

eyes darted up and down as if she didn't know where to look. She wrapped an arm around her midsection as if it could cover her exposed skin. He placed his hand on her wrist, withdrawing her protective arm, and before she had a chance to say anything, his lips were on hers.

Chris had never experienced anything so sensual in his life. The herbal smell of her shampoo. The feel of her velvety wet skin under his fingertips. The sound of the shower as it pattered on their bodies and the curtain. The taste of chocolate liqueur on her lips. And most of all the sight of her. Rebecca, wholly and completely as God had made her—utterly beautiful.

By the time they had emerged from the shower he knew how the night would end. He couldn't conceive of anything other than taking her in his arms, laying her down on her bed and making love to her. If any contrary thought niggled its way into his brain, it quickly died of neglect.

He led her to her bedroom where he dragged his hands through her still damp hair, and she communicated nothing but her desire for him. He couldn't sense the slightest bit of hesitancy in her eyes, her touch, or on her lips. The music from the other room poured in, its relentless beat and frantic rhythm driving him. He couldn't have chosen a more fitting soundtrack if he'd tried. He'd listened to this song dozens of times and never noticed its eroticism. The singer's ardent falsetto was tinged with a gentle desperation as he sang of lips, love, and crashing waves. A nebulous sense of inevitability permeated both the music and Chris's mind.

Rebecca breathed heavily against his face, and moving her lips against his cheek, she asked, "Dave Matthews?"

He hadn't even thought of it. A low laugh rumbled through his chest as he clasped each of her hands in his, pinning them above her head as she climbed back onto the bed. He leaned down to kiss her neck as he answered. "Yes, Dave Matthews."

It felt so good, so true, and so right.

Until it didn't. He didn't know how long they lay there together, but when he held her in his arms, her head resting on his chest and her arms wrapped around him, the depth of his feeling for her and what they had shared overcame him. He kissed her head and squeezed her, smiling at the contented sigh she released. He studied his arms protectively around her, and as his heart rate returned to normal, his gaze settled on his hand.

It had been near perfect. Better than he had expected in every way. With one glaring exception. And then it hit him with full force. His bare hand. His wedding band (and its smaller companion) resided in a small bag at the back of his sock drawer, where it would remain until his wedding day, when he would wear it as a sign of his love for and fidelity to Rebecca. The night would have been perfect. Save for one thing—Rebecca wasn't his wife.

She must have felt him tense because she lifted her head to look at him.

"I know," she said, and the regret that hung in her tone told him she understood completely, and she shared his guilt.

After a few moments of silence he blurted, "I have to go."

Rebecca seemed startled as he pulled himself from her embrace and sat up. She looked pained as she sat up, too, pushing her damp hair behind her ears.

"I know it was wrong, Chris. I regret it, too, but please, please stay with me tonight."

"I can't." He didn't like being short with her, but he would suffocate if he didn't get out of her apartment. He grabbed his clothes off the bathroom floor and dressed. Rebecca, still not wearing anything, followed him out to the living room.

"Please, Chris. Please don't leave me tonight. I need you here. Stay with me."

"Why, so I can wake up in the middle of the night and feel you next to me, and repeat everything that just happened?" He hated how angry his voice sounded. He had to get out. Now.

"No. No, I just feel—"

"For God's sake, Rebecca, put something on, will you?"

She looked down, suddenly shamefaced, and tears sprung

from her eyes. She covered her mouth as a sob escaped. And instead of taking her in his arms, holding her close, and comforting her, he turned and ripped the quilt from the back of her couch and tossed it to her. He headed for the door, nearly tripping on a pile of wedding presents amassed in the entryway. It was the middle of the night, he was half drunk, and he had no idea how he would get home. He only knew that he couldn't stay there.

***

Rebecca had known from the sudden quiet that something was wrong. For the last half hour, Chris had done nothing but tell her he loved her. He couldn't stop saying it. Then he grew silent, and she knew he felt it, too—the guilt.

What should have been a beautiful expression of their married love was, in hindsight, a stark contrast. It was a sin. Rebecca felt conflicted—sorry that they had offended God, had betrayed their convictions, and given in so easily to temptation—did they even try to resist? But yet she felt loved—more than that, cherished. She had no idea that Chris could be so tender yet, at the same time, so passionate. She shuddered when she recalled the feel of his hands on her bare skin. She thought she'd be nervous on their wedding night, but from the moment his lips had touched hers in the shower she hadn't felt even a twinge of anxiety, only a compulsion to keep going, to give herself completely, finally, to the man she loved.

She glanced at her nightstand and noticed the basal thermometer lying there. She and Chris had been learning a natural method for spacing children, and she had been recording her waking temperature each morning and charting her fertility markers. They were ready for a baby right away, but based on the suggestion of another couple at their parish, they decided it would be easier for them to learn the method now rather than later while she breastfed a baby. She jumped from the bed and quickly opened the drawer, unfolded her chart and studied it. Suddenly their utter lack of control after all these months made some sense.

She was ovulating. No wonder her resistance was so low.

He drank a few too many beers, and there she slunk around in poorly-concealed Spandex, reeking pheromones. She drank that bottle of liqueur. She even invited him into the shower, albeit to put out a towel, but still. So many bad decisions. Why couldn't she have stepped out of the shower and grabbed a towel herself? What was a wet bath mat compared to your immortal soul?

She had to call Chris. Maybe he wouldn't be so hard on himself. She called, but he didn't answer. She texted and got no response. Six messages and more than fifty hours later, she still hadn't heard back from him.

24

Fool to Think

Tuesday morning, Rebecca opened the door to Abby and her kids. "We're dropping off a couple of wedding presents. Somehow they keep ending up at my house. Probably Aunt Maggie's fault." She wrinkled her brow and looked Rebecca up and down. "I thought you'd be at work."

"Home sick."

"Okay, kids. Back up." Abby shooed her children behind her and switched the baby to the arm farthest from Rebecca.

Rebecca sighed. "Come in. It's more of a mental health day. I'm not contagious."

Giving her sister a wary glance, Abby motioned for her kids to step in and followed them as Rebecca closed the door behind them. Rebecca went to the bookshelf and retrieved a new puzzle she had bought for the kids' next visit. "Why don't you guys take this and work on it at the kitchen table?"

Ricky plucked it out of her hands and made a beeline for the other room, Emma on his heels.

Rebecca took the baby from her sister's arms and kissed his chubby cheeks before hugging him tightly. Tears threatened to spill out of her eyes.

"What are you making? It smells heavenly."

"Oh, there are macaroons, marble cheesecake brownies, and there's a lemon Bundt cake in the oven now."

"What the heck, Rebecca? Are you having a bake sale? Because if you eat all that you're never going to fit in your wedding gown."

The tears fell at the mention of her wedding.

Abby took the baby back, sat on the couch, and waited for Rebecca to join her.

"So, do you want to tell me what's got you so upset that you've resorted to maniacal baking?"

Rebecca wanted to use an innocent-sounding euphemism:

"Chris spent the night" or "Chris and I slept together," but Chris had neither stayed nor slept. Could she say they "made love?" That's how she had thought of it at the time, but in the light of day when she hadn't heard from him since, she wasn't so sure. Only one honest answer came to mind, and she blurted it out.

"Chris and I had sex."

Abby took a hard look at her. "And it was that bad?"

"Abby." She knew Abby's opinions on premarital sex all too well. In spite of that, she had hoped Abby would be supportive, not laugh it off.

"Cause I always imagined he'd be good in bed."

The blood drained from Rebecca's face. Here she sat, her heart riddled with shame, hurt, and fear and the best her sister had to offer was either to make light of the situation or, even worse, admit she lusted after Chris.

"Abby, he's my fiancé. He's going to be your brother-in-law." As she said it, she half-wondered if that was even true anymore.

"I'm sorry, but you can't bring home a guy like him and not expect me to wonder. What's the big deal anyway? The wedding's in three weeks."

"You don't get it at all. I thought you and Joel waited."

"We did. It was more his thing than mine. We had already done everything *but* that anyway. He wanted our wedding night to be special. It wasn't such a big deal to me. What happened?"

"Spandex, hormones, pheromones, and alcohol."

"You had me at Spandex. I want details."

Rebecca sprung from the couch and started pacing the small room. "Abby, I have no intention of discussing that with you now or ever. It's what happened afterward." The tears started to fall again.

"What happened?" From Abby's pinched expression, Rebecca thought she had finally realized the seriousness of the matter.

"Waiting until our wedding night was important to both of

us. We've been very careful about it. Then Saturday night we were both drinking and..." She debated how much she should say. "We used really poor judgment and exercised no self-control whatsoever."

Abby's face sagged with disappointment at the lack of details. Too bad.

"As soon as it hit us what we had done, Chris emotionally withdrew. He couldn't get out of here fast enough. I've been calling and texting him since then, and he won't respond." Rebecca sobbed as quietly as she could into her hands so as not to draw the attention of her niece and nephew.

Abby's free hand rubbed her back. "You haven't talked to him since?"

Rebecca shook her head and quickly grabbed the box of tissues from the coffee table.

"That numskull."

"Abby, what if he...if he doesn't...he doesn't love me anymore? The wedding ..." A fresh round of tears formed, and Abby pulled her into a hug.

Rebecca felt a tugging on her leg.

"Aunt Becca, you crying."

Sweet little Emma. Rebecca pulled away from her sister and wiped her eyes. "Yes, sweetie, I'm sad."

"Why you sad?"

"I feel like I've lost my best friend."

Her little niece was supposed to say something tender and insightful, wise beyond her years. Instead she said, "I poopy."

Rebecca sniffed and got a whiff of the horrific odor emanating from the little girl's rear. Her eyes grew teary again from the stench.

Abby excused herself to change the offending diaper, and Rebecca sunk back into the couch. Now that she had begun to verbalize her fears, they were all running roughshod over her wounded heart. What if Chris didn't want her anymore? Maybe he had lost his respect for her. The wedding was less than three weeks away; everything was paid for and in place. She didn't think she could bear the embarrassment of calling it all off.

In a minute, Abby returned rubbing moisturizer into her clean hands. "Sorry about that. The demands of motherhood stop for nothing and no one. You'll see."

"Will I?"

"What's that supposed to mean? Listen to me." She waited until Rebecca lifted her teary eyes to look at her, and then Abby took both her hands in her greasy palms and squeezed them.

"I don't know what's going on with Chris. You guys are both such goody-goodies it's hard for me to imagine this happened let alone that he is acting like such a blockhead about it. But I do know this: That man loves you, and that doesn't change overnight. I would bet his absence has more to do with him than you."

"What do you mean?"

"I'm guessing he initiated it, right?"

Rebecca thought back to the shock of him climbing into the shower with her. Him leading her to her bedroom. "Yes, but I didn't object."

"Doesn't matter. He feels responsible, Rebecca. Guilty. Probably ashamed of himself. If he was sober enough to do the deed, he was sober enough to know what he was doing."

Rebecca's face heated. They had known *exactly* what they were doing. He may not have been in condition to drive home from Craig's, but neither of them was really drunk. The alcohol obliterated their inhibitions. No, their consciences.

Abby squeezed her hands again. "Am I right?"

"Yes."

"Then that's it. I know it is." Abby released her hands and scooped Ian off the floor where he teethed on Rebecca's dirty flip-flop. "He's had enough time for self-flagellation or whatever you guilt-ridden fish eaters do behind your hair shirts."

Leave it to Abby to offer comfort with a hearty side of religious slurs. She reached for her purse on the floor, pulled out her cell phone and started tapping. "This has gone on long enough. I don't give a hoot about his guilt trip. He needs to man up and get his keister over here."

***

Father John pinned Chris with a solemn look. "Well, your first sin may have been fornication, but now I think you've followed it up with a total lack of charity."

"What do you mean?"

"Chris. You made love to your fiancée, and then you left her there when she told you she needed you. I understand you wanted some time to sort things out, but that was two days ago. You haven't even reached out to her to see how she's doing. Hasn't she called you?"

"She's left me six messages, but I haven't listened to them."

Father John massaged his brow with his fingertips. "Chris, set aside your own guilt and shame for a minute. Think about the conversations we've had about Rebecca and the skewed view she had of sex. She has no recollection of having two loving parents in the home, so she had no example of married love. Her father is a verbally abusive man whose streams of vile putdowns seem to center on Rebecca's imperfections and baseless accusations of 'whore,' slut,' and the like. He twisted her notions of purity, chastity, propriety, and sin at every possible turn. And to top it off, she had well-meaning abstinence educators telling her girls who committed sexual sins were no better than a used tissue or chewed up bubble gum.

"Now, I know she's been tearing through Theology of the Body books, and you've had a tremendous positive influence on her, but think about this from her perspective. She finally caves. Finally falls. And instead of you holding each other up, you leave her even when she begs you to stay. How do you think that made her feel?"

Chris couldn't even meet Father John's eyes. Elbows resting on his knees, he trained his eyes on the carpet and bit back a four-letter word. Well, he tried, and then he let it fly as he threw his baseball cap to the floor and crushed it under his shoe. Kicking the chair or knocking a stack of papers off the desk would have been more satisfying, but he couldn't do that to Father John.

"How could I be such a thoughtless, selfish jackass?"

Father John waited a beat. "Is that a rhetorical question?"

"Not really. Am I going to be a terrible husband? Maybe I'm not what she needs. What if I'm a selfish jerk?"

"I think you're doing exactly the right thing. I hear marriage is an excellent cure for selfishness. Add a couple kids or three or more, and it gets even better."

Chris didn't say anything as he picked his flattened cap off the floor and tried to reshape it.

Father John sighed. "Do you still love her?"

"Yes, of course, I do."

"Do you intend to go through with the marriage?"

"Yes. If Saturday night had happened *after* our wedding, you'd be looking at the happiest man in the world."

"I absolved you a half hour ago. You need to do your penance, and you need to forgive yourself and Rebecca, although I think you've decided to take all the blame on this. You need to move forward. You need to be there for her. Show her the kind of husband you intend to be. Are you going to up and leave every time there's trouble? Because this won't be the last time. I dare say it won't be the last time you struggle with sexual sin, even in marriage. Or are you going to stay with her and get through things together?"

Chris's phone buzzed in his pocket.

"I think you should look at this one."

Chris lifted his hip and slid the phone from its holster. He swiped at it a couple of times and gave a half grin. "It's from Rebecca's sister, Abby. She says, 'Call my sister within the next ten minutes or I'm taking a contract out on you. And not on your head.'"

Father John recoiled. "Ouch."

"Classic Abby."

"I've got to get over to the school. You can have the office for a few minutes. Call Rebecca, and let Erica know when you leave."

"Thanks, Father."

"No problem." The door shut halfway and then reopened as Father John poked his head back in. "Chris, I know you've got your own troubles, but if you could spare some prayers for Kimberly, I'd appreciate it. They're taking her off the ventilator today."

The door closed with a click, and Chris leaned back in his chair. Damn, he really was selfish. Here they'd spent all morning talking about his problems and what were they compared to a young woman's life?

He swiped some more at his phone and in seconds Rebecca's voice filled his ears. A wave of calm swept over him. "Rebecca, we need to talk. Where are you?"

***

"Can I come in?"

"Of course."

The tears already leaked from her eyes, and they welled in his eyes, too. Once she closed the door behind him, he pulled her close to him, letting her cry against his chest while his tears fell into her hair.

After a few minutes, he took her by the hand and guided her to the couch, taking a seat across from her on her coffee table.

"How do we start?" she asked, clearing her throat and wiping the tears from her cheeks.

He released his hand from hers and cupped her face in his hands. He stared into her teary, reddened eyes, and his gaze lingered as he aimed straight through to her soul.

"Like this." He leaned in and kissed her. Without rekindling the unfettered desire that had gotten them into trouble, he reassured her neither his love nor his desire for her had wavered one bit. She wasn't a wadded up tissue or old gum or whatever other ridiculous thing someone said. She was as beautiful and precious to him as ever.

Would it be too much if he got down on his knees? He thought about how he had treated her, whipping the blanket at her and storming out like a petulant child. No, it might not be enough. The knot in his gut tightened. He'd be lucky if she heard him out, let alone forgive him.

He held onto her hands again and shifted onto his knees in front of her before he began a litany of *mea culpas* he had rehearsed on the way there.

"I'm sorry I had too much to drink. I'm sorry I asked you to come get me. I'm sorry all I could think of when I saw you was, well, what we ended up doing. I'm sorry I didn't just put out a towel for you like you asked. I'm sorry I got into the shower with you. I'm sorry that at the half dozen or so chances I had to stop that I didn't. I'm sorry that I was so curt with you when it was over. I'm sorry I walked out on you when you begged me to stay. I'm sorry I didn't answer your calls. I'm sorry I didn't listen to your messages. I'm sorry for being so selfish—I didn't even think about how you felt." He stopped and took a breath, giving her a sad smile. "I'm sorry this will detract from our wedding night. I'm sorry we're going to carry the consequences of this with us into marriage." He realized this last one was the biggie. The one that undermined everything they had built their relationship on. "I'm sorry I betrayed your trust. Please forgive me."

Her chest rose and fell with a deep breath. She shut her eyes for a second and reopened them. "I do."

An invisible load lifted from his shoulders. She forgave him. It was more than he deserved.

"Now it's my turn. I'm sorry I didn't change my clothes before I came to get you. I'm sorry I didn't get my own darn towel. I'm sorry I didn't stop things."

"That's it? Your list is a whole lot shorter than mine." He smiled, and at last she smiled back.

She squeezed his hands tightly and tugged them, helping to pull him up off of his knees and back into a sitting position. "Chris, it's not like we're the first couple who have ever given in to temptation. After you left, I looked at my chart, and I think I know what was going on."

Her chart? What did that have to do with anything? "What do you mean?"

"I know I'm still kind of new to the charting, but I think I was ovulating, which would explain why my libido was in overdrive and probably why yours was, too. Add that to the fact the beer impaired your judgment, Lady Godiva impaired mine, and I sashayed around here in Spandex. It was a recipe for—well, I hate to call it a disaster. Makes sense though, doesn't it?"

Chris raked his hand through his hair. "It does. But if you were ovulating, then..."

"I could be pregnant. It's a possibility. We'll know in a couple of weeks."

He leaned back, rubbed his palms up and down his thighs, and shook his head. "I never thought I'd get myself in this position. Worrying about a pregnancy."

Compassion filled her eyes. "It's only a few weeks until the wedding. Everyone would think it was a honeymoon baby."

He nodded his head, but he couldn't speak. He knew they would love and cherish any and every child they conceived no matter the circumstances, but this was not how he wanted it to happen. He took a deep breath and let it out slowly, trying to ignore the new ache in his chest. Nothing could be done about it now.

"Are you going to be okay here tonight? I have to take care of some things today and run into work, but I can come back and stay if you want. On the couch."

"I'm fine. It was just Saturday night. It felt like..." She looked down and bit her lip.

"Rebecca?" He had hurt her so much. He had been so wrapped up in his own shame that he'd been oblivious to the pain he'd inflicted.

"It felt like a one-night stand when you left. Like you got what you were after, and you were done with me. That's why I needed you to stay."

Unbelievable. "Rebecca," he said as he smoothed her hair with his hand. "How could you think that?"

"I know. It's not what I thought. It's what I *felt*. And without you here to contradict it...it...it just hurt is all."

"I should have looked at it from your point of view. I'm sorry. I was so disappointed in myself—so angry with myself. I mean, we wait twenty-four years or whatever and then three weeks before the wedding? Really? I couldn't stand being in my own skin, and I had to get out. But believe me, please, when I tell you that when we made love, the only thought in my mind was that I love you. I guess by definition we used each other, but that was not my intention at all. I swear. I love you, and I was sorely misguided, but I wanted to give myself to you and be one with you because I love you so much."

"I know. I do believe you. It's all you kept saying the whole time. You must've said it, like, a dozen times."

Chris moved next to her on the couch and pulled her against him so that she could lay her head against his chest.

"I want you to know I can't wait to be your husband and not just because of the sex, but because I truly love you, and I want to spend my life with you."

He loved the feel of her hand rubbing circles on his chest. When she stopped he looked down at her, and she smiled. "Our honeymoon is going to be a lot of fun, isn't it?"

"Mmmm...I think so. To say I'm looking forward to it would be a gross understatement." He enjoyed the feel and scent of her hair under his chin. "You know, morality aside, if you had asked me before Saturday, I would have thought that, uh, what we did would take the edge off. Sort of like a snack before dinner."

Rebecca amazed him by finishing his thought. "But it was more like an appetizer. The kind that makes you realize how hungry you really are."

"Exactly." He enunciated every syllable for emphasis. "So it's not just me, huh?"

"Nope. Not just you. It was a mistake in a lot of ways." She leaned back, and he was able to look into those warm, brown eyes that he loved so well. "You know, it wasn't all your fault. I did nothing to discourage you. I have no doubt that if I had asked you to stop you would have. I encouraged you, maybe not with words, but in every other way."

He shrugged. "I'm supposed to honor and protect you, not lead you into sin."

"That goes for me, too. You know, after she sent you that

text threatening you with castration, my crazy sister actually said something kind of profound."

Chris cocked an eyebrow. Abby was intelligent, but he had yet to hear her say anything that indicated serious introspection.

"I know what you're thinking, but I think she hit the nail on the head with this."

Rebecca moved over to the coffee table where Chris had been so they could see eye-to-eye again. "Let me think of how she put it."

He waited while she gathered her thoughts.

"She said that marriage isn't the happily ever after. It's the rocky, brush-covered path that'll get you there. You're going to trip and fall. You might even take a side trail that gets you lost and confused and you'll have to fight your way back. Every last vice, fault, and rough edge will be exposed, but you'll never have to travel alone, and if you hang in there it'll perfect you like a refiner's fire."

"Abby said that?" He was incredulous; he couldn't help it.

Rebecca laughed. "Yes. After I confirmed she wasn't body snatched, I kissed her. I've been so focused on the wedding and our wedding night that I kind of forgot the purpose of the whole thing. It breaks my heart to think I'm going to hurt you and disappoint you a thousand times over, but I know I will. And you will. But I love you with all my heart, and I'm going to promise before God and our families and friends that I will forever. This," she said as she gestured around them, "these last few days, doesn't mean we've made a fatal error. We screwed up. We go to confession, and we get back up and dust ourselves off and keep moving in the right direction."

Profound gratitude for Rebecca and for a God who brought them together filled his chest. He moved forward in his seat and taking hold of her hands, pulled her into his lap.

"How did you know that was exactly what I needed to hear?"

She smiled and kissed his cheek, then his ear, and his neck. "Because I needed to hear it, too."

"The wedding night's going to be . . . different." He rubbed her back and tried to make sense of his muddled feelings. "I know we're forgiven, but I still feel—"

"Yuck?"

He chuckled. "Is that the technical term for it?"

She nodded. "I guess there's not much we can do about it now."

Was there anything they could do? An idea formed. "No... but what if we did something that maybe made us feel less 'yuck' and made the honeymoon sweeter?"

"Such as?"

"Lay off the heavy kissing until the wedding." Not that he wanted to—ever. But, it would sort of give them a clean slate.

She traced a finger along his cheek and chin then tapped his lips. "It's a good idea. We can't undo what we did, but this'll make things more special."

***

Rebecca turned left and then right in front of the full-length mirror and admired her reflection. "What do you think?"

Abby stared and smiled. "I think it looks perfect, which is a good thing because this is the final fitting, and the wedding is a week away."

That's it? No cutting wit? No snide comment? "It does look good, doesn't it?"

She stepped down from the pedestal, and Abby helped her remove the gown. Abby waited outside the changing room door while she slipped on her jeans and shirt. "So, did Dad say if he's coming or not?"

Rebecca's mood plummeted. "He won't commit. When I ask, he says the same thing he said the first time Chris and I went over there and told him we were getting married."

"What's that?"

She opened the shuttered door and handed the gown to the seamstress. "He says, 'I'll never approve of it.'"

"You know, Rebecca, it might be better if he stayed away."

Rebecca took her purse back from Abby and swung it over her shoulder. "That's what Chris says, but Abby, it's Dad."

"I know, I know."

They walked to the counter where Rebecca handed the girl her debit card to make the final payment on the gown. Her eyes darted to the speaker mounted on the wall above them. "Abby, listen. What's this song?"

"Not sure. I've heard it before though."

"We need to figure it out. And then I need to borrow your husband."

"Okay, but I thought we'd start the swapping *after* the wedding."

Rebecca rolled her eyes. "I figured out what I'm going to give Chris for a wedding present, and I need to practice on Joel."

25

Lying In the Hands of God

Chris sat in the front pew wiping his sweaty palms on his tuxedo pants when Father John crossed the altar and stood in front of him.

"How's my bride?"

He always suspected his friend had a soft spot for Rebecca. Now his admiration was apparent. Father John blinked and gave his head a little shake as if he couldn't believe what he was about to say. "She's stunning."

"Is she nervous?"

"About marrying you? Not a bit. She's worried her dad's not going to show though."

Chris glanced at his watch. A reasonable concern. The wedding would start in fifteen minutes. "He's not coming. I knew it, but she kept holding out hope. What do we do?"

Before Father John could answer, Alan slid into the pew next to Chris.

"Alan, did Rebecca's dad get here yet?"

"I haven't seen him. Do you think he's going to show?"

Chris looked at Father John. "No, I don't."

"Abby told me something at the rehearsal dinner last night. About her dad."

Chris and Father John both turned to Alan and waited for him to explain.

"She said she hadn't told Rebecca, but apparently Abby had it out with their dad last weekend—about the wedding." Alan scooted in closer to Chris and Father John and lowered his voice.

"He told her he doesn't want to hurt Rebecca, but he can't in good conscience support her marrying you." Alan seemed aggrieved by all this, even though it must seem to him like they were splitting hairs over religious nonsense. "He said he couldn't support her apostling or something like that?"

Father John leaned forward over the pew. "Apostasizing?"

Alan met his gaze. "Yeah. I think that was it. Sorry, I'm not familiar with all the religious terminology."

Father John shook his head. "No, that's okay, Alan."

Alan's head moved back and forth between Chris and Father John. "Anyway, that led to a big row, and Abby told him if he didn't love his own daughter enough to wish her well in her marriage, then he should just stay away."

Chris rubbed his sweaty palm over his forehead. A headache threatened. He didn't doubt that Rebecca's dad loved her, even if he did a dreadful job of showing it. His absence would break Rebecca's heart, but Chris wondered what he would do differently if it was *his* daughter he truly thought was jeopardizing her soul.

Surveying Alan and then Chris, Father John clapped his hands together. "Here's what I suggest you do."

***

Rebecca stared into the mirror and pushed a stray hair beneath the comb holding her veil in place. The urgent knock on the door made her jump. Her hand flew over her heart. Five minutes until the ceremony. Finally, her dad had made it.

"Come in," she called toward the door. When the door opened, she was stunned not to see her dad or Abby, but Chris. He looked so handsome in his tux that her knees actually felt weak.

He gave her the biggest dimpled smile. "I'm here to walk you down the aisle, Rebecca." He took a few seconds to look her over from the long tulle veil that hung past her shoulders to the beaded sweetheart neckline of her gown, the cinched waist, and the full, flowing skirt with intricate beaded designs.

"Wow." He stepped toward her and lifted her hand to his lips, kissing her knuckles right next to the beautiful ring he had given her. "You've brought another one of my fantasies to life." He tugged on her hand, slid it under the lapel of his jacket and laid it over his heart. "Do you feel what you do to me?"

Rebecca finally found her voice. "Chris, you're not supposed to see me before the wedding."

He released her hand, but his blue eyes still focused on her. "I don't believe in that superstitious nonsense. I'm here to walk down the aisle with my bride."

He was being so sweet, but she knew what he had come to tell her. "He's not coming, is he?"

He shook his head and held her gaze. "No, sweetheart, he's not coming."

Rebecca fanned her face, picked up her train with her left hand, and started pacing the tiny room. "I can't cry, my makeup will run."

"So, don't cry."

Easy for him to say. Both of his parents sat in the church eager to be part of one of the most important days in their son's life.

She wouldn't be able to hold back the tears much longer.

"Rebecca, look at me."

She turned to see Chris with the right side of his jacket hanging loosely behind him. He had slid the suspender from his right shoulder and was in the process of unzipping his pants.

"Chris!" She couldn't keep the alarm out of her voice. What on earth was he doing? Any minute a knock on the door would signal it was time to begin and for some unknown reason he was disrobing.

"You're not going to cry, you're going to laugh." Chris pushed the right side of his black pants down far enough for her to see his hip, which was covered in black ink.

"You got a tattoo?" What was he thinking?

"Not a permanent one. This is why I didn't want to sleep at Alan's place the last two nights after my lease ran out. He thought it would be funny to tattoo me with a Sharpie."

Rebecca took a step closer. It said, "I love Rebecca" using a heart symbol for "love."

She didn't cry after all. She laughed. "How did he do that without waking you?"

Chris tucked in his shirt, zipped his pants, and slipped the suspender back over his shoulder. As he slid his arm back into his jacket and shrugged to adjust the fit, he whispered in her ear. "Alan knows something you don't. I sleep naked."

He took a step back and gave her another dimpled grin. Then she laughed again and couldn't stop laughing. In fact, she laughed so hard she feared her makeup may be ruined by happy tears.

A knock sounded on the door, and Abby stuck her head in. "Get it together, you two. We're up next."

***

Chris missed out on that magical view of Rebecca walking toward him from the back of the church, but having her on his arm eliminated every last trace of nervousness. His heart swelled with pride just having her by his side. Father John was right—she looked stunning, and her appearance only captured a fraction of her interior beauty.

He tried to focus on the Mass, but his mind raced in a million directions settling periodically on the folds of white tulle that scratched the stiff fabric of his jacket. Each distracting rustle diverted his attention to the resplendent woman beside him. When it was time for the homily, he made a concerted effort to pay attention and to remember what Father John said to them.

"I'm blessed to witness the marriage of two dear friends." Father John smiled at both of them. "I met Chris and Rebecca at different times, different places, separated by almost a decade. Neither of them were Catholic at the time. And, no, I did not introduce them. Some would say it was a chance meeting. I think Chris and Rebecca would disagree."

Chris squeezed Rebecca's hand as he remembered the first time he saw her. The ear-piercing screams of a child had *caught* his attention, but the pretty girl desperately trying to soothe the child *held* it.

Father John glanced at his notes and then back at him and Rebecca. "Most of us are familiar with the Sting song, 'If You Love Somebody, Set Them Free.' Now, you can interpret that sentiment in a lot of different ways, but I believe it is more accurate to say that if you love somebody, *you* set them free. I propose that today Chris and Rebecca will be set free.

"I see some of the looks from the guys here. I know what you're thinking. Free? Chris is about to be shackled to the old ball and chain." A smattering of laughter erupted.

"But in a few moments, when Chris and Rebecca confer the sacrament on each other, they will mirror the image of God in a special way. We all remember St. Patrick, right? That holiday when we drink green beer?"

More tittering. Their guests professed a mixture of all faiths and no faith, but most were non-practicing Christians, and if they thought they could slump back in the pew and wait for the kiss at the end, they were mistaken. Father John would catechize them without them even knowing it.

"St. Patrick used the shamrock to show that God is a communion of three persons—Father, Son, and Holy Spirit. And we know from the fourth chapter of John's Gospel, the beautiful reading that Chris and Rebecca chose, which I just read, that God is love. Today, by and through their love, Chris and Rebecca become one flesh, one body. As male and female their married love, the physical union of their bodies, manifests the love of God. Now, I see some people squirming in their seats, but come on, we know what's going to happen tonight, right? Chris, you *are* taking Rebecca on a honeymoon, aren't you?"

Chris smiled and nodded. With laughter from behind him, he doubted Father John could hear him, so he held up his right index finger and made a zero with his left hand.

"He's signing ten days for me. That's a serious honeymoon, folks." More laughter followed. "Here's a couple that takes their vows seriously, because that's what they'll be doing—renewing the vows that they take freely here today to be faithful to one another and open to life.

"We all know that we are more than our bodies. We're body and soul, but the soul is rather useless when it comes to the material world. Souls can't speak or hug. They can't sing or dance. They can't laugh or cry. And they can't make love. But with our bodies, we can communicate from the depths of our souls. We can love and be loved. And isn't that what we all want? To love and be loved. Today and for the rest of their lives, Chris and Rebecca are free to love and be loved. They are free to make their very lives, their very bodies—which we know communicate the deepest stirrings of the soul—a gift to one another.

"Well, you might say, that's all good for Chris and Rebecca, but what does that mean, really? What's the big picture here? Do you see how this freedom, this total gift of self is like an echo of the greatest gift ever given?" Father John turned and gestured to the crucifix suspended behind him. "The gift of Christ's flesh, his body, for the life of his bride, the Church."

Chris had heard these words before; they had drawn him to the Church. He'd never *felt* the truth of them until now. The awesome responsibility he undertook by making Rebecca his wife humbled him. And scared him. And, geez, did a tear just roll down his cheek? Good thing they were facing the altar rather than their guests.

He swiped at his cheek, bumping Rebecca's arm, and she nudged him back with her elbow. He cast a sideways glance at her, and she smiled. Tears dampened her cheeks, too.

"That, my friends," Father John said, gesturing again to the crucifix, "wasn't easy. That required sacrifice and suffering. So much suffering that as he hung there, Jesus called out to his Father, 'Why have you abandoned me?'

"Chris and Rebecca, like all of us, will suffer. We don't want to think of the suffering because today is a happy day. We're going to leave here and celebrate. We're going to eat and drink—there is an open bar right? And we'll laugh and dance, and that is as it should be.

"I wish you could see what I see standing here: the joy on Chris and Rebecca's faces. They're both wiping tears from their cheeks, but they're not sad. They're overcome. They're filled with joy."

Well, so much for hiding the tears. Chris sniffed, and then

pulled the handkerchief from his interior pocket and handed it to Rebecca. She dabbed around her eyes, still trying to preserve her makeup.

"As their friends and their family, it's our duty to support them in their vocation—their marriage. They're going to be on such a high at first that they won't dwell on each other's faults. But given time, they will. They'll get on each other's nerves. There will be money problems. Health problems. Problems with children."

Father John's gaze settled on him and Rebecca then and his tone softened. "There will be in-law problems. Problems they brought with them from their families of origin. And none of us escape our fallen natures, making us susceptible to temptation and sin and, therefore, suffering."

Chris wished Father John had prepared them for this. Now they were both a wreck. He could see Rebecca's shoulders shaking in his peripheral vision, and he looped his arm around her to soothe her. He also wished they'd had someone record this so they could remember it. Maybe Father John could give him a copy of it, although it looked like he was winging it off his notes.

"When the time comes, hold them up. Encourage them. Babysit their children so they can go on a date. If they're an inspiration, tell them. If they're failing miserably, and they need correction, tell them. Gently. Above all, pray for them."

He looked at Chris and Rebecca a final time. "Pray for each other. Pray with each other." He paused and looked down at his notes and then back up at them. Chris rubbed Rebecca's back gently, the smooth satin so cool and soft beneath his fingers. "Rebecca Ann Rhodes and Christopher Aiden Reynolds: 'This is the day the Lord has made, let us rejoice in it and be glad.' . . . Let's do this."

26

Stay

The music stopped, and Chris looked around to see if he could find a reason.

Rebecca strode toward him, and he excused himself from the conversation with his college friends.

She moved with ease, her train pinned up and her skirt gathered in her left hand. "Excuse me, gentlemen. I need my husband."

She wrinkled her nose at a couple of ribald comments and a modicum of laughter as she and Chris left the table and headed for the dance floor.

"Do you want to dance?" he asked her.

"In a little bit. First, I want to give you your wedding gift."

Before he could ask any questions, Joel stepped in front of them and set a chair in the middle of the dance floor. He grinned and winked at Chris as he walked away, and Rebecca held onto the back of the chair, motioning for Chris to take a seat. The lights came down, the heat of a spotlight hit him, and then widened so that a large area around him illuminated.

Rebecca stood in front of him and adjusted his black bowtie. Her eyes danced and the corners of her mouth verged on turning up into a huge smile. She leaned over far enough to give him—and only him—a good view of her cleavage. *Have mercy.*

"So, are you going to give me a lap dance in front of 150 of our closest friends and family?"

Her breath tickled his ear as she whispered, "I thought I'd save that for later."

She glided off before his addled brain could get a coherent response to his mouth. He pressed his sweaty palms out against his pants.

Rebecca said something to the DJ and then took the handheld microphone he offered her.

The room grew quiet, and Chris turned his attention back to the DJ.

"If I could have your attention on the dance floor, Rebecca would like to sing something for Chris."

Sing? For me? In front of all these people? Not a trace of nervousness showed on her face or in her movements. She exuded composure and confidence. The music started, and she moved into the light, lifting the microphone to her lips as the sounds of a banjo being strummed filled the room. It sounded vaguely familiar, but he couldn't place the song. She began to sing, and the sound mesmerized him.

Her warm, rich voice evoked longing. They only word for it was sultry. There may have been other people in the room—a lot of them—but this performance was all for him.

She walked in a circle around him as she sang, inching closer as she went. He recognized the song now, but he found it hard to believe it hadn't been written for them. She sang about a jar filled with sand and catching fireflies, and he closed his eyes for a couple of seconds as the memories scrolled before him like a slideshow.

When she got to the first chorus, he thought she might turn and sing to the hundred or so awestruck people who had no idea she could sing like this. She didn't. Her unwavering gaze stuck to him.

What you've given me is sweeter than honey
What you've shared is stronger than steel
You were sent from heaven
To save my life
So now I can give it to you

As she began the second verse, she moved closer and sat in his lap. Dumbstruck, he put an arm around her waist and made a conscious effort to burn this memory into his brain. Somehow she managed never to lose eye contact with him while she undid his bowtie with one hand, letting it hang loosely around his collar.

Another chorus followed and a last verse, but he had lost concentration. *This magnificent creature is my wife? I am blessed beyond belief.*

As she reached the final chorus, she took his hand and brought him to his feet. Eye to eye, with the poufy layers of her dress pressing in on his tux, this last refrain seemed more intimate than the others.

You were sent from heaven
To save my life
So now I can give it to you

He suddenly wished he had booked a room in this hotel. One he could take her to as soon as she was done singing.

The music went on for a few seconds after she had turned off the microphone, and the first hint of disquietude showed on her face as she bit her lower lip. "Well?"

The room erupted in applause and whistles, and everyone stood. What could he possibly say that would tell her how deeply grateful he was that she had done this for him? What it meant to him to hear her sing. How his heart overflowed with love, pride, desire, and humility all at the same time. As he opened his mouth in the hope that something capturing a fraction of that emotion would come out, the metallic clatter of spoons against glasses broke his concentration.

He was off the hook.

He wasn't eloquent enough to convey his feelings with words, but he could do it with a kiss. If their guests thought they were going to glimpse another peck on the lips like they had the half dozen other times they had tapped on their glasses this evening, they were mistaken.

Chris pulled Rebecca to him, and he knew she could see the tears in his eyes. For once he hoped what was in his heart was written all over his face. Her hands, one still gripping the microphone, wrapped around his neck. He kissed her, his heart racing as her soft body leaned into him. She kissed him with an abandon he had never felt before. Suddenly the merit of waiting almost three weeks to do this became apparent. It was new again—cherished and pregnant with purpose and meaning.

A tug at his sleeve finally pulled them apart as Abby stood amid a bevy of Rebecca's friends and family pressing in on her, raving about her voice and her performance.

Chris couldn't imagine going back to chatting with his college buddies or elderly relatives, so after a few of minutes, when the music started back up, he stole Rebecca for a couple of dances. Feeling like his feet had finally returned to earth, he and Rebecca went their separate ways for a short while before the DJ started in on some special dances.

Chris planned on dancing with his mother. Had Rebecca's father shown up, she would have danced with him as well. Apparently no one got the message to the DJ that the father-daughter dance was a no-go. He introduced Rebecca and her father.

Rebecca stood across the dance floor from him, her eyes wide and her face pale. She didn't need this reminder that her father had chosen not to be a part of one of the most important days of her life. Before Chris could decide what to do, his father stepped in and extended his arm to Rebecca. A slow smile spread across her face as she took his arm and walked to the dance floor with him. Never had the contrast between his father and Rebecca's seemed so stark. Rebecca's father had spent years diminishing his daughters' self-worth whereas his own dad had spent that time building his sons up.

After the dance with his mother, somehow several of his cousins cornered Chris and pulled him to the bar for a round of shots. When his cousin Joe learned he worked at a brewery, he recounted his experience with home brewing and peppered Chris with questions. About ten minutes into Joe's travails with hops, Alan came up alongside him. He jerked his elbow against Chris's ribcage.

"You've got to see this."

Chris tuned into the seventies Redbone song blaring from the speakers behind him as he watched Abby, Jamie, and Rebecca at the opposite end of the dance floor. Rebecca's gaze was fixed on him, and she leaned forward, one hand pressed against her thigh while she used the other to beckon him with her index finger. She sang along with the refrain, "Come and get your love."

An ear-splitting grin covered Chris's face.

"I've never seen Rebecca so...so, uninhibited," Alan said. "It's captivating."

Chris hadn't noticed Father John alongside Alan until he spoke.

"She's blossomed."

He looked over to see his friend smiling, too, as Rebecca continued to tease Chris.

"She told me, you know," Chris said, still smiling at his bride.

Father John glanced at him. "Told you what?"

Chris didn't know why he brought it up now of all times. "That you were her first kiss." The song ended, and a group of young women quickly encircled Rebecca.

"I didn't know it was her first. I should have guessed."

"Must not have been much of a kiss," Chris said, draining the few drops left in his shot glass.

"Obviously it wasn't with the right guy."

Chris smiled, grateful that he *was* the right guy. "Your homily today was perfect. Thank you."

"I don't deserve the thanks. It was off the cuff. My notes were a reflection on the first reading you chose from Genesis. The Holy Spirit led me somewhere else."

"Well, I'm glad you followed." Chris forced himself to look away from Rebecca and make eye contact with Father John. "Hey, have you heard how Kimberly is doing?"

Father John reached into his pocket and pulled out his cell phone. "I got a text this morning from her mother. She regained consciousness last night, thanks be to God." Father John glanced heavenward and his eyes glistened. "I talked to her mother before the reception. Kimberly had gone to Catholic Charities after all. They had worked out a plan for her to leave, but her husband lost it on her before she could go."

Chris heard what was unsaid: "It wasn't my fault. She didn't nearly die because I pushed her off on someone else instead of dealing with my attraction to her." Chris pulled his closest friend into a hug, slapping him on the back a couple of times for good measure.

He let go, and Alan's arm clapped his shoulder, his whiskey-laden breath curling around his ear.

"What are you still doing here, anyway? Go get your hot wife and get out of here."

"I agree," Father John said. "You put in enough time here. You should get Rebecca and go."

"I think I will." They had a long ride ahead of them, and he had enough socializing; he wanted to be alone with Rebecca. He excused himself, shaking both Alan and Father John's hands and handing a business card to his cousin Joe before he crossed the dance floor.

"Mrs. Reynolds," he said, standing behind her as she talked with a young woman he hadn't met. When she didn't respond, he touched her shoulder and said again, "Mrs. Reynolds." This time she turned toward him. "You're going to have to start answering to that, you know."

"I know. Maybe it will help if you whisper it to me all night long."

He grinned, more convinced than ever that it was time to go. "I've come to get my love."

"It's about time," she said grabbing him around the waist.

He grinned again, and seeing the playfulness in her eyes he asked, "What have you been drinking?"

"Water with lemon." She smiled and stared at him a second longer. "I'm drunk on love." She giggled and leaned into him.

He rolled his eyes.

"I'm high on you?" she tried, laughing.

"Enough with the cheesy lines." He wrapped his arms around her waist, too, and leaned his forehead against hers. "Are you ready to blow this Popsicle stand?"

She kissed him, her hands tugging on the lapels of his tuxedo jacket. "Yes. Let me say goodbye to Abby."

"Okay. I'm going to try to sneak out. I'll meet you in the

lobby in a couple minutes."

Chris got out in a few minutes with only one handshake, two slaps on the back, and one messy kiss from his Aunt Lydia. He wiped his cheek with the back of his hand as he entered the lobby. He sighed and took a seat on an upholstered bench as the photographer approached. This wedding business exhausted him.

"You leaving?"

"Trying."

"We need one more shot."

Chris leaned his head from side to side, and his neck cracked with each movement. What did it take to get out of this place? Chris paced around the lobby for a few minutes, trying to avoid eye contact with any of the guests passing through.

Abby appeared, bouncing Ian on her hip. "Trying to get out of here?"

"'Trying' being the operative word." He leaned into Ian and gave him a little tickle on his chest that he knew would elicit a giggle. "Hey, Ian. How's it going? I'm your uncle now, buddy."

Ian smiled then leaned back precariously, forcing Abby to grab onto him with two arms.

"You're a lucky man, you know," Abby said.

Chris gave Ian another smile and then straightened and looked at Abby. "I do." He hoped the sincerity of those two words assured Abby that he treasured her sister beyond measure.

Abby wrinkled her brow and frowned. Instead of satisfied, she looked almost irritated. "I should tell you that she's a lucky woman, too. You're a good guy, and you're good for her—that whole guilt trip abandonment thing notwithstanding."

"Not my finest moment, and it won't happen again, but thank you, Abby." No wonder she had looked perturbed. It had probably been difficult for her to spit out that compliment.

"This may not make sense to you, but Rebecca is more Rebecca with you."

She might not have expected him to understand that, but he did. "Become who you are," he murmured.

"What did you say?"

"Become who you are. It's something Pope Saint John Paul II said. I thought it was an interesting statement. I didn't really get it until now though. Rebecca has become who she is meant to be." He wanted to say "in Christ," but that would be a conversation for another day.

Abby seemed nonplussed, and Ian stretched toward the ballroom. "I'll drag her out of there for you. You deserve some time alone." She reached up and kissed Chris's cheek, and gave him a side hug with her free arm. She turned and started toward the door and then turned back, her voice elevated because of the distance. "You two better get working on some cousins for my children."

He opened his mouth to answer, but she cut in.

"Unless...Rebecca complained of queasiness this morning. I dismissed it as nerves, but is she pregnant already?"

Chris's cheeks heated. The pretty dark-skinned girl who worked as a receptionist in Rebecca's office strolled into the lobby. Rebecca would be humiliated if she or anyone else knew tonight wouldn't be their first time. He hadn't shared that information with anyone but Father John. He figured Abby knew and probably Joel as well, but it wasn't anyone else's business.

Chris made a downward motion with his hand trying to tell her to lower her voice. "No, Abby," he hissed. "She's not."

Her reply came at the same volume as before. "All it takes is one good swimmer."

Abby should win an award for the sheer number of cringe-worthy statements she could pack into a conversation. He'd sooner die than discuss his sperm motility with his sister-in-law. Thank God she resumed her mission of finding Rebecca. She must have been successful, because in a few minutes his bride emerged from the ballroom.

***

"I'm so sorry. People kept stopping me." Rebecca huffed an exhausted sigh as she came to a stop in front of Chris.

"Tell me about it." He kissed her forehead where a few of her long bangs were coming loose from their comb. Lowering his voice, he said, "Our fashion plate photographer wants one more shot. He says I should, and I quote, 'carry my woman out of here.' I won't tell you what else he said I should do with you."

"Really? Ew."

"Yeah. I said if he ever spoke about my wife that way again, I'd crush his expensive lenses under the heel of my motorcycle boots."

"I love it when you get all chivalrous." Rebecca leaned into him as he slung an arm around her shoulders. Worn out from hours of socializing, her introverted nature had re-asserted itself. "Where is he?"

"Restroom." Chris nodded toward the men's room. "He said he'd be right out."

In seconds he returned, and Chris swung Rebecca up into his arms. "You're not as heavy as I thought," he said with a half grin.

"You will pay for that later, Mr. Reynolds."

"And how do you intend to get your retribution, Mrs. Reynolds?"

She snaked her arm down and around his side and tickled him until he almost dropped her.

Chris carried her through the double doors laughing as the photographer took a stream of successive shots. He deposited her on the sidewalk outside where the sun had now fallen completely beneath the horizon.

Rebecca kept her arms wrapped around Chris's neck and stood on her tiptoes to whisper in his ear. "Someone implied once that if I left a wedding with you, you would expect certain, uh, favors."

Chris grinned and lowered his mouth to her ear. "I can't speak to the past, but starting tonight I'm expecting a helluva lot more than that."

A chill ran up Rebecca's spine, and she savored the feeling of their life together unfolding before them.

As they neared the curb, someone called Rebecca's name.

Her dad approached from the parking lot dressed not for a wedding, but in casual clothes.

"Dad. You're a little late." She adopted a flat tone, but reminded herself to be kind. Maybe he wanted to apologize for skipping the wedding.

"Chris, I'd like a few minutes alone with my daughter."

Rebecca slid her arm beneath Chris's jacket and around his waist so that he knew she did not want him to leave her. "Whatever you have to say to me you can say in front of Chris. We only have a few minutes though before we leave on our honeymoon." She would not allow him to drag this out or in any way spoil their wedding night.

"Fine. I think this marriage is a huge mistake, and I couldn't come and support it."

"You've made your opinion clear, Dad. Why are you here now?" Did he think they didn't know this already? They were married now; couldn't he leave it alone?

"Please, Rebecca, I'd like to speak to you in private."

"No. That's not possible." The muscles in her neck tensed and her heart rate crept up.

He shook his head, which angered Rebecca. He acted as if she was foolish for refusing to allow him to divide and conquer.

"You haven't consummated this marriage yet. You can still have it annulled."

Rebecca let out a humorless laugh. "You can't be serious. You need to accept this, Dad. We're married. And the sooner you get out of our way, the sooner we can take care of the consummation part."

Rebecca marveled at how easy it was to say that to her dad. Not long ago, she couldn't muster the courage to stand up to him about trivial matters, let alone tell him to get lost so she could make love to her husband.

Chris's arm wrapped around her torso and with it, his warmth and strength. She realized a large part of her newfound confidence came from him and his love.

Her dad protested. "You're still pure, Rebecca. You can still find someone else, but this is your last chance. After this, no one worth having will want you."

She wanted to put him in his place. All the words were there, ready to spill out. He would consider her worthless if he knew she'd already lost her virginity. She gritted her teeth and breathed a large intake of air, ready to fire off the words with machine-gun precision.

Chris's grip tightened around her, and his fingers dug into her ribcage. He had to know she verged on unleashing the fury of their sexual sins on him. She couldn't think straight about it now in her anger, and out of respect for Chris, she tamed her tongue. Chris would say it was none of her dad's business, and that he'd only use that information to hurt her.

"Dad, we're leaving now. I'll call you when we get back." She turned and walked toward the limousine that pulled up alongside them.

Despite the tension she felt in Chris's arm, he hadn't spoken. Thank God he hadn't let her out of his reach.

The limousine door clicked open, and he held it for her as she descended carefully into the seat, trying to keep her dress from dragging along the gutter or getting caught in the door.

Her dad approached the vehicle and got in one last command. "Be smart, Becca. Make sure he uses a condom."

With his hand tightened in a white-knuckled fist, Chris slid into the seat and slammed the door behind them.

Her dad's words hit her like a punch in the gut. He wanted nothing more than to separate them. Not to mention he knew that as Catholics, contraception was anathema to them.

Chris helped arrange her skirts, and she couldn't comprehend his ability to remain so stoic about this. Especially that last comment in which her dad had relegated him to the role of poison papist seed bearer ready to impregnate her. Chris brought her life in so many ways, and she happily awaited the day she could tell Chris he'd brought life to her, inside of her, in yet another way. It made her father's remark even more offensive. She leaned over Chris and pressed the button to lower the window.

"How dare you come here and try to ruin our wedding night. If you hope to have any relationship with your grandchildren—and God willing there will be a bunch of them—you had better think long and hard about what you say to me and my husband. Chris is my first family now. Maybe if you had come to our wedding and listened to the readings, you would understand that a little better." She expected him to say something. Yell, plead, complain, anything, but he looked as if he'd been slapped, and he stepped backward in silence.

With one touch of Chris's hand to the door controls, the window rose as the first tears escaped her eyes. "Please don't let him rob us of our joy tonight, Rebecca."

Sadness sounded in his voice. Poor Chris. He had really tried with her dad; she knew he had, and yet her father continually rejected him.

Rebecca raised her head. "I won't." She sniffed and wiped the tears that had rolled down her cheeks. There was a knock on the window and even though the tinted glass between them muffled Dad's words, anyone with the most rudimentary lip-reading skills could make out his meaning as he bit out a three-word insult.

Leaning to the side, Rebecca tried to avoid Chris's arm as he twisted in his seat, yanking off his tuxedo jacket. His hand tightened around the door handle as he let out a growl. "That's it. He crossed the line."

Rebecca reached across him and stilled his hand. "We're not going to let him do this to our wedding night." He didn't move for a full half a minute, and then he pulled her into his arms as he told the driver they were ready. They rode in silence for several miles.

"I want to know where we're headed."

"Curious, huh?" There was a smile in his voice. "South."

"That's it? South? As in the Carolinas or the Caribbean, or the Antarctic?"

"As in the Blue Ridge Mountains of Virginia."

She should have known he'd want to go to his beloved mountains. Then a stab of panic hit her. "We're not camping, are we?"

His shoulder shook against her as a loud laugh burst from his lips. "No, I'd actually like to *stay* married to you. We're spending ten days in a remote, luxury cabin in the Shenandoah Valley. There's a waterfall, a fireplace, and a hot tub. And it's fully stocked. With any luck, we won't see another soul the whole time."

"It sounds perfect. Thank you." She turned and gave him a simple kiss that immediately changed the mood. "So, we've got, what, a three-hour ride?"

"Yes." His blue eyes were bright and simmering with affection. "Alone together at last." Careful not to snag her hair, he lifted the comb holding her veil in place, and swung it over her head, setting it to rest on the seat beside her. Once the white tulle cleared his line of vision, Chris's gaze swept over her face. He smoothed her hair where he had loosed the comb. "You're beautiful."

"I think you mean that," she said, recalling their first date.

She had never felt so contented as when she leaned in against her husband—*her husband*—and it all began to sink in. As she rested her head against his shoulder, all the day's excitement and tension melted away, leaving her spent. She eyed the limousine's interior and wondered if there was any way for them to sleep comfortably with her gown taking up so much space. It wouldn't be a bad idea to rest now and conserve their energy for later.

Chris looped his arm around her shoulder, and his hand ran up and down her arm is if he were trying to warm her. "How about a toast?"

He slid forward on the seat and reached for a bottle of champagne chilling in the limousine's small bar. He poured a glass for each of them, handed one to Rebecca, and took his place next to her.

The moon peaked out from over his shoulder, reminding her of nighttime rides as a child and being awed at the moon's ability to follow wherever she went. Like in her *Harold and the Purple Crayon* book, the moon remained a fixed and ever-present anchor when she felt lost. In its waxing or its waning, eclipsed, or covered by clouds, the moon abided. A fiery ball looming large on the horizon, or a nearly-invisible obsidian disc in a starlit sky, the moon abided.

Her gaze drifted back to Chris. She prayed their love, like God's, would abide from this day forward through all seasons, all travails, every high and low. An anchor when the world threatened to throw them off-course.

Lines creased Chris's handsome face as he held up his glass. He was beat, too, but it didn't stop his mouth from lifting in a smile big enough to show his dimples.

"Here's to Holy Matrimony, wedded bliss, and a whole ten days of seclusion."

They clinked their glasses and sipped their champagne.

It was her turn. She wanted to say something witty, but something different filled her heart.

"I went looking for yogurt, and I found love beyond compare, faith that can move mountains, and a husband whom I adore. What more could there be?"

Chris set their glasses aside. His voice rumbled low and soft in her ear, his breath warm. "Stay with me and find out."

Acknowledgments

Thank you to my husband, Michael, and my children Michael, Felicity, Miriam, and Jacob for their patience and support. Thanks, too, to all those who read my manuscript and offered suggestions: Christopher Blunt, Erin McCole Cupp, Ann Frailey, Father John Mulcahy, Barb Szyszkiewicz, and especially Theresa Linden. Theresa, you've made me a better writer and *Stay With Me* a better book. To my fellow 10 Minute Novelists and members of the Catholic Writers Guild, your generosity in sharing your knowledge and encouragement on this writing journey has made all the difference. Finally, thank you Ellen Gable Hrkach for your support and encouragement and taking a chance on an unknown author.

About the Author

Carolyn Astfalk resides with her husband and four children in Hershey, Pennsylvania. For ten years, she served as communications director for the Pennsylvania Catholic Conference (PCC), the public affairs agency of Pennsylvania's Catholic bishops. The PCC advocates for religious liberty, pro-life, pro-family, Catholic healthcare, and Catholic education issues before state government.

Carolyn's column on state and national news related to the PCC's interests appeared regularly in Pennsylvania's diocesan newspapers. She also appeared on the state-wide television program PCN Live and was a guest on then-Bishop Donald Wuerl's television program, "The Teaching of Christ." In 2005, she resigned from the PCC to be home full-time with her children.

Carolyn is volunteer chairperson of Real Alternatives, Inc., a non-profit, charitable organization that administers alternative-to-abortion funding in Pennsylvania, Indiana and Michigan. She is a member of the Catholic Writers Guild, Pennwriters, and the Pennsylvania Public Relations Society. Her writing has appeared in *New Covenant* and *Lay Witness* magazines. *Stay With Me* is her debut novel.

Published by Full Quiver Publishing
www.fullquiverpublishing.com